EAT
YOUR
HEART
OUT

EAT
YOUR
HEART
OUT

EAT YOUR HEART OUT

COURT LEGACY: BOOK 5

EDEN O'NEILL

CONTENT WARNINGS:

EAT YOUR HEART OUT is a dark new adult college romance recommended for readers 18+. Please see the author's website at www.edenoneill.com for all the book's content warnings.

PROLOGUE

Bru – age 15

Cissy Armstrong had blonde hair. Cissy Armstrong liked to sway when she walked, and Cissy Armstrong wore heels when she was like fifteen. She also sported a full face of makeup and showed way too many teeth when she looked at me.

Like now.

She had a grin for days, and when she swayed, she made her blonde ponytail move intentionally. Cissy Armstrong didn't actually sway. She just wanted to make her ponytail move. She wanted to be cute.

Apparently, she wanted to be cute for me.

"So, this is the lunchroom," she exclaimed, again, showing teeth. She had so many they nearly didn't fit in her face. She bounced. "And anyone who's anyone sits over there."

She directed her finger to a table full of jocks and cheer-leaders and was basically the opposite of any table I ever sat at. The scrawny poor kid whose dad was fucked up didn't sit at the popular table.

But this was a new school.

There were always new schools, but this was the first I'd ever been hugged up on by, who was clearly, the head chick at the school. Something happened the summer I turned fifteen. I looked different and actually filled out the clothes my sister, Sloane, got us from the secondhand clothing stores. My dad wasn't the one to buy us clothes.

My dad didn't do anything.

Of course, Cissy invited me to sit at her table and pointed out everything along the way. We had the Model UN kids who were basically future politicians and influential figures, and if one didn't happen to get a seat at the table with the *it* kids, the Model UN table was a close second. They weren't as popular as the popular kids *today*, but they would be one day because they were projected to rule the world.

And yes, she actually said that.

We also had the chess kids, the mathletes, and anyone else who could be considered smart or would, I don't know, actually change the world one day without bullshitting their way through it with words and politics. This was the table I'd normally be sitting at, but I was never under any circumstances allowed to sit there.

According to Cissy.

Cissy wanted me close. Cissy grabbed my arm, and Cissy waved at her other cheerleader friends when we got to her table. I didn't want to sit at the table with Cissy. Sure, popularity would be a nice break after being treated like a social reject for most of my life, but Cissy Armstrong kind of freaked me the fuck out. It was like my psycho flag went flying.

I started to sit with Cissy, not really given much of a choice, but feet away, I noticed another table. A girl sat there, and I noticed her because, well, she was the only one sitting there. All the other tables had people in them.

Not hers.

A redhead, she sat staring out of the window. It'd started to snow in New York City, and she stared at it from a table that had no lunch.

She just stared.

Cissy immediately noticed me staring at the table, and when she did, she smirked. In fact, she'd gone from sugary sweet to full demon in the face.

And so, my psycho radar was wrong.

I actually got chills when she stopped full stop before our table, her arms crossed, her grin evil. She tipped her chin. "Oh, and we definitely don't sit with her. She's a fucking freak."

I nearly cringed, but all Cissy did was bump a short laugh.

"Hopeless," she exclaimed, unprompted. "Her dad died, and like, it's sad but she's gone full zombie since it happened."

She tsked her tongue, actually tsked it like she hadn't said that girl's dad died and she had the audacity to be sad about the fact.

"She's also, like, a total burnout," Cissy continued. "So, no, we don't sit with her."

We don't sit with her. Like this was some fucked-up lunch-room hierarchy and she called the shots.

I supposed she thought she did.

And with that, I eased my arm away. Needless to say, I'd seen all I needed to see when it came to this chick.

"Bruno? Where are you…"

I didn't stick around to watch Cissy's mouth part. Instead, I sat at the redhead's table. She wore all black and had a face full of freckles. They were freckles I saw once close up because she didn't wear any makeup outside of red lipstick. It made her lips bright and just as bold as the auburn waves on her shoulders. She also didn't automatically smile at me just because I was a boy and sat at her table.

If anything, she sneered.

Her reaction was the complete opposite to Cissy, who basically forced her tits in my face the moment she got assigned to show me around the school today. She was class president and something I got to hear all about as she used any excuse she could to touch me, or rub up against me. I had to admit, at first, I liked the attention. I wasn't used to it and definitely not from the popular girl in school.

It was fake, though, phony just like Cissy, and even though this girl snarled at me when I sat down, at least I knew that response was genuine.

Not taking offense to it, I gazed away. I immediately opened my milk and started eating my lunch, but that was when the huff sounded from across the table.

"What do you think you're doing?"

Since the redhead opened dialogue, I stared over at her. I confirmed the snarl, and for some reason, I wanted to smile at it. I resisted, though, shrugging. "What?"

She made a look like it was obvious. "What are you doing?"

"What do you mean?"

She looked like she wanted to slap me, legit. Her shoulders dropped. "Why are you sitting here? You shouldn't be."

I noticed she said I *shouldn't*. Not that I couldn't. I turned, directing a finger at Cissy's table. "You see that table over there? More specifically the blonde sitting at that table?"

Right away, she saw Cissy. I mean, the girl was snarling in this direction. I couldn't determine if it was at me or the redhead, but at this point, I was well aware of the fact I'd probably just given up my chance at popularity at this new school.

"Cissy Armstrong?" the redhead questioned, and I nodded.

"Yeah. I'm hiding from her," I said, and the redhead's lips parted. "She showed me around today. I'm new, by the way. Name's Bruno. Bruno Sloane."

I noticed right away the redhead didn't give me her name.

She crossed her legs. "Okay, so why are you hiding?"

I mean, I didn't want to put Cissy's shit out there but... I opened my hands. "She kind of freaks me out."

That was putting it mildly, and though I hadn't been trying to make a joke, I hoped for a smile out of the redhead.

I didn't get one, but almost found something better when she lowered her shoulders. They relaxed.

Like she relaxed.

Her defenses weren't so high up, and sitting this close to her, I did kind of see what Cissy was talking about. It was hard not to notice the bags under the redhead's eyes, or the fact she couldn't quite focus on me. She seemed not quite all there, but in a way that was more familiar to me regarding depression.

Sadness.

I knew that well, saw it every day at home. I'd lost count of how many schools I'd been to. My dad chased jobs. He'd have good days and bad, and eventually, a boss wouldn't hold a job for someone who just didn't show up to work.

Being here was new, New York different. I'd lived in the Midwest my whole life, but Dad got a tip on a job here. He'd brought me and my sister, Sloane. Our mom died when we were kids.

Sloane was only a year older than me, but she generally made the bulk of the money in our household. We couldn't rely on Dad, so she always took part-time work and did odd jobs. I helped out too when I could, but generally, Sloane wanted me to focus on school. She was in school too but didn't take it as seriously as I did. She said I was smart and was going to do something one day. She skipped school today to work, but I probably wouldn't see her anyway since this school's campus was so big and she was a year older.

The redhead gave no response to what I said about Cissy besides looking out of the window again. I was sure she was just misunderstood, and I knew that too. You got to be whoever you wanted when you came to a new school, but eventually, people found you out. A guy's personality would show, and they'd find out I was just a nerd and label me like they did this girl.

I wasn't sure of the redhead's story, but her otherness I definitely got.

"Fawn Greenfield," she said after a while, and I looked at her. She tipped her chin. "I'm Fawn."

She's Fawn.

I smiled at her. "Hi, Fawn."

She nodded, sitting back. "And I guess you can sit here, but you probably shouldn't."

Again, she said *shouldn't*. I put my milk down. "Why's that?"

Once more, she gave a look like it was obvious. She gazed around. "Because no one does."

I got that too. I got being the one no one sees.

I got being broken.

I saw that every day with Dad, and before she gazed away at the snow, I leaned forward. "Well, I'm okay with that. I'll probably be here two seconds before I have to move."

I felt vulnerable admitting that but saw no point in hiding from her or judgment. Again, I'd probably only be here a little while.

I got her attention with that, her lips parting. "Why?"

"Dad's always between jobs." I picked at the plastic on my sandwich. I shrugged. "Has a hard time keeping work, I guess. Mental health stuff."

I felt really, *really* vulnerable saying that, and I did gaze away this time at Fawn's snow. I found her name interesting, Fawn, and the snow seemed fitting. A fawn in the snow.

"Well, maybe it won't be that way this time."

I glanced at her, instantly discovering something curious.

A smile. Fawn *smiled* at me, and though it was faint, she did.

I think right away she saw that I saw because she pushed back her hair, fidgeting. "I mean, it sounds like that sucks, so yeah. Maybe it won't be that way this time."

"Maybe." I sat back. "You, um, think I can sit here longer if it isn't? If I'm not here just two seconds, I mean."

I'd like to sit with her, I think. I would.

Fawn did that mouth-parting thing again, and instead of responding, she nodded. It was quick and almost shy and made her face red. It'd been red when I came over, but I think just out of agitation that I'd joined her.

That didn't seem to be the case now, and I smiled at my food. Maybe I would be here longer than two seconds.

Maybe this time it would be different.

CHAPTER
ONE

Bru – the present

"How the fuck do you two even know each other?"

My brother's words had bite to them.

His gaze matched.

Ares Mallick came at Fawn and me hot when we'd come in, but he wasn't the only one who was pissed the fuck off.

Which was why I was cutting him off from Fawn again.

I cut off his view, cut off any and all contact he could possibly make with her. He didn't have any right to it according to what she'd told me at the airport.

"I'm going to need you to clarify something for me first, bro," I said, slipping my hands in my pockets. My brother was taller than me, but I noticed he'd gotten leaner since I'd last seen him. I assumed that was because he wasn't playing football this year. He actually went by Wolf on the football field, and people called him that. He was clearly still a gym rat, though. His angular jaw was chiseled and defined, and because Wolf was my adoptive brother, we looked nothing alike. He had a tan to his skin that I didn't have, his parents a mixture of races. His hair was darker than mine too, and more often than not, he kept it back and out of the way. It was long and curly, so I got that. He did that today, and I think I only picked up on his leaner build because I myself had been packing on the pounds in the gym. It'd been something to do between classes.

Yeah, something to do.

Wolf's reasons for not playing football recently weren't unknown to me and was almost the reason I didn't go away to school this past semester. My brother had been going through it, and I wanted to be there for him. What I hadn't expected when I came back from a semester overseas was all this, though. What Fawn had told me was insane.

Fawn Greenfield…

Behind me, she was looking at everything but Wolf, and it'd been so long since I'd seen her. Been around her…

Gazing away, I faced my brother. "I want you to explain to me what happened last semester. What happened between you and Fawn."

My brother blinked then and with good reason. I was still having a hard time digesting what she'd told me, and even seeing Fawn at all had been crazy. I'd actually been trying to figure out what I was going to say to my family about my last semester when I saw her.

And then, well, I saw her.

She'd been there right in the middle of Maywood Heights International Airport. She had her phone in hand, and I thought I dreamed her up at first. It'd been a really long time, and I greeted her, of course. We were catching up when she said she missed her flight home and the alternative was her going back to her school, Pembroke University. I was familiar with it since my brother and sister went there, and she was talking like she was going to spend the holidays on campus.

I didn't know why my first instinct (after chatting with her for like a minute) was to invite her home with me for Christmas. She probably thought I was a freak, but it'd just been so nice to see her. I'd been really in my head when I saw her, and yeah, it'd been nice.

I had to say not much changed about her, but then on the other hand, so much had. I recognized her right away, bright red hair, freckles, red lips. She'd worn lipstick back then too, always did, and it always made her look like a vintage photo. One of those classic ones of old Hollywood starlets. I remembered thinking that even back then.

What had been different was the automatic smile she gave in my direction to someone, she clearly, hadn't recognized. I'd changed quite a bit from the brief time we'd gone to school together, but despite not knowing who I was, she had just smiled at me. The old Fawn I knew hadn't done that. She was guarded *heavily*, and it took some time to crash through that exterior.

In fact, I didn't see anything of the old Fawn until she had mentioned my brother. It came up when I'd been asking her about coming home with me. I explained my family dynamic, how I was adopted, and as soon as she found out who my family was, her entire demeanor had changed. She'd locked up again.

She got guarded again.

I was covering her at this point because, for some reason, my brother was getting closer to her. His two piercings in his left nostril rose and fell when his nose flared. He was angry I brought her here, but he wasn't the only one who was angry.

I put a hand on Wolf's chest, his heart racing behind it. "Bro, explain to me. *Now.*"

Because my shit was racing too. I was *angry* too because no reason in the goddamn world warranted the kind of behavior Fawn explained to me.

And definitely not directed toward her.

It'd been a long time, but I knew Fawn's story. I knew what she'd been through. I also knew she'd been a friend to me no matter how brief the time. We'd both had some bullshit happen to us back then.

And we'd managed to find solace with each other while within it.

I got Fawn's hand then, mostly because my brother was still stepping up on her. She started backing away, and I wanted to let her know she was okay. I had her, and she was good.

Right away, she gripped my hand, and distracted by that, I glanced down. My brother gained then, and it took a second to distance him.

He sneered at me, Fawn, then for some reason our hands, which I found odd. He bared teeth. "You told him, Red? You fucking *told him?* How do you guys even know each other—"

"You have *no* right."

I blinked for a few reasons. One was because my brother had given Fawn a nickname. I mean, it was an obvious one. She was a redhead, but that was... different. Another was because I was still kind of thinking about my hand holding Fawn's. We used to do that a lot too. We were friends, but there were a lot of moments either one of us just needed a little security in the past. We needed a kind gesture from a familiar face.

We needed a friend.

I wasn't able to think about it long because she let go, which brought me to the other reason I blinked. She'd been the one to tell my brother off after what he said and was now stepping up *on him* with her finger in his face. She legit walked up on him, and even though she was like over a foot beneath him (everyone was with his height), she stood tall. She stood confident. I'd seen that before too. Fawn Greenfield stood up against her bullies.

She always had.

· · ·

Fawn

This was a bad idea. Terrible.

And yet, here I was.

Here *we* were, Wolf and me, and him driving me *fucking* crazy. Here he was getting a reaction out of me, and that pissed me off so fucking much.

I shook my finger at him, actually shaking, and I know I surprised him. He closed his mouth after I snapped at him, and he didn't do that.

And to see him...

This sucked. It *killed*. My chest borderline caved in looking at him like I'd been socked in the freaking chest. Some of his hair had glided out of his bun, the curly strands wavy.

Gorgeous.

His jawline cut sharp, more defined like he'd been sculpting himself more than bulking up. Of course, he was still huge and completely all-encompassing.

Completely intimidating.

I couldn't let him intimidate me. Not this time. I hadn't wanted to come here today and confront him, but since I was, I had to stand my ground.

I had to stand up for myself.

I was doing that by getting in his face, and even though he smelled like literal heaven, I didn't back down. I wouldn't. I wet my lips. "You're completely and ridiculously unbelievable. Do you know that?" The audacity he had for coming at me. The audacity he had for getting *mad* at me, all things considered. "I owe you nothing. Nothing, do you understand that?"

I really hadn't wanted to come here today. I'd wanted to go home, but something happened when I saw Bruno at the airport.

Bru...

He looked so different now, completely different. For starters, he was like two Brunos with his size. He had arms nearly as big as Thatcher Reed's beneath his jacket, which he'd put on after I ran into him in the airport. Thatcher was Wolf's childhood friend, and the guy was huge, just like Bruno.

I guessed it was Bru now. He'd asked me to call him that when he'd seen me at the airport, and how crazy that had been. I hadn't seen him in years, and even though I hadn't, it'd been like no time had passed seeing him. He'd been a rock for me back then, a kind face in the midst of so much trauma.

But then you left.

I had to after what I did to Cissy Armstrong. She'd locked me in a car knowing I was afraid of them after my dad died. He'd died in a car crash, and I'd been at the wheel.

She knew that.

I didn't regret standing up for myself, but I did regret what I'd done in retaliation. I hurt her physically, badly. It'd been so bad and completely out of character for me. I had to leave school after, leave Bruno, and things got so much worse after that. I got worse.

Bru stood there, and I couldn't forget the look on his face after I told him what his brother did to me. How confused he'd been...

How angry.

I'd never really seen Bru's angry side when we'd gone to school together. He'd always been that comfort for me, but the moment he found out about Wolf, he'd been furious. Immediately, he'd wanted to confront Ares, and I should have just let him.

But for some reason, I came with him.

For some reason, I wanted to step in and retract everything I said. I wanted to go to Ares himself and stop Bru from confronting him. I wanted to *stop this* like I wanted to protect Wolf or something, and that didn't make any fucking sense.

But doesn't it?

No, it didn't. He'd hurt me, and regardless, I didn't end up doing anything anyway when I saw him. It was like just being in front of him locked me up. It always locked me up, and I was tired of this shit.

Wolf started to open his mouth, but I wasn't going to let him talk. He'd done enough talking, and it was my turn now.

"Red…"

But then he said that, *Red*, and he looked at me in a way that made me feel seen. It made my entire being blaze like I was bathed in fire and not given the courtesy of an easy death. A bullet to the heart would have been easier.

It was easier.

I backed away, unable to do this. Bru started to reach for me, go to me. I had to put up that barrier too because he had a way of making me feel seen as well. He gave me support in some of the worst moments of my life. He gave me his friend-ship, and even though it hadn't been for long, that meant something to me. It made me stronger, and I didn't want him to see how weak his brother made me. Bru had seen too many instances of me being weak in the past, and I refused to let him see that side of me again.

Ashamed, I ran off, and even left my bag. Bru had gotten both mine and his inside before we'd seen Wolf.

"Fawn!"

I think it was a combination of them both that called me, but I wasn't able to identify if that were true. I opened the door, but stopped when I physically couldn't go any farther.

I think three guys the size of literal marines had some-thing to do with that.

CHAPTER
TWO

Ares

The wrong time for the guys to come over. The wrong fucking time even if I had asked them. I'd wanted to tell them something and planned to do so tonight.

I'd planned to tell everyone really, and *I'd planned* for the kid, aka my little brother, Bru, to be part of that.

But then he'd done this.

Then he'd brought *Fawn*, and what in the literal fuck?

"Fawn?" Dorian had said that, my best friend from high school and my whole life. He was flanked by our other best friends, Thatcher and Wells, and all three of them were clustered in the snow and gazed inside the house. They were studying Fawn, and I was too.

I couldn't help it.

I hadn't been within five feet of Red for months. I'd seen her, but I definitely hadn't let her see me. She was hard to miss on campus, and intentional or not, I did see her.

I was around her.

More often than not, I witnessed her striding across the quad or studying in the library. Too often than not, I was aware of her brushing snow off her shoulders when she came into a building or kicking that same snow off her boots. She didn't like snow. In fact, it annoyed the fuck out of her. She always appeared increasingly frustrated when she did have to rid herself of it. Like she didn't live in the Mid-fucking-west and had to deal with it like everyone did in the winter.

But that was just her, Red.

Red...

Her face was full of color, her tan freckles blending into it. She always flushed cherry red when she was frustrated or scared.

When I made her come.

That Red was my favorite, the one where I had her writhing beneath me, calling my name, and taking her to her high. I brought the madness out of her, her freak, and for so long I tried to control it. I did that, and she couldn't control me.

Yeah, about that...

That wasn't the Red I'd seen today. She'd been pissed at me in her little puffer coat, the one that did nothing for her curves and hid all her tattoos. I used to like licking her tats. I bit and flicked my tongue across every visible inch of this girl only a matter of months ago.

But that wasn't now. Now, I was trying to keep her from destroying the last fucking shreds of anything stable I had. Now wasn't the time for all this. It couldn't be the time.

"What, uh," Dorian started, coming inside. I wasn't surprised. Dude had open access to my window since we were kids and snuck in all the time to game or chill. He was doing that even more so now since he was dating my sister, Sloane, but even before that, he'd always made himself at home in my space.

The same went for Wells and Thatcher, who definitely

exchanged a glance before they came inside. All my friends were big fucking dudes, but they definitely had to make room for Thatch, who was the biggest. Thatcher closed the door before wrestling snow out of his dark hair, the cross earring in his ear dangling. He'd flicked it but stopped everything he was doing when Bru came up behind Fawn.

He'd been faster.

The kid didn't use to be faster than me. Not even when we were on the football field in high school did he outrun me, but I'd let myself slip in the past few months. A lot of stuff had changed, and the kid himself had certainly contributed to that.

Bru hadn't even looked like himself when he'd come in, and I think I only glossed over that due to the appearance of Fawn. She'd distracted me, but seeing him behind her now, I definitely noticed he'd grown like three sizes. Not in height but mass, and even though he wore a coat, he was stretching the seams of it.

Yeah, a lot had changed.

Those changes were far from the reaches of my mind at the present. I didn't have the mental bandwidth to address them, as Dorian's, Thatcher's, and Wells's shock at seeing Fawn transferred to surprise at seeing Bru, then shock again.

I appeared then, right then, and they saw me well. I was a part of all this too and came forward.

But that didn't mean I had anything to say.

I didn't know what I could say or should. I didn't know what the fuck was going on or how my little brother knew Red.

"Hey, Prinze," Bru led in with. He always called Dorian by his last name. "What's up?"

Dorian obviously didn't know what to say either.

My buddy D, as eloquent as he was, appeared to be at a loss for words. He was but did hug my brother.

"Hey. You're home," D said, patting Bru's back. Dorian

expected my brother home after Bru had been away at school for the semester, but I highly doubted he thought the reunion would be like this.

The same clearly went for Thatcher and Wells because after their hugs, Wells mouthed, "What the fuck," over to me. He was getting shaggy these days since he'd grown out his hair a bit. It was still electric blond everywhere but the roots. The fucker didn't bother keeping up on dyeing it.

"Uh, yeah, got in a bit early," Bru stated, stepping back, but when he did, he was right in line with Fawn. He stood beside her, *with her*, and unreasonable agitation unfurled inside of me. I didn't forget how he put his hand on her before, and although it might not mean anything at all, I was always territorial when it came to Red. I obviously fucking loved my brother, but it didn't matter who was close to Red. This was *Red*.

My Red.

Of course, this was unreasonable, and once more, I didn't care. Regardless, acting on anything other than standing here wasn't a good idea. At least, not until I knew what all this was.

Bru gestured to Fawn. "I ran into Fawn at the airport."

"Wait. You two know each other?" Thatcher asked that, and ironically had already gotten more information than I'd been able to. The kid wouldn't answer me when I'd asked, and Fawn definitely hadn't.

She stood there, shifting in her snow boots. Wrestling with her hands, she had her sight on nothing but the door when earlier all she'd wanted to do was call me on my shit.

"We do." Bru gazed down at her. "We went to school together briefly. High school."

What. The. Fuck.

I felt like I was having an out-of-body experience right now because what were the fucking odds that my little brother went to school with my ex-fake girlfriend? What were the odds that they'd run into each other and that meeting would result in this?

This...

I didn't know what this was, but I assumed this was all Fawn. This was her trying to teach me a lesson for breaking things off with her. I'd done that when shit got too real for her during our fake relationship and the lines got blurred. I'd wanted to spare her.

I'd wanted to save her.

I'd needed to get her away from me, and it was the only thing I'd ever done right for her. She and I didn't belong together, point-blank. I wasn't the good guy. I was the one dads had shotguns for to protect their daughters from. I'd used Fawn. I *used* her.

Then had the nerve to fall for her.

The sins didn't even end there. In fact, they were so fucking evil and sick that most days, I had a hard time even looking at myself in the mirror. I kept seeing the monster that did that to her, the selfish prick who'd done it for his own gain.

No matter the severity of the reason.

As far as I was concerned, I'd allowed Fawn Greenfield to go on and live her life, but now here she was about to decimate my already fragile life. This almost seemed like poetic justice. Fitting.

But that didn't mean I was going to allow it.

My brothers, Dorian, Thatcher, and Wells, didn't need all this shit to air. It would just fuck them up and be unnecessarily cruel on an already bullshit situation. Bru clearly already knew something, but he didn't know everything.

It wasn't possible.

Fact of the matter was, I had strong reasons for getting into a fake relationship with Fawn. They were messed up, fucked up, but the kid would hear me out if I just got a second with him. He'd be pissed at me and probably wouldn't understand, but he'd hear me out. He'd give me *time* and more than I seemed to have in this moment.

I started to step forward and take Bru aside. I just needed that second with him and would do anything for it.

"Yeah, Bru brought me over for dinner, but I obviously didn't know he was Wolf's brother."

I paused after what Fawn said, but mostly because the kid did. His attention made a beeline for her, his brow jumping, and mine did too.

She didn't know…

I found that hard to believe. She'd been angry before she even walked through the door. I knew because I'd seen that as she'd entered. Bru had also said he'd brought her here to spend Christmas break with us, not just dinner.

"Fawn?" Bru started to say, but Red cut him off. She physically got in front of him, standing between him and the guys.

"I, uh… I came over for dinner and had no idea." She placed a hand on her head, laughing when a second ago, Red wasn't laughing. She'd been pissed at me and handing me my shit, but she *hadn't* been laughing.

She appeared to be now.

"Obviously, I realized the connection when I got here," she continued, putting her hands out toward Bru, then me. Her smile escaped during the latter, but she didn't scowl at me like she had been. She put off indifference. Like it didn't matter that I was standing here before her.

Like I didn't bother her.

But I did, though. I knew I did, and I'd seen that before when she'd come inside.

She chewed her lip in front of my friends. "The whole thing was terribly awkward as you can imagine—"

"Fawn." Bru shook his head at her. "What…"

He didn't finish, but he didn't need to. Fawn wasn't telling the truth, and that was very apparent when she smiled at him…

Then said she had to go.

My friends and I watched as she thanked my brother for his invitation for dinner, then politely declined. She thanked him for that and only that and made no reference toward staying for the holiday. She made no reference toward me, or our fake relationship. She just thanked Bru for dinner, *lying* right there in front of Bru, my friends, and me.

I just didn't know why.

This girl had every opportunity she could possibly have to put everything I'd done out there. I mean, she already had to Bru to some extent.

And she was leaving.

"It was good to see you," she said to my brother, and even gave him a hug. It didn't bother me. Not like it had before when he'd touched her. It was friendly. These two were clearly friends. She faced me. "Wolf."

Wolf…

And that was all she said before aiming for the door. She grabbed the handle of her rolling bag too, but something had me cutting off her escape.

I put my hand on the door, not letting her go, and I didn't realize why until I was looking down at her, until I was smelling her…

Drowning in her.

Red always smelled like sugar. She always smelled warm and good, and that was just who she was. She was standing there, right there, and protecting me. She was protecting her evil.

Her monster.

Her lips trembled a little, those red lips I'd tasted. I wanted to taste them now. I wanted to taste them so bad.

"Buddy?" Dorian's blond eyebrows narrowed at me, and it took me a minute to realize Red and I weren't alone. That it wasn't just her and me, and we weren't in the reality of my own creation. I was the reason everyone was here and confused. This was me, all me and a fake relationship I'd started.

My gaze hit Bru then, that reality there. His frown was deep on me, heavy, and I made a choice in that moment. I knew if I just took him aside, I could weather this current storm. I could give him the reason why I'd done what I had to Fawn, and he'd give me his confidence for as long as I needed him to. He would because we were brothers, and Dorian, Thatcher, and Wells wouldn't have to know about anything that happened last semester. I'd come out unscathed...

And Fawn would look like the fool.

"We were fake," I stated, looking at her when I said it. "Everything. It was fake."

I was outside of my body hearing the words, and I didn't care about anyone's reactions to them. I just wanted Fawn's. I wanted her clear from this.

I wanted her out.

Her head shook when I spoke, and her face managed to get even redder. She blinked. "Wolf?"

Confusion lined her raspy voice, awe. She didn't know why I was doing this, and I liked to say I didn't know why either.

But that'd be another lie.

I stepped close to her about the same time I heard a shift to my left and gazed up to find my father on the opposite end of the foyer.

He wasn't alone.

He had my mother with him. Her coat was still on, and my father had his on too. In fact, the only person who'd removed hers was my sister, Sloane, who was also standing there. She stood between them.

And I couldn't breathe.

A pin drop could be heard in that moment, and even though my parents' house had vaulted ceilings, I could hear my own breath. I could hear Red's who was right there in front of me.

"What was fake?" Dad asked, casually taking off his coat. I looked a lot like my father, dark hair, curly. He was the tallest person in the room outside of myself, but his confusion was evident upon seeing what he was seeing. He knew Fawn and I had broken up, but here she was standing in front of me. "Son?"

My mom had the same question, that same confusion in her dark eyes. She had shopping bags in her arms, and my sister did as well. The three of them had gone Christmas shopping, and I'd bowed out because I was a moody prick.

Dad had his own bags. They were currently on the floor as he must have placed them down to take his coat off. He wasn't picking them up, and my sister, Sloane, wasn't moving toward Bru or her boyfriend. This was unusual considering she hadn't seen our brother in months, and anytime Dorian was in the room, my twin had blinders. She'd normally be in his arms in seconds, but currently, she had fingers to her lips. Like she was trying to determine what was going on here and was just as confused as our parents. They all must have come through the back entry and happened to come in right at this point in the conversation.

Everyone was confused, clearly. Dorian, Wells, and Thatch also stayed in place. They weren't moving, and their heads were cocked while looking at me. The only people who weren't confused were Bru and Fawn. Bru was holding his big arms and looking like some kind of pissed-off dad. Like he was waiting for some kind of explanation from his son who'd fucked up. Actually, Fawn was the only one who wasn't looking at me, but she did when I gazed at her. She probably thought I'd lie and throw her under the bus in that moment.

I mean, I had before.

"Fawn and I, our entire relationship, was fake," I said, refusing to break eye contact with her now that I had it.

I think it gave me strength.

CHAPTER
THREE

Fawn

"So, um…" Wells Ambrose acquired a couch cushion beside me and dropped his arms between his long legs. He was the lankiest out of all the Legacy boys, but he was still solid. He played football like the rest of them too, so that much was a given. He opened his hands. "How did this all happen?"

Thatcher Reed gazed over from his easy chair, and Dorian Prinze did the same from his position by the door. I was surrounded by Legacy boys, and people on campus called them that because of the influence they came from. Their families were rich, powerful, and I managed to get caught up with all of them because of Wolf.

I can't believe he told the truth.

I was left without any allies here in front of the Legacy boys. Shortly after Wolf's confession, he'd been ushered away, and that went the same for Bru and their sister, Sloane. Their parents called a family meeting, and Bru had had no choice but to attend.

Of course, that hadn't sat well with the rest of Legacy.

Things had gotten elevated before Mr. Mallick shut things
down and called the meeting. They'd gotten *loud* as the
Legacy guys had their own questions about the whole fake-
dating situation.

This is such a mess.

I knew it would be, which was why I wanted to stop all
this. I hadn't wanted all these people hurt in all this just
because Wolf was completely screwed up.

Yeah, keep telling yourself that was the only reason you did it.

I would tell myself that. Wolf had been cruel to me, sick
and cruel and terrible. A fake relationship was unfortunately
only the tip of the iceberg when it came to the reaches of his
cruelty. He'd used my internship with the *New York Times*
against me, as well as threatened my enrollment at my
college, Pembroke University. He dangled them both above
my head to force me into doing what he wanted, and let's not
even go into how far the whole fake relationship itself had
gone. It had gotten physical in the end, sexual, but if things
had only stopped there, I would have been okay. Wolf was a
gorgeous guy, and I could fuck him with no strings, if
anything as penitence, but that wasn't what had happened.

That was when his savagery took on a new level. Things
had gotten physical. They'd gotten intense and lines had
gotten completely eradicated not just blurred. I hadn't been
wrong for sleeping with Wolf countless times. Where I'd gone
wrong was thinking those times meant something to him.
He'd led me to believe something and ended up using me in
more than one way.

"Better yet, why did this happen?" Thatcher Reed put his
phone away. He'd been tapping on it and restless like the rest
of these guys. He frowned. "Why would he do this?"

I definitely didn't want to be here, answering these
questions.

Bru, where are you?

He was somewhere in this gorgeous house, the place

decorated with winter flourishes and twinkling lights. The Mallick family clearly got into the holiday spirit. I'd spotted at least three Christmas trees on the way into this room, and I'd only seen three rooms on the way to this one. I rubbed my hands. "He, um, came to me toward the beginning of the semester. Wolf did."

I had Dorian Prinze's attention now. The big blond shifted from his position at the door, and he hadn't left it. He was the only one standing in the room and had his meaty arms crossed. He kept staring out of the door like he was ready and waiting to take action. I didn't know what kind, but I assumed that had something to do with the family meeting going on somewhere in this big house. Honestly, they probably wouldn't even have been excluded from it if not for the explosion in the foyer. These guys had big personalities, but Mr. Mallick wasn't having it. With just a word from him, they exited the room, and they'd gone like soldiers. They undoubtedly respected him.

I released a breath. "He came to me saying he needed a fake girlfriend and blackmailed me into doing it." I watched the guys' reactions to that, each of them exchanging glances with one another. "He threatened an internship I had with the *New York Times* and my enrollment at Pembroke if I didn't do it."

Thatcher's and Wells's mouths parted, and a heavy confusion laced Dorian Prinze's eyes. Thatcher scrubbed into his dark hair. "But why?"

I really, really didn't want to answer that. At this point, I didn't care about putting Wolf's business out there, but this was personal. This was a family, and these guys were his family too. I'd seen their connection, their brotherhood. There were a lot of people affected by Wolf's actions, and I didn't want to be the one to tell them why he lied.

I really needed Bru and hadn't realized the extent of that need until he'd been forced to leave too. His attention had been on nothing but me before he'd left, and it reminded me of when we'd been in school. We hadn't known each other very long, but we had quickly formed a connection and he'd been there during some really dark times. He'd been there when I couldn't see beyond my trauma. My dad had died in high school, and Bru knew what it was like to see someone going through tough times. He'd had a parent he basically had to take care of due to mental health issues, so he knew how to deal with people who were suffering…

Who were fragile.

It was like we'd stepped back into old roles when he took my hand in the foyer. He'd been a lifeline instantly and with no questions asked. That was just Bruno Sloane.

Bruno Sloane-Mallick now.

This was all so complicated. This was all so messed up, and I hated this. I hated it for everyone, but I hated Wolf even more. I hated that he'd done this, and that I'd contributed to it. I especially hated how I kept *thinking* about him, and that he was somewhere in this house too. I loathed that I wondered about what he was going through and what he was feeling while he did. I hated that I wondered if he was okay.

Like he ever, *ever* had the right to get that from me.

Maybe this was some residual Stockholm syndrome. Maybe I'd fallen for my bully, but I couldn't let myself go back to that place. It broke me the first time. It broke me so bad.

I breathed into my hands. "He said he did it for you guys."

"What?" Dorian stayed at the door after his question, like he was locked there, but that certainly hadn't stopped his quest for answers.

I nodded. "He said he didn't want you guys to worry about him. He wanted to show you he'd moved on and that he was okay." I swallowed. "That he was okay after his cancer."

Of course, this behavior was the opposite of okay, and the reaction to what I said chimed more than one curse in the air.

"That motherfucker," rolled out of Thatcher Reed's mouth. He wet his lips before working his jaw with his beefy hand. "He would."

He would.

This behavior appeared to be not so crazy in this circle of guys, but that didn't mean they were happy about it. Frustrations rang across all three of them. Especially Dorian who still hadn't left the door. He was cracking his knuckles as he gazed away, and that was when Wells leaned forward.

"So, it was all fake, then? All of it?" he asked me, and Thatcher lifted his head. He'd been staring at the floor. Wells shook his head. "For weeks, just fake?"

I started to speak, but hesitated a beat. I think that had something to do with Dorian. I gained his attention, and the intensity of his stare could only challenge one person. Wolf was also very intense when one happened to receive his full attention. He didn't go in weak about it. He made you feel it, and I borderline suffocated beneath it.

I had been suffocated and was so tired of the lack of air. I was tired of feeling like I was drowning all the time. I'd tried a lot of vices in my life, but none were as raw and visceral as Wolf Mallick. He was the worst fucking high, and coming down had one hundred percent killed me.

"It was fake," I told the room, and I said that with confidence. It wasn't possible to fall in love with something that wasn't real, and even though Wolf had told the truth tonight, I doubted that had anything to do with me. He didn't love me, never had.

And to that he'd been clear.

CHAPTER
FOUR

Ares

"You really paraded this girl around *like an object* for weeks, Ares? Lying to us... What in God's name were you thinking?"

My mom had always been the hard-ass between both of my parents. She was the one who voiced her opinions while my dad typically sat back in the supportive role. That went the same for this moment, my mom basically chewing me out in front of my siblings. Sloane couldn't even look at me during all of it, but Bru was doing enough of it for the both of them. The kid had been giving me nothing but the stink-eye this entire time, like he had nothing to do with this moment.

He didn't have anything to do with it.

In my mind, I knew that, but that still didn't stop me from being pissed off at him. Was that illogical and completely fucked up? Yeah, but that was me.

The fuckup.

I was fucked up, and my entire family (and the guys) were seeing that now. Thatch, Dorian, and Wells were somewhere in the house with Fawn, and that was honestly where I wanted to be. I didn't want to be around the guys right now. They'd be giving me just as much of a handling for what I'd done, but I did want to make sure Fawn was okay. That was illogical too, but I couldn't help feeling that way.

She shouldn't have been here for all of this.

I cut a look to Bru then, and he cut one right back. He had his own words to say about all this undeniably, and I was sure I'd hear them just like the boys later.

And Sloane.

Like stated, my twin couldn't even look at me. She'd stopped looking about the same time I'd been forced to admit why I had done all of this. I told my family I hadn't wanted them to worry about me, and a fake girlfriend had been the solution. I told them what they needed to know in that moment, and yeah, it was the truth.

Mostly.

The lies still continued here in front of my family, but I was giving them what they could handle at this point. The night had turned into something else, but this version was just as fucked up.

I lifted my shoulders after what my mother said, and with barely a response from me, she frowned. She still basically had her coat on, even though we were inside my dad's office with the fireplace going. She pushed her hand into her dark hair, and after her hand dropped, my dad reached for it. He was able to do that now that she'd stopped pacing. He sat in one of his leather easy chairs while my mother had completely abandoned the one beside it.

"Tell me you at least took care of Fawn's internship," Dad said, and yeah, I'd been forced to admit that too, the blackmail. He actually already knew about her internship since he'd technically met Fawn before. It'd been at her internship interview, but she hadn't been my girlfriend then.

Your fake girlfriend.

My dad wet his lips, and his patience was thinning, considering his terse expression. "Son?"

"Yes. Yeah." I dropped my head, too many eyes on me. Normally, I was strong enough to stand in front of my parents regarding anything I'd done. I didn't back down from my fuckups, but disappointing them in this way hit hard. It reminded me of all the other times I'd disappointed them in the past when I really had been fucked up. Shit got so dark back when I was in high school. Since my sister, Sloane, hadn't always been with us, I hadn't handled that well. She'd been taken from us, stolen.

She was here now obviously, and her disappointment hit just as bad. She sat on the couch next to Bru. She had her feet up on the sofa, and her oversize hoodie completely covered her leggings. It looked like one of Dorian's since it said Pembroke Football.

"You know, I really don't know what's worse, Ares." Dad guided Mom over to the arm of his chair. Slinging an arm around her waist, he managed to get her to sit instead of pacing. His eyes narrowed. "The fact that you did all this, or the only reason you came clean was because your hand was forced. Because your brother ran into Fawn at the airport and you had no choice."

I glanced over at the kid in that moment, and if it was possible, he appeared madder at me than anyone. I mean, my mom was pretty pissed, but red had completely colored Bru's tightened jaw. I figured his anger was because he knew Fawn, and well, because what I'd done was pretty fucked up.

"I know the answer to that," Mom answered for my father, and he apparently did too because he shook his head.

"And you said you know her from high school?" Sloane asked, facing our brother. She hadn't gotten the reunion with him she'd probably wanted. The two were so fucking close, but all that was rushed due to all this shit. She placed a hand on his arm. "I don't remember seeing her."

"Well, it was a big school, and we lived in New York for only like a minute before Dad forced us to leave," he said, referring to his bio dad and Sloane's kidnapper. Bru's biological father had been forced to take Sloane by a third party. The man had been threatened, and it was understood by everyone in this room he'd been guilt-ridden about it. That was all a story for another day, but the signs were there according to Sloane and Bru. The man was severely depressed, anxious, and the result led to Sloane and Bru basically raising themselves.

There was so much trauma in this fucking room, so much goddamn trauma, and all I'd done was add to it. The story surrounding my sister's reunion into my family was a long one, and though it certainly didn't end happy, it had started to gain some light. It had until I'd gotten sick.

I rubbed my hands in front of the fireplace light, and all eyes were gratefully on Bru at the moment.

"I hadn't seen her since then," Bru continued. "I was still in disbelief about that when she told me about Ares."

"Which is why you actually brought her home, then?" I asked, knowing I really had no fucking right, but I hadn't forgotten what he said about that whole Christmas thing. He said Red was his guest but she hadn't even fucking wanted to be here. In fact, she'd tried to stop this whole thing, lie for me...

"Actually, no. At least, not at first," Bru quipped, instantly jerking me out of my thoughts. His lips turned down. "I invited Fawn, initially, to spend Christmas with our family. That'd been before you and all that." He tossed out a hand before facing our parents. "Fawn missed her flight back home to her own family. She was talking like she was going to spend the holidays on campus, but rather than let her do that, I extended an invitation for her to stay with us."

Red had been trying to go back home? To her family?

"Of course, that all backfired when she found out who my

brother was." The kid was shooting daggers at me with his eyes, and it'd been a long time since he'd looked at me so cold. We hadn't always gotten along, the kid and me. Things were rather tense when my sister came back, and neither one of us was sure how to adjust to our roles as Sloane's siblings. We'd gotten around it, though, and I'd literally die for this kid. He was my brother, blood or fucking not.

I didn't know the details surrounding his friendship with Fawn, but a friend would care about another friend. He would if he wasn't an asshole, and Red deserved to be cared about. She deserved more than that…

If I'd done any type of caring, none of us would be here right now, and I was surprised to hear what Bru said about Fawn's family. Red had been kind of estranged from them since her dad died. She'd distanced herself and closed off.

We were so much like each other.

Just tack on another reason why I needed to stay the hell away from her. My parents sighed yet again.

"Of course, she's welcome here, son. That is, if she still wants to," Dad stated, eyeing me. My dad was never the stern one, but I never fucked up in front of him either if I could help it. My father was laid back, so when he did crack enough to show his anger, that felt ten times worse than seeing Mom's. It meant I broke him, and I hated that. He glanced at my mom. "Though, this does complicate things."

I didn't understand, nor did Bru or Sloane. They finally let up with their leering in my direction to study our parents. Reaching down, Mom grabbed her handbag, then handed my sister a green envelope.

"What's this?" I asked, but instantly shut my mouth when I got that heat from, like, everyone in the room. My dad's eyes held nothing but warning. I wasn't to talk, not right now.

I stayed silent, watching as my sister opened the envelope. The front of it said, *"To the kids,"* and when she opened it, a handful of tickets fell out.

Plane tickets.

"The Reeds have some property in South Carolina," Mom said, referring to my buddy Thatcher's parents. "They have a house, and the families all planned to spend Christmas down there together. Escape the winter and my parties, which I know you kids hate."

We didn't hate her holiday parties. Well, my siblings didn't hate them. Again, I was a moody prick and didn't like anything that was considered social outside of hanging out with my friends.

If I didn't already need another reason to feel guilty. I'd clearly been taken into consideration when it came to these plans. At least, when it came to my parents and our family's involvement.

"I can stay home," I said, doubting anyone wanted to share physical space with me anyway at this point. I'd most certainly have to deal with the guys too after all this, and they wouldn't be happy I lied to them either.

"Full of solutions tonight, aren't you?" My dad's back hit his leather chair. He opened his hands. "And just because you're in college doesn't mean you aren't going to be punished for what you did and how you treated someone, Ares. Lying to us is one thing, but what you did to Fawn was truly appalling. It is, and definitely not the kid your mother and I raised."

He didn't need to tell me what I did was awful. I knew.

Dad sighed. "Make no mistake, you will be dealt with, but in the interim, your mother and I need you kids to pack. Our flight for South Carolina leaves in the morning. As far as Fawn, *your mom and I* will talk to her. We have no problem with her coming along, but I highly doubt she'll want to be around Ares after all this. She probably won't, and we wouldn't blame her."

I wouldn't blame her either.

"Bru, if you could get her into a room after we talk to her

and something to eat?" Mom requested, her smile small. "We planned a formal dinner tonight to welcome you home, love, but…"

"I understand and no problem." Bru's attention cut to me, still pissed at me, and I didn't judge that either.

"Any other announcements or surprises?" Dad opened his hands. "It'd be nice to have a normal Christmas once we're down there, so if you have something, get it out right now."

My dad said this, but now wasn't the time for any kind of announcement. Not if he did indeed want us to have a normal Christmas.

And that much I knew.

My kid brother's gaze hit the floor, but Sloane eyed me. I hadn't known I had a twin for a very long time, but once I had, I was hard-pressed to keep shit from her. She was worse than the guys with her probing gaze. It was like she saw me inside and out.

Which was why my gaze hit the floor too.

CHAPTER
FIVE

Ares

My parents dismissed me after our family meeting. I'd been strongly advised to head to my room and pack and didn't dare attempt to determine the fallout of my actions tonight. I didn't dare see the guys. I didn't dare see Fawn, but what the fuck would I fucking say anyway?

There wasn't anything to say.

I'd made things right. At least, where she'd been concerned. I *let her go*, and there was no way in hell she'd be going out of town with my family and me. She wouldn't, and I wouldn't even have to stop her. My dad was right. She didn't want to be around me.

Even if she did try to save me.

I tried not to think about that part today. If I did, I'd think about the reason I cut off ties in the first place. The lines had been more than fucking blurred back then.

For both of us.

My bags packed for South Carolina, I attempted to get some sleep that night. I knew this was pointless. I didn't sleep. I'd already been having a hard time before the semester began, but it was even worse these days. My body didn't like beds no matter how soft.

Even still, I attempted, but my eyes opened at a tap to my window. Sighing, I sat up and didn't even bother looking.

It was always the same person.

Instead, I gave my buddy Dorian some light when I tapped a digit on my beside lamp. Of course, that was after I worked some of the kinks out of my back and the feeling back into my limbs. I'd fucked up and slept wrong.

I was clenching and unclenching my hands by the time Dorian was standing in front of me, and I was surprised I hadn't heard the taps sooner.

I'd shut off my phone.

Had that been weaker than shit to do? Yeah, but I didn't need it from my buddies right now. My parents showed disappointment through headshakes and lectures.

My friends showed it through anger.

Anger, I could take, but not right now when all this shit was fresh. I was also still dealing with my own internal shit, so no. I couldn't handle anything else they had for me at the present.

Lounging against the wall, Dorian crossed his legs at the ankles. His blond hair was fingered through, and he had a look about him that mildly disturbed me. Normally, he'd come into my room raising hell after the kind of shit I'd pulled.

Instead, he was *calm*.

I mean, he didn't look happy, but he was quiet, and the eeriness of that hit the room like an air horn in a library.

I shrugged. "So—"

"What are you going to do?" His head cocked at me, his dark eyes focused. That really tripped me out because he was calm, controlled. He shook his head. "What are you going to do about all this?"

Alarm bells hit my head. I was unsure of what he was talking about, and it was weird him coming at me this way.

Deciding not to panic, I put my hands together. I thought he'd be yelling at me for lying to him. Lying to everyone. "What are you—"

"Fawn, man," he stated, and his expression could cut. He threw a hand out. "*Fawn* and the fact that you're clearly in fucking love with her."

I blanched, not expecting *that*. I mean, out of all the things the guy could say.

But then again…

This was D, and out of all the guys, we were the closest. We basically came out of the womb being best friends, and though the same went for Thatcher and Wells, Dorian and I were closer in age.

I let out a breath. "I don't know what you're talking about."

"Like fuck you don't."

I got up, easier to lie when I wasn't looking at him. It took me a second. Again, I was stiff, but once I got moving, I was okay. I grabbed my phone, and when I decided to tap on some random app and distract myself, Dorian swiped it.

He fucking threw it.

Normally, I'd have the dude on the goddamn floor right now for something like that. I didn't care if I was stiff or not. No one took my fucking phone, and whether we were evenly matched or not, I would have laid out my friend. I would if I hadn't already fucked up and lied to him about shit. "D—"

"Don't fucking lie to me." He was in my face, his finger in my face. "You owe me some truth, don't you fucking think?"

I did owe him truth, so much truth.

I stayed silent, and when he laughed, I maintained it. We wouldn't be talking about Fawn. Because if I did, I honestly didn't know what would come out. Fawn Greenfield was like truth serum to me.

She exposed me.

I'd seen that in full blast tonight. She had an effect on me I didn't like, so no, we weren't talking about her.

"This fake relationship. Fake." He'd air quoted that last word. "I mean, who do you think you're fucking playing?"

"Lay off, D."

"Lay off?"

"Yeah, fucking…" I got in his face but stopped. "Just don't. I played that girl. I played her for you fucks so you wouldn't worry about me."

"Yeah, we're not even going to go into that shit. If we do, I will lose my shit."

I'd rather that actually. Anything but this. "Nothing happened between Fawn and me. It was all a lie."

"I didn't ask if something happened. I know something happened. You forget I heard you two fucking on more than one occasion."

I closed my mouth. "We were, and it was casual."

"Fucking, right." Nothing but sarcasm passed Dorian's lips. "It was casual like when Sloane and I were hooking up."

He was saying the kind of shit that would lay him out. I accepted that he was with my sister, but we had a gentle-man's agreement I was never to hear about any of that shit. Like ever. "Watch yourself."

Ignoring me, he just closed more distance. I had height on my best friend, but he had mass. The fact was even more so now because he was doing college football, and honestly, these days, I wasn't sure I could take him. Not like before. Dorian's eyes narrowed. "I didn't ask if something happened between you. That much was a fucking given. What I asked was what are you going to do about it? Because something did happen, and you are in love with her."

There was no question, only a statement.

"And I swear to God, that's the only reason I'm not punching you out right now," he continued, laughing a little.

I was obviously testing him here. "Because shit got complicated, and your ass fell in love. I blame your continued idiocy, aka lying to us and not coming clean sooner, on that because I know what that shit does to you."

I was sure he did with my sister. I swallowed. "I'm not in love with her. That was all a lie. We were a lie. It was fake."

"Yeah, that's what she said," he stated, and I hadn't been prepared for that.

Nor the stomach clench that came with it.

Swallowing, I studied my friend, and Dorian paced a bit before wetting his lips.

"So, how about some truth now from you?" Dorian braced his big arms. "Come on, Ares. You know, I know you."

I'd been saved from the stupid response I know was about to come out of my mouth. The door swung open, and through it came a girl who looked like me but was shorter and wasn't as much in her fucking feelings.

"Well, since you're up," my sister, Sloane, quipped, and I had to say, she didn't appear any less pissed than she had downstairs. She started to get in my face too until Dorian shifted positions. He got the underside of her arms in the delicate way a quarterback received a pass. My buddy was just as good at that as calming my sister.

Because that's what he did as soon as she stepped up on me, but the action definitely wasn't *for me.* Things were still fucking heated between Dorian and me, and my sister was the only thing that could ever divert his attention. She was riled up, and he wanted her to feel better first and foremost.

The *babys* and *little fighters* in her direction told me that. *Little fighter* was his nickname for her.

"Dorian," she warned, but she was a sucker for him too. He did calm her down, massaging her shoulders, but the dynamic of the room shifted again when my bedroom door apparently became a revolving one.

"Since we're having a meeting." The kid made his appearance, and fucking hell, if he hadn't gotten bigger since I'd seen him. Bru was wearing a cutoff tee like me, and his arms fucking bulged.

I'd have asked him more questions if, I don't know, he hadn't been ruining my life earlier with Fawn. I almost wondered if she'd be flanking behind him, and I still had fucking questions about that.

I squeezed the bridge of my nose. "Kid—"

"Hello?" Wells's snowy-white head popped into the room, and what the fuck? Like clockwork, Thatcher's head appeared above him. Thatcher had the hood of his hoodie pulled up over his head, and both my friends pushed open the door fully dressed. Everyone else was in bed clothes, and even D had come in wearing lounge pants below his short coat.

I wasn't sure where my friends had headed after I'd been sent to my room, but I got an indicator when Dorian asked why Thatcher and Wells were still here. Apparently, they'd all gone home to pack, and Thatcher shrugged.

"We came back for some answers. The kid let us in," he said, then tossed his huge ass on my bed. The fucker launched himself, shoes and all, and I growled.

"Please. Make yourself at home," I cut, and Thatcher tipped his chin.

"Don't worry, my guy. We will." Thatch threw his hands back behind his head while Wells joined Dorian and Sloane on the window seat. There was plenty of room since Dorian had gathered Sloane on his lap. She was wearing another one of his hoodies and sleep shorts, and though she'd come in on fire, she wasn't talking. She had her little arms folded, mean mugging me.

My eyes lifted to the ceiling. "Why are you guys all here?"

It was a fucking town hall going on in this bitch, and all of Legacy was here, aside from Thatcher's sister, Bow. I was sure I'd be seeing her soon since the families were spending

Christmas together. She was in high school, and unlike the rest of the people in this room, she wouldn't give me a hard time. That was just Bow, the nice one.

That wasn't my buddies, and I knew exactly why they were here, them and Sloane and the kid. Everyone was pissed at me, but I didn't think I'd have to deal with that tonight.

Wells smirked. "Why aren't we here? The fuck was all that earlier tonight—"

"And by that, you mean the whole goddamn semester." Thatcher sat up. He tugged down his hood, and his metal earring hit the light in my room. "You really thought we'd want you to fucking lie to us? You and—"

"Fawn." The kid was coming out to play with his anger now, and I'd seen it well.

I was still trying to wrap my head around it.

I wasn't certain if Fawn had told him the reasons why I'd done what I had, but if anyone knew about protecting someone, it was the kid. He'd made the ultimate sacrifice for our sister in high school, and though I'd understand annoyance with me if he knew Fawn, I would have thought he at least got it.

Again, I still had my own questions, but I thought it best to keep them silent at the moment in a room full of pissed-off people.

Bru raised his hand, the guy sitting in my desk chair. "I mean, how do you even know Fawn to blackmail?"

"Oh, we know the answer to that," Thatch cut in, and I folded my hand over my face as he put out there *that* connection.

"You're kidding," Bru stated, and Wells shook his head.

"Wish he was, and you obviously never really forgave her for all that," Wells chimed in with, but that was when I lifted *my* hand.

"I was over that and hadn't lied about that," I admitted, making more than one eyebrow jump in the room. I had a big reason to have beef with Fawn over an episode that occurred in high school, a huge reason, but I truly had been over it. Had I felt that gave me license to rope her into all this fake-girlfriend shit, sure, but I hadn't been mad at her.

Knowing no one in this room would understand why, I, once more, kept my opinions to myself. That was when my sister laughed, and I truly didn't like her mad at me. Sloane and I hadn't gotten a lot of time together over the years, and I even stayed in the Midwest for school to be closer to her. The time had been great for us to get to know each other, so I didn't like wasting the time we did have on drama.

This couldn't be helped at the present, and I watched as my twin scrubbed at her face.

"You know, I warned *her* not to mess with *you*," she shot, and Dorian rubbed her arm. She wasn't having it, though, shaking her head at him before snarling at me. Her dark eyes pierced. "You made me look like an idiot, a fucking idiot, and what you did to her…"

Biting her lip, she gazed away.

"It was just awful. Horrible," she finished. "And for what? For us? Bull-fucking-shit. This was for you. For *you*, Ares. Fuck."

"Fuck is right." Thatcher leaned back. "I mean, I've done some fucked-up shit, man, but…"

I think we all had, all us guys anyway.

It seemed everyone had put me in my own league here, which said something. I gazed away. "Look. I know you're all pissed—"

"Damn fucking right. I mean, what the fuck?" Wells passed a hand over his head before looking at Dorian. "Right? Tell him what a fucking idiot he was."

Normally, he would. In fact, Dorian would be doing all the talking.

He wasn't tonight, and I guess I was the only one who

knew why. He'd come in here hot, but it wasn't so much about what I'd done.

I glanced away when D's dark eyes hit mine. My friends were all pretty intuitive. It came with the territory of us all knowing each other for, like, ever, but Dorian thought he got a read on something deeper tonight. Clearly.

"Not sure what else there is to say," he said, and my mouth parted. His fingers grazed my sister's arm, his attention moving to her. "We should probably all get to bed. It's getting late, and everyone's got early flights."

This was facts, but I was still surprised he shut the conversation down.

I was even more so relieved.

I really didn't need my buddy tossing around his "theories" right now. It would just make everything more complicated.

And things were complicated enough.

For some reason, my friend was saving me from further complications, and I could only gather he had his own reasons for that. He stood, taking Sloane's hand. She got up too and clipped me on her way out of the room.

I got her shoulder. "Little—"

"Don't even, Big," she said, calling me by the nickname she gave me. I was *big* and she was *little*, a name I'd given her. She frowned. "You made me look like a fool tonight, and what you did to Fawn was just disgusting."

I swallowed. "I know. I—"

"Well, I'm glad you know." She nodded, then headed toward her room. At least, that was where I assumed. Dorian started to go with her, but I cut him off.

"Hey," I said, my voice low. "I know everyone is pissed, but I need you to make sure this is a good Christmas for my family." We needed to have a good Christmas. Just one after last year. My jaw moved. "You know last year was rough, and you can be pissed at me all you want, but I just need you to do that. For my family, do that."

Last year had been rough. I had fucking cancer, and pissed off at me or not, he had to help me keep things calm this year. D got trying to make things better for family when things got tense. He did because he'd asked me to help do that for his own family in the past. We had a long history, my friend and me.

I knew asking this of him was shitty, terrible, but I was doing it anyway.

Dorian's eyes were cold in my direction, and when he shook his head at the floor, I knew he'd help me. He would because he was ride or die.

He put his finger in my chest. "I will do that, but respect-fully, Ares, deal with your shit." He backed off. "And don't you dare ask me for anything else until you do."

I would ask for context, but I wasn't sure I needed to after how he'd come in here.

Instead, I let him go, and though Thatcher and Wells clipped me too when they eventually made their way out, I knew Dorian would relay the information. He would, and our other best friends would give me the same unsaid promise. The guys and I looked out for each other, regardless of how pissed we were. When it came to our families, we looked out, no questions asked.

The kid was flanking Wells and Thatch, but I trailed after him. "Hey, kid—"

"What, Ares?" Bru turned around, and I didn't like how pissed off looked on him. The kid was usually pretty easygo-ing, but I got it.

I eased my hands into my sweats. "I'm assuming Fawn's going back to campus in the morning." I hadn't heard what happened after I left, and upon mentioning Fawn, Bru laughed.

"You'll be happy to know Fawn will be spending

Christmas by herself." His eyes narrowed. "She is going back to campus. Mom and Dad asked her to come with us, but she politely declined."

I figured as much, but I didn't like that she'd be spending Christmas by herself. If the alternative was being around me, though, she was better off. "I don't like that she's spending Christmas by herself, but I think you and I can both agree, we shouldn't be sharing space. I was shit to her."

"And I still don't get why even after hearing all of it." He braced his arms. "Honestly, Ares, I didn't even believe it when she told me. I didn't believe my brother would lie to his family and his friends, and for reasons I'm still trying to wrap my head around."

So Fawn had told him, but he just hadn't believed. He thought I was better.

He thought I was good.

"You know that girl is one of the nicest people I've ever known," he shot, making me blink. "She was so cool to me, which I didn't always get moving around as much as I did."

He was right about that. It even took the guys and me some time to warm up to him when we all first met. Granted, there'd been a lot of factors going on back then, but still.

"So she was your friend." I was more so telling myself that, and that definitely sounded like Fawn. She supported the shit out of me on more than one occasion when I certainly hadn't given her a reason.

I really didn't want her to spend Christmas alone, and actually, if I was hell-bent on torturing myself, I'd be bugging the kid and asking him where he put her up. I'd be at her door like a sick fuck doing sick-fuck things. Things like pleading with her when I had no right.

Things like being on my knees for her.

Shit like that wouldn't be helpful, but mostly, for her. I may look like the asshole right now to my friends and family, but I'd be that. Fawn didn't need to be around me right now. Now was a bad time, terrible.

"She was and a good one, a great one," Bru continued, and I gazed up. Bru shrugged. "It was brief, but yeah."

I figured because of what he said earlier, how he'd moved. That part still confused me a little since I'd believed him and Sloane had lived in the Midwest their whole lives.

I asked the kid about that, and he ended up bumping his shoulders again.

"We weren't in New York long enough for it to count," he said, and when I nodded, he sighed. "Anyway, I'm going to bed. I love you, dude. But you're making it really fucking hard now after what you did."

I understood that, respected it, which was why I did let him walk away. "I really don't like that she's going to be alone," I said, his back to me. "And I'm sorry things happened the way they did."

I truly was, honest. I hated I got her wrapped up in my stupid fucking life, and I meant that.

His back to me, Bru sighed again. "Maybe give that apology to her, bro," he said, though that was something I knew I couldn't. More complications would come that way. Fawn had told me she loved me once.

And I couldn't risk that love again.

CHAPTER
SIX

Ares

My parents wanted the house up at a certain time, and though I got up, I didn't get out of bed right away. Call it wanting to avoid the inevitability of the day, but I dragged my fucking feet and had a long-ass shower. The first person I ended up seeing was Dorian, and he was sneaking out of my sister's room.

I shook my head that he wasn't even bothering to act like he hadn't stayed over. I adjusted my shoulder bag. "Morning."

"Morning." He had a shoulder bag too and apparently wasn't bringing a lot for the trip. "Sleep good?"

"Decent."

This exchange was definitely out of formality. He wasn't making eye contact with me, which meant he was clearly still pissed. I pointed at his bag. "When did you get that?"

If he had stayed over and hadn't gone back home, it was weird he had his things. He shrugged, mentioning something about getting here a couple hours ago. That didn't mean he hadn't stayed over, though, and knowing him, he probably had. I started to say I'd see him down at breakfast when the door behind him opened and my sister came out.

Sloane was definitely prepared for a day of travel. Her sweats mirrored mine, and upon seeing me, she ignored me for her boyfriend.

This was all to be expected considering, well, everything, and the fact only emphasized the reason I didn't feel like fucking getting up.

"You tell him?" she asked, talking about me but not to me. Dorian got a handful of her hip when he brought her close, and though the question had been directed at him, he placed his dark eyes in my direction.

"Can't see why we should," he said, and my eyebrows narrowed. Dorian's head cocked. "After all, what they had was fake, right? Shouldn't bother him."

What the fuck?

And with that, the two headed down the hall like they hadn't stated some ominous shit.

Meanwhile, I was hot on their heels. "What are you talking about?"

They didn't tell me, their own conversation far more interesting than me breathing down their necks. It must have been because they continued a duo exchange all the way up into my kitchen, which was busy as fuck. Normally, my parents' staff would be making stuff, but with the early hour (and us leaving town), it seemed my parents let them have the time off. The busyness came from Wells and Thatch, who had everything in my parents' fridge out on the goddamn counter.

"The fuck you two doing here?" I asked, Dorian and Sloane leaving my ass. Right away, they took seats at the bar, but cut me a look before they did. Their heads lowered, they started another quiet exchange. Meanwhile, Wells was in front of my parents' stove while Thatcher handed him shit. I headed over to them and the mess. "What are you guys doing here?"

"Relax. We figured we'd all head over to the airport together," Wells countered, actually making some pretty kick-ass smells with whatever he was making. Upon further observation, it looked like some kind of omelet and potato combination, and Wells did have skill when it came to the kitchen. His grandparents were celebrity chefs, and his dad was a restaurant franchise owner.

His logic was sound about the travel, and my parents did say all the families were flying out together before dismissing me.

I didn't particularly like that my friends were making such a mess before my family was about to make their way out of town, though. I barked that over to them and got a dismissive wave from Wells and an eye lift from Thatcher.

"Whatever, bro," Thatch huffed, obviously still in his feelings too. I'd give my buddies time, but we really needed to be on the same page about not making Christmas shitty. Thatcher leaned on the counter. "You tell him?"

This was directed at Dorian, and as soon as he said it, Wells stopped cooking. His spatula had left the pan and everything, and the rage of clearly being left out of something summoned something fucking feral inside me. I opened my mouth to unleash it, but stopped at the sight of another party. Red and my brother entered the kitchen then.

I thought she'd left.

I supposed I'd assumed she had, and I did have another reason for not getting up out of bed right away. I'd wanted to give her time to leave, but I guess I hadn't done a good enough job.

She stopped upon seeing me, and though she'd been wearing that bulky-ass coat last night, she wasn't now. Now, she was wearing a fucking top that showed off her tatted arms and exposed the swell of her tits like it wasn't fucking below freezing outside. There was a reason my parents were getting us out of town for the holidays, but Red didn't seem to care about that, the cold.

No, she didn't care, and the red instantly hit that gorgeous swell. This girl flushed something crazy when she was uncomfortable, nervous, which she obviously was upon seeing me. At some point, Bru noticed his venture into the kitchen was solo and stopped himself. He glanced at Fawn before finding me, but his exchange *with me* was a quick one. Like everyone else, he wasn't too happy with me, and his attention was dismissive before facing Fawn.

"You're fine. He's not going to do anything," he said, like I'd literally go over there and eat her if no one else was in this kitchen. Thoughts of feasting had been on my mind upon seeing her in that *fucking top*, but not in any way that didn't have her tits in my mouth...

That pussy on my tongue.

The urge to let this chick sit on my fucking face hit like a son of a bitch, and that was so fucking dangerous here, now. Growling, I headed over to the other side of the kitchen. Putting my bag down, I sat next to D and my sister, and the two looked at me. Dorian was *really* fucking looking, and I shook my head when I assumed why.

Relax.

I was hard-pressed when I was in the same room with Red. Eventually, she believed my brother enough to continue her journey into the kitchen, and she wore those shredded-up jeans she always rocked. The ones that showed the tats on her thick thighs, and I literally had to put my hands on my dick. The asshole was trying to split my *fucking* jeans.

Like my buddy Dorian knew, he cocked his head at me. In fact, he basically had his entire body in my direction, and I was saved when my parents entered the kitchen.

"Good. You're all up," Mom said and smiled to her right. The only people sitting on that side of the room were Bru and

Fawn, and Mom gave a nod in that direction. I didn't know what to make of that and couldn't when my dad came up behind Mom.

"We have an announcement," he said, claiming my focus. He put an arm around Mom, but despite making the declaration, all eyes headed toward me. They weren't watching my dad for the announcement, which one hundred percent set off red flags.

Especially when Fawn's attention hit the wall.

CHAPTER
SEVEN

Fawn

I knew Mr. Mallick's announcement. This whole room knew. The only one who didn't was Wolf, and that was because he wasn't there this morning when everyone else had been up and moving. Even his friends had been here. They'd got in before Wolf had made his way downstairs, and now, they were all staring at him. They were waiting for his reaction.

And he was surely about to give it.

I rejoined the conversation about the same time Mr. Mallick stated all the buses coming into Queenstown Village were canceled due to inclement weather. Pembroke University, my university, was located there, and the snowstorm that was apparently going on over there was legendary. Nothing was getting in or out of the city on wheels, which meant I was stuck here in Maywood Heights.

I was stuck here.

I studied that play over Wolf's face, that reality. Shifting, his dark eyes bounced over to me, but I glanced at the bar. He didn't know, but he wouldn't have to worry about the next thing his dad said. I had no intention of accepting Mr. and Mrs. Mallick's offer no matter how generous.

"We've once again extended our invitation for Fawn to come to South Carolina with us," his dad said, and though I knew it was coming, my stomach did clench. Escaping this fucking cold sounded heavenly, but not if I had to share any type of space with Wolf. It wasn't happening.

Ever.

I hated him, my feelings for him or not. I still had them and wasn't in denial about that. The dull ache of it only infused my hate. A part of me did want him to suffer by knowing I'd be around, but the feelings came back and stamped it down. I wanted to be fucking petty when it came to this guy, but I knew I couldn't.

Last night had taught me that.

I'd obviously tried to save him again and still didn't know why he'd told everyone the truth. It really had to have been a guilty conscience. His whole family was in front of him, and he just couldn't lie to them anymore.

"But we want to make sure she's comfortable," Wolf's dad continued. His eyes were narrowed hard at his son, and I wanted to dropkick myself that I felt any kind of way about that. His whole family was so mad at him, and I shouldn't feel bad but I did. I was a part of that lie. "So, if you decide you have a problem with this decision, you will be staying home. This won't be a reward, though, and your grandparents, Grandma Evie and Grandpa Jim, will be monitoring your house arrest. They won't be able to make the trip due to work obligations but understand you won't be leaving this house under their watch. You won't do anything, and though your mom and I don't love that things will be that way, if you disagree with the decision—"

"I don't."

I actually had to sit down...

Because I'd been standing.

Well, I'd been about to stand. My feet braced to the floor, I was midway there because I'd been about to formally put my position out there. I appreciated Wolf's parents being nice to me, but I wasn't going on this trip. I didn't know what I'd do as an alternative. Probably an Airbnb or something…

But then Wolf said that, his expression completely stoic. He shrugged, bracing his big arms. "I don't mind. Why would I?"

Why would he.

The fact that it was possible… freaking possible for this guy to do that.

To cut me again.

I was so fucking tired of feeling the hurt from this guy. I was over it, *spent*, and he was right. Why would he care? He'd told me he felt nothing for me when I'd been pouring my heart out to him months ago.

"That okay with you, Fawn?" Bru sat next to me, redirecting everyone's focus. He'd been there the whole time, and despite all this mess, he thought about me in it.

That was another thing Wolf ruined. I hadn't even gotten to catch up with Bru before I'd made the connection between them. It was like Wolf had charged a runaway train through Bru's invitation to spend time with his family.

To spend time with him.

He'd always been so kind to me, and when I'd seen him at the airport, I couldn't help taking his invitation. It had come at such a needed time when I'd been avoiding my own family. I'd missed my flight back to New York on purpose. I'd been weak because being around my mom and stepdad just reminded me of how truly fucked up I still was. I never really recovered after my dad's accident and being around family hurt. I didn't want to hurt. I wanted to be *free*. I wanted…

Bru eased in front of me, cutting off my sight from his family. He cut off my sight from Wolf, who hadn't even been looking at me, from behind him. He didn't care, the fucker staring at the bar after what he said. It was like I didn't even warrant his attention enough for a response.

I probably didn't.

He literally ruined everything, and I hadn't always been broken when it came to my family. I'd been getting better for a time. Better because of him.

I stared at Bru, genuine concern in his eyes when he looked at me. I had a feeling if I didn't go, he'd stay. He'd ruin his life for Wolf too. Bru was on college break, but I knew he'd spend it with me. The old Bruno would have done that.

And so would the old Fawn.

The old Fawn wouldn't have allowed an asshole to break her, and she would have nutted the fuck up so her friend didn't ruin his Christmas plans. She would have been there for him so he could spend time with his family. I wouldn't let Bru ruin his holiday, and I wouldn't let Wolf destroy something else. He had enough power when it came to my life.

It was time I took some of it back.

CHAPTER
EIGHT

Fawn

The time between me accepting the Mallicks' invitation to go
to South Carolina and the house going into overdrive to make
flights was a quick one. I offered to pay for my own flight, but
once again, Mr. and Mrs. Mallick were generous. They not
only covered everything, but managed to get me on the same
flight as themselves and the rest of the Legacy families.
Things were moving.

This was happening.

People scattered in the kitchen, but Wolf was the first one
to leave it. He'd basically had smoke on his heels after my
decision, grumbling about having to get some last-minute
things. I'd be an idiot to think that wasn't about me, but I
didn't give a fuck. I'd given way too many to him and the
situation he put me in. I was tired of taking the blame, and I
wouldn't from here on out.

My immediate concerns more so lay with travel from here
on the way to South Carolina, but those were stamped down
at the present when a shuttle bus pulled up to the Mallicks'

about a half hour after the decision made in the kitchen. I assumed Mr. and Mrs. Mallick called one of those because of the large party, but this completely worked for me. I still didn't get in cars and wasn't sure how to broach the subject with Bru and Wolf's parents. I wasn't sure if they knew about my impairment.

If Wolf had told them...

Bru didn't know, and that had been deliberate. We'd gotten here on a bus last night, but that was only because I'd lied to him about having an issue with rideshares. I'd told him I didn't like getting into strange people's cars, and though he knew about the fight I had in high school with Cissy Armstrong, I didn't think he knew the extent of my issues with cars in general. I think back then he just thought my anger lay with being locked in a car by my bully.

I hadn't let him in.

I was still very guarded back then. Hell, I was still guarded *now* and didn't want him to see how weak I was. I was sure if he did know about my issue back then, he logically would believe I'd be over it now. I wished I was, but I wasn't.

In any sense, I had escaped that possible hurdle, but I wasn't sure if that would remain constant all the way down to South Carolina. I wanted to take Bru aside and actually talk to him about everything. There were a few things I wanted to talk to him about just in general since we hadn't gotten the chance, but he quickly got caught up in the fray of the last-minute travel hustle and bustle. His parents requested him and the Legacy guys to bring down all the bags and help with the bus loading, and rather than be in the way of all that, I escaped outside.

I took a breath.

I think it was the first one I'd taken since this all started, and I welcomed it.

Breathe. Just breathe.

My phone chimed off shortly after stepping out into the brisk air, and taking it out, I got a sad emoji from Bru.

Bru: Sorry, I have to do all this bag stuff. I'll try to make it quick.

He managed to get a smile out of me in that moment. Again, thinking about me. I hadn't gotten a lot of that lately, so yeah, that meant something.

Me: It's cool. I wanted to take a walk anyway before we leave. All this was a lot, so yeah.

This felt like a massive understatement, and I did take that walk as Bru texted back. His little message bubble popped up, and I smiled again.

Bru: Why am I not surprised life with you now is just as exciting as it was back then. *laughing emoji*

It had been exciting, but not only in the bad way that was Cissy Armstrong. Actually, before all that, it'd been cool, fun, and I recalled the days that it had been. Bru and I certainly cut our fair share of classes out of boredom, and when we had, we'd gone on the school's roof.

It'd been nice up there, peaceful. The school's groundskeeper kept pigeons up there. The guy kept them locked up, of course, but Bru and I would just hang out and listen to them. We'd take our backpacks and lay them out on the roof as pillows. After that, we'd just watch the sky, the pigeons flapping and cooing in the background. Some may find all that chaos the opposite of peaceful, but I would have done anything back then to get out of the chaos of my head.

I supposed Bru shared that same thought back then, because we didn't really talk up there. We just existed.

Again, it was peaceful.

Bru: Anyway, see you in a bit. Want to chat before we go. I'll grab you before we leave.

I wanted to talk too, and hoped, as I shoved my hands in my pockets, I'd nut up enough to tell him about everything with cars. It was still hard for me to talk about, but I felt I gained a little bravery after I circled Bru's neighborhood a couple times. The front door of the house was open when I came back, but so was the bus.

I headed toward the latter. If the door was open, the guys were probably still moving things in and out. I didn't want to be in the way, so I decided to just find my seat. I planned to sit at the front of the bus, but a wolfish specter stopped me in my tracks.

Blood literally pounded in my ears, Ares taking up about a bus seat and a half with his broad frame. His eyes closed, he had his hands tucked under his arms, his earbuds in and a hood up under his thick jacket. Chunky curls had pushed their way from beneath the hood, and when his nostrils flared, so did the gold hoops in his nose. He had two on one side that lay close together. I had one myself, silver.

Why are you looking at his nose?

Why was I looking at him at all, and I didn't anymore when I rushed past him. I basically ran and didn't stop until I made it to the back of the bus.

But that certainly hadn't stopped his effect.

His familiar spicy scent filled half the damn bus, and I resented it immediately. I resented the feeling it gave me, and how it reminded me of Christmas morning. Call it being in the midst of the holidays, but I hadn't really been able to place it before. It had always just reminded me of home and that welcomed feeling of security.

Safety.

That was such bullshit when it came to him, and of course, he noticed someone pretty much sprinting past him. He navigated that large body in his seat, and since he was a full head above it, he hadn't had to turn much. Instantly, we locked eyes, and when I thought he'd dismiss me and turn back, he didn't.

He got up.

Like actually got up, tucking away his phone and everything. My throat closed in like I was going into anaphylactic shock, and I didn't breathe once when he grabbed his seat and stepped into the aisle.

I shrank immediately, not knowing what to do, but it turned out I didn't need to at the sound of voices. Soft, feminine, they caused Wolf to turn around.

Cursing, he shook his head and didn't give me another look before he retook his seat.

What the fuck?

I didn't know what was up, but he was back in his seat by the time two girls made their way on the bus. One, I recognized right away. I mean, his sister looked just like him except for the fact she was a girl and a fraction of his size when it came to overall bodily dimensions. If Wolf was a girl, he'd definitely make a pretty one, and that fact was proven with his sister, Sloane. She had a short coat on and her curly hair up, and even though she wore oversize sweatpants and high-tops, she was still a freaking knockout. Actually, because of her laid-back dress, the juxtaposition between her and the other girl she was with hit a little harder. That girl also had her hair up, but her black wool coat and heeled booties were certainly different from Sloane's airport attire. Her friend even wore stockings, which was different, and she was a whole head shorter than Sloane.

Both girls stopped in front of Wolf, and Sloane borderline sneered at him.

"Why are you here and not helping the other guys?" she asked, her frown evident. I'd certainly seen some of that in the kitchen, but not just from her.

It seemed Wolf was on the bad side of a few people in his life, but as I didn't care, I stared out of the window. I had my camera bag, which more often than not doubled as my purse since I didn't like to leave it around. It was my father's and meant a lot to me. I held it close as I studied snow-coated trees but couldn't help when Wolf's voice divided my attention.

"Already loaded everything Dad wanted me to load," he said, pointing upward, and I blinked. I hadn't noticed the bag storage before. I supposed I'd been too busy trying to get away from Wolf, but the evidence of his claim was there. Bags lined pretty much the majority of the bus (on both sides), and I was wondering if he'd left anything else for the other guys to bring on.

Wolf lounged back in his seat. "Figured it was best I get out of the way after that," he said, and I glanced up to curiously find my own bag. It was right above my head, which was obviously a coincidence. He wouldn't have been able to know where I would sit and wouldn't have cared enough to make sure I had access to it.

Coincidence.

It definitely was one, and something about what Wolf said made Sloane laugh. It was dry and accompanied her headshake.

"Probably a good idea," she said about the same time the girl she was with lifted her hand at Ares. She said *hey* to him, her voice high-pitched, cheery. It was certainly the opposite of the energy given off by both twins, and with a chin-tip, Wolf gave her back her *hey*.

The exchange was brief, but I think only because the smaller girl tugged Sloane's sleeve. Sloane spotted me then, and both girls made their way back to me.

Awkward, I just kind of sat there and let it happen, well aware Wolf was gazing back here too. I wondered what he'd been about to say to me before, but stopped. I really didn't give a fuck what he had to say, and odds were, he'd probably been about to chastise me for my decision to come along. That'd been his MO in the past.

Cutting off my attention from him, I lifted a hand at Sloane. She waved, and her friend *really* waved. I mean, the girl waved so hard I thought she'd take off in flight, and seeing her close up, I took a moment. She had red cheeks. Like redder than mine, which said something as I got really red on my best day. I did when I was embarrassed or nervous, or for any reason since I was a redhead and, well, genetics. This girl wasn't one, a brunette, and had a face that struck me as so familiar when she got close. Bright blue eyes, she appeared doll-like and mantel ready.

"Hey, Fawn," Sloane said, and the girl was bouncing beside her. Like she was excited, and that kind of made me smile. I didn't know why. It was just the girl's energy maybe. Sloane put an arm around her. "This is Bow Reed. Thatcher's sister."

Thatcher Reed, of course, and I did see that now. Despite being the biggest Legacy guy, he was a pretty boy. He didn't have this girl's face, but they were clearly related.

I shook Bow's hand, and she did that just as hard as the wave. I laughed. "Hey."

"Hi. Oh my gosh, it's so good to meet you," she piped, and I grunted when she completely abandoned the hand-shake and hugged me. She got me hard for a little thing, and there was no question this girl was a Reed. She hugged like a bear, and her brother looked like one. She froze. "Sorry. I get excited."

Almost instantly, she let go, and I waved off what she said. "It's cool."

"I just feel like I know you, I guess. I've heard a lot," she stated, and I was sure she had. From what I understood, the Legacy kids were really close, and I could imagine it was no different with Bow.

Wolf caught my attention again, and at least this time, he was aware no one cared for him to be a part of the conversation. He turned back around, his head on the seat, and I shook mine.

Sloane noticed, and both she and Bow frowned.

"I'm glad you're still coming despite what an ass my demon of a twin has been to you," Sloane shot, audible. She tossed the words directly in Wolf's direction, and if he heard, he gave no reaction to them. He might not since he had his earbuds in before.

I had a feeling Sloane wouldn't have cared regardless, and I sat back. "I guess I decided I'm not going to give any more of my energy away." I'd given him too much, way too much.

I noticed a slight shift of Wolf's head, and maybe he was listening.

You don't care if he is.

Eventually, I would believe that to be true, and I knew I would, the longer I stood my ground. Ares Mallick didn't own me. Even if we both believed he did for a semester.

My throat clenched again, and Sloane and Bow both nodded at me.

"Definitely get that," Sloane said, her lips turned down. "And I've said it before, but I am sorry. So sorry for how I acted when we first met. How I treated you…" She eyed her brother over her shoulder. "I'm definitely regretting a few things."

She wasn't the only one, and the sound of the bus amplified in that next moment. Bow's brother, Thatcher, had two large duffels on his meaty shoulders, and Wells pulled up with a couple behind him. Thatcher had to turn sideways just to get into the aisle, and both boys had to lower their heads to navigate the area.

"Incoming!" Thatcher announced before charging down the aisle and pretty much barreling through his tiny sister.

"Thatcher!" she squealed just as Sloane got the back of her coat. She pulled Bow and herself into the nearest seat, just missing the football player.

"You asshole!" Sloane barked, but all Thatcher did was laugh.

He angled around. "What? I warned you guys." With a

wink, he started to load the bags up top, but Sloane had made her way into the aisle and launched herself in his direction.

Thatcher dropped his bags then, nothing but laughter on his lips, and Sloane would have gotten to him if not for Wells. Quick, he put himself between both of them, and Sloane seethed in his direction.

"Whoa now, princess," Wells stated, his hands up and guarding his friend. He was lucky he had height on him, or otherwise, Sloane would have punched over him. Wells laughed, dodging strikes. "He's sorry."

"Like fuck he is." Sloane managed to get a sock into Thatcher's arm. He had a thick puffer coat on, and with his size, I doubted her small fist hurt.

Even still, he made a show about being injured, rubbing his arm. Wolf was completely turned around in his chair again. He started to get up (I assumed to stop everything), but Bow de-escalated the situation when she tugged Sloane's arm.

"He's not worth it," she said, sticking her tongue at him. It was literally something a sister would do to her brother, which made him laugh. This got Thatcher another punch from Sloane, but he chose not to do anything about it.

Wolf faced the front again after he did, which pretty much confirmed he'd been about to do something about the chaos back here.

And you care because?

Since I didn't, I stayed in my own corner. Thatcher loaded his bags, and Wells did the same across the aisle from him.

"Watch out, squeak," Wells said, apparently referring to Bow who was in his way. Her face shot up in color, and when she didn't move, his eyes lifted. "Earth to squeak? You want me to avoid hitting you in the head with these or not?"

This guy's bedside manner could use some work, but I wouldn't say I was surprised. I had my own run-ins with both him and her brother. These Legacy guys were a special breed, and no one drove that point home more than a certain someone in the front seat.

Wolf seemed to be keeping toward his own corner at the present, but it seemed Bow didn't need any help when Sloane stepped in. Sloane smirked, her arms crossed. "Hey, Wells?"

"Yep?" He was stowing the bags at this point, because Bow had sat down. Currently, he was forcing her to look at his abs when his short coat crept up and exposed them.

Sloane cocked her head. "Fuck off."

His head shot around, and Bow grabbed Sloane's coat. She said Sloane's name low, but all Sloane did was shake her head.

"No, he's always messing with you," Sloane said, her hand up. Bru mentioned excitement with me, but his family certainly had their own brand of excitement. It might have started again had not both Bru and Dorian Prinze made their way on the bus. The two had a handful of bags, but even with them, they hadn't matched what was already on the bus. Wolf had clearly put some work in, but it was the least he could do for lying to his family for so long.

He was acknowledged by Dorian, but just barely, and Bru's glance was cordial but nothing more than that. These people were steamed with him, and after this bus trip (and we were no longer sharing space), I had every intention of not making any of that my business. I'd be avoiding a certain wolfy asshole as soon as the opportunity allowed.

That started now, as I watched these boys stow the rest of the bags, then pound fists. Wells still appeared a bit prickly after Sloane's comment, but he kept his mouth shut when Dorian asked him what his problem was. Dorian had his arm wrapped around Sloane at that point, and I assumed Wells's silence had something to do with that.

A mumbled "nothing" came out of Wells's mouth, which made Thatcher bark a laugh. Wells punched at him, and the two continued to jostle each other until Dorian barked at them to cut it out, and Sloane sighed at Dorian to cool off. The dynamic was so familiar it kind of hurt. They were all that way too when Wolf and I had been fake-dating.

Fake.

I had forgotten that then, but I didn't now. Now was a new era, and when everyone started to head toward the front seats, I got up to follow. I suppose I wanted to be a team player and not wallow, but I was surprised when Bru held back.

"Hey, can we, uh…" he said, waving to hang back with him. He gestured to a seat, which I took, and when he joined me, I was well aware of the lack of space. He had to fold himself in, and I really didn't know this Bruno. He'd changed a lot physically, and I'd joked with him about that at the airport.

"So, I guess I wanted to give you a way out," he said, and I looked at his face for the first time. He was flushed, his dark hair strewn about. He waved a hand through it. "There's still time, and you're not locked into anything."

I didn't understand and paused when he got closer. He smelled like sea breeze and ocean, and I remembered that.

Maybe not everything had changed. His smell was the same. I recalled that on the roof as we listened to pigeons and studied open air for minutes, hours.

"You don't have to go," he said, the reason for his closeness. He got real quiet, only the two of us back here, which was obviously his intention. His head lowered. "If you're saying yes for the sake of being polite… for my parents, you don't have to. They'll understand if you don't want to go. We all do."

I glanced up and over his shoulder, a third party to this conversation. I wasn't surprised to see Wolf's head angled back. He wasn't making it obvious, still under his hood, but he was a part of this conversation.

At least, he was trying to be.

Maybe he knew that Bru would be the one to try to fix all this. Maybe he wanted to look like the bigger guy, say I could go, and that he didn't mind. All the while, he knew his brother would try to do the right thing and give me an out. He would if he knew Bru.

So maybe a lot really hadn't changed.

Bruno Sloane-Mallick may look different, but he was still that same guy. That *nice* guy and completely the opposite from his asshole brother.

I faced him. "If I stay, you will too."

The look on his face said everything, his lips coming together. He massaged his jaw. "Please tell me that's not why you're going." His hand dropped. "Because of me."

It was part of the reason, and I wouldn't lie about that. I shrugged. "Tell me it's not true."

If he could, I would stay, but all he did was shake his head.

He propped an arm on the seat. "Well, would you look at us? Years pass, but we're still the same."

"Idiots."

How many times did I cut class only for him to do the same and vice versa? How many times did only one of us have a bad day, but we both ended up on that roof?

How. Many. Times.

Too many to count, and when he laughed, I did too.

"Taking off in about ten minutes, kids," came from the front, Mr. Mallick. He had a couple bags too and mentioned the Reeds, Thatcher and Bow's parents, would be joining us on the bus. It seemed they had just arrived with Bow, but the other Legacy parents would meet us at the airport.

Mr. Mallick got off after he loaded the bags. I didn't know why, but I assumed he'd return with the rest of the parents. Bru edged close. "There's still time for you to change your mind."

"Will you?" I cocked my head, and when I got another

laugh, I knew my answer. "Well then, I guess we're both going to South Carolina."

"I guess so." His smile was easy, also familiar. He smiled so easy, effortless. That was something I always admired about him. Despite his tumultuous home life, he always came to school with a smile and a laugh. And one better, he always had one to offer me.

I wished I'd been able to do that for him back then. Unfortunately, I'd been in my own trauma, and though I still wasn't better by any sense of the word, I was stronger. I could be strong and be there for him. He wouldn't lose out on his Christmas because of me, and this was me returning the favor for all those easy smiles. For all that kindness he so effortlessly gave. It had meant the world to that broken, fucked-up girl back then.

It had meant everything.

CHAPTER
NINE

Ares

I didn't know what I'd been about to say to Red on the shuttle that morning. I guess I'd been confused why she'd said she was going to come. I may have said I had no problem, but I certainly hadn't meant that. I guess I assumed, regardless of what I said, she wouldn't go.

I assumed wrong.

Going to talk to her had been impulsive, but I wanted to question her and establish that hard line. Red had gotten ideas in her head about us before, and I wanted to clear up any confusion. She and I weren't anything, and we were never going to be anything.

I think that'd been what I was going to say.

I honestly didn't fucking know, and she avoided my ass like she already knew that hard line. She appeared to be establishing it herself, and though I hadn't heard what Bru had been saying to her at the back of the shuttle, I figured he'd been trying to give her an out. That was something he'd do, but nothing must have come of it. Red did go with us to the airport on this trip, and right away, I got separated from her and my friends. My parents may have gotten us all on the same flight as the rest of the Legacy families, but they had me sitting at the back of fucking economy.

I supposed I got the extra ticket they purchased.

I was being punished by my family, but I anticipated this. What I hadn't anticipated was being separated from everyone, again, on our layover. There was some confusion with my ticket, and I'd been placed on another plane for the second flight. Something about overbooking.

"Sorry, critter," my mom said when delivering the news to me. She and Dad were the only ones to greet me when I finally got from the back of the fucking plane. Apparently, the guys and everyone else were rushing to get on their second plane, which left my ass at the airport.

Once more, I was being punished.

Of course, I said nothing. I nodded, and I was happy Mom hadn't seemed as pissed at me. She'd been running her hand through my hair when she called me by her nickname for me, and Dad let her for a bit before nudging them both along. I couldn't get much of a read off him, but he did tell me to check in as soon as I boarded. He wanted to hear from me, which was good.

I had a lot of time to think on that plane by myself, and I did a lot of fucking thinking. There were a lot of things that needed to be said, and I had yet to say them. I had my reasons for basically hurting everyone I'd ever loved. I had a lot of collateral damage on my hands, but the worst by far rested with one person.

Why did you do that? Think that?

My thoughts had automatically placed Fawn amongst the ranks with my family and friends. I did that, and I couldn't fucking do that.

Dangerous.

It was the only word that kept coming to mind when I thought of her. Danger. Pure and unadulterated.

And you're fucking toxic.

Swallowing, I stared out the window of a Tesla, my ride from the airport to the Reeds'. I'd been given the address for the property and got to sit with more thoughts on my way there in the rideshare I got.

I closed my eyes to them, trying to think about anything else but Fawn fucking Greenfield and what I'd done to her. There were so many other things to think about, but for some reason, I was holding my fucking breath until I did get to the Reeds'.

Until I saw the shuttle.

It was a second one and different from the one that'd taken my family and friends to the airport. It was one that was supposed to be there, and I knew for a fact it had taken everyone who'd been on that first flight to the Reeds'. It had because I'd arranged it.

I ran my tongue in a dry mouth, my focus moving to the property my Tesla pulled up in front of. How Thatch and Bow's parents had managed to get a mansion in the middle of fucking nowhere South Carolina was beyond me, but they had. It had a body of water alongside it, docile and temperate, and the whole thing was nestled amongst a never-ending landscape of tall trees. The house itself kind of reminded me of the Reeds' own home in Maywood Heights. Large brick home, columns. The place looked like it had stepped out of time, and the environment was basically jacket weather. It was enough to never make me go back to the Midwest during the winter again. It was cold enough to freeze a guy's dick off back there right now.

My mother definitely had something about moving the Christmas festivities over here. I was sure the decision was made by her, Dad, and the other parents, and the holidays appeared in full bloom here. Dusk was bringing out the brightness of the holiday lights on the white brick home. The place was dripping with them, and each set of windows held an evergreen wreath and silver bow.

I thanked my driver before getting out, a feat in itself since I was stiff as fuck. The back of economy had been a bitch on me.

Adjusting, I passed the shuttle outside of the house, and there was movement on it. I peered in and noticed Dorian and his dad in there. They were getting bags, and I waited by the bus until they were standing in front of me.

Dorian and his pops, Royal, looked like fucking twins, and it was always a surprise to not see him in a suit. He always wore one in the business he was in, investment banking, but today, he was dressed down in a sweater. The Prinze family owned the majority of the banks in Maywood Heights.

His hands full, Royal offered me an arm nudge when he passed me and was one of the rare parents who hadn't scowled when they saw me at the airport. The parents had all clearly caught wind of what I'd done, and those who didn't give scowls (the moms mostly) just looked sad and disappointed. Wells's mom, Cleo, couldn't even look at me.

I hadn't gotten that from Royal, though, and he asked me if I was okay when he saw me with my things. I assumed the question came because of my lonely flight, and I told him I was fine before asking if I could help with anything.

"We got it. It's the last of it anyway," that came from Dorian upon watching the short exchange I had with his dad. Normally, Dorian was the one who didn't hold on to anger. The guy was abrasive as fuck, but he burned fast and leveled out even faster.

That wasn't today.

Today, I got to watch my friend's back. He passed me, following his dad into the house.

Fuck.

As it turned out, he saved me from a distraction because I

wanted to get inside anyway. I hadn't known why until I crossed the threshold into an overly decorated foyer. I smelled sugar amongst the twinkling lights, something floral behind it. It was distinctly unique.

Distinctly *her*.

Someway, somehow, Red managed to make this whole big-ass house smell like her. She always held this light scent, soft, feminine…

My blood simmered the moment I smelled it, and I didn't fucking like that.

You need to talk to her.

It was important we kept our distance this trip. I'd like to say that was mostly for her benefit, but I knew what would happen if I was within a decent proximity of this girl. I'd *act*, and since I didn't know how I would, I decided a confrontation was needed sooner rather than later.

"What's up?" I found Thatcher and Wells first, the pair of them on the floor playing video games. They were in a grand room with a Christmas tree that made our nine-footer appear small.

I'd passed some of the moms on the way into the room, my mom with them. They'd been moving things around, unpacking and getting things settled. I'd gotten only small pleasantries for the most part, but I did get asked how I was doing by one. That came from Dorian's mom, my god-mom. I was close with D's parents since I was over there so much as a kid. Dorian and I were the closest in age out of our best friend group, and I wondered if Royal's laid-back disposition outside had anything to do with his wife's.

My god-mom, December, never could really be mad at me, and she hugged me before I left with my things. I hadn't even gotten that from my own mother. She asked me how my flight was and everything, but beyond that…

Yeah, I was in the doghouse with everyone, and I didn't get much more than a chin-tip when I approached Thatch and

Wells. I left my duffel and coat on the couch. "Where's everyone else?"

I didn't want to just put it out there, asking where Red was and all that. But even without me saying anything, all I got was a shrug from the pair of them. I frowned. "You don't know where anyone is?"

I'd seen most of the moms. They were all there with the exception of Billie, Dorian's god-mom. Apparently, she and LJ (Dorian's god-dad) hadn't arrived yet, and the dads were in town getting some supplies to feed all the people in this big-ass house. The Reeds kept a couple of cars down here, and December said they took one of those.

"Lost track after we got in." Thatch didn't even look at me, and though Wells did, it was brief.

I growled. "You fuckers going to be in your feelings this whole trip?" I got it. They were pissed, but it was going to get old real fucking quick. Besides, I needed them on the same page with me about keeping the peace while we were here.

I would have assumed Dorian relayed that information, but with the way they were acting, I wasn't seeing it.

"You don't really have a say in how long it takes me to get over what you fucking did," Wells stated this, frowning. He scrubbed through his hair, only blond until it got to the root. "I think the girls are upstairs."

"And Bru?" I'd gotten the information I needed. I figured Red was a part of the "girls," but I didn't need them to know I was looking to talk to her.

"Probably, yeah." Again, no look from Thatch.

Sighing, I started to go, but rerouted. I ripped the PlaySta-tion cord out of the wall, and that got a slew of obscenities from Wells and a chest bump from Thatcher. He got in my fucking face too, but I pushed him back.

"Whoa. Come on." Always the fucking peacemaker, Wells put a hand on both our chests. "We don't need this shit. We fight and the parents come out? That makes this shit worse."

"So D talked to you, then? About making shit peaceful for Christmas?" I asked, and the aversion of eyes told me all I needed to know. I angled until I got their attention back. "So I don't need to stress how we need to be acting down here?"

That was why I'd pulled the cord out of the wall. To get them to listen to me.

"No, but you're a bastard for even fucking asking." Thatcher gave me his back. He plugged the PlayStation back in before sitting down, and Wells joined him.

"Yeah, fucked up using your cancer and cheaper than shit."

Wells was right saying what he did, but what I needed from them was true. "So y'all understand the assignment, then?"

I got a couple of grunts and not a lick of eye contact this time. The sighs from them both came after, though, and I knew I wouldn't have to worry about them.

They were my best friends.

They were, and even though they were mad at me, I knew they'd get over it soon. Us guys were never upset with each other long. No matter what the fuckup.

My sister on the other hand...

Dark eyes narrowed in my direction after I knocked on my twin's door. Sloane stood puffed up before me, and her arms were crossed in front of a big-ass room. It was large enough to fit two king-sized, four-poster beds and each one was draped in silk.

I gazed above her, unable to help wandering eyes considering who I was looking for. "Hey. Sup?"

Apparently, I wasn't worth the response because Sloane left my ass at the door. The chill my twin was giving off gave the guys a run for their money at this point, but that wasn't foreign to me. She'd been prickly since this morning.

In any sense, her opening the door gave me license to come in, and though I scanned the room, no one turned up but Bow. She was unpacking a bag into a set of oak drawers. Meanwhile, Sloane was on one of the four-posters, her ankles crossed and cell phone in her hands.

"Little, how long you going to stay mad?" I asked her, and unlike my boys, she wouldn't put on the peace just for my benefit. Sure, she wouldn't make things difficult for our parents. She'd do what she could there in general, but no false pleasantries would be had both in front of or behind closed doors. That was just Sloane and something I was learning really quick about how she operated. I liked to say it was because she was a chick, but that wasn't true. She'd be pissed because she wore her heart on her sleeve.

Because she was like me.

When I was pissed, people knew, and that went the same for her. I didn't care who was watching. I ripped my hood down. "Little—"

She fled the bed and escaped into a connecting bathroom. The door slammed so loud I felt that shit in my kneecaps, and when I turned, Bow was biting her lip.

"She needs time," was all she said, always the nice one. She gazed up from her folding. "Did you need something? I can tell her."

Bow Reed was much too sweet for the likes of Legacy. We were all a bunch of fucking grumps. Meanwhile, she was the light. Always had been.

Even still, she didn't need to know I was looking for Red, and when I asked her the same question I'd asked the boys, she glanced up.

"The boys are somewhere in the house."

"I saw Thatch, Wells, and Dorian, but I didn't see Bru."

"Probably in his room," she said, tucking some jeans into a drawer. "I think I saw Fawn with him."

Bow Reed was my saving grace right now, but I didn't let that show. I asked her where Bru's room was, and after I got that information, I excused myself. I thought I had all I needed to say planned out, but it escaped when Bru opened the door. He also was in a room with two king-sized beds too, and though I hadn't wanted to instinctually glance over his shoulder for her, I did.

Red, where are you…

"Can I help you?" Just as rigid as the rest, Bru rested his thick shoulder against the door. He'd changed into jeans and a T-shirt, and I still didn't get how this dude was so fucking jacked.

"I see you've been working out at school," I stated, casual. I took the opportunity to do a once-over of my brother's room, but still wasn't seeing Red.

Bru crossed into my line of sight. "You here to ask me about my workout routine or…"

Normally, I didn't take shit from the kid, but I let him have that one. I was in the fucking doghouse, so I let him. I frowned. "Bow said you and Red were up here."

"Yeah. *Fawn* and I are," he stated, making me look at him again when he puffed up. Guy was acting like her goddamn keeper right now, but I did get it if he was her friend. I'd treated her like shit, so I got it.

"So, where is she?" I was proud of myself. I asked the question without fucking snarling, and Bru's brow jumped.

"Why?"

"Obviously, because I want to fucking talk to her."

"Yeah, but why, and what's with that nickname?"

My eyes rested on the ceiling. "She has red hair."

"Yeah, but why did you nickname her? Was that something you guys did when you were faking, because you obviously don't have to put on now."

The kid was legit testing me right now, and I didn't have time for it. Instead, I braced my arms, trying my best not to appear pissed the hell off. "Obviously. It's just what I call her. I call you the kid. That's just what I call her."

Fucking relax.

My brother definitely noticed the elevation in my voice, his frown heavy, weighted. "Why do you want to see her?"

"Maybe to fucking apologize? You're the one who told me I should."

"Okay, well, you should probably actually want to fucking apologize."

"I do." I spoke through my teeth. "I owe her that. Now, where is she?"

Bru simply stared at me, and I questioned my ability to allow my brother to continue living in that moment. He was coming between Red and me, and no one fucking did that.

So dangerous.

This stressed the reason I was here right now. Fawn wasn't the only one who needed a line drawn. In fact, I probably needed it the most.

Well aware of that, I waited patiently. Well, as patient as I could with a rapidly beating fucking heart.

Bru sighed. "She does deserve that, but you can't. At least, not right now."

"Why?"

"Because she's in the shower."

What. The. Fuck.

"Shower? Whose shower?"

Bru's brow lifted slow. "Ours?"

"What the fuck do you mean? *Yours*?" I did start to move into the room then, but he cut me off.

"Bro, what's your deal?" In my aggression, it took me a moment to realize my kid brother had handfuls of my hoodie.

Because he was holding me back.

He had a physical *hold* on me, but I wasn't thinking straight. "What do you mean yours?" I repeated, seething. "You and Red…"

"Are rooming together," he said, and I was on him at this point. Chest to chest, I was so close we barely had a nose of space between us. Bru had my shoulders, bracing them *hard*, but all I was seeing was red.

Red...

I didn't see her, not in the room, and the longer I didn't, I felt myself losing my shit. I felt myself panicking, and through my haze, my brother made me look at him.

"Ares, what's up? Ares?" He was shaking me, making me physically fucking look at him. "Bro, what's wrong? You okay?"

No, I wasn't fucking okay. No, I wasn't good, and I needed in that room right now before I landed him on the floor.

But the kid was bigger than me, stronger. In his time away, he'd gained the advantage where I'd lost it.

I lost it.

So much I lost, Red somewhere in this fucking room in *my brother's shower*.

"Ares, look at me. Fuck. You're scaring me."

I was scaring myself because in that moment I did almost hit him. I had my fist raised, ready and willing to destroy anything that was coming between myself and that girl right now. The girl I'd pushed away. The girl I made think I wanted nothing to do with.

That I didn't love.

I didn't love her. I couldn't, and I ended up throwing myself off my brother.

"Ares. What's going on? Ares?"

I tried to walk away, but Bru got my arm. He flung me around, and I had my fist raised again. It'd been instinctually, but I lowered it when his eyes flashed.

The way he looked at me...

A deep, unsettled expression fell across my brother's face, but I didn't think it had anything to do with my raised fist. He hadn't looked at my fist at all, his focus more so on me. He had a concern etched across his face I didn't like, and my heart stopped when he glanced back. He gazed into an empty room, but I heard that shower now. The door was in the same place Sloane had escaped into to get away from me in her own room.

The muted pitter-patter of running water hit the hallway, but unlike before, I wasn't running to get to her. I was stuck, nailed to the fucking floorboards because my brother's attention returned to me.

And his look didn't sit well.

His eyes had twitched wide, his head shaking.

"Ares," he said again, less panicked and something else. He stepped forward. "Ares, did something happen?"

Did something happen...

"Between you and..." He didn't finish, staring back into that room once more, and the longer he did, my stomach twisted up. Like someone had socked me in the fucking gut with a baseball bat, then left me there, weak.

Broken.

I did feel weak in that moment, and my swallow was hard when the kid closed more space.

"You're acting jealous," he concluded, my gut clenching more, my chest. He pointed back toward the room. "Why are you acting jealous?"

Why am I acting jealous...

His head cocked. "Like it bothers you that Fawn's in my shower right now."

I noticed he said *his* this time. Not *theirs*.

My heartbeat thrashed, but my choice of words had to be careful here. Dorian had already had his suspicions about Red and me.

I think my silence made things worse in the end, and the kid's confusion only twisted into more concern. His breathing had stopped. Like he wasn't breathing, anticipating.

"Ares?" he repeated, but his continued proximity halted.

Another made an appearance, and I couldn't be happier to see one of my best friends.

"Everything okay?" Dorian asked, bag-free. It was weird to see everyone in not just hoodies and sweatshirts. The guy was in jeans and a T-shirt like Bru. Dorian cuffed his arms. "What's going on? Everything good?"

No. Not by a long shot, but I wasn't getting into that shit. "We're good. Just talking."

Right away, the kid's attention zoomed to me, but I wasn't making eye contact.

I couldn't risk it.

I prayed on everything I had that he'd let what he had been trying to get at go. At least, at the present.

Please.

I dared to look at him again, and his eyes narrowed.

"Just talking," he said, playing along, but I knew it was just because Dorian was there. The difference between Bru and the other guys was he didn't call shit out. He didn't put people on the spot and never would.

He was better.

He was so much better than me, and in that moment, I let him be that way.

An arch hit Dorian's eyebrow. He obviously wasn't convinced things were good, but I doubted he had the patience to deal with more shit.

I certainly didn't.

Instead, he nodded, his hands slipping into his pockets. "Well, I guess I came to say don't plan on doing anything tonight. Making plans or anything like that."

"Why?" the kid asked, and Dorian just stamped his boots in front of me. He liked to wear these old military boots. The dude was richer than Midas but liked to thrift to accomplish his style. He had since high school.

"Because thanks to this one," he stated, pointing at me, "the dads are making us go to the fucking ballet."

Holy fuck.

"*The Nutcracker* is in town," he said, his dark eyes narrowed, *charged*. I was definitely putting my friend through the wringer right now, all of them. The only reason the Legacy fathers would make us all go to the ballet was because one of us guys fucked up. In a nutshell, our dads scheduled ballet outings to humble us. Their logic was it made us better men to see the delicate ways male leads handled female ballerinas on stage. It was a reminder for us to step up our own games. Ballet outings were reserved for offenses against a woman, and it didn't matter who caused the offense.

We all went.

It'd been a while since I was the screwup, and I guess my dad's punishment was starting. My gaze hit the floor. "Sorry."

"Yeah." D left my ass, and I started to leave as well, but the kid got my arm.

"Kid," I warned, so much warning there. Now wasn't the time.

I could still hear her *showering.*

I needed to leave *now* before I did something about that, but my brother's hand didn't leave my arm. "Ares—"

I worked my arm away, a feat in itself.

It hadn't been abrasive.

I controlled myself, and I was doing so now as I made myself walk away from him and the situation. I was choosing to believe the best-case scenario here, that being that my parents had set up Fawn in Bru's room intentionally. That they'd done that because she was an added guest and would need a roommate placement. *This* made sense to me, the only scenario here.

I refused to entertain any kind of alternative.

CHAPTER
TEN

Bru

"You're lucky we love your idiot ass."

I glanced up from my cell phone. Thatcher had let into Wolf shortly after Wells had regarding the whole ballet thing.

It saved me from having to do the job.

I had more on my mind at the moment, my thoughts lingering on a certain confrontation during which my brother lost his shit and freaked me the hell out. I was still freaked the hell out, confused.

Not that my brother would look at me.

He had his eyes on the road, Dorian Prinze at his side. They'd both been very quiet, but Thatcher and Wells had enough words for all of us.

Thatcher grunted. "I should be resting off my fucking jet lag, but here I am in this tight-ass tux suffering for *your* fuckup."

I knew the feeling, my own tux tight as fuck. It appeared all our parents had managed to hide away our tuxedos, the surprise of this ballet field trip sprung on us.

I'd be lying if I said all this wasn't familiar, though. When one of us messed up, our dads took us to the ballet. That was just how things were. They wanted us to treat women better, and I got that even though I'd never been the reason for the outing.

This particular one hit close to home, though, and currently, I was trying to explain to Fawn none of this was her fault. She was trying to take the blame for this outing for some reason after I'd explained what was happening tonight.

Fawn: I'm so fucking sorry. This sucks.

It did suck, but it wasn't her fault.

Me: It's cool. Ballet isn't that big of a deal.

I'd seen this one before at least, and I'd also be lying if I said it was unusual Fawn was trying to take the blame for this. It reminded me of high school and her dad's accident. She'd been trying to take responsibility for that too. It wasn't something she really talked about, but I picked up on it.

This girl had trauma, trauma like mine, and *my brother* had taken advantage of that. He currently was lifting his eyes in the passenger seat while Prinze drove, his hair up and in his own tux. I saw him well through the side-view mirror. The Reeds had a couple of Escalades, and us guys drove one to the theater while the Legacy dads tailed us. The fathers weren't letting us get away, and we'd all be seeing the showing of *The Nutcracker* tonight.

Wolf sighed. "Jet lag. Really?" Wolf stared back out of the window. "It took two hours and a layover to get here, dude."

Where was the lie, but I wasn't saying shit. Not when I was angry with Wolf too.

For a few reasons.

We'd be talking about what happened later, because no way in hell did my bro manipulate Fawn into getting into a fake relationship, then have something tangible with her.

Physical.

I wasn't even going to wrap my head around that one.

Mostly because it wouldn't even get that far. I knew Fawn, at least I had, and a guy like Wolf *wasn't* her type. My brother was arrogance and a growl. Loved the dude, but that was straight facts, and Fawn hadn't typically gone for guys like that.

At least, back then.

Add that to the fact that my brother didn't date, and anything between Fawn and Wolf wouldn't be happening.

I wet my lips, going back to Fawn. I hadn't brought up how my brother had acted in our room, and I wasn't going to until I talked to Wolf.

Me: I've seen this one. I like it.

Fawn: Yeah, but you shouldn't have had to go.

She was right, and as I continued to talk her down, I got to hear more of Thatcher. I fully supported the reaming, so I had no intention of cutting it off. Thatcher had worked his dark hair around in frustration, both the crosses dangling off his ears dark metal. They matched the black-on-black situation he had going with his tux, and the dude looked more like a gorilla than he already did in his formal wear.

"I still don't fucking care. I should be enjoying my fucking Christmas break and not this shit," he seethed at Wolf, and when Prinze told him to relax and calm down a bit, he didn't. Thatcher shot a hand in Wolf's direction. "No, we're all supposed to suffer for this dude's fuckup?"

I couldn't make out what Wolf said, but it sounded like something resembling a curse and a few other choice words. Whatever they'd been, he shut them down, and that was also weird. Fuckup or not, Wolf Mallick always stood up for himself.

Curiously, he wasn't. In fact, the guy had been falling on the sword since I'd come back. He had barely even tried to defend himself when I came at him, which was something that didn't happen. My bro and I had our history when it came to conflict. It wasn't so often these days, but it happened, and when it did, we handled it like dudes. Shit got heated, but the guy had barely raised his voice today. He'd been the pinnacle of calm until he hadn't.

I still didn't know what that was about, and tonight, he appeared to be checking himself again. He held his tongue after what Thatcher said, and oddly enough, it was Prinze who whipped around and told Thatcher to shut up.

"Like you have the right to say shit at all," Prinze cut, facing forward now and taking an exit.

We hadn't had to drive far to get into town, but long enough that Wells nodded off. After he got in his reaming, he tucked his hands under his arms and put his head back to the window. He'd gotten the seat between Thatcher and me.

Prinze frowned into the rearview mirror. "How many fucking times did Wolf and I have to drive back to town for your fuckups senior year?"

Let's just say more than one, and that was within the first month of Wolf and Prinze going off to college. I remember because all that shit went down before Wolf got sick.

It'd been a shit time, for everyone a shit fucking time. I attempted to reach my brother again through the side mirror. We clashed gazes this time, but I only got him for a moment before his attention drifted to the road again.

You can't run forever.

We'd be talking. He had a lot to answer for, and I was starting to think I didn't even know him. My brother could be a bully. I knew because I'd seen it, but he never did shit for no reason.

Hurt people…

He'd hurt *her*, and I didn't get that. Fawn was so fucking nice, and she'd been through so much shit. I wasn't lying to Wolf when I'd said how cool she'd been to me. She had managed to make another shit move not so shitty.

She'd been my friend.

Fawn: Thanks for letting me room with you. I really hope I'm not putting anyone else out.

She'd been worried about that, but I assured her she was fine. My parents proposed she stay with me because I had the only room with an extra bed. They asked Fawn, and she said she'd be cool with it if I was. I was of course. We were friends, so of course.

I smiled.

Me: You're fine. Seriously.

Honestly, the only person she'd probably be inconveniencing was my brother. He was rooming with Prinze, but I had a feeling my sister would be in his bed. Didn't really want to think about that, but if they got up to stuff, I could see Wolf wanting to take ownership of my extra bed.

Voices rose again, and Thatcher was pointing at Prinze this time. Thatcher snarled. "You know what? Whatever, and why the fuck have you been so cool about all this?"

"Right. Dude would usually be big mad right now." Wells was up a little, his wool hat flipped down over his eyes. It wasn't really cold outside. Especially in these stuffy-ass tuxes. I assumed the choice was for personal style and maybe even to help him sleep. He bunched his hands under his pits. "Probably more so than the rest of us."

"Yeah," I said, that curious too. Prinze was the closest to Wolf. Therefore, he'd generally be the most betrayed. Or at least would feel that way.

Prinze glanced over at Wolf, who was still gazing out of the window. Prinze frowned. "I guess I don't see the point. Doesn't help."

It didn't, but the guy was never logical. In fact, he was just as hotheaded as Wolf on his best day.

The weirder-than-shit award was being passed around tonight.

Fawn: I guess I believe you. I'll see you when you're done. I'll try to stay up, and I'm sorry again.

I really wished this girl would stop apologizing. After all, she was in this mess because of me. She'd admitted she only came because she knew I'd stay in Maywood Heights. Stay with her.

I put my phone away. I did want to broach the subject of what happened with Wolf earlier, but I needed to talk with him first.

I needed answers.

I had so many questions on my lips by the time Prinze pulled up to the valet. I had to put them away (temporarily) to get out and navigate all the traffic outside the theater. A lot of people were out for tonight's show, adults in tuxes and formal wear running after kids in sparkly gowns and tiny tuxedos. The guys and I blended in amongst them, waiting for that second Escalade to unload behind us. The fathers didn't make us wait long and resembled mafia dons when they eased out of the darkly tinted SUV. Most of them sported black-on-black like Thatcher, calm in the chaos as they stepped onto the pavement and buttoned their jackets. Thatcher's dad had gotten out first, and since I was closest to him, he shook my hand.

"Bru."

"Mr. Reed."

"Enough with the Mr. Reed stuff," he stated, genuinely grinning at me. Mr. Reed and I had always been cool. Thatcher and Wells were in the same year as me, so I spent a lot of time over at both the guys' houses senior year. Mr. Reed clasped my shoulder. "Call me Knight. You're family, boy."

I watched a few mouths part at that, my brother's included. Wolf had been more discreet about it, but Thatcher wasn't. Thatch's head cocked. "But you make us call you 'sir.'"

Mr. Reed shot a look over at his son, and instantly, Thatcher stiffened.

Thatcher's throat flicked. "I mean, Dad. Sir. Dad-sir?"

This appeared to be acceptable to Mr. Reed because he nodded, and Wells barked a laugh so hard I thought he'd get a look too. He did get Mr. Reed staring coolly at the hat on his head. He tipped his chin at it, and right away, Wells ripped it off his head.

Mr. Reed eyed my friends. "That's because none of you boys are Bruno Sloane-Mallick," Mr. Reed boasted, and the other fathers had made their way over at that point. My own dad was included in that number. Ramses got my shoulder and grinned at me just as hard.

"Never do have to worry about Bru," he said, the pride swelling in his eyes. Almost instantly, I shifted in my shoes, my hands in my pockets.

"So true. Some of you boys could learn a thing or two from him." This came from Jax, Wells's dad. The guy had taken up real estate between his son and Thatcher. He studied them both. "We've never had to be out here for him."

"Or hop a red-eye," LJ stated, Dorian's god-dad. LJ didn't have any children, but he was here on these outings just like the other dads. He and the fathers were all childhood friends, and he showed up just like they did. "And I have to say. That's getting kind of old."

From what I'd heard, LJ and his wife, Billie, had planned to come out for Christmas with the rest of the Legacy families, but not this early. I'd heard some of the moms say the pair had been on the other side of the world making real estate deals. LJ was in real estate like some of the other dads.

But he was here now, and we knew why we all were. The focus hit Wolf at that moment, and our dad stepped over to him.

"How about you lead the way, then, huh?" Ramses stated, my adoptive father and my dad in every sense of the word. I'd joined the Mallick family at seventeen, but they hadn't hesitated to give me their last name and make me one of their own. I'd become an instant family member, Ramses and

Brielle, my adoptive mother, so giving. When they found my sister (their biological daughter), they certainly hadn't had to include me with her.

But they did.

My brother's eye contact I didn't miss. It drifted my way after our dad brought an arm around me too. The three of us scaled the steps together, the others behind us, and I was happy to have all the focus off me. The dads always did that when we were all together. I was Bruno Sloane-Mallick, the golden boy.

Mr. Perfect.

The heavy weight of that I felt bog me down all the way into the theater. The dads had gotten us a couple of boxes. They always placed themselves between us guys, so we'd focus on the show rather than talking. They also took our cell phones too, but I noticed I was the only one who got to keep mine when Ramses made his rounds to retrieve them.

He nodded at me before taking his seat between Wolf and me. He always did that too, both of us his sons.

The guys noticed I got to keep my phone but didn't say anything about it.

Mr. Perfect.

Suddenly anxious, I shifted in my seat. The show hadn't started yet, and most of the dads were still up and talking.

Thatcher hit Wells's chest. "Incredible Hulk over there too big for his seat," he said, snorting. The comment barked a short laugh out of Wells, and I studied the fathers before flipping them both off. I normally was up for a little handling, but this wasn't the first comment made about my size. I'd been hearing it since I'd gotten home and not just from my friends.

"Guess all them heavy-ass books," Wells joked, then shut up when he got squeezed between his dad and Mr. Reed. Thatcher quieted too, and I was grateful. I really wasn't trying to have the focus on me. The last thing I wanted.

My jaw moving, I actually watched the show that night. One, because we were supposed to, but the main one had to do with control. I had a focus point, and I wasn't jumpy. Calm.

And I needed calm.

CHAPTER
ELEVEN

Bru

"Wolf!" I jogged toward him.

He'd booked it the moment Prinze pulled up to the Reeds' house.

The fact that my brother was trying to avoid me was apparent, and he'd been doing a pretty good job tonight. After the show, the dads and LJ took us to dinner. We hit up a local Jax's Burger franchise. Jax's was owned by Wells's dad, and Wolf had made sure at least one body was between us all night. If it wasn't a dad, it was one of our friends.

I picked up my pace. "Wolf?"

"Kid?" Wolf turned around, but I noticed not until there was a decent amount of lawn between us and the others. Everyone was still unloading out of the damn cars. Wolf tucked his hands under his arms. "What?"

Finally making it to him, I slowed down. He'd undone his tie like most of us, his hair down and his jacket off. His white shirt hung loosely off his big shoulders, his tux in general way roomier than mine, and I'd been envious of the fit. My own had been tighter than shit. "You know what."

I had to say, I nearly applauded my brother in that moment. He growled at me, *a reaction*, which let me know he wasn't drugged or dead. I considered both with how laid back he'd been acting since I'd gotten home.

Wolf scanned across the lawn at the others lazily making their way toward the house. He appeared hesitant to allow others to be privy to this conversation.

Which set my hackles the fuck up.

Prinze, Wells, and Thatcher passed us before Wolf angled toward me, and he didn't speak until the door shut behind the three. "You're getting at shit that doesn't exist."

"Really?"

"Really." He waited again. A couple of the dads moved past us. Wolf smiled at them, tight, before facing me. "You're working up bullshit that, again, isn't reality."

"You were acting jealous." I was never one to beat around the bush, and my candor elicited another sharp growl in my direction. "Don't lie to me. I'm not fucking stupid."

I knew what I saw, which made no fucking sense. My brother didn't get jealous over girls. Again, loved the guy but dude knew he was a fuckboy just like the rest of our friends outside of Prinze. That was just how these guys were, and there was never any judgment there. I was the last person to preach about how people should live their lives.

Especially after last semester.

I had my own shit, but at least I was the only one affected by my actions.

"You aren't stupid, but you are coming up with the wrong conclusions."

"How so?"

"Fawn and I had a business arrangement."

My mouth closed for a second. "A business arrangement."

He nodded. "I controlled everything she did. My property."

What the fuck?

"And anything you *think* you saw before was just some residual shit. Territorial."

He was speaking so coldly about her. So cruel. "What are you talking about?" This wasn't my brother. He didn't do shit like this. Treat people this way... I closed the distance. "You do know what she's been through, right? Her dad—"

"Yeah, I know all about that."

I blinked. Fawn hadn't been forthcoming about the terrible things she'd been through when I knew her. I'd found out through the grapevine back then, and that hadn't been something we talked about on the roof. We didn't talk about anything meaningful. I think she'd been afraid to let me in, and I hadn't really wanted to pressure her.

Honestly, I was shocked he knew anything about her beyond the rage he apparently had. "I don't believe you. That you'd do that. That you're that..." My breath was harsh. "That you're that cold."

I really wanted to believe him better than that. I mean, he said he knew her history, and Wolf didn't treat people like an asshole for no reason. I knew his reason, the one he gave, but it was weak and hadn't made sense to me.

Wolf wet his lips. "Well, believe it. Now, if you'd excuse me, I need to go to bed. I basically have to do anything the parents fucking want me to do while we're here. That includes waking up at the fucking crack of dawn and baking with the moms."

I got his arm.

"Kid, if you don't let go of me right fucking now, we're going to have a problem."

We were going to have a problem, and that started with me. "I don't believe you."

"What?"

"I don't *believe* you, Wolf," I said, and I did let go but only to confront him full on. So he'd look at me.

So he'd face me.

"You had a reaction before," I explained, and it was one that had freaked me the fuck out. It scared me. He'd gone all apeshit, but it hadn't scared me in a way that caused me to fear for my life.

I feared for him.

I'd never seen my brother have a panic attack, but I'd heard about them. He had looked on the cusp of heading to the floor, and yeah, that freaked me out. I had been scared but for him.

"Like I said..." He shrugged. "It was residual shit. Bullshit."

I scanned his eyes. "You're sure?"

"Positive."

And then, he was leaving, and I think that only had about fifty percent to do with me. The rest was Dad who'd come around, and he called out to Wolf as he walked away.

"Remember. You're to be around for anything we need, son," Dad said, and Wolf bobbed his head once in acknowledgment. His hands in his pockets, my brother strode away, and Ramses sighed in his wake. "What am I going to do with him?"

This was a rhetorical question, and in the silence, Dad squeezed my arm.

"And thank you for paying attention tonight," he said. "For being the example? The other boys really could learn a thing or two from you, and I'm so proud your mom and I don't have to worry about you."

I had paid attention tonight. At one point, Thatcher and Wells had fallen asleep, and Prinze and Wolf were in and out. The latter two had been awake, but barely, and I was sure my focus was for different reasons.

I closed my mouth, my smile strong on my father. He and Brielle had said that a few times since I'd been back, that they were glad they didn't have to worry about me.

That they were proud.

They said they were proud of me for taking life by the horns and branching out. They'd let me find my own way after high school and hadn't even blanched when I'd decided to cross an ocean to go to school. They were proud of me and happy for me.

I owed my adoptive mother and father so much, my throat tight when I nodded at my dad. I put on a strong face for him and was proud of myself that I didn't let my anxiety show.

My restlessness.

It had hit hard tonight, and I'd felt the trigger of it the moment the dads had all showered me with all that praise. I'd been in a constant state of restlessness after that, and Thatcher's and Wells's comments about that Hulk shit hadn't helped.

Calm.

Smoking seemed to be the only thing these days to help me fight my body's urge to physically expel energy. It wasn't the solution by any means, but it ebbed the pulse charging through my veins.

My fists.

Going back to the house wasn't an option right now, and I texted Wells and Thatcher to cover for me when I went behind the house to smoke. It had kind of been unsaid that we'd be doing that for each other since we all smoked weed.

I took mine out back farther into the woods. I didn't want to risk one of the parents being on the back porch and seeing the light. Thick smoke curled from my lips, and I physically felt myself calm down.

Calm.

Breathing exercises helped too, but not when I was so

amped. I related with my brother on the whole panic thing. I'd never had an actual attack, but it felt like I handled my shit worse.

I still wasn't sure what to make of Wolf and all this stuff, but at the present, I was more concerned with myself. I needed to calm the fuck down.

Closing my eyes, I let the back of my head touch a tree. My muscles loosened up a bit, not as tight, but I looked up when some brush hit my face. My eyes shot open and a short shriek hit the air before someone fell from the tree and was suddenly in my arms.

What the hell?

Something sweet and floral smelling surrounded me, and I nearly lost my footing *and her* when Fawn crashed against me. She had her camera cradled in her arm, the other one wrapped around me.

"Fawn?" She'd mostly landed on her feet, but I had to keep her there. "Hey."

She was panicking a little, her face exploded in color. I didn't know from how high up she'd fallen, but far enough to freak her out. She was breathing rapidly, *harshly*, and after I got her on her feet, I directed her to look at me.

"Fawn." My thumbs brushed the flush in her cheeks. Adrenaline charged my heart too, and that'd been before she fell. There was a reason I was out here smoking weed. "Fawn, look at me."

She was now, and I calmed as she did. I was grateful for that. Before she fell, I'd had enough energy pumping through me I thought I'd punch a tree.

The urge wasn't there now, my breathing mellow. The weed had helped before, but this was better.

"Holy fuck, Bru." She pushed her hair out of her face, still in my arms. She laughed. "Shit. I almost killed you. I'm sorry."

She hadn't almost killed me. In all actuality, she'd ended

up easing me off a fucking ledge. Things were getting dicey there for a moment, dark.

"What were you doing?" I asked. We both realized I still had my arms around her at this point, and rather awkwardly, I let her go. I immediately realized the loss of the warmth, but it was chilly tonight. Even in my tux. "You okay?"

"Yeah, and…" A flash of panic struck across her face. That was until she realized she had her camera. She sighed. "You saved my camera."

"I saved you." I was laughing now. She could be cute sometimes, panicking more for her camera than herself.

Real cute.

I directed a look to the ground before wrestling a hand through my hair. "And you're okay?"

"Yes, and thank you. Fuck, that was stupid." She arched her neck, staring up into the dark tree. I guess there was a little bit of light since the Reeds had various ones posted throughout the grounds. "I was trying to get a shot of a bird."

"A bird?"

"Yeah, an owl. Trying to stay loose, you know? Since I'm here." She was looking up again, and I fought my smile. I forgot about her love and drive for photography, and I knew what that and her camera meant to her. The camera was her dad's, and they shared that same passion for taking photos.

Fawn's drive was one of the things I'd admired about her back in the day. She used to carry her camera around with her everywhere. I angled close. "Did you get the shot?"

"Not quite." Her focus returned down here, and when she did, we were a few inches away from each other. She'd been that sweet smell before, flowers or something like that. Her blink was slow. "It moved."

"Ah," I said, noticing the slight twitch in her throat, a swallow. She rerouted her attention to the tree after that. I smiled a little. "I can help."

I heeled my weed butt. I'd dropped it when I broke the fall

of an unexpected photographer. Laughing to myself, I scaled the tree and think I surprised Fawn and me both when I did. I mean, I was still in this tight-ass tuxedo, but I managed without ripping anything.

"You know, it's probably gone," she said from below. She laughed. "What are you doing?"

"Do you want to take a photo or not?" She hadn't been far off the ground and thank God for that. She could have broken her neck. I reached for her. "I see it."

"Really?" Taking my hand, she climbed up to meet me. I got her secure, and once she got herself situated, I put a finger to my lips.

She spotted the owl right away. The thing had its back to us. I made a noise with my hands, and not only did it turn around but opened its wings.

"Holy fuck," Fawn whisper-shouted. Acting quick, she picked up her camera, snapping a photo. "Holy fuck, Bru. Are you like an owl whisperer or something?"

Not really, but it sure looked like it when the thing show-boated the way it did. That'd been a nice little surprise. I'd just been trying to get its attention so she could see it. I shrugged. "I know an animal call or two."

"Really?" After she got her shots, I helped us both out of the tree. Not far from the ground or not, the distance was dangerous, and I was there to catch her when she came down. It was the right way this time, and my hands didn't leave her until I knew she was stable, her curves in my hands.

I felt that heat leave again when I let go of her, and I wasn't sure I could blame that on the fact that it was chilly and she was just, well, a human person. That she held heat my hands missed, warmth...

I think Fawn noticed my fingers accidentally brushed her skin before I let go. Her own fingers lingered over that sliver of charged flesh that exposed beneath her hoodie.

She tugged it down. "So, they're teaching animal calls in college?" she asked, her tone playful and even teasing. It was nice to see considering how everything had been with Wolf and everything.

I nudged a stick with my patent leather shoe. "Nah. Not really. I did some volunteer work at an animal reserve last semester. Volunteered there and a few other places. Just trying to stay busy."

And it worked for a time, stamped down my energy. I had a lot of it.

Anxiety bloomed in my chest again, made me shift. Fawn asked me if my volunteer work had to do with my major, and I was glad. It made me focus on other things. "Undecided."

She nodded, and I was also glad when she didn't ask any more about it. I'd have to tell her how I deep dived into every area of focus under the sun. How I'd gone looking for something just to stay busy.

And how it ultimately hadn't been enough.

I'd had a difficult semester, but unlike most, it hadn't just been the casual stresses of term papers and final exams. It'd been some deep fucking shit.

Trauma shit.

Rather than focus on that now, I smiled at her. "If you want, I can help you find some animals tomorrow. Get some more pictures to help you stay loose."

The alternative was me doing something a lot less productive. Like smoking weed and shit just to do *something*. I still hadn't told my parents about what had happened last semester, and with all this shit with Wolf, I wasn't planning to right away.

I also wanted to help her, be there for her. My brother had treated her like shit, and though I knew that wasn't my fault, I wanted to do what I could to make up for it. Once more, I knew this wasn't my obligation but...

I wanted to help her, and this shouldn't surprise me. That'd been the way we'd met back at school.

"I'd like that," she said, and for some reason, my insides did funny things. Things like dance and hop and shit. She grinned. "I'd like that a lot."

I'd like to help her a lot.

A lot.

A lot.

Something twisted her expression in that next moment, pulling me out of my thoughts. Her mouth parted. "How was the ballet?"

So that was the reason for her sudden shift, her focus suddenly on my tux and not the conversation. "Wasn't bad. I have seen this one before, so no, it wasn't bad."

Smile again, please.

I liked it when she smiled. I liked it even more when I made her happy. I remember it being a drug back then too.

Another drug…

Fighting that thought, I watched her shake her head. She played with her camera's strap. "How did he act?"

Seeing as how *he* probably meant my brother, I didn't ask her to elaborate. Regardless, though, I wasn't quite sure how to answer.

Fawn wrestled through red strands. "You know what? Never mind. Sorry I asked. I don't care." A curse left her lips. Like she was chastising herself for asking.

I eased my hands into my pockets. "Fawn?"

"Ready for bed? I am." She looped her arm in mine, a friendly gesture.

I nodded, not sure if that was more for her or myself. "Sure."

Her smile returned then, and since it had, that might be why I let where we'd been headed go. She clearly didn't want to talk about my brother, and my brother didn't want to talk about her. They were two people who didn't want to talk

about each other, and I thought I'd gotten her reason considering how he'd treated her.

I wasn't so sure now as I walked Fawn into the house, but
I did escort her. I was tired too. Dog tired.

Always tired.

CHAPTER
TWELVE

Ares

Numb. That was what I wanted to feel. It was the only way not to feel anything at all, internal, external…

I'd been on autopilot that morning with the moms. I couldn't tell you what tasks I did for them, or what they were baking. I just knew the moment my own mother told me they were good with the help, I headed out.

I ran.

My feet hit ground, jogging the best way not to feel anything. I tired my shit out and worked myself to the point of exhaustion.

I was exhausted.

In every way I could think of, I was, and I couldn't see a way around any of it. I'd dug myself too deep. Buried.

Numb.

I honest to shit couldn't feel any part of my body by the time I got to the harbor. The local town was decorated in holiday lights just like the theater, and I came across the ocean breeze exhausted.

Spent.

I was used to feeling too much these days, and it was like someone knew when I got a text.

Remember to reach out when you get back, the text said, and I didn't bother looking at the name of the person who sent it. It was always the same person these days.

Instead, I pocketed my phone, a glutton for punishment when I pulled it out again. A second text buzzed against my leg.

I know you don't want to, but I think it's time we explore our other options.

Numbness hit me again, illness. My stomach clenched, and I thought I'd be sick, but I breathed through it.

I wasn't trying to deal with reality right now, so instead of texting back, I just put my earbud back in. My music playing, I tried to drown out the sound of thoughts and bullshit with heavy metal. I circulated between that and hip hop, and I thought it did the job I needed it to until I escaped the harbor and ended up in front of a coffee shop. We had that chain back home, back at college.

Wetting my lips, I went inside, and I had no idea what I was doing. I just knew I was heading up to the register, and the next thing I knew, I had a coffee.

I didn't even drink coffee.

I hadn't for a while, but the drink in my hand I knew all too well. A blond espresso latte with oat milk and heavy foam. And sweet.

So sweet.

I'd joked with Red she'd rot her teeth out with this shit. She used to order one when we had our coffee dates. They were things we'd staged to look like a couple, mandatory...

"Anything else, sir?" the barista asked me. She was giving me the fuck-me eyes, but I hadn't even noticed until directly spoken to. I didn't notice those things anymore.

Not for a long time.

I told her no then mentally dismissed her, not knowing what I was doing when I headed over to the milks and sugar area next. I added extra sugar. Red liked sugar.

What are you doing?

I knew what. I was ordering a girl her favorite coffee when *I* was the one who created a clear boundary. *I* was the one who wanted nothing to do with her.

Also me, adding more sugar to an already sugar-laden drink. Red always did that, adding sugar on top of sugar.

Stop.

I didn't, suddenly determined to make it perfect. I'd had a shit morning, shit texts, and adding sugar to this damn coffee right now was the only thing that was making me feel less like shit. It was making me feel.

Numb.

I wanted to feel nothing. Fuck had I wanted to, but everything inside me was pulling at me to get this drink right and get it to her. I didn't know what I'd say once I did, and she probably wouldn't even open the door for me.

I wasn't caring at this point, but glanced up when someone called my name. No one should be calling my name. I didn't know anyone here.

"Eh. Got enough sugar there?"

My brother, Bru, had a coffee in his hands and a sweatshirt on. It was a gag gift with a tipsy elf on it and eggnog in his hands. My mom had gotten all us kids one a couple Christmases ago, but none of us wore them outside of Christmas Day.

My brother would, probably to make her happy. He was the perfect son my parents had finally gotten. I wasn't perfect, far from it. Bru cocked his head. "Bro?"

I added too much sugar, ruined it. Even still, I passed it off. "Hey."

"Hey." He got close, but when he did, I gazed over his head. It was easy to do considering I had height over him and like everyone else besides my father. I hadn't been looking for anyone, but I wasn't surprised to see he wasn't alone.

That he was with her.

Fawn had her camera in her hands, wearing a sweatshirt too but not Christmas-related. She wasn't into that corny shit, and she still wore those ripped-up jeans. The ones that showed off her tats and had me gripping this damn coffee.

What do you know? You do feel something.

I did and fuck me for it. *Fuck. Me.* I had no right.

None.

Tell my eyes that, my heart when it felt like slamming through my rib cage. It was rare I could just look at Fawn. Normally, she caught wind and was snarling at me.

I laughed to myself, laughed because I loved that fucking shit. I was so toxic I enjoyed that I drove a girl completely insane.

I loved…

Bru, of course, had his focus on me, and I think, at that point, I hadn't given a shit. He'd accused me of some stuff last night, and though he wasn't far off, I just didn't care anymore.

He can't take this.

This moment he couldn't have, but it turned out to be short-lived when Fawn finally did glance up. We clashed gazes right away, and I stepped forward. Like I was pulled or something.

Hey, Red.

It was like we were in our own silent conversation, and one I desperately wanted with her. I thought when I did finally get to talk with her, I'd threaten her, but those weren't the thoughts floating around in my head.

A hand formed around my arm about the same time, Fawn's expression twitched. Wincing, she shifted her attention to her camera and was doing God knows what with it.

She was pressing buttons, but I was sure only to distract herself.

"We went out this morning. I was helping Fawn find local wildlife, so she could take pictures and help her stay loose."

Right. We weren't alone, Red and me. I slid my gaze to my brother. "Oh, yeah?"

"Yeah." Bru's tone and expression had been accusatory last night. In fact, he'd come so hard at me I was sure he'd blow my shit out of the water the next time I saw him. He was so close with what he'd said last night.

Spot on.

He and Dorian hadn't compared notes, and though that was obvious, I figured it'd only be a matter of time. I swallowed. "That's cool."

It wasn't cool, them hanging out, and I didn't know what to feel about it.

My phone buzzed, another text, and it was like it tugged me back into reality. Everyone in my life was mad at me, so only one person would be texting me.

Ignoring it, I picked up my ruined coffee. "Got to get this to Mom," I said, a lie, clearly. This shit would be going into the garbage the moment I got outside.

"All right. Cool." It wasn't cool, and my brother's words were a lie too.

He watched me leave the shop, but he wasn't the only one. I knew what it was like to have eyes on you. I knew because I was normally the one doing the watching. I'd done my fair share of stalking this past semester.

And it didn't stop just because my fake girlfriend and I had broken up.

CHAPTER
THIRTEEN

Fawn

"Did something happen between you and Wolf?"

I stilled, my hands gripping my camera. Bru eased into the line of my sight after what he said, his hands together.

Dammit.

My heart was still racing after seeing Wolf, and I hadn't yet recovered from it. He'd been half dressed, sweaty. I mean, he was covered up, but he'd cut the sleeves off his hoodie. He must have been more focused on his runs lately because his body had transformed into that of a runner. Less bulky, and more toned. This was something I'd noticed before, the guy still ridiculously huge and his presence the same. He had his hair up and sweat glistened along his brow. It glistened everywhere, his arms, legs.

I got all that in the two seconds we'd made eye contact before I'd severed it. I mean, I'd taken a full inventory of the guy down to his Nikes.

And I still hadn't answered Bru.

I didn't know how to. I didn't know what to say. Had something happened between Wolf and me?

And had it even counted?

I didn't feel it had. It couldn't if it was one-sided. I glanced up. "I didn't want it to."

Bru blanched. "What do you mean you didn't want it to? Like he..." His gaze shot outside, his eyes suddenly cold. He faced forward. "Fawn, did my brother make you do something you didn't want to do?"

It took me a second to realize what he was getting at, and after I did, I waved what he said off right away. It hadn't been like that.

The truth of it was I'd been stupid. I fell in love with someone who wanted nothing to do with me.

Stupid.

I had been in love, so fucking in love it drove me crazy. *He* drove me crazy. "I just mean, the platonic parameters of our relationship were something he clearly set, and I got stupid."

"Stupid?"

I nodded. "I don't want to talk about it, Bru. It was dumb. I was dumb."

So dumb.

And I wanted to cry now, even dumber. I started playing with my camera again, and out of nowhere came Bru. He placed his hand on the strap, making me deal with shit.

Making me face him.

He was never one to make me talk about my problems, like his brother in that way. But unlike his brother, he never pushed once I gave him an in. That had been Wolf. Once he got a thread, he unraveled it. He bled it out of me.

He made me feel things.

He made me feel like he was there for me and created a space where I could trust him. This was such bullshit, epic shit.

"Fawn, did you," Bru started and was so kind. This day

had been great before his stupid brother. I mean, he'd gotten up at the crack of dawn with me and helped me find deer and shit. His eyes narrowed. "Did you fall in love with my brother?"

I thought I had, believed I had, but how could I have when it was never real?

It was real for you.

"That wasn't love, Bruno," I said, the truth, then shrugged. "Anyway, nothing was ever real for him, so it couldn't have been real for me."

Bru's attention shifted outside. I didn't know what he was looking for, but something had him working his jaw. "You sure he doesn't feel the same about you?"

I blinked, but then, well, I laughed. It was dry as I shook my head. "Pretty sure it was just physical for him, and thinking about it, I think that was the same for me too."

And maybe, if I drilled that into my head enough, I'd believe it. Someday...

I'd been overzealous with my thoughts, my words. Bru's hands came together, and when he studied the table in deep thought, I realized what I'd said. I just put that out there that his brother and I fucked. I rubbed my temple. "That was TMI."

And well, weird. That was just the ease of Bruno, though. Easy. I felt like I could just talk to him, and I should be able to.

I rubbed my hands, shifting. I had made things weird and didn't know how to address it.

"It was honest." Laughter touched his voice, but he was being kind again. It was weird, and I shouldn't have said it.

But why shouldn't I have?

Bru and I were friends, and we should be able to talk. This was his brother, but we had a history too.

Friends.

I didn't know why this felt awkward, besides, well, the

obvious. I suddenly felt the need to apologize, but the moment passed.

Bru braced his arms. "And you don't feel anything for him? I mean, not anymore."

I swallowed. "It was physical like I said. That was it. The end."

The belief felt like my mantra at this point, but that seemed necessary. It had to just be physical for me, and I did like having sex with Wolf.

A lot.

We connected on this visceral level, and it was something I'd never experienced.

And might not ever again.

I saved that thought for myself this time, shrugging, and Bru was in deep thought for the second time today. His fingers danced along his coffee cup, and I nudged his knee. "I'm sorry I made things awkward."

Right away, his hand lifted, his smile back. It didn't quite reach his eyes, and that just felt like more of his kindness. "Not my favorite topic, my brother's sex life, but I'm glad you told me about it. We should be able to talk. We're friends."

That was how I felt too.

Then why did it feel so weird?

I shifted in my chair again, awkward.

"Definitely explains a few things, though," he said, his eyes narrowed. He didn't elaborate, and since his brother wasn't my favorite topic either, I let what he said go. Odds were, I just wasn't good at hiding how his brother affected me, and he'd picked up on that.

"So, uh, we still have some time before we head back for lunch." Bru got up. "Want to check out the scene more? Get some more pictures?"

We kind of wandered into the back part of town this morning after miles of woods. I liked the look of the harbor and wanted to take pictures. I eased out of my chair. "Sure."

I'd like that and loved spending time with him. We'd had so much fun. In fact, I couldn't remember the last time I'd felt so free, so good.

It was good with Bru, easy. He never failed to take my worries away, and if I was smart, I'd invest a lot more time into that relationship. Things were always good with us and good wasn't bad.

Again, it was easy.

CHAPTER
FOURTEEN

Fawn

The Legacy parents and their kids decided to do some shopping later that afternoon, and I opted out of going. I claimed illness, something I ate during lunch.

The reality was they'd all piled into cars to do their shopping. The town was within walking distance, but it was far enough where people wouldn't generally walk there. At least not these families. They had a private chef for all their meals on top of the beautiful mansion we all stayed in. Needless to say, they'd all chosen not to huff it through the woods, and I wasn't surprised.

Still, I couldn't do cars, and I had too much pride to tell Bru and his family the truth. I'd gotten lucky again when we all arrived at the airport. There'd been a shuttle, and I hadn't had to say anything about my aversion to small vehicles.

I supposed that afternoon my luck ran out, and before Bru could protest and miss out on an opportunity to hang with his family and friends, I'd been proactive. I'd pretended to sleep after announcing my food poisoning, but not before sending him a text. I requested over-the-counter meds to help with my stomach, weak I knew, but it worked. He had checked on me, but he ultimately left when he'd seen I was asleep.

I guessed Wolf Mallick wasn't the only liar around here.

I'd spotted Wolf at lunch in passing. It'd been brief because, despite all the families being under one roof, they hadn't all eaten at the same time. I'd met everyone between the airport and just being under the same roof, and it was overwhelming what a family bond all these people had. Some of the parents were godparents to a few of the kids, but even without the tie, they were family.

Family.

I'd gotten quite a few texts from my mom the past couple of days. She did that, checked on me, but I never had much to say to her. I had no problem with my mom or stepdad, Anton, but it did hurt to talk to them. I just kept remembering how I had family, and I'd ruined it. My dad would still be alive if not for me, and I held that weight long past the time of his accident. It pushed me in every way to succeed and let him see I wasn't wasting my life.

The sacrifice he made.

He was the real reason I wanted that internship with Kurt Ackerman from the *New York Times*. He was also the reason I went to Pembroke, my dad's alma mater. I wanted to follow in my dad's footsteps, and ultimately, work at the *New York Times* myself. My dad had worked there too, and we always used to talk about where my office would be. He'd take me on tours of his office when I was young, holding my hand. We were so happy, so fucking happy, and I'd taken that for granted.

There was no sleep for me that afternoon, fake illness or not. I changed into a plaid button-up instead of my hoodie since it wasn't as cool outside, then headed out. I scouted the woods for subjects to photograph. Nature wasn't typically my focus, but it was the next best thing I had to hone my craft. I usually focused on people or human interest when it came to my photography like my dad. A photojournalism major, I captured stories of individuals and documented the power we all had to influence our communities. It was something my dad had done as well, something we'd shared.

I snapped a photo of a creek after I got deeper into the woods and chastised myself for not getting the right angle. There was no excuse not to get a perfect photo out here. The lighting was perfect.

I attempted again, getting some plant life in there. I knew what those were thanks to Bru. As it turned out, he held a cornucopia of plant knowledge on top of what he knew about animals. He'd showed me all kinds of things this morning during our venture out.

I smiled to myself, not really knowing why. I liked Bru. Hell, I really liked him, and the pair of us being thrust back into each other's lives only reaffirmed that. He was a great friend and had all the qualities in one I'd been hard-pressed to find since. I had friends, of course. I had Heath, my ex-roommate, and a few others in our photojournalism program, but I'd be lying if I said I ever let them get too terribly close to me. We were all friends at the surface level, but I always kept a wall up.

Not always.

There had been a time after Bru where I'd let my walls down, but that'd kicked my ass and then some.

Cursing myself for taking another crappy photo, I hunkered down for another shot, but nearly dropped my camera in the creek at the sound of twigs snapping behind me. I whipped around, my back up, but I went ramrod straight at the sight of someone else.

At the sight of *him.*

Ares stood still several feet behind me, his hand pocketed in a pair of dark joggers. He fingered through his thick curls and was mid-turn like he was on the cusp of spinning around.

Had he been following me?

This I didn't know, but he was behind me now, *striding toward me.* I was spinning, grabbing my camera bag and putting it on my shoulder. I escaped the creek, then hopped down to some brush on the other side of it.

But he was faster.

Of course, he was, those godforsaken long legs of his. He used them and barely allowed me to get a second or two ahead of him.

"Red, wait. *Fuck.* Wait—"

"Don't call me that." His hand briefly landed on my shoulder, but I ripped it away. Even still, that didn't stop the hot sear that scorched through my button-up after he touched me.

Or the race in my heart because he did.

I'd managed *for days* not to talk to this fucker. Yet here he was tormenting me. I bared teeth. "Are you following me?"

"What?"

"I said, are you fucking following me?" He'd take me for an idiot if he claimed anything else. Before I saw him, he hadn't exactly looked like he'd been trying to come to me.

Ares had his hands laced above his head, his hoodie exposing his abs, and I wanted to burn my eyes out of my head. I couldn't stop *looking* at him. I couldn't stop being aware of him like some psycho, Stockholm syndrome freak. He wet his lips. "I was just checking on you."

I had to have looked like I was slapped. "Checking on me?"

"Yeah. You lied, right? About being sick?"

My mouth parted, and he huffed.

His expression fell. "I mean, come on. It was obvious."

He was joking, right? A joke.

I barked a laugh, and it was loud enough to send birds flying out of the trees. "You're a joke."

And I wasn't hearing this.

I shot around, but Ares sprung and got a hold of me. Jerking, I worked him off, then immediately raised my fists.

His dark eyebrows basically hit his hairline, and it was him to bark a laugh. "What are you going to do with those, Red? Hit me?"

He'd deserve it, more than deserved it. I balled my fists. "If I need to."

The threat struck an easy grin across his lips and sent my tummy into a tailspin.

I wished it had been because I was sick.

I wished a lot of things were happening right now, but zero of them had to do with him, me, and him laughing at me in these fucking woods. I dropped my arms. "Fuck you, Wolf."

Another wish I had was stronger words. I wanted something harder that cut deeper.

It was the least I could do.

I had nothing heavier in my arsenal, and since I didn't, I had to settle for leaving. Gripping my camera bag, I attempted to do just that, but right away, Wolf strode behind me.

"Red—Fawn. Would you wait?"

I didn't and made strides to pick up the pace no matter how futile. I knew he was faster than me, but I had to try.

I had to.

This was my only thought as I broke off into a sprint. I wasn't a fast runner. Hell, I wasn't a *runner*. Like zero physical activity outside of my photography work. I also wasn't the lightest girl, but I gave it my best damn shot to get away from this asshole.

He'd broken my heart.

Into a million fucking pieces he had, so, yeah, I did what I could to get away. He caught up with me about the time I passed a tree, and when he worked me around, I gave him no fists this time.

I just spat.

It landed right in his stupid, fucking face. His pretty face crafted by the fucking gods. Wolf probably shouldn't be considered pretty. He was an asshole and a monster.

But that didn't stop how beautiful he was.

Physically, aesthetically, he was perfection, and there was the rub. He was this terrible person wrapped up in this gorgeous package.

The better to deceive you with, my dear…

He really was a big bad wolf, a beast.

And he was letting me go.

He did in order to use his hoodie sleeve to wipe the spit away. He stared at it. "I deserved that."

What?

I honestly didn't believe what I heard, so angry, shaking. Wolf put more distance between us, but once he did, he sighed.

"But even still, you lied, and I'm going to walk you back to the house now."

I was still trying to recover from the fact that he said he deserved being spat on. "What are you talking about?"

The look he shot me…

Frustration came to mind. Especially when he scrubbed his face. He tucked his hands under his arms. "Come on, Red. You lied, and now you're in the woods taking pictures by yourself when there could be drifters and shit out here. It's not safe. Dangerous. Now, you need to come back to the house—"

"You are joking." This was a joke. Had to be. "You have to be joking."

His lips thinned into a hard line. "I'm not."

"Oh, you gotta be." I was laughing, like hysterically at this point, which had Wolf eyeing the trees. I crossed my arms. "You want me to actually believe you care?"

I wasn't buying it. Not for shit did I buy it, and in the next moment, Wolf was shaking his head.

"I'm not joking. You're out here by yourself, and you don't know the area."

I was still laughing, rubbing the tears out of my eyes.

He frowned. "Fawn…"

"I'm sure I know it better than you," I said, still laughing. "Bru showed me around."

We'd gone all through these woods this morning, and though I didn't believe what Wolf was saying for shit, I felt the need to stand up for myself. He was playing some game, clearly, but if it was to make a fool out of me for not knowing what I was doing out here, he wasn't winning there. I did know what I was doing, and that was thanks to his brother.

At the mention of Bru, Wolf bristled for some reason. His arms dropped, and the next thing I knew, he was the one laughing.

"Right. You and my brother," he said, the words laced in what could only be sarcasm. He smirked. "Best buds."

I bristled this time. "What's that supposed to mean?"

"Just what I said. Best buddies." A muscle feathered his jaw. "Have to be since you guys are all shacked up and having slumber parties."

I was all out of laughter at this point, just straight confused now.

What. The. Fuck.

I didn't just hear what I did. He didn't just say what I *thought* I heard. I raised my hands. "You are kidding. You are *fucking* kidding. Where are the fucking cameras?"

I spun around, my hands out and everything. Wolf's expression cooled. "Fawn."

"Where are the cameras, Wolf?" I got in his face, and this was the biggest mistake.

I could smell him.

The spicy notes of his aftershave or whatever hit me like a tidal wave, and I physically wavered where I stood. I didn't back off, though, call it pride, and I got great satisfaction when his nostrils flared and his jaw clenched in front of me. The sun glinting off the double piercings in his nose, he obviously didn't like me being in his face. I stood tall. "We have to be on some hidden camera show, because no, you did not just say you had a problem with your brother and me sharing a room."

That meant he was jealous, and though I'd seen that before, it'd been just as much of a joke as this conversation. Wolf had once said he didn't like other people touching his things, but I wasn't his thing, and he couldn't control me.

He'd freed me from that.

He probably thought the freedom came from ending our fake relationship and getting out of the way of my internship. But the real freedom had come from those last words he'd shared with me.

"I don't do girlfriends, and even if I did, no way in the goddamn stratosphere would she be you."

Those words hit me hard today, and though they'd killed then, they made me strong now. They gave me reality, and now, I could see the forest for the trees when it came to him. This man was arrogant. This man was selfish, and he loved having ownership of something. He loved control.

Wolf squeezed the bridge of his nose. "Forget I said anything, but just please come back to the house and get out of the woods. It's about to get dark, and you shouldn't be out here by yourself. Outside of people, there's wild animals too."

He was the only animal I saw in front of me. "You really expect me to believe you give a shit? About me?"

His throat jumped. "No, Fawn, I don't want you hurt. I mean, why do you think I'm out here?"

More of his arrogance, or his stupid territorial caveman

crap. And I guess my well-being didn't apply to my emotional state. If it did, he wouldn't be here at all.

I didn't say any of my thoughts, and now, he was pacing for some reason. He lifted a hand. "I mean, it was obvious why you didn't want to go out with everyone else."

"Really?"

"Come on. You know it was." His lips turned down. "You're really going to make me say it?"

Pride kept me silent again, and maybe something else. I wasn't stupid enough to address that other thing, my hands coming together.

He stopped pacing. "You and I both know you don't do cars."

I expected the words, but even still, I felt slapped across the face with them. That he was out here to address that very thing.

That he *thought* to address it.

I didn't do cars, and out of everyone, he was the only one to know that. Bru hadn't even put the pieces together about all that. I'd never told him, not even back then.

Why hadn't I?

Why had I told *Wolf*, but I hadn't told Bru who was a genuinely true friend? Even now, I hadn't nutted up enough to tell him.

Even now.

I was fighting tears at that moment, mostly out of frustration. "You really expect me to believe you're out here because of me." He didn't *care*. He didn't... "You're an asshole, and you're cruel, and I need you to stay away from me."

This was more games. More *lies*, and I was going to leave before I did something stupid. Something like cry in front of this fucker and show him something I didn't want him to see.

I didn't even want to see it myself.

It might break me, so leaving was the best decision.

"Red—"

I swung because Wolf grabbed me.

It'd been instinctual.

I hadn't punched him, but the slap that struck his face hit so hard the sound radiated off the trees. A deep red bloomed across his golden cheek, and when he faced me, I thought he'd be angry. I mean, I'd hit him, and he should be angry.

Not sad.

Something weird twisted his handsome features, something that turned down his lips and made my heart race. I think I was angry that he wasn't lashing out. That he wasn't being his dicky wolf self.

I swung again, anger driving me this time, but he cuffed my wrist. He had a history of playing sports and caught me effortlessly. My third swing landed in his other hand, and he put both to his face. He put my hands right over where I slapped him.

Stop.

He wasn't stopping, and the next thing I knew, he backed me against a tree. He was just looking at me, staring at me so deep. That same pained expression laced his dark eyes, and I bit his lip.

I just wanted him to stop.

I wanted it gone, whatever sadness on his face gone, but once I started, I couldn't stop.

And he didn't either.

Wolf let go of my hands, deepening the kiss. He shoved his hands under my plaid button-up, palming my breasts, and I groaned.

Stop.

But I didn't want to. I loved it when he touched me, died for it. I pushed my chest out to meet his hands, and he growled so deep I felt it in my teeth.

"Red..." He dragged his mouth across my cheek, deep diving into my neck. He bit me, and I cried out. "Red, you have to stop me."

The words only warmed my blood. He'd said something similar before when we'd been together. I hadn't stopped him then, and I had no intention of stopping him now.

Instead, I pushed up his hoodie, making him take it off. His necklace hit his golden chest. He and his sister had matching ones.

Wolf's body had changed since the last time we'd been together. He was more svelte and chiseled like stone. A Greek statue came to mind, but whatever he decided to change about his body, he was still Wolf. Powerful. All consuming...

And he tasted like sin.

Our tongues dueled, teeth clashing, clacking. I bit his lip again, and he rewarded me by tongue-fucking my throat.

This is bad.

This was so bad, and I didn't want to do this. I didn't want him, but my body was doing the exact opposite thing that my mind wanted. It was like it remembered all those days he made me feel like pure heat, liquid and molten everywhere.

Feral.

"Fawn... Fuck." I was making him feel that way too, his hands on me, feeling me everywhere. He had me turned against the tree now, his fingers at the clasp of my jeans before he all but ripped them down my legs.

Stop this.

No.

It was like the angel and the devil. The angel was telling me this guy was a monster. He was a demon, and the only thing he was seeking was physical pleasure. He wanted nothing to do with emotions. He wanted nothing to do with me, and he proved that when he so brazenly shoved his hand down my panties. I cried out, and his teeth skidded my neck, biting me.

"I want you so fucking bad," he gritted, his fingers on the verge of fucking me, parting my folds. He spun in my juices, and I whimpered so bad tears pricked my eyes.

He kissed the pulse at my neck, as if soothing me, but I didn't want to be soothed. I wanted to be fucked and satisfy that itch only he could fulfill. I couldn't see anything else when it came to Wolf Mallick.

And I didn't want to.

Right now, I didn't. *My body* didn't. It ignored the hurt and the pain of the past, giving in to complete pleasure. It made me absolutely sick, but I couldn't help it.

Wolf's lips dragged absolute fire across my skin, and despite his fingers being so close to my entrance, he still continued to play with my folds. He parted them gingerly, strumming my clit with teasing strokes, and I bit the inside of my cheek so hard I tasted blood. He was right there, but he wouldn't do anything else. He breathed heat over my neck. "Let me fuck you, Red."

God, please.

I felt the words fall out of my mouth, but not by my own volition. They were body only, no mind here.

Only sex.

That was what I told myself, my panties ripped when Wolf bent me down over a tree stump. That was also what I told myself when he ripped my shirt open and shoved his hand into one of my bra's cups. My flesh spilled between the spaces of his lengthy digits, and he tweaked my nipple so hard I thought I'd come on his hand between my legs.

He growled then, his cock out when he casually ran the tip along the seam of my ass. It rubbed against me lazily, teasing like he was questioning this.

But we'd already started.

We already made it to the point of no return the moment I let him put his hands on me.

The moment you kissed him.

I was aware of my sins, and right now, I didn't want to repent. I just wanted to be *fucked* and only be him.

"Red..." Wolf hugged me, easily driving himself to the hilt

with one, charged thrust. His roar rumbled against my back, his hips driving wildly in quick succession. He was losing control.

But I already had him beat.

I let this guy fuck me on a dead tree, bark scraping against my chest, Wolf's digits digging into my breast. He'd ripped my bra at this point, the thing basically torn in half, and the only purpose my button-up served was to cover my back. The buttons had popped off the moment he'd gone for my breasts.

There was something forbidden about all this, being half naked and fucked in the woods. I didn't consider myself into exhibitionism, but I knew, if I had an audience, I'd probably come right there.

"Look at me, Red," Wolf coached, his hips still charging, dick tunneling. His hand caged my face, guiding me to look at him, but whatever he saw made his lips part and his hips eased to a stop behind me.

I think it was the tears.

I didn't know why I was crying. I think because all this felt so good. Because it felt so goddamn *heavenly* to be beneath him again. Because I knew once we stopped what would happen.

Because I knew this didn't work.

We didn't work. Wolf didn't love me.

Just sex.

I grabbed his hips, making him fuck me at this point. He'd stopped, and I didn't want him to.

"Fawn…"

I faced down, using his body as much as he was using mine. I dug my hands into his hips, pushing my ass back against him. Grabbing my hands, he forced them off him to the tree.

"Fawn," Wolf repeated, his voice laced with something. Whatever it was caused a jump in my heart. Especially when I saw him weave our fingers together. I used to watch our hands when he'd take mine during one of our coffee dates or our strolls across campus. The time we spent together had been for appearances, but every time he'd taken my hand, my foolish heart had betrayed me. I had let myself feel something every freaking time.

"Hey…" His lips were on my ear, but he wasn't kissing me, a swallow in his throat. "We don't have to do this."

My fingers tightened around his, and working my hips, I pushed back into him. A feral noise erupted from his chest, rolling right away into my back, and when I put his hand on my breast, I felt his hips pick back up. He couldn't resist my tits. Never could.

Just sex.

I told myself that as I steeled my heart. I locked it up in a vise just as tight and clamped down as his was. I lost myself in the pleasure, the pain.

Why don't you love me?

The words ached inside me, so much *pain*, but I made the pleasure override it. If he could use me, I could use him too. This was a mutual exchange, and I could put my emotions aside.

"Red…" The word touched my ear strained. Like there was ache in it too. *Impossible.* He hugged me. "I hate what I'm doing to you."

No, he didn't. Because if he did, he'd stop.

I ground my ass into him, holding him right back. His weight, his hold was always enough to send me over the edge. I intended to reach my peak that way and by my own terms, but then, I did something stupid.

I let him kiss me.

Wolf had my face in his hand again, but he wasn't kissing my mouth. His lips and tongue rolled down the trail of my tears, and the moment he did, warmth blazed into my tummy.

Just sex.

The crest rose so quick, that climb right at the precipice. I crashed over in a wave of fallen stars. Dead, broken stars.

Only sex.

The heat of the orgasm flooded my body the same time Wolf's cum exploded inside me. He hadn't put on a condom. Whether he trusted me to still be on birth control was up for debate. I was, but he didn't know that.

Maybe he didn't care. Like most things he was just a selfish fucker. He may have come into these woods to check on me, but he didn't care about me. Not really.

I flattened against the stump, partially from the lack of energy, but mostly because Wolf weighed a ton and he was on top of me. I liked his weight and even enjoyed how he milked himself inside me.

Just sex.

It was just sex, and the moment he pulled himself out, I decided I had my good time. I got up, immediately pulling up my pants.

"Fawn?"

There was a reason I hadn't looked at Wolf. I hadn't wanted to *see* him, but I did when I turned my eyes in his direction. His jeans open, he was naked from the waist up, his large body rising and falling with rapid breath.

His hair just fucked.

It was just as wild and all over the place as mine probably was, and it took me a second to realize he'd called my name because of what was in his hand. He held his hoodie, lifting it in my direction.

My shirt was ripped, my bra *in shreds*. He really had torn it in two. The front was hanging by a thread, my nipples basically out.

He cringed. "Fawn—"

I didn't want his help, instead tying my button-up and covering myself.

He drew forward. "Fawn..."

If he called my name one more fucking time, I'd break. I'd *crack*. Reality hit me in that instant, and the way I was wrestling my clothes on was all too familiar. That last time we were physically together I'd had to do that.

Once he was done with me.

He'd treated me like a whore then, and I took great satisfaction that I was returning the favor. I grabbed my camera after I clothed myself, leaving him, and refused to turn around when he called for me again.

"Fawn, please. I didn't," he started, his steps falling in behind me. He stopped. "I didn't mean…"

I would never know what he was going to say. He didn't finish, and I didn't stick around to listen. Nothing but filth ever came from his mouth.

Lies.

I wasn't strong enough to hear any of it then and was proud of myself when I continued walking on to the house. I didn't even stop when a roared, "Fuck!" blasted through the trees behind me. I felt the word in my bones, but I left its effect at the door of the Reed house. I closed the door to it.

Just like he'd closed the door to me.

CHAPTER
FIFTEEN

Fawn

"I slept with Wolf."

Three days it took me to come find Bruno and tell him the truth.

Three. Freaking. Days.

He sat on his bed behind his laptop, but the moment I rushed in, out of breath and most likely red as hell, his brows jerked up. His mouth parted. "What?"

God, he was going to make me say it again. I rubbed my arm. "I slept with Wolf."

Slept with were the wrong words. There was no sleeping. We'd fucked like animals, then I'd left him in the woods, ashamed as fuck and frustrated.

Why did I do that?

I hated him. *Still* hated him, yet for some reason I'd given my body over to him freely.

Bru had clearly heard me at this point, or at least understood me. He had a far-off expression on his face, and I think I only broke it because I eased over. "Bru?"

I suddenly felt vulnerable about being here, telling the truth. I'd wanted to tell him right after it happened.

So why didn't you?

Maybe it was that same reason it had felt awkward to talk to him about all this before. Bru and I had a history, and in some ways, it was more complicated than the situation I had with Wolf. We'd been friends back then, good friends.

But there had been these moments.

I hadn't been able to identify them back then. That was mostly due to trauma and how fucked in the head I'd been. My emotional damage hadn't computed letting anyone in during that time period in my life, and when I'd been getting around to easing past that, Cissy Armstrong saw fit to crush my progress. She'd been into Bru back then and picked at me, gnawed until her jealousy drove me to do something stupid. She hadn't liked my friendship with Bru and had hurt me because of it.

I'd hit back harder.

This was a simplification of the damage I'd ultimately done. I regretted the actions I'd taken to remedy my problem, but they had happened. I'd acted, and I'd been forced to leave my old school, and consequently, my friendship with Bru behind.

And now, things felt weird with him, and honest to God, probably because of me. I'd read into those little moments back then. Like they could have been something when they could have just as easily been the new kid being nice to the broken girl. Bru was nice, and now, I was making our adult friendship weird long after the feelings surrounding those tiny moments had passed. After I'd grown up and moved on.

After I'd gotten stupid and fallen in love.

The brevity of my stupidity hit in waves these days, and I hugged myself waiting for Bru's response. He still didn't have one, his hand running over his laptop.

He closed it slowly. "Okay."

"Okay?"

Say something else, please.

I kind of wanted him to scold me for being so dumb, and I deserved a double scold for waiting so long to talk about this. He invited me to, but I still went all hermit and closed into myself. The past few days, I'd basically been anywhere I assumed Wolf wouldn't be. That included this house and the majority of the property surrounding it. I'd used the excuse of going out to do some shooting when anyone asked, and that included Bru himself. He'd offered to go with me (on multiple occasions), but I'd shut that down.

Again, old habits.

Even he couldn't get anything out of me. He couldn't but his brother could.

Stop thinking about him.

I closed my eyes. "It just happened." And once it had, I couldn't stop thinking about it. How much I liked it...

I wasn't even going to *touch* that one now, refusing, and I studied Bru's slow nod.

"And, um..." Bru placed his laptop off to the side, his eyes narrowed. "It was consensual?"

The fact he was talking to me like a friend about all this despite Wolf being his brother made the guilt sit even heavier. I should have told him about this days ago. "It was."

And you liked it.

I wouldn't tell him that, refused to voice it. If I did, I would have to address the little devil living in my head. The one that said I regretted what had happened, but not that I'd done it. It was in direct conflict with what I was feeling emotionally when it came to Ares. I couldn't *stand him*, but the sex had been, well, how it always was when it came to him and me. It'd been earth-shattering. Ridiculous.

Amazing.

The guy just got my body. Even when he was wild and

untamed, which he'd been. I mean, he'd ripped my fucking bra in half.

I pressed my palms to my eyes. Though, I was sure Bru had no idea why.

And he was too quiet.

I made bravery my strong suit when I dared to gaze up. Bru was sitting back and had pushed his glasses into his hair. He really did look like one of my younger professors, and I did notice when he was in here on his computer, he had readers on. Actually, whenever I did see him in the past few days he'd been on his computer. I didn't know why since we weren't in school right now, but figured he was just scrolling.

"So, um, there really was something between you, then." He studied me. "Between you and him. There was something."

I'd told him before it had been one-sided, and the other day, it had just been sex. I still loathed Wolf.

But I wanted him.

I wanted him in that deep way and that heat we'd always been able to create. We were good at it. Fucking great. I breathed into my hands. "I like having sex with him."

My words were so low, but he completely heard them. His brow twitched before lowering slowly.

And he'd called me honest before.

I wanted to be and did feel guilty about how long it had taken me to come to him. I wasn't sure why I'd waited so long now.

Bru's gaze traveled across the room. Like he was trying to solve the most intricate problem with the way he circulated. His hands came together. "So, what's the problem, then?"

My brow jerked up this time. "What do you mean?"

"I mean." He paused, shifting. "You said this is just physical, right? That he used you…" His sight wandered once more, deep, penetrative. I didn't know what he was thinking about, but he was bracing his arms now. He shrugged. "Why not just do that? It can be that simple. You and him in a consensual situation."

I understood why he was shifting now, what he was proposing. My mouth parted. "You're serious."

"I mean, you're two adults. Consensual." He was scrubbing into his nut-brown-colored locks. "You like *doing that* with my brother." His face charged red. This entire topic was completely uncomfortable for him, and it was weird talking about this. I think I'd laugh about it all if I wasn't in such shock. Bru's head cocked. "If that's what you want, it can be only that. Especially since you said that's all he wanted out of everything too."

It'd been obvious. We were in a fake relationship, and he'd decide to eat his cake on top of having it. Literally.

And you thought he had feelings for you.

He'd been a good actor and an excellent liar.

And my chest stung.

Bru was right that I didn't have to get played this time. Not if I didn't want to. I could have consensual sex with Wolf if that was what I wanted. I could because I liked having sex with him, and it didn't have to mean anything. It could be no strings attached. No ties.

No love.

"Fawn?"

Bru tugged me out of thoughts that were getting too deep, his frown heavy. He opened his mouth, but instead decided to close it.

"Was just going to say whatever you do, it should be what you want," he said, nodding. He smiled a little. "You should have that. You deserve it."

CHAPTER
SIXTEEN

Ares

"Seriously, bro. Can you fix your attitude shit? You're literally sucking the energy out of the room."

I turned my head on the window seat. Thatcher was killing shit on the wall-sized TV in his and Wells's room. All of these rooms had TVs, but he'd brought the PlayStation up here after I'd ripped it out of the wall downstairs.

I supposed he thought he could protect it a little, which was funny. Currently, Thatch sat next to Wells, who had a popcorn bowl in his lap. Both had game controllers, but only Thatcher was talking shit to me while they played. I frowned. "The fuck you going on about?"

"Just what I said. Your energy is all fucked." Thatcher jerked right, then left. They looked like they were playing some kind of first-person shooter. Thatch frowned. "You're staring out the window like some sad-ass puppy."

I opened my mouth to retort, but then Wells nodded. He shoved his hand into a bowl of popcorn the moms made last night. It was cinnamon flavored or something. Wells chomped kernels. "For real, and it's legit killing both our vibes."

The fuck did I care about their vibes? Taking the pillow from beneath my head, I tossed it at them both and immediately regretted it. The first reason was because I missed when they dodged, and all the labor got me was them both flipping me off. The second was because I was now without a fucking pillow when it'd taken me the better part of an hour to get comfortable on this fucking seat made for normal-sized people.

Growling, I attempted to alleviate the problem when I tugged my hoodie off, leaving my T-shirt on. I balled it up and shoved it under my head, but even still, it wasn't doing the job of the pillow. I had my legs up on the wall to straighten out my back on the seat.

"Bro's mad because we're speaking facts," Thatch continued. He was on his back too, thumbs flicking the controller on his bag-ass chest. He smirked. "And you do look like a puppy. A sad-ass, *pathetic-ass* puppy."

"Fuck *you*," I seethed, this dude fucking lucky I wasn't trying to do anything to mess with my back. I'd worked it to hell three days ago, and it'd been temperamental every day since.

Since the day you fucked up…

I had fucked up. I'd fucked up so bad, but I just couldn't help it.

She'd been so soft.

Red's taste I hadn't forgotten. I couldn't forget that shit even with a lobotomy. But the body did have a way of forgetting, self-compartmentalizing. If it didn't, I would have fucked Red days ago when I'd seen her in those jeans and that fucking top that made her tits look like literal heaven.

And her smell.

So fucking soft, so *floral*. That shit messed me up so bad. I got fucking crazy, and I'd over-extended myself in the woods.

I had to get in as deep and as hard as I could with her beneath me.

But then she'd started crying.

That was what made me stare out the window. That was what tightened my fucking chest and made it hard to breathe these past few days. I hadn't left this room despite it being Thatcher and Wells's space. I was basically sleeping in here since Dorian and Sloane took every available opportunity to fuck in my room. They had to be discreet about it with the parents being around, and since D and I shared a room, that was their hook-up spot. When they weren't doing that, they were just hanging out in there. Usually Bow would be in there too hanging with them, but one person that wasn't was me.

My sister was still mad at me, and I felt like I hadn't seen Dorian in days because of that. She'd been very obvious about not wanting to share space with me, and since she didn't, Dorian got put between a rock and a hard place. I wasn't his favorite person either considering all the drama in the past few days, but we were still boys. With Sloane being mad, though, he essentially had to choose between her and me, which meant there wasn't any choice. He was with her, and I was stuck with Thatcher's and Wells's asses. I loved my buddies, but they could be annoying as shit in large doses. They didn't let up with their ragging, and that shit got old.

I sighed, in my fucking feelings, but I didn't care. I hadn't known what to say to Red, so I stayed the fuck in here. I didn't want to hurt her anymore.

I hurt enough for the both of us.

I'd wanted to throw up after what happened in the woods. How she cried. How she'd made me *fuck her* even though she was crying. The whole situation had been fucked up, and my chest seared.

Red...

I closed my eyes, in agony for us both. I just had to get through this trip. I did that, and we wouldn't have to see each other anymore. Did it suck knowing I'd have to probably stay in this room on the days leading up to Christmas with Thatcher and Wells talking shit? Yeah, but at least they were talking to me again. They hadn't been in their feelings and got over my lying shit easy. Were they still mad at me? Probably, but I didn't give a shit.

I got some grumbling after I tossed shoes at them. They talked more bullshit, because this time, the shoes landed. They had a look like they might attempt some retaliation, but I sat up, so they settled back into their positions. They were still intimidated by me, which was good. I had lots of years of tackling them both into submission if they pissed me off.

I was utilizing that history now despite a few things changing. I brought a foot up and stared out into the woods again. A knock hit the door, and when Thatcher called for whoever to come in, they did.

"Is Wolf in here? His mom said that—"

My head snapped right, so hard in fact I'd probably be regretting that shit. My spine and back in general were doing pretty good today, but I didn't need to grant them a reason to give me problems.

Red paused by the door, and I had to say, she made an appearance. Both Thatcher and Wells stopped playing their video game, and I had stopped breathing.

I think that had something to do with her coming over.

Red stalked over was more like it. She had her little arms crossed, and what could only be described as determination wove tightly in her flushed features. A rosy tone bloomed hot all over her body, and I was aware because I was taking inventory of said body. Her crossed arms hugged those big, beautiful tits of hers, her flower tattoos in a flourish over her full arms and thick thighs. She wore her shredded jeans, and I got peeks of her water-colored flowers. Lightly colored blooms I wanted to lick. Suck.

The same went for the koi tat swimming along her shoulder, her freckled skin an abyss I wanted a summer fucking pass to. That and her ass, and if I'd been paying attention to anything but that and the rest of her, I'd realize she was standing in front of me pissed the hell off.

Which she was.

I'd seen Fawn red before. I mean, she was *always* red, but there wasn't an inch of her that wasn't reaching the tone of her freckles. She was also breathing heavy, and my heart raced. I swallowed. "What—"

"I want to have sex with you."

The fuck...

No words. Like zero fucking words, and her hands moved to her hips. She appeared less angry and more impatient now. Her head cocked. "Did you hear me?"

Yeah, I heard her, and Thatcher and Wells did too. Their players had completely died on the screen at this point, the pair frozen just like me. I cut to Red. "What are you talking about?"

Impatience had been correct. Fawn tapped her sock-covered foot, shifting. "Just what I said. I want to have sex with you. Hot, *consensual* sex." She rose and dropped her arms. "I'm not sure how else I can break that down."

I had no idea what the fuck was going on here, but my attention rerouted when Thatcher sat up and ripped the bowl of cinnamon popcorn out of Wells's lap. Wells barked a protest, and Thatcher waved him off.

"I need this more than you," he said, and my jaw clenching, I growled.

"Get the fuck out of here *now*," I seethed before going back to Red. I didn't know what the fuck she was talking about. If she'd lost her mind or what, but regardless, I didn't need them here for this.

"This is our room, bro." Thatcher lay back, shoving popcorn down his esophagus like this was a matinee. He waved a hand. "Y'all go ahead and continue."

Growling again, I left them and the situation when I got a hand on Red. She yipped out her little retort, but I didn't give a shit.

"Wolf, let *go*. What the fuck!"

Her attempts to jerk away from me were futile. I was stronger than her, and I enforced that strength all the way into Thatcher and Wells's bathroom. I locked the door and didn't let go until after I did.

Red balled her small fists in front of me, looking all cute and shit, and it reminded me of when she threatened to punch my ass out in the woods. She pointed at me. "That is the *last* time you put your hands on me without my permission. You understand me? The absolute last fucking time. Touch me again unless I want you to, tell you to, and I'll scream for this whole fucking house to hear."

She was being entirely serious, her chest rising and falling with rapid breaths.

And why was my dick hard?

Something about her telling me what to do. One hundred percent, I wasn't into that shit and dropped chicks who'd tried for less. I didn't have time for it, and there were easier lays.

But when Red did it...

Yeah, my shit was fucking *hard*, and I'd adjust it if she wasn't fucking snarling at me. She might say something else to me if I did, and the asshole in my pants just might get a little harder. I pushed some restless curls out of my face. "Okay."

I mean, what else was there to say? And why the fuck had she come in here the way she had? Saying those things...

Her nod was curt after her statement, and words left me. She'd gotten what she wanted, and my fucking cock was *hurting*. What the fuck? She eyed the bathroom. "Is someone sleeping in here?"

She noticed my bedding in the tub, and it was a surprisingly decent place to sleep. It wasn't comfortable by any means, but it was big. It had to be to accommodate Thatcher's ass, and sleeping there was certainly better than running into Dorian and my sister.

I kept my shudders at the thoughts internal, and these days, it didn't matter where I slept anyway. I didn't get comfortable and got the same hours of sleep regardless of what I did. A strong reason for that was Red and all our drama shit.

At least, recently. I licked my lips. "What—"

I cut myself off by my own accord. I raised a finger to Red, indicating one moment before I crossed over to the door.

I threw my fist into it.

One sharp hit and several curses sounded from the other side. I laughed. "Get the fuck away from the door before I end you."

"Fuck you," drifted back in to me, a combination of Thatcher and Wells and their nosy shit. I got more cursing before their voices trickled away, and when a door slammed, I realized they'd left. I guess if they couldn't listen in, they weren't going to bother sticking around.

Little asswipes.

These were my friends, but again, they were at least talking to me and without attitudes. Pretty much everyone was talking to me these days, but I was still getting cold shoulders from the adults. My parents…

"Wolf, why are we in the bathroom?"

That's right. Red.

I shifted, propping a foot back against the door. "You tell me."

We wouldn't be in here if she hadn't come in like a fucking hurricane. She was a category five at this point, and I watched as she worked her hand through red strands. Her scent hit the air, and I did adjust myself.

Relax.

It'd been impulses that had gotten her beneath me in the woods, and her mentioning my brother. I didn't like them hanging out together. Platonic as it seemed to be or not. This girl was mine. Fucking *mine*.

Relax.

It was hard to with Red's tits like a foot and a half away from me. This girl had curves for fucking days, and the way I'd fill my hands with them. Fill them with *her*, licking her. She turned me into a beast that I didn't like.

But these days, I'd been trying to be better. I tried so damn hard. I mean, I let her *go* no matter how pointless the attempt. She was still in my head, and I couldn't control it.

You're a monster.

I knew this, but I had tried. I did for her.

And she was coming over to me, no makeup on her face. Her lips were naturally red even without her usual lipstick. They were freckled like her skin, plump.

"I want to have sex with you," she repeated, and the front of my joggers threatened to split. *Fuck.* She shrugged. "You and I like having sex, so we should just have sex."

We'd had sex, and it'd been a mistake. It got her back in my head again, my chest...

Ignoring the tightness, I shook my head. "I heard what you said. I'm not hard of hearing."

"Are you sure? Because I've had to repeat myself several times."

Red's sass never failed to do something for me, but in this case, it was pissing me off. I braced my arms to keep from grabbing her. "You know what I mean. Why are you saying this? Asking this?"

Why was she in this bathroom with me? Being in any type of proximity with this girl was dangerous, and that episode in the woods had taught us both that.

I mean, she'd *cried*.

I'd made her cry and being with me did that to her. I could

physically feel her anguish, how I was ripping her apart just as much as she was doing me in. It was painful to be with her too. Like a bleeding-fucking-wound painful.

So why would she want that?

This didn't make any sense, and that was outside of the fact that she hated me. What I'd done to her made sure of that. Purposeful.

My throat locked about the same time Red wet her lips. She navigated over to the sink, and I studied every move. The way her ripped jeans hit her thick thighs just right. The way her top revealed a sliver of her stomach when she lounged back.

So. Fucking. Soft.

I think she knew how she affected me, but she also knew how I affected her. The sink was the farthest spot she could get away from me. She folded her arms. "We were already having sex before I complicated things."

My head tilted, and her jaw moved.

"I'm just saying we should again. I like having sex with you, and this time it won't be complicated." She frowned. "I'm not asking you to do anything you weren't already doing."

The words cut in a way they shouldn't. I intended for her to believe what happened between us meant nothing.

She thinks you used her.

And why shouldn't she? My stomach tightened. "Where's this coming from?"

"What do you mean?"

"Exactly what I said." I mean, had she gone insane or was this a strike back? Something to get at me, hurt me. I pushed off the door. "No way in hell you'd actually want to do something like that."

And certainly not with me. She was essentially proposing a friends-with-benefits situation. Except we weren't friends. The opposite.

You'd made sure of that.

The irony in all this was crazy. How I'd gotten her to be my fake girlfriend, and now, she was in here saying this stuff. I didn't believe it. No way.

Her expression tensed, and what I'd mistaken as anger before wasn't. This was anger, Red at the height of it. Her nostrils flared, nose ring moving with it. "Are you saying a girl can't proposition a guy to fuck without complications?"

"Nah." I stopped in the center of the bathroom. "I'm saying you can't." Or had she forgotten how we left things?

I didn't think she had, all that all over her face. She wet her lips. "Like I said, that won't be a problem." She studied her nails then, as if this whole conversation was just us talking about the weather. Who was this Red? I didn't know her. Her lashes lifted. "Things aren't complicated anymore, and I certainly won't be the one to complicate them."

Because she didn't love me.

This was what she was insinuating, and I hadn't expected those words to cut. This was good she felt that way. I hadn't wanted her to love me anymore.

This was good.

I forced down the thickness in my throat, watching as Red slinked over. She pushed off the sink with confidence, and though she'd had that in the past, it had always faltered when it came to me. I did things to this girl and even thrived off that.

That was back then, *before* things were complicated and I did fuck up. I should have never asked her to be my fake girlfriend. No matter what the reason, I should have never asked her. It was impossible to establish a line with her.

Hopeless.

Red was too close to me, her hips nearly meeting mine. Any closer, and she'd get a rude surprise from my Johnson.

Too close.

I could taste her. In my fucking mouth, I could taste that

sweet, juicy Red. I could feel her curves against me, the memory of their softness a hard thing to let go of. The way those flushed ass cheeks would hug my dick...

I forced those thoughts away. "What are you doing?"

Stupid shit. She did get too close and pretty much had her tits in my face. Her head cocked. "I don't see the problem. We like having sex together." She popped up on her little toes, wrapping her arms around me, and I growled.

It was in warning.

She ignored it, using my neck and the tips of her feet to get closer to my height. I had a lot of inches on this girl. I did on all girls, but they never fit me the way Red did. I couldn't break this girl. She was unbreakable. Body, or mind.

"You're playing with fire, Red." Another warning, her lips getting closer, her fingers in my hair. "Don't."

I wasn't fooling around, and when she tugged my hair free, curls spilling down the side of my face, I turned the tables. Pivoting, I had her against the door.

My hand around her neck.

I bracketed her throat, the delicate flick under my hand. "I said don't."

A hint of fear flashed in her hazel eyes, like she wasn't quite sure what I was going to do.

But wasn't going to stop it either.

I did stop it, letting go before I did something dumb that she and I would regret. She didn't know what she was asking, and I did think she'd lost her mind. The real Red, my Red, would never chance putting her heart on the line like this. I lifted a finger. "You don't know what you're asking."

She had no idea, none, and surprise lassoed me when she smirked. She legit smirked in my fucking face, shaking her head.

"Whatever," she said, pivoting and facing the door. She gave me that beautiful ass of hers when she went for the knob. "Maybe Bru wants to hang out."

Lightning struck slower. Daylight filled a *fucking room* at a snail's pace compared to how quickly I had her back against that door.

My hands on her.

I had her hips in my hands and her bottom lip between my teeth. I did nothing else. I didn't trust myself.

"Say that *again*," I warned, slowly grinding my cock into her. I had to. My dick was fucking swollen. Painful. "Say that shit again."

Her smirk had returned, but this time, it didn't piss me off. It just made me harder, steel. She brought her hips against me. "I said I was going to go hang out with your brother."

She knew what to say to me, to get a reaction out of me. My hands moved to her throat. "One more time, and this time, think hard about your next words." I eased toward her ear. "Otherwise, you may have them choking around my dick."

I heard the words, even felt my vocal cords make them, but I had no control here. I had zero at the possibility she'd go hang out with my brother right now. That she'd be anyplace but here with me.

Beneath me…

I couldn't stop the thought, blinded by it. She was getting a rise out of me, which was obviously intended.

My grip tightened around her windpipe, but the way Red hiked up her hips to meet my lazy thrusts no one would know. She even got my hips, making me hit harder, faster. Her smile was coy. "Maybe that doesn't sound so bad."

Oh, fuck.

She reached between us in the next moment, her hand on my cock, and I sucked in a breath. "Stop."

"I don't think so." Again, I didn't know this Red. Her neck adjusted in my hands, her palm massaging my dick through my joggers. A thin layer of cotton kept me from completely blowing a load in this girl's hand right now.

Stop this.

But it was like in the woods, Red bent over a stump as I fucked her into an oblivion. I had blinders on when it came to this girl. "Red…"

We shouldn't be doing this, my cock actually fucking her hand now. My hips rolled in a slow thrust, my eyes rolling back when she started playing with my balls.

Fuck it.

My last layer of sanity left me, my mouth on hers, my tongue down her throat.

Christ.

Literal heaven. Red's whimpers cut off when I teased her tongue, then bit down on her lip. She squeezed my balls in response, and I groaned.

She laughed. "Now, that wasn't so hard." She thought she had the power right now.

I was going to show her different.

Working her hair around my fist, I ended the kiss and guided her head back to the door. Her mouth opened like she was ready to receive my cock, and I made her fist it.

"Take me out," I said, standing there waiting. I told her I'd cut off her smart mouth and watched as she wet her lips again. Arousal inundated my body and settled hot into my dick, the fucker stiff as hell and pulsing. "Now, Red."

I wasn't joking. Lifting my shirt out of the way, I revealed my abs. Her gaze flicked down instantly, her eyes hungry. I knew what she liked just as much as she knew what got to me.

Her hand eased inside my joggers, exposing my hip tat, and I gave no reaction to her fingers wrapping around my length, squeezing me. My grip pressed into her windpipe. "I said out."

She was playing with me, this sick fucking game she was playing to make this happen. I didn't know what had gotten into her, and I needed to stop this.

I was hard-pressed when she did pull me out, and I had her on her knees before she could get to me more.

Fucking hell.

I brought her hair back, this girl sexy as fuck on her knees for me. Her freckled tits were spilling out of her top at this angle. I dragged my finger across the swell. "Show them to me."

I needed to see them, would fucking die if I didn't.

Red didn't disappoint. She worked her tank straps down, then unclasped the back of her strapless bra. The cups eased below her breasts, and I was in heaven. They were that perfect flush of red.

Flawless.

I tweaked a nipple, and her mouth fell open. I guided her head up, flicking her tongue with mine.

Her moan in my mouth was deep, her hand returning to my cock, my balls. She teased me, squeezing, and when all that became too much, I drew her mouth away from mine. I directed her mouth toward my dick instead, a bead of pre-cum on the tip. Red had confidence up to this point, but she hesitated before receiving what I showed her. Perhaps, she forgot how big I was.

"Suck," I coached, pushing past her flushed lips. I watched in awe, my cock disappearing inch by inch past her bruised mouth. I sucked air through my teeth. "More."

I knew she could take more because she'd done it, her eyes widening below me. She'd been trying to challenge me before, fuck with me, and now, it was time she showed up to the mat.

And show up she did.

She took me right down, gagging, and I didn't hold back while I was in. I fucked her throat with easy thrusts, as equally angry as I was frustrated.

But not at her.

I didn't want to do this, do this to her, and had done

everything I could to step away. I physically made myself put distance between us last semester.

And it had nearly killed me.

Every day knowing we were on the same campus. *Every day* knowing what I'd said to her and the look she had given me once I had. I'd broken her, and I had to live with that. I had to live with the pain I'd caused her.

I had to live with being away from her.

That had been the hardest part, and the ache of that loss caused me to numb. I didn't feel anything these days. At least, not mentally.

I was feeling this.

I was dying on the inside feeling this, Fawn's hungry moans on my cock like a symphony arranged just for me. Her choking was the added percussion, her fingers digging into my hips.

On my tat.

The tattoo on my hip she felt up, her hand running down it, her fingers pressing into it. I couldn't take it once she did that, all of that shit too much. I removed her from me, then brought her up to my mouth.

Big mistake. It was a fucking *huge* mistake kissing her. Her taste combined with mine maddened me.

It made me drunk.

I had her pants down, rolled down and off with her underwear.

The same went for her shirt.

The girl completely naked, I had her up on the sink before I thought better. She'd basically hopped up there herself, eager, ready. She let me strip her bare, then got up on that sink like that hadn't been the position she was in the last time we'd fucked.

I couldn't do it then, my cock out and hurting between us. I couldn't fuck her in the same way I had before I'd shattered her. We'd fucked, then I'd had her clean up and move on like what we'd done had meant nothing.

When it meant everything.

I started to go for my pants and pull them up, but Red didn't let me. Grabbing the back of my neck, she forced a kiss on me so hard I thought she'd fuse us together. She tasted me, slow nips to my mouth, and I groaned.

I'd thought this before, but I didn't know this Red, her hands on my face, her mouth deepening the kiss. Next thing I knew, I was doing the same. I was right back with her, and once I was…

I guided myself inside her, Fawn widening her thick thighs. She had tats up her inner thighs too, lightly colored flowers disappearing when I entered her.

"Fuck…" I dragged the word over her mouth, the pair of us kissing outside of our mouths. We were all tongues, taste. My hips slapped her inner thighs with aggression. It was too much.

It hurt.

It hurt so fucking bad and worse than any physical pain. It hurt like someone was bleeding me out, then left me there in my own blood. Being inside this girl…

Loving her.

My hand caged her throat, the only thing I could do to hold on to my own emotions. I felt like I was being split apart even though I was the one who was fucking her.

"Don't stop," she commanded, hungry Red back, confident Red. She wrapped a leg around my hip, her mouth to my ear. "Fuck me like I'm yours."

She was mine. She'd never stopped even if she believed that. I'd placed a claim on her a long time ago. I'd braced the back of her neck. "Fuck me like I'm yours."

It was the only thing I could think to say that wouldn't scare her. If she knew the truth about what she did to me.

That I never stopped being hers…

I came with the thoughts, my dick pumping heavy streams inside her. I didn't even wait for her, and I knew she hadn't come by the time I finished.

That didn't stop me from getting on my knees.

I licked her cunt, my cum leaking out of her. I flicked her clit with a hurried tongue, taking her to the brink, and she didn't last long. She cried out, her fingers fisting my hair. She ended up biting her arm to muffle the sounds, but I wasn't quite sure that was enough. She very well might alert the house to what was going on in here like she'd threatened.

I found myself not giving a fuck at that moment and saying to hell with the consequences. I'd given up so much, but I wouldn't give up this. Her orgasm was mine.

Mine.

I kept the word internal as her cream filled my mouth, as I sucked down her essence combined with mine. Her body twitched, satiated above me.

I stood once I knew she was done, wiping my mouth. I kissed her, then tugged her off the sink. She'd voiced thoughts about someone sleeping in here, and she was about to make it to my bed.

I took her into the empty whirlpool with me, kissing her and making her wrap her legs around me. We were nothing but sheets and each other, and I wasn't letting her go. I knew I would, but right now, I wasn't. I was about to make this last for however long I could.

Which meant I was saying to hell with everything again.

CHAPTER
SEVENTEEN

Ares

Red and I fell asleep in the tub.

I fell asleep.

This shouldn't awe me as much as it did. I'd fallen asleep before with her hugged up against me. Sleep wasn't comfortable by any means in the tub, but I'd managed despite not being able to find comfort anywhere on any mattress. Over the past few months, I'd grown used to that shit, I guess, but I found sleep with Red. She smelled like flowers and heaven.

And she was gone when I woke up.

I hadn't gone looking for her. What happened between us shouldn't have happened, and I had no intention of getting into a friends-with-benefits situation with my ex-fake girlfriend.

More like enemies with benefits.

Red wasn't my enemy, but I was hers. I'd put her through hell, and I wasn't going to fuck with her heart that way.

Even if she didn't love me.

Regardless, I couldn't handle the back and forth. That was

selfish of me to consider my own feelings. They were low on the reasons a FWB situation wouldn't work for us, but the added stress wasn't good for me. I wasn't supposed to be in fucking stressful situations.

Eventually, I unfolded myself out of the tub. I couldn't tell when, but it was late. I avoided people for my own sanity, but by the time I did run into folks the next morning at breakfast, I found out very quickly no one had heard Red and me. The pair of us were passing ships in the kitchen, and no one stared at us.

That fact hadn't stopped me from staring at her, though, but she gathered her grub quickly before exiting the room. The parents' private chef usually kept food around, stacks of pancakes and waffles while holiday music played for whoever passed through. Red had made her circulation through the kitchen swiftly, and I honestly think she didn't see me before cutting out of the room. Between the Legacy kids and our parents, there were over a dozen people moving around through mealtimes.

No matter. I had every intention of finding her and talking to her later. I wanted to make it clear what had happened yesterday was a mistake. It was a mistake I wasn't comfortable with, but I found the discussion had to wait when my dad said he and the other fathers needed me that morning. My punishment was still in full swing, and this morning, I got to play workhorse.

The dads piled into cars that morning, the trip to the hardware store a quick one. They needed bricks to build a burn pit behind the Reeds' house, and I got the job of loading the bricks.

Lucky me.

The job went to Bru and me, as he tagged along too. My buddies had been invited to help, but they'd all opted out, and I would have too had I not been forced.

But I had been. I passed Bru on our ins and outs of the

store with bricks. The dads had told us what they needed, then proceeded to let Bru and me do the work. I had no idea why the kid had volunteered, but it was something he'd do. When it came to brown-nosing, he won the award.

I was obviously grumpy this morning. My back still ached due to the tub, and I wasn't used to all this manual labor shit. I didn't lift in the gym anymore, just doing cardio these days.

I grunted after dropping the last brick, and it took me a second to angle up and get my back right. Bru set his stack with ease beside me, the guy looking like he was feasting on 'roids with the way his muscles bulged in his T-shirt. I may be a little paranoid, but it felt like he'd been eyeing me since breakfast.

He was eyeing me now, as I stretched out. "You good?"

Nah, but he wasn't going to know that. I told him I was cool, then got away before he could ask me about anything else. I ended up running into Dad, who asked me the same question. He caught me mid-stretch inside the store. I waved him off. "Yeah, I'm fine."

"Okay." His hand clasped my shoulder. He and Dorian's dad, Royal, had been chatting about something with Wells's pop, Jax. I didn't know where everyone else was, but I assumed somewhere in the store.

The small conversation continued after my dad excused us. He asked if I'd come with him to go look at art supplies at the craft store next door, and I did.

Even if my stomach was in a clench.

My dad and I shared our love for art, my father prolific. One could find his work all over the globe. His use of steel and metalwork was legendary, but he ended up going more toward the business side of the art world. He owned many art galleries, but that didn't stop him from being a complete badass at what he did.

The craft store was limited in materials, but Dad found some stuff he could use to sketch. He asked me if I needed anything, and I grabbed some charcoal so he wouldn't look at me funny. I hadn't sketched in weeks, months.

"So you'll forgive me for tricking you and getting you away, but I wanted to ask you about something," Dad said, the pair of us in line at the checkout. He pivoted in my direction. "You changed your major."

This wasn't a question, and my stomach had *locked* when he said he had something to talk to me about. This direction wasn't so bad, though, and I shrugged. "Yeah."

I didn't know how he'd found out, but I wasn't surprised he had. My mother used to teach at my university. She still had colleagues there who were friends, and my dad was a part of that circle. Even without that link, he was *my father* and everyone at Pembroke University knew him. He donated money since it was his alma mater, and since he was prolific, he was like a god to the art department there.

Dad's brow jumped after what I said, perhaps surprised with how casual I was about changing my major. This shouldn't surprise me at all. Art was my life, but things had changed.

I had changed.

Of course, my father didn't know that. His head cocked. "Any particular reason for that? And I wasn't snooping in your life, FYI." He laughed. "It happened to come up over lunch with some friends from the university."

Some of my professors, I could imagine, and I had just changed before the semester ended. I worked my hand through my hair. "Just felt I was being pulled in a different direction."

"Again, any reason? You know I've never pressured you into going into the family business."

I supposed he could assume that was why I'd changed, for him and to go that route. I changed my major to art business instead of sticking with actual application. I wet my lips. "I know, but after everything with my cancer, I guess my thoughts just changed on some things. My priorities or whatever."

I wasn't exactly lying to my father. I always had intended to get involved with the family business. Half of my father's empire surrounded real estate and development, but the other half had to do with his art. He was an artist through and through, and getting involved with his galleries would keep me in that world. I wouldn't have to let go of it completely.

I worked my fingers involuntarily. My dad started looking at me in a way I didn't like.

He eased close. "I know your health scare took you through the wringer, but you know, you don't have to be scared anymore, right?" He put his arm around me. "You keep up on your check-ups. You're doing what you need to do?"

I nodded at the question. My parents had started taking a hands-off approach to my health after I'd asked them. I'd told them I wanted to be responsible for it on my own, and they had backed off. They did with the caveat that I would keep up on my care and let them know the minute something was off. My cancer diagnosis had nearly broken my family.

Again.

We'd had so much shit happen to all of us. Shit regarding my sister, and so much other *crap*. My family was strong, but they could only handle so much. They could be broken, shattered.

Dad rubbed my shoulder. "Promise me you're not putting your life on hold because you're worried."

"Of course not," I said, shaking my head. "I really do want to get involved with the business."

No lies there, but lies were so easy these days. Sometimes I didn't even know what was real versus the truth.

And my dad was smiling again. He squeezed my arm, and almost instantly my stomach settled. He wasn't looking at me like he was before, his own worry in his dark eyes. "Well, I'm not going to lie, I would love to have you involved." He shook me. "Just as long as you know you don't have to do that for me. I promised myself I'd never let that happen after the pressure I felt from your grandpa growing up."

As far as I knew, my dad and grandpa had repaired that relationship, but I could see him still worrying about repeating history when it came to Sloane, Bru, and me.

I smiled. "I know. And since when have I ever done something because that's what you wanted me to do?"

I was a little asshole, and we both knew that.

Dad laughed before bringing me in, hugging me. It was a strong hug, a great hug, and I didn't want to let go.

I did, though, eventually, made myself. We wrapped up at the checkout, then made our way back outside.

The dads and Dorian's god-dad, LJ, were all outside the hardware store chatting. Since they were, I offered to take the stuff Dad and I bought to the Escalade. Dad thanked me, and once we parted, I headed toward the SUVs we all took into town. I found the kid lounging against one of them, his thumbs tapping on his phone.

I passed him, putting the bag in the SUV through the window.

"You and Fawn talk?"

I froze, easing back out. "What?"

The kid's eyes were on me, his thumbs hovering over his phone. "Just wondering if you talked and worked things out."

My mouth parted. "We talked."

Did she talk to him, tell him what she'd approached me with?

My brother's nod was curt between us, and I guessed he had no other questions because he opened the Escalade and got inside. I stood by the door before he could close it. "Did she talk to you about what she talked to me about?"

I figured I'd ask since, you know, all these questions were being put out there, and I got my answer when Bru averted his eyes.

I blanched. "She did talk to you."

"All that's none of my business."

"But she did talk to you." I angled until I got his attention, his eyes. "She did, right?"

Which explained all the *eyeing* he was doing at me this morning. I thought I'd been paranoid. Fuck.

"She did, but again, all that is none of my business."

"Then why do you know about it?" I was kind of pissed now, that shit personal.

Calm down.

The kid was calm for all of us and must have been doing some of the same calming shit Fawn was on. She'd come on to me in a way that was completely different than who she'd been. There'd been no emotion there. She'd wanted something and approached the situation with intention.

And she'd gotten it.

I'd given it to her, thought with my cock, and apparently, my brother knew the details about it. He forced his hair out of his face, rubbing his neck. "We're friends, Ares. She had some concerns, and we talked about them."

"What kind of concerns?"

A crack in the armor, his eyes narrowed. They cut at me, and I was grateful for some emotion between us. His jaw shifted. "I won't talk to you about that. Fawn and I are friends, so we talked, and I won't fuck with that friendship by telling you what we talked about."

"Well, what about our friendship?" I got close. Or had he forgotten that we're brothers? Not all brothers were friends, but the kid and I were, and he was keeping shit from me about Fawn.

He put a hand out. "Don't put me in between you both. Don't you fucking *dare.*" He put a finger in my face. "You treated Fawn like shit, and it took all I had to be neutral about everything when she talked to me. I did that *because* you and I are friends. Brothers." His nostrils flared. "Now, again, I will emphasize anything to do with you two is none of my business. I just ask whatever you decide to do that you're honest with her and make whatever your intentions are for that relationship clear."

Because he thought I was playing with her, fucking with her. I forced out a breath. "Look. I don't know exactly what she talked to you about regarding her and me, but..." I rubbed my mouth. "Moving forward there won't be anything. Not physical. Not anything."

We'd be adding gasoline to an already flammable situation, and *I* couldn't handle it.

It nearly killed me the last time.

Bru wouldn't look at me, puffing up. I didn't see the kid angry a lot, but he'd been nothing but angry since he got back into town. That was on me, and I didn't like putting him in the middle of all this.

He put his hand on the door. "Just make your intentions clear, Ares."

And then he was shutting the door in my face. I cursed, but didn't make him talk to me. I had a feeling that would just make all this worse.

My phone buzzed.

My anxiety was on one hundred these days, but for some reason, I thought answering a text was a good idea in that moment. My texts weren't good lately, but I glanced at my phone anyway.

Fuuuck.

Tits. Beautiful, rosy tits were on my phone screen. An arm held the swell up, nipples covered, and the curve of the softest-looking stomach exposed beneath. Her jeans were open below, lace panties peeking out…

I bit my knuckles as another text rolled in.

Fawn: Did you get the text?

Oh, I fucking got it. She showed me everything but her fucking nipples.

That came next.

Blood rushed to my dick, Fawn on her back with the camera above her. It was at this point I was easing as far away from the Escalade as I could. I had my back to it when the texts came in, but wasn't taking any chances my brother could see what just buzzed onto my phone.

What is she doing to me?

Her lips were bright red, and I was well acquainted with the shade. I'd had it on my cock more than once.

I groaned.

The next text message came in quick, but I was afraid to look at it. I ended up reading it through squinted eyes, worried what I'd see would have me heading off to the closest bathroom to jack off.

Fawn: Not sure how long you'll be out, but I'm in my room. Plan to be here all day editing photos.

The next picture was her under some sheets. She had her laptop on her lap but she still clearly had no shirt on. The bedding covered her chest, but her skin was exposed, her shoulders naked and a veil of her bright red hair hanging over one of them. She looked like a literal wet dream, her tatted arms all flushed and perfect.

I think I was drawing blood with as hard as I was biting my fist at this point. I kept envisioning the teeth marks I could make across her freckled skin, her voluptuous chest, her round stomach…

No, *fucking no.* I started to text back, but hers came first.

Fawn: Anyway, no pressure. Come if you want. Or don't. Whatever.

Whatever? Really?

She was playing a game, and not going by any kind of rules that could be considered fair.

Me: I'll come by, but we're going to talk.

Fawn: Okay, but I don't plan on wearing any panties. Just FYI.

The groan settled deep in my chest, and when the next text buzzed in, I ended up rushing past the dads and going back into the hardware store. I found the bathroom and didn't come out until I was done. Fawn's picture had been taken under the sheets this time, and though that darkened the image slightly, I still made out what she showed me. She wasn't wearing panties.

And I was fucking screwed.

CHAPTER
EIGHTEEN

Fawn

I answered the door naked…

I told him I wouldn't be wearing any panties.

I think Wolf didn't believe I would do something so bold, and I'd surprised myself. I was secure with my body, loved my curves, but being with Ares had always been intimating. I hated the fact, but it was, and he could make even the most confident girl question herself. Being in his presence was just daunting in general, so that went double for being naked in front of him, vulnerable.

But I'd done it. Oh, how I'd done it. I mean, I snuck a peek through a crack in the door first to make sure it was him when he knocked, but I did. He just stood there, unblinking, and I didn't let him question anything.

I just pulled him inside.

Things were kind of a blur after that, tangled tongues and mouth kisses. Wolf had his hands everywhere even as he protested.

"We shouldn't," he dragged across my lips, my neck. "We can't."

But we were, and I didn't let him stop. We stumbled toward my bed, shedding our clothes along the way.

I had him naked in seconds.

I was the aggressor here, the one in control, and not only did that seem to completely do it for Ares "Wolf" Mallick, but he let me. He allowed me to navigate, the driver.

And even helped me ride him.

He guided me up, and that was it, his cock between my legs, tunneling deep. I threw my head back, my hands lost in the sea of my hair. Wolf fisted my ass cheeks to the point that he pinched my skin. He was making his mark as he dragged his fingers along my flesh, but I was making mine harder.

Watching him be fucked beneath me... his head back, his jaw clenched tight. He'd come to my room today with some reservations, clearly.

They were long gone as he gripped me into riding him harder, faster. His eyes popped open, and in the same moment, he drew his hips up. He fucked me aggressively from below, his flesh slapping mine while my breasts hit my chest.

"Fuck, Red. *Fuck*," he gritted, palming my breasts. He sat up and drew a nipple into his mouth. "You're so fucking hot. So perfect."

I wasn't letting his words affect me, clearly sex-driven, lust-laden. He wanted my body only, and I wanted his too.

Get out of your head.

This guy wanted ass. He wanted a lay. The difference between now and how it was before was that I accepted that and wanted the same. I preached that to myself as I picked up the pace of my hips and refused to think that I was claiming him. That I wanted to fuck all those other girls he'd been with before me out of his head. The ones that most likely didn't look like me...

I shut off my brain, all of this was physical only. It had to be.

"Red…"

I came first this time, Wolf biting and teasing my breasts, my nipples. He flicked the beaded peaks, alternating between them as he watched me. It was so intimate, *too* intimate.

I closed my eyes, not letting myself see him. If I did, it made all this intimate for me too. I'd cross a line I didn't want to cross and refused to.

"Fuck," he ground out, the word humming over my nipple. It popped out of his mouth, and the next thing I knew, he was hugging me.

This was intimate too, his high. He filled the condom in between my legs, and he actually thought to put one on this time. I hadn't known why since he hadn't bothered before but had today.

His cheek touched my chest while he milked me, right over my heartbeat while he hugged me close, tight.

Disconnect.

I made myself, letting him hold me, his cheek rubbing against me. His forehead replaced it eventually, damp, warm. His hair was down and his thick curls were completely in my face.

The smell simmered my blood, the temptation to play with them there, but I resisted. That would be intimate, and I wouldn't let myself.

I was proud when I'd been able to remove myself from the situation, when I'd been able to get off him after we both finished and ease beside him. I did that with intention, easy.

"Wait. Don't go."

But then, he said that, drawing me back into his hard embrace. He adjusted behind me, and I glanced back to see him working off the condom. He dropped it in the trash can beside my bed.

He was right back with me after that, his forehead on my shoulder. "Stay. Don't leave."

This was my bed, my room, and we were crossing a line here.

Tell my body that when my eyes closed, my ears that when I fell asleep with him softly breathing in my ear. I once again preached to myself. It wouldn't hurt just to be like this for a few minutes. I shared this room with Bru, but he'd texted me he was going hiking with Wells and Thatcher after he got back from the store. Wolf and I had a few minutes to be like this. I had a few minutes to nap, and they didn't have to mean anything. I'd done that in the tub too when Wolf and I had been together yesterday. It had meant nothing then.

It meant nothing.

———

He was drawing on me.

A lazy digit glided across my back, invisible figures etching into my skin. I didn't know how long Wolf had been doing this, but he had while I'd been napping.

You should stop him.

I didn't, desperately trying to figure out what he was creating. Wolf was an artist, but I'd rarely seen his work. He was rather protective over his art, and as an artist myself, I never pushed.

I assumed he was creating something from thought, but as I lay there, I realized he was scrolling letters. I could identify an occasional *I* or an *F*. There were so many, though, and I couldn't string any of them together.

A part of a letter started, bigger than the rest, and I wasn't quite sure it was a letter.

But then, he stopped.

He'd done so when I drew in a breath. I think from anticipation of what he'd been making. I wanted to know, but something ate at me. I shouldn't want to know. I shouldn't care.

I turned around, his dark eyes on me. He was like a foot away from my face, and I made out his dark freckles. He lifted his fingers. "Hi."

"Hi." I moved, creating distance, space. It was needed. I gazed around. "I fell asleep."

Wolf nodded, sifting through his wavy hair. "I did too for a bit. It was nice."

It was nice, but I wouldn't tell him that.

"Bru didn't come in here, but I locked the door just in case." His attention hit the door, but then he faced me. "I didn't want him walking in and accidentally seeing us. Seeing you."

I'd say how thoughtful, but the action could very well be because he was a complete caveman. Marking his territory and making sure only he saw me naked. I huffed. "He's out hiking with some of the others. He'll be gone for a while."

I didn't want to say I'd insinuated to Bru earlier I'd be occupying the room, but I had. Bruno Sloane-Mallick was too good of a friend. He remained impartial to all this shit I had going on with his brother. I didn't tell him Wolf would be swinging by here, but I figured he could have assumed.

Wolf's nod was curt. He lay on his back, and I took the opportunity to get up. He was smelling too good beside me, and I didn't like how fuzzy my head was getting in result.

"What's, uh… what's with the rush?"

We didn't rush was my first thought following what he said. We fell asleep so we didn't rush. Also, why shouldn't we? We already fucked, hadn't we? If anything, he'd overstayed his welcome, and I'd allowed him.

I wasn't anymore, easing to the edge of the bed. I reached for my shirt and a glance over my shoulder told me Wolf watched me. His focus burned hot into my back. I tugged my shirt down. "No reason."

I was being good about sounding impartial, unaffected. It was one of those situations where I hoped I could speak into existence what I wanted to feel. To fake it until I felt that way.

I learned from the best after all.

Another glance, and I observed Wolf on his arm. I was tugging my panties on, but he wasn't even watching. His lengthy, naked form was halfway beneath my bedding, the sheets rested at his chiseled hips. His gaze was far off, his fingers dancing on the fitted sheet.

He outlined his mouth. "Well, if there's no rush, you should stay, then." I turned completely in his direction, and his big shoulders shrugged. "If we have time, you should just stay for a little bit."

"This is my room."

"Let me stay, then."

I was surprised to hear this, that he wanted to stay. He had some protests about doing all this at the door earlier, as well as yesterday. My head tilted. "And do what exactly?"

"I don't know, hang out?" His sight flicked down to the sheet. "There's no harm in occupying each other's space for a little while. You can tell me about your semester and…"

My breath stopped, and his Adam's apple bobbed up and down.

He lifted a hand. "We can just talk."

Talk.

It was crazy what he was saying about no harm. This was harmful. It was *cruel*, and shaking my head, I stood. I started gathering his clothes in quick time, and Wolf rose from the bed. "What are you doing?"

I was getting his stupid things.

Then threw them in his face.

He caught them. He blanched, but he caught them. They fell into a heap in his muscled arms, and I was shaking, livid. I pointed toward his things. "Put them on, then get out."

My words were shaking too, goddamn me. My throat

went tight, and I noticed Wolf wasn't moving. Why wasn't he moving?

My fists knuckled. "I said get out, Wolf. *Now*. Don't make me say it again."

I'd scream if he didn't. I felt on the cusp of it if he didn't move his ass. The urge to do so buzzed hot in my throat, but the urge to cry hit worse.

I wouldn't, though. I refused in front of this asshole.

Wolf's mouth parted. "Red…"

"Get out." I was so close now, my eyes fucking cloudy. I blinked it away. "If you don't get out now, I swear to God I'll scream."

"What did I do?" He was up from the bed now, but he wasn't dressing. His bundled clothes gave him modesty, but not much. His mouth parted. "Red, I just wanted to talk."

See, that was the problem.

And why didn't he see that?

Why was he *being* this way? Ruining things…

I was crying now, and I hated myself for every tear. Wolf's eyes shot open. Like the sight of them horrified him. He started to come over, but I stiffened up so much. He raised a hand. "Red, what's wrong?"

"*You're* what's wrong. You *asshole*. You. Are. What's. Wrong." I gave him my back, shaking, gasping. "Why do you have to ruin everything? Why do you have to fucking ruin everything!"

He couldn't just let me have this. He couldn't just not be himself and let me have this. He had to make things weird. He had to be a monster and continue to do this shit to me.

I cried into my hands to keep quiet. I'd raised my voice before, and I didn't want to bother the house. I just wanted him out of here and away from me.

"What do you mean I ruin everything—"

"I mean, you couldn't just let me have this." I whipped around, raising and dropping my hands. Wolf's face had bloomed in color, a terror in his eyes that read nothing but fear.

Worry.

Sniffing back tears, I refused to believe any of that concern had to do with me. He was probably unnerved I was being so loud. I pointed at him. "You had to be weird and make things fucking weird." I clenched my hand, unable to stop shaking. "You can't handle this arrangement. Not me, you, and I need you to get out now because this is over."

"Red—"

"It's over, Wolf." I was in his face, the frustration and anger rattling me to my core. "You are vile, and you are cruel, and I refuse to give in to whatever game you're playing. You're trying to confuse shit. Fuck with my emotions…"

It was emotional warfare, which was the same thing he'd done for an entire fucking semester. He must truly be unhinged, a psycho who got off on that sort of thing. He was playing more games here today, and I was done with all this shit.

I was done.

Wolf stood before me with a fallen expression. If fact, it was so close to the way he stared at me in the woods. I kissed him just to make him stop it, but now, I saw the look for what it was. It was sympathy. He made me cry and saw me as something to sympathize. He swallowed. "There is no game, Red. I…" He stepped forward. "I want to talk to you. Please, I need to talk to you."

He reached for me, but I angled back.

He cringed. "I swear, it's no game. I'm not playing with you."

And what else could it be? I was clear about our arrangement. I wanted sex and sex only. There was no emotional shit. No talking. No napping…

Cuddling.

He pushed me past my boundaries, and I fucking fell for

it. I did, and I guess I was the true idiot here. I pointed toward the door. "Get out of my room and get out of my life. You and me are *done*. You understand me? Done."

"Red—"

"Get out!" I held my arms, gripping them.

And he finally moved.

I averted my gaze, as he quickly dressed, and this was to protect me. I didn't want to be affected by him anymore, physical or otherwise.

I didn't move, not one inch until he finally did make it to the door. He opened it, and at that point, I was giving him my back again. I didn't know how long he stayed there, watching me, but eventually, he closed the door behind him. The emotions lanced me then. They racked my body in an emotional influx I wasn't equipped to handle. I fell to the floor, pushing my face into the side of the bed.

It was all I could do to silence my screams.

CHAPTER
NINETEEN

Ares

"What the hell is wrong with you!"

I nearly dropped the bricks I had. I'd been stacking them out back for the dads' burn pit with Dorian, Wells, and Thatcher. Bru hadn't been a part of the help, but I could see why now as he stalked toward me, yelling at me.

Fuck.

I was regretting letting my friends help with the bricks. The guys had seen me out back here moving at a snail's pace. Bru and I had unloaded them into the shed earlier today, but as I knew my dad would ask me to move them to the site where the pit would be, I decided to get a jump on that. It was probably stupid not to ask for help in the first place, but I'd been doing some stupid shit.

Epically stupid.

That was all coming full circle, as I set the bricks down. Bru pushed himself between Thatcher and Wells to get to me. Everyone had stopped, even Bow and Sloane who were playing a game of checkers nearby. They had one of those oversize sets in the grass nearby, the ones that unrolled into a rug. They'd been playing for something to do since Sloane was waiting for Dorian to finish up with the bricks. She still wasn't trying to be around me and frowned from the ground when Bru passed her. "Bru?"

The kid ignored her. He ignored everyone to cross the five or so feet to get to me. He was amped the hell up, his face beet red, and it was all aimed in *my* direction.

Fuck, she talked to him.

That much was a given, and though I'd anticipated this, I didn't aim to have this talk in front of the guys and our sisters. I was still trying to wrap my head around what happened between Red and me earlier that day.

"You really just can't not treat people like shit, can you?" Bru barked at me, and I'd never seen him this way. I mean, I'd seen him pretty pissed, but this appeared to be another level. He had his teeth bared, snarling. "What about *make your intentions clear* did you not understand?"

The siblings and friends had made their way over. They clustered behind Bru, but Dorian eased his way to the front of the group. Rather quickly, he was between the kid and me, and I didn't need my buddy hearing this. I didn't need any of them hearing this. Dorian raised his hands. "What's going on?"

It was like the kid hadn't heard him and only got closer to me. I kept my focus on him. "Let's go talk."

"We are talking."

"Bru? What's happening?" Sloane made her way to her boyfriend, then quickly intercepted her brothers. She expressed concern in Bru's direction. Probably because he was red as fuck. Again, I hadn't seen him this way, and Sloane's eyes twitched. She faced me. "What did you do?"

What didn't I do to piss people off? What wasn't I doing to fuck up everything royally in my life? I'd literally fucked over everything. Everything good. Everything worthwhile.

Everything I loved. It was starting to not feel worth it, and I hadn't made my intentions clear with Red. I'd made things confusing as shit, and she was right.

I just didn't care.

I was so fucking tired. I was done, and if things were going to be fucked up, I might as well get a shred of something good. I should get something I wanted, needed.

I wet my lips, ignoring Sloane, the guys, Bow, and their probing eyes. I angled in front of Bru. "This is between her and me, okay? I'll talk to her."

I loved these people, but this conversation wasn't for them. It was for Red and me, and the only reason we weren't having that was because she'd kicked me out. I was trying to respect that and give her distance, but I would not be discussing any of this in front of my friends and family.

No sooner had the words left my mouth than the kid started to laugh at me. Like right in my face, he laughed. He laced his fingers above his head. "I really got out of the way for you to do this shit."

I blanched. "What do you mean?"

"I mean, this is all my fault. I actually suggested she talk to you. Go to you…" He was clenching his fists like he'd punch something, and that something felt like it was about to be my face. He was physically shaking for some reason, and I wasn't the only one to see this.

Dorian stepped in then, but he wasn't pushing between myself and the kid. He faced Sloane. "We need to let them talk. They've obviously got something to talk about."

I wasn't surprised he was backing me up. Especially because the two of us were clearly talking about Red. Dorian still had his theories about that situation, and he was protecting me now, again, in front of the group.

He really was too good of a friend to me, him, Thatcher, and Wells. Thatch and Wells had been all questions when Red came into their room the way she had yesterday, but they dropped them when I refused to talk about it. I was sure all the guys knew what was up at this point when it came to Red and me.

My gaze averted, lost, but I was rocked back into the conversation when my brother snorted like a bull in front of my face. He laughed. "You know, I actually thought you cared about someone else besides yourself. Thought it made sense with how crazy you've been acting, but that was *clearly* bullshit. The start of this whole trip should have told me that."

I swallowed. "Kid—"

He basically got nose to nose with me, mere inches between us. "You stay away from her. You understand me?" His throat flicked. "You're killing her."

My gut clenched, aware of the feeling. Hurting her was killing me too.

But it had nothing on loving her.

I thought my brother might leave after what he said, but he put no distance between us. He stood there, and I thought he actually would hit me. Thatcher put a hand on Bru's shoulder. "You should go take a walk, kid. You're coming in real hot right now."

So, I wasn't the only one to notice. I got it. He and Red were friends, but this was intense. As far as I knew, he and Red hadn't spoken in years, old friends but nothing that warranted this kind of aggression.

The kid blinked, blanched. It was as if he was in some kind of haze, and once he got out of it, he rubbed his face.

He pivoted then, stalking away, and I had nearly a dozen eyes studying me.

"You guys are talking about Fawn." There was no ques-, tion in my sister's statement, and it was obvious considering what the kid said. Sloane's arms folded. "Seriously? Did you do something else to her?"

Again, I wouldn't be talking to her about this, but it

turned out I didn't have to. She ended up shaking her head at me, then running after Bru. Bow followed her since she went wherever my sister did.

Dorian pointed at me. "Don't go far. We need to talk."

I supposed he would want to do that, make me face some shit.

Cursing, I threaded my fingers on top of my head. Dorian headed in the same direction as his girlfriend, and when Wells and Thatcher stayed, I averted my gaze once more.

"What's going on between you and Fawn, Wolf?" Wells asked, and the question wasn't foreign. The pair of them had been all questions when Fawn propositioned me for sex, but I shut them down just like I would now.

I picked up my bricks, passing them and finishing the job I started. I ignored the generalized pain the labor caused my body but was hard-pressed to do the same for the ache in my center. That shit lingered. This thing with Fawn wasn't just killing me. It was destroying me piece by piece.

Nerve by nerve.

CHAPTER
TWENTY

Bru

"I'm an idiot, aren't I?"

I turned my head to see Fawn, her body stretched out beside me. I'd found her lying on our bedroom floor about an hour ago and joined her.

How did this all become such a mess?

I'd been trying to give Fawn space since I'd found her crying in our room about two days ago. It hadn't been obvious crying, and she'd attempted to hide it. She'd missed dinner, and I'd come to check on her.

Only to find her in tears.

I sighed after her question, aware the only idiot in this room was me. I was the one who had told her to talk to Wolf.

I thought he…

Well, I didn't know what I thought now. I just knew my brother had been acting weird and him having feelings for Fawn seemed like the only way to justify his recent actions. He wasn't acting like himself and him getting too involved with his fake girlfriend seemed like the only answer.

All he did was hurt her.

I felt like I didn't even know my brother and definitely couldn't look at him right now. I even refused to go camping with him and the other guys. It came up about getting a trip in before Christmas in a few days, but I stayed behind.

I think Sloane did the same in an act of solidarity. Word of what happened between Wolf and Fawn traveled quick through our ranks. At least, when it came to us kids. I think we all weren't trying to bring any drama in front of our parents during the holidays, and with Sloane staying behind, Bow did too. Dorian tried, but my sister convinced him out of it. Something about her wanting him to have fun with his friends.

Basically, shit had hit the fan around here, and as much as I wanted to blame Wolf for his stupidity, I had to take some ownership of what had happened. Had I not convinced Fawn to go talk to Wolf, what had ended up happening wouldn't have happened. My brother clearly didn't love her. If he did, he wouldn't have treated her the way he had.

My cheek touched the carpet, my fingers laced on my chest. Fawn stared up at the ceiling, the glow of our fireplace flicking warmth across her cheeks. All I could think was how much of an idiot my brother truly was and how much I was for subjecting her to him. I swallowed. "You're not. I'm the one who suggested you go to him."

Honestly, my brother's feelings were only part of the reason I'd pushed Fawn in his direction. Of course, I cared about my brother and wanted the best for him. Idiot or not, I thought he was getting in his own way, so when Fawn had come to talk to me, I'd guided her to approach him, but that was only because I thought I'd picked up on something on her end too. I thought maybe what they'd had started phys-ical and shifted into something else. That they had both gotten in over their heads and whatever they'd had turned into something more.

I wasn't sure of Fawn's feelings for Wolf, and because I didn't know, I'd pushed her. I wanted her to figure out her feelings for herself, and if she truly could find happiness with my brother, I wanted her to have that, both of them.

I cared about them.

All my meddling did was work shit up, and I should have known better than to listen to my instincts. They'd been terrible lately and completely unreliable.

"You were just trying to help." Fawn turned fully in my direction, and I fought my eyes from closing at how floral she smelled, how familiar. I'd had such a crush on this girl back in high school. I hadn't acted on it then. I hadn't wanted to take advantage of how vulnerable she'd been after her father died, and then, she was gone. A memory.

History.

Today, I was scared of that history. I feared I was latching on to something and using it as a vice. How easy it would be to read into old emotions and use them to not feel anything.

My mouth dried. "Ever think about when we were in high school?" The words rolled out of my mouth, but once they did, they itched to tread on. "About what might have happened if Cissy hadn't pulled her shit?"

I didn't know why I asked her this. I think because, like her, I had my own feelings to figure out. I needed to know if I was reading into things.

Fawn blinked a little, the bright flames of the fireplace bringing out her hazel eyes. "In what way?"

In the way a boy loved a girl, and I think I had loved Fawn. What I didn't know was if that love was just friendship now.

My jaw moved. "I wonder if we had something back then." I swallowed. "Or if we would have had something if you hadn't left. You and me, if we would have had something."

This was a shit thing to ask after all this drama with Wolf, but it was something I needed to know.

Fawn's gaze hit the floor, and I felt like a giant asshole. I shouldn't have said such things. It was stupid and completely inappropriate after everything she'd been through.

But then she grabbed my shirt.

She kissed me, hard, and it happened so fast I didn't really have time to react. I just knew Fawn's mouth was on mine, and once it was, I closed my eyes.

I felt.

I sunk into it, working myself into the depths. I wanted to feel something so badly.

Because it was better than everything else I felt.

I had so much rage these days, anger and giving in to something else would be a welcomed relief. I wanted to unearth those old feelings, but when the kiss ended and I was staring at Fawn's flushed lips, all I saw was a friend. It was a different kind of relief I felt at the realization, a relief for her. Fawn Greenfield was too good to be wrapped up in more shit.

"Bru?"

I blinked, so much concern in Fawn's eyes. She looked worried, truly worried.

Her head tilted. "You okay?"

I wasn't, but that had nothing to do with her. I smiled a little. "Fawn, I think we're just friends."

It really was a relief actually. I didn't want her to have to put up with more shit. My brother had given her a mountain-full already, and I didn't want to add to it.

I had my own mountain.

Last semester hadn't gone the way I'd liked. It hadn't by a landslide. I had thought being away in another country would help, but all my problems did were chase me. They'd *hounded* me until I'd given in. I'd been a shaken bottle ready to explode.

And I had.

I had so bad, and that mountain I had I still climbed. I could definitely see what all this was now with Fawn. I think I'd wanted to lean into those old feelings and use them as a crutch.

A vice.

I tried to silence the little destructive voice in my head, and there was a lack of surprise on Fawn's face after what I said. She nodded. "I know."

She knows.

She stared at the fire, playing with her hands. "Back in high school, I think it was more complicated for me, and I did wonder for a time after I initially left." She studied me. "But that changed."

I guess it had, for both of us it had.

I wasn't sure when it had for me. Possibly it was just time and moving on, growing up.

Her lashes flicked up. "But I hope we can still be friends. I'd hate to lose that for a second time."

I would too, and it hadn't been her fault. It wasn't hers any more than it was mine. We both moved on. We both changed. My smile returned. "You'd be hard-pressed to get rid of me this time."

I'd love to be her friend. I was a good friend and could support the shit out of anyone else.

But when it came to myself…

I wasn't so good to me sometimes and let my shit eat away at me. A direct example of that was my last semester, which I still hadn't told my family about, my parents…

Mr. Perfect.

The label haunted me. I was never perfect even back when I knew Fawn. I busied myself by taking care of my dad and helping my sister take care of our family. I did anything I could not to feel anything back then.

Like now.

Fawn squeezing my shoulder broke me out of my daze. Her head cocked. "You okay?"

There was that question again, and once more, I overcompensated. I put on that Mr. Perfect grin, making sure everyone else was feeling good. "Fine, and we won't forget each other this time. We'll check in and not lose touch."

"Promise?"

I nodded, my grin genuine this time. "I promise."

And I planned to keep that promise for her. If she ever needed me, I'd be there. No questions asked and hoped I could keep that same promise for myself. That I'd reach out if I needed her.

"Knock. Knock."

Thatcher's sister, Bow, peeked her head in. Her cheeks colored. "Sorry. I heard voices and knocked, but no one answered."

Not many could blush harder than Rainbow Reed, and she was the complete opposite of Thatch. For starters, she could be shy, and her brother was arrogant as fuck. Loved the guy, but he was. I laughed. "You're fine. What's up?"

She tiptoed her way inside the room like she'd break it with her mere existence. She really was the opposite of her brother. She let the door close behind her. "Sloane and I were wondering if you wanted to both go to a holiday party."

I sat up, and Fawn did too.

"Well, Sloane's wondering. We both heard some of the locals talking about it when we went in town for coffee today. It's a college party." Her cheeks brightened. "We both thought it'd be a good idea to do something fun since we're all home anyway. I suggested a movie, but Sloane remembered the party."

That didn't sound like a bad idea to me, and it'd be nice to get some movement into my body. I got kind of stir-crazy when I sat for too long.

I tried to ignore the reason why and redirected my attention to Fawn. "What do you think? Wanna go?"

Her mouth parted. "Is it, um, far? I'm not sure if I, um…"

She started to fidget for some reason, playing with her hands. I almost asked what was wrong, but then Bow spoke.

"Not far at all. We're probably going to walk since it is so close. It's just behind my parents' property a few houses back."

Fawn's hands relaxed. Actually, she visibly relaxed, and I wondered what was up. I also wondered why she asked, but maybe she didn't want to stay out super late. Some of these properties could be pretty far out and required a long drive to get to them. It was also already getting late.

"Well, that sounds fun if you want to," Fawn stated, and suddenly, she was asking me the question. She smiled. "Do you want to?"

"I'm game if you are," I said, since she seemed to be okay now.

Bow nodded. "I'll let her know. Honestly, I think she's lost her mind." She rocked on her sock-covered feet. "If Dorian finds out, he'll be pissed."

I lifted my eyes, but didn't question why she said what she did. Dorian and his protective shit when it came to my sister was legendary. I obviously appreciated him looking out for her, but the dude was completely over the top sometimes.

I pulled out my phone. "I'll text him we're going, and that I'll be with you guys." It might not matter but it was worth a shot, and these dudes could get handsy at these parties. I didn't want dudes messing with my sister either, or Fawn and Bow. "You can go ahead and let Sloane know we're going. I just need to get some shoes on."

Fawn might want to get ready too, and she was already up on her feet.

The door closed behind Bow, and I almost walked into

Fawn since I just sent off the text to Dorian. I laughed. "Sorry."

"No problem." She didn't move and studied the door before facing me. She frowned. "I guess I just wanted to check in. You were kind of spacing before Bow came in."

And she was already keeping her promise to me, checking on me. "I was, but I'm good. You good?" There was a moment I questioned that when Bow came in as well.

Fawn waved me off. "I'm fine. And this does sound fun. It's going to be fun."

I agreed it sounded like fun, but I also felt we were talking about something without talking about something.

That's just you.

It was just me, me and my secrets, and if I did have some kindness when it came to myself, I would have shared that fact with her. Instead, I just smiled again and let her get ready.

I was already breaking half our promise.

CHAPTER
TWENTY-ONE

Ares

I HATE THIS.
I NEED U.
FORGIVE ME.

My stick dragged through the dirt, the same three sentences
drawn over and over again.

I HATE THIS.
I NEED U.
FORGIVE ME.

I forgot how many times I drew the letters, probably about
as many times as I did on Fawn's back before she kicked me
out of her room. I used her freckles, the tiny imperfections
like stars forming a constellation. They were perfect in their
imperfection, unique like snowflakes. Art.

I HATE THIS.

I NEED U.
FORGIVE ME.

I'd drawn a heart after that last set of sentences on her back. Well, I'd started to until she woke up, which was just as pathetic as me drawing words in the first place. I had no right to do any of that, none of it.

I HATE THIS.
I NEED U.
FORGIVE ME.

Even still, I drew them at my feet now, but Dorian's curse gave me pause. I'd been using a stick to draw in the dirt at our campsite, but I'd been doing so discreetly. I didn't need any of my buddies asking questions.

They were already asking too many questions.

Using my shoe, I rubbed the sentences out, my attention drifting to Dorian who sat across the campfire from me. Thatcher and Wells had left to go get beer. Apparently, the two cases we'd picked up on our way out here wasn't enough. We hadn't even had to use our fake IDs, getting shit like beer and illegal substances easy when you were us. Thatcher merely had to drop his dad's name who owned half the properties out here.

Dorian was texting quickly on his phone, his expression tight and twisted in consternation. I tipped my chin. "What's up?"

"What's up is your sister and her ability to literally drive me fucking crazy," he grunted, his thumbs moving in rapid time. "The kid says she's going to a college party. Her, Fawn, and Bow."

I sat up, Fawn's name on his lips.

"He said he'll be with them, but I don't fucking care. You know how fuckers are at those things."

I did know. I was one of those guys. At least, I had been before the whole Fawn-and-the-fake-relationship thing.

You know it started before that.

It had actually, well before. The fact of the matter was I hadn't been that guy since I'd found out Fawn would be coming to my school.

I wet my lips, gazing down.

"I'm texting Sloane," Dorian said. "She has no business being at a random party with some drunk college fuckers."

I agreed, but I didn't know why he was bothering. This was my twin we were talking about, and she was headstrong. Just like Red.

I dragged my stick again, ignoring the tight pull in my chest. I'd be on my phone too. Except it wouldn't matter. Red wouldn't answer me.

My grip on the stick tightened, and it took me a second to realize Dorian called my name. He had his mouth open, his hand up and the light of the fire flashed in his dark eyes. "Did you hear me?"

I hadn't. Well, I heard my name but that was it.

He raised and dropped his hands. "I asked why you're not doing anything. Fawn's going to this thing too."

I was aware, but *he* was aware I'd made anything having to do with Fawn not my business. Of course, he'd eventually come back to me after chasing after Sloane, Bru, and Red that day, but when he'd gotten back, I'd essentially told him shit wasn't his business and to back off. It hadn't sat well, and I think if my mom hadn't come out and let us know food was ready, some shit might have gone down. My friend had been really good at watching my back. He'd even made good on his promise about keeping things peaceful in the house with our families. The drama had been nonexistent since we'd all arrived here, and the parents were barely even side-eyeing me now. *That* had been because of Dorian, and Thatcher and Wells by proxy.

They did whatever Dorian wanted, and usually, I did too. I respected him, loved him.

I was sure it wasn't looking like that these days, but I didn't care. I knew I'd have to come to terms with some of the choices I'd made, but today wouldn't be that day. Not with Christmas literally days away.

Nah, that wasn't happening.

I ground my stick in the dirt. "You said the kid will be with them, right?"

"Yeah…"

I shrugged. "Well, he's got it, then."

"He's got it?"

I nodded. "He'll keep eyes on the situation." I firmly believed that, and that he would protect my sister, Bow, and Fawn.

But that didn't mean it was easy to say.

In fact, it was the hardest thing I had to fucking do to remain impartial and not do something about shit myself. The jagged parts of wood on the stick cut at my fingers, the pain welcomed.

"I don't get it, Wolf. I mean, do you actually think we're all idiots or is there something else going on here? Something I'm not getting?"

An ice bath hit me, froze me, and I glanced up to see my buddy frown. He'd all but forgotten his phone, looking at me.

He lifted a hand. "Well?"

Well.

I decided to choose my next words carefully here. It felt important. "Look, when it comes to all the stuff with Fawn…"

"Oh, we don't need to talk about Fawn."

That surprised me, him saying that. He and the other guys had been doing nothing else but trying to get me to talk about Fawn after all this recent stuff.

Him doing the opposite now felt like a trick, so I stayed silent, and Dorian laughed.

"That whole situation is obvious regarding how you feel about her," he continued, my heart thudding. "That shit isn't up for debate. What confuses me is why you continue to deny it, and why you did all that shit with a fake relationship in the first place."

My throat thickened, tightened. "I told you why." And we already had that discussion. The topic was over, squashed.

At least, I'd thought it was.

Dorian was already shaking his head in the breeze, the wind picking up and catching his blond hair. It hadn't been chilly tonight but breezy. His frown deepened. "Yeah, you did all that shit for us and got in over your head with the girl you did it with."

"Dorian—"

He directed a finger at me. "No, you've done enough talking, and I'm going to do some now. I let you have your space to deal with shit you're clearly not dealing with, but I'm not a fool. None of us are. There's something fucking weird going on with you, and that goes way beyond you burying your feelings for your ex-fake girlfriend."

My eyes closed. "D…"

"No." He was up now, on his feet. It gave him an intimidation advantage I didn't normally put up with, but I found I couldn't move in that moment. Challenge him. He hunkered down in front of me. "You're an asshole, Wolf. Hell, we all are, and when it comes to any of us guys, we'd do much worse than creating some fake-relationship bullshit if we knew it'd help a situation. If we knew it'd *help*, but what you did didn't help. All it did was create mess and hurt everyone."

I knew that, aware of that.

Dorian rubbed his jaw. "We've all done some fucked-up things. Like I said, we'd do worse *if it meant something*, but what you did, man? It was just *cruel*. It was cruel to Fawn, and fuck, it was cruel to us too. You know, we'd never want you to do something like that. Not for us."

My jaw moved, and Dorian shook his head.

"You're acting strange, man. And we've all seen it." He stood up, finally giving me breathing room, distance. He laced his fingers above his head. "The kid's been back a minute and a half, and he saw it too. He was wondering why you'd do something so fucked up, and we didn't have any answers."

I knew they'd compare notes, talk, but I figured that would mostly be about things between Fawn and me.

Not this.

This had me quiet in ways I shouldn't be, but I couldn't bring myself to get in my buddy's face and defend myself. I found myself listening, waiting.

Hoping.

I shouldn't be quiet right now, but I was. Dorian braced his arms. "You just haven't been acting like yourself, and I've been trying to support you. Give you space. We all are."

I dropped my head, and Dorian sighed.

"But I'm starting to regret it. I physically feel your distance, and we all feel that too. Like we've lost you even though you're right in front of us."

The words lost themselves in the trees, the breeze. It picked up in foreboding ways and even waved the fire.

I got chills from it, a deep and visceral feeling that settled into my bones. My mouth dried. "D—"

A raindrop hit my face, then another. It came down in a soft trickle, and Dorian cursed.

He pulled his hoodie's hood up. "Brilliant. Thatch was supposed to check the fucking forecast."

That should have been our first mistake, leaving him to do that. With the weather nice, we all decided to go camping, but getting rained on out here in our tents wasn't what had me searching the sky. I scanned and soft illumination brightened the sky.

No.

I stood then. Where there was lightning there was thunder, and that wasn't good.

"Ares, what's your deal, bro?"

Dorian was asking because I still had eyes on the sky. I did like I could change it, the downpour. It all came down in a whoosh, but where Dorian started to retreat and head to one of the tents for shelter, I stood firm. It hit in a soft roll then, the thunder. It was like a caged animal ready to strike. Meanwhile, my heart shot up in my fucking throat.

"Ares, bro. What are you doing? Get in the fucking tent!"

I wasn't, dragging him out of it instead. He started to protest but I shook him to look at me. "Where's that party?"

"What—"

"Where's the fucking *party*, D? Is it far?" I had no transportation, no means to get out of here but to go on foot.

Get to her…

I had to. I had to get to Red. She was afraid of *fucking storms*, and Thatcher and Wells had the goddamn car.

I got in Dorian's face. "Did Bru tell you? Sloane?"

"Yeah, but—"

"Drop me the pin."

He did, seeing I was serious, his light-gray Pembroke Football hoodie dark now. He was getting drenched in the rain. We both were. He tapped his phone. "You want to go or something? You acted like you didn't fucking care not two seconds ago."

He was right about that, but he was also right that I'd been acting, and according to him, poorly.

My phone buzzed with the pin, and I scanned it.

"Fuck, I'm not getting any reception out here now. Maybe it's the storm?" Dorian was raising his phone to the sky, using his hand to shield it from the rain. "I just sent you that pin, but now, I can't get a text out to Wells and Thatch. If I can get a hold of them, they can come back and take us to that party —hey. What are you doing?"

He saw what I was doing, reaching in the tent. I grabbed my hoodie, and once I had it on and my hood up, I pivoted. I headed directly into the storm, jogging, and he called after me.

"You're not seriously going to run all the way there, are you?" he asked, his voice amplified. The rain was coming down in sheets at this point, currents. "Wolf, it's five fucking miles!"

I didn't care, not caring, and I only picked up the pace when the sky flashed with light and that thunder turned into a growl. I didn't know if the storm had made it to Red yet, but it would, and my gut told me that. I hadn't been listening to my gut lately.

If I had, I never would have allowed myself to fall in love.

CHAPTER
TWENTY-TWO

Fawn

"Any reason why you're choosing to be a creep by hanging out over here drinking instead of dancing with the rest of us?"

Bru glanced up after I called him out, that drink in his hand, a beer bottle. We'd gotten to this party almost an hour ago, but he hadn't danced, not once. He laughed. "I'm being a creep?"

I mean, he had been in this dark corner the whole night. He kept a constant eye on Sloane, Bow, and me, but he hadn't done much dancing. Actually, he hadn't done any dancing at all. I frowned. "What's up?"

I worried about him. He'd been spacing out before we left the house, and there had been all that stuff *with us*. I wasn't entirely sure what drove me to kiss him, but after, it felt like a weight of awkwardness had been lifted. He'd told me he'd wondered about things in our past, and that kiss had felt like goodbye to all that in a way. It wasn't a sad goodbye, but the opposite. It was like a clearance toward a path forward. I felt like I got my friend back, and I think that'd been where all the awkwardness from before came from. I did know where the two of us were at regarding our friendship, but Bru was still figuring it out. That was something I think I knew deep down. We had a history, and he had a what-if when it came to us.

I think the only reason I hadn't was because I had moved on. Had it been stupid to fall in love with someone who only wanted to use me? Yes, but it had happened. It was even more stupid to think I could separate sex from emotion, and a small part of me had been glad Wolf fucked up that whole plan. I was aware of what would happen eventually if we continued down the path we'd been on. I'd get attached to him. I wouldn't want to let him go, and I...

I squeezed Bru's shoulder, pushing that all away, forcing myself. "It wasn't that kiss, was it? Did I make things awkward?" I thought we'd closed that chapter, but maybe he was still working things out.

Bru smiled at me, a small one, before lifting his hand in Sloane and Bow's direction. With her height, Sloane was pointing out that she and Bow were going to the bar. The holiday party was put on by a local frat at one of the nearby cabins. I'd heard they had rented out the place, and even though it was on the smaller side, it housed a lot of people. It was also loud as fuck, and I could barely hear my own voice when I spoke to Bru.

Sloane and Bow made their way to the bar, and after seeing that, Bru redirected his attention to me. He really was a good guy and looked out for his family, his friends. His head tilted. "No, I'm glad you did that. I think it's great we're just friends, and I'm glad that's cleared up."

I felt the same. "What's going on, then?"

"You can tell something's wrong?" He had to lean in to speak, the decibels in this place seemed to grow louder and louder. Bru laughed. "And here I was trying to keep shit to myself."

"You forget we were friends."

"Are friends," he said, lifting a finger, and I nodded, smiling. He lifted his shoulders. "No big. Just lost in my thoughts a little."

"Want to talk about it?" I sat on the arm of his chair. I was nudged in the process, this place really packed.

Bru started to open his mouth, but Sloane and Bow cut through the crowd. They had drinks in their hands, red Solo cups, and Bru frowned at them. He pointed. "You never set those drinks down, did you?"

Sloane's dark eyes lifted toward the ceiling decorated with holiday lights. They dripped down and twinkled bright in red and green. Sloane laughed. "We literally just got these drinks, and before you ask, no, I didn't let the little rabbit get any alcohol."

She nudged Bow, and I assumed *little rabbit* was her nickname for her.

Bru nodded. "Yeah, you know Thatcher would kill my ass."

"Which is completely ridiculous because he totally drank in high school." Bow rolled her eyes. "Anyway, I wanted soda."

"And, *Dad*, we only came over here to let you know we're going to the bathroom," Sloane chimed in, and when Bru started to get up, Sloane lifted a hand. "I think we can handle this on our own thanks."

Bru was looking some kind of way about that, but he did sit down. He eyed Sloane. "Keep your phone on and handy in case I text."

Sloane saluted Bru, which made him shake his head. She asked if I wanted to go as well, but Bru and I ended up deciding to get our own drinks. He needed a new beer, and I still wanted to know what was wrong.

"So?" I questioned, settling against the bar. I got a soda too since I didn't drink. "You're not avoiding this."

"And what is *this* exactly," he asked, but he wasn't talking about whatever alcoholic concoction he got the bartender to make him. There'd been several kinds of alcohol, whiskey, but currently, he just nursed the drink, staring at it.

I eyed him. "The conversation. What's up?"

I didn't hear his sigh over the volume in the room, but I'd seen it. He shook his head. "I guess I'm just having a hard time quieting my thoughts." He studied the bar. "My last semester kind of sucked, and I'm trying to figure out how to talk to my parents about it."

I couldn't fight my brow from lifting. I had no idea he'd been struggling with something.

That was because you'd only been thinking about yourself.

This stuff with Wolf had made me crazy, and if I hadn't been thinking about that, I maybe could have spared some thoughts for my friend. "Did you, like, flunk out or something?"

This would surprise me. I recalled Bru being really smart in high school.

A smile lifted his lips. "I wish it was something like that honestly," he said, giving me pause. He wished he would have flunked out of school? That seemed very unusual, and I watched as he sucked back his drink. All the liquor didn't even faze him. He barely had a reaction to it before stamping his cup down. He sat back. "That would be easier to explain to my folks. *Normal.*"

"What do you mean?"

The smile remained on his lips, but it was a fake one. I knew because I'd seen it back at the house before we'd left. He faced me. "I'll figure it out. Seriously, I don't want you to worry about me."

I couldn't help it though. I mean, he was my friend, and I started to say that, but I was nudged again. In fact, I was rocked forward, and the guy who'd done it spilled half his drink on my jeans.

He laughed after, mumbling sorry before walking away, and I got off my chair. "Asshole!"

The guy flipped me the bird. Like legit lifted his finger as he folded back into the crowd. He didn't even look at me, and before I could say anything about that, Bru charged past me. Quick, I barely saw him, and when I did catch up to him, he'd made his way in front of the guy.

"How about a real fucking apology, man?" he questioned, his arms folded. His words had been clear, calm, but nothing about him looked it. His face charged red, and he put a finger in the guy's chest. "You spilled beer on my friend, so now, you're going to apologize to her."

Bru was a big guy, a huge guy, but so was the guy who'd spilled the beer. In fact, he had height on Bru, and I didn't like where this was going. I touched Bru's arm. "Hey. Don't. I'm good."

"Nah. He needs to apologize to you. A *proper* apology." He spoke to me, but he had his focus on the guy.

The dude laughed again. "Fuck off, bro. You're at *my frat's* party, and maybe if that chick didn't take up as much surface area as she does, I wouldn't have spilled my drink on her."

He was obviously calling me fat, which was weak. Guys like that took cheap shots, but I didn't give a fuck about what he thought about my looks. I started to tell him that, but Bru's fist came out of nowhere. He hit the guy right in his jaw, and I'd never seen such a thing.

Bru landed him out. Like *one* punch, and the guy was on the floor. Someone in the room shouted. A scream followed, and I didn't realize why until it hit me that Bru went to the floor with the guy. He got on top of him, his fists flying.

He didn't stop.

Hit after hit Bru's fists came down. They drove into the guy's face, the same area over and over.

"Bru!"

He didn't hear me, continually socking the guy. Blood left the frat dude's nose, his mouth, and all of it covered Bru's fists. The frat guy didn't even have his eyes open, clearly unconscious, and I grabbed at Bru's shirt. "Bru, stop! You're killing him!"

Bru stopped then, froze. His hand came up, and he stared at it with wild eyes. It was like he'd gone into some kind of violent haze.

And he was shaking. He was shaking so bad when he got up and looked at me. "Fawn..."

He almost sounded confused like he had been in a haze. He glanced down at the frat guy, and his eyes twitched wide. As if he was seeing what he'd done for the first time, which didn't make sense. I stepped forward. "Bru—"

He backed off. Like I'd burn him if I touched him. People were still screaming, and some guy was on his knees tapping the frat dude's face. Eventually, the frat guy woke up, shaking his head. Regardless, someone said to call 911, and Bru looked at me. He lifted his hands. "I should go."

"Bru—"

"I need to find my sister, Bow, I..." He started to walk off in a random direction, but I guided him another way.

"No, I'll find her. I'll find them. You go." He probably shouldn't stick around any longer anyway. Someone could call the cops or something.

He didn't even argue. Like he really was completely out of it. It scared me as much as what I'd seen him do. I'd never seen him act in such a way, so violent.

I lost him in the crowd of people, and once the frat guy was up on his feet, people started to calm down a bit. A couple dudes got him on the couch, and I left to find Sloane and Bow. It wasn't a huge house, but there were a few bathrooms.

I ended up on the second floor, and it was much quieter

up there. I called out their names, opening random doors. Eventually, I tried to call them both, but the reception was kind of shoddy out here, and neither call went through.

That was when I heard the rumbling.

It was low at first, tame, but then it crashed and roared. The dimly lit hallway exploded with light, lightning flashing through the window.

Oh, God. No. Please.

Rainfall charged above me. It hit hard, and I fell to my knees.

No…

I grabbed my legs, but when lightning hit the hallway again, I crawled into another room. I didn't know where I was or what kind of room it was. I just knew I was in a corner, my arms around my legs, as I prayed for silence. Relief. I closed my eyes, and all I could see was my dad's car flipping and me inside it at the wheel…

My dad.

I saw him in his final moments, my father. I saw the life leave his eyes as he reached out for me. I drove, and he wanted to *save me*. I watched my father die in that storm.

And a part of me died that day too.

CHAPTER
TWENTY-THREE

Ares

By the time we got to the remote cabin surrounded by woods, we were soaked. I say *we* because Dorian ended up sprinting the five miles with me. He was ride-or-die and barely asked any questions along the way. I told him the situation anyway, though, and he already knew about Fawn's aversion to cars to some extent. I never went into details about it with him, but he knew she didn't like them.

Dorian hadn't known anything about the storm thing, though, but I knew he'd probably be alongside me even if he hadn't. I hadn't been treating my friend great lately, any of them, but they were there for me.

Hang in there, Red.

The storm had gotten worse by the time we crossed the threshold of the party, and Dorian and I nearly got side-swiped by an ambulance half a mile away. There weren't a lot of properties out here, but apparently something had happened at one of them.

"I finally got a text out to Thatcher and Wells," Dorian

huffed, tugging his hood down. He was out of breath like me, and our hoods had been pointless. We were both dripping wet, and the only reason our cell phones had survived was because we'd shoved them down our fucking boxers. Dorian tapped the phone. "I told them where we were, but my texts to Sloane and the kid failed."

He'd attempted to contact my sister and Bru since they'd be with Fawn, and I'd been desperate and tried Fawn myself. My shit hadn't gone out either and...

"Hey. We'll find her," Dorian said, squeezing my arm. "We'll split up. Cover more ground that way. I'm sure everyone's together."

I was sure they were all together, but what he could never guarantee was that everything was fine. It wouldn't be.

Not in this.

The house fucking rattled, and the only reason no one inside was freaking out was because they were drunk and partying, unaffected. Storms didn't get to them the same way it did to Red.

I'd seen firsthand what the torrential elements could do to her. She shut down, and Dorian barely got the words out before I left him. I folded into the fray, sending rapid texts to Fawn along the way. They were texts I wasn't sure would go through, but I tried anyway.

Me: I'm at the party.

Me: It's storming, and I needed to make sure you're okay.

Me: Please answer if you can. I just want to help.

In what way I could help, I didn't know. I just know I'd been there during one of her shutdowns, and after, she hadn't been so scared. I prayed that my presence here would make things better and not worse.

"Have you seen a redhead?" I asked random people. They were too busy partying and shit to give me the time of day, and I had to shake a few people. "She's got bright red hair. Freckles. She might be wearing something that shows her tattoos. She's got a koi fish on her shoulder and watercolor flowers down her arm."

I left out how perfect they were and what they allowed her to mask, her vulnerabilities. Fawn liked to come off as this confident ball breaker, but she had a delicate layer she never addressed. She hid from it and never let people see when she needed help.

She was like me in that way, the pair of us so goddamn alike. I never let people see my weaknesses either, my vulnerabilities...

The group I talked to had no information, and the next, the same. I went from room to room out of luck and with no sighting of Red, Bru, my sister, or Bow. I was beginning to wonder if Dorian and I had made it to the right cabin. With our phones' reception being spotty, our navigation hadn't been the best. At some points, we were literally running blind.

"That girl who came with the crazy dude? Yeah, I've seen her," some guy said after I gave him Fawn's description. The whole "crazy dude" comment set off alarm bells, but my focus quickly transferred when he pointed directly above. "Pretty sure I saw her go into a room upstairs. Last door down the hall."

That was all I needed, my steps quick. I found a stairwell, and the cabin crashed with so much thunder I nearly grabbed a wall. The storm could be heard a lot louder upstairs, and I wondered if she'd even still be here to find. Who knew when that guy had seen her.

That was if it was her.

I almost hoped I didn't find her. Actually, I internally prayed that I didn't, and that she was back at the Reeds'. Maybe the storm hadn't reached the Reeds' house yet despite it being so close. I reached for all kinds of hope in that moment because I didn't want to see her.

No, I didn't want to see her like this.

I didn't even have to call out for her in the end, because the instant I opened that door at the end of the hall, there Red was. She was tucked tight in a corner on the floor, her head down and her arms curled around her legs.

And she was shaking.

Red…

I rushed to her, another thunderclap behind me. The room filled with so much light, lightning. It was so bright for a moment it appeared as if someone flicked on a light switch, and the walls thrashed with waves upon waves of rain. "Red?"

She didn't hear me. I was standing right in front of her, and she didn't hear me, her head down. That last crash of thunder had her digging her nails into her arms. There were already marks there, red trails. She was on the cusp of drawing blood, and I hunkered down. "Red, look at me."

Her head shot up, probably because I was so close. Her eyes flashed wide, and she backed into the corner so hard. She backed *away from me*, and my chest felt slammed, socked.

Instantly, I backed away, but when the room filled with light, absolute terror filled her eyes. Tears streamed down her cheeks, and she shook her head. "No…"

But she wasn't speaking to me. Her head whipped around every which way, like the walls were literally crowding around her. Another thunderclap hit, and she croaked out a noise like a wounded animal. It was screechy and horror-filled and made my stomach clench violently. She sounded like she was in guttural pain and had no means or hope to stop it.

Her face pressed into her legs, and I ignored the voice in my head, the one telling me to back off and back away. I *ignored* the one telling me to leave her so I didn't make this worse. I got her arms. "Red…"

She stiffened up, curling into herself, but I guided her to

look at me, focus *on me.* "Red, listen to my voice. Focus on me. Stay with me."

She needed an anchor, something else but the storm around her. I knew that because I'd had my own panic attacks in the past. My sister being taken from my family caused a lot of trauma in my life. For many years, I tried to find her myself, but no matter how long I'd looked or how far I'd gone, I never did. I was literally riddled with anxiety at some points in my life, and the only way I was able to come out of it was by staying in the present and focusing on something.

I brought my hands down Red's arms. "Just listen to me. Just stay here..."

She did for a second, her eyes on me. But then the storm had its angry way and threw itself at us. I felt the thunder in my teeth it was so loud, but my reaction to that was limited. Red grabbed me, and the next thing I knew, she forced herself into my chest. I was dripping wet, but she grabbed me.

She hugged me.

"Please," she cried out, sobbing against me. "Please, make it stop. *Please.*"

I felt like death, like *I died* because she was in so much pain, and all she had was me to help. She had me who she hated, her enemy.

But she wasn't mine. She'd never been, and I brought her closer into my chest. "You hear my voice, Red? My breathing?" Her nod was light, timid, and I swallowed. "Focus on that. Breathe with me. Take in lots of breaths."

She did, the two of us in sync. We had to start again each and every time the storm threatened to shake her, but I brought her back. I always brought her back.

"You're doing so good," I coached, pushing her hair away. She was basically in my lap at this point, but I held her tighter. She couldn't be close enough. "Just keep breathing. You're doing so good, baby."

She was doing good, perfect, and I couldn't help what I said. I felt a claim over this girl I had no right to.

Despite my words, she didn't shy away. If anything, she did the opposite. Her arms looped around my neck, she brought herself closer, her breaths even with mine, and I hated myself in that moment. I did because I allowed the proximity, and even though she was in her own personal hell, I wasn't. Her closeness brought me life, and I couldn't help it.

I think I might have been doing the same for her because despite the storm, she fell asleep in my arms that night. She did despite her fear...

And the warmth of her enemy's arms around her.

CHAPTER
TWENTY-FOUR

Fawn

I woke up in a place I didn't recognize and with memories I didn't like that I had. The majority of them had been with Wolf, his arms around me...

I sat up, feeling drugged. I'd cried myself to sleep last night, and I remembered that. I also remembered a voice telling me things would be okay. He'd told me what I was feeling was scary, but I'd be all right. I'd get through it.

Swallowing, I felt a dry mouth and squinted into sunlight. I recognized this room as the one I'd escaped into last night, but I had no idea I'd been in a bedroom. I was on a bed and under sheets.

Why was I here?

I pushed the bedding off. Wolf obviously had let me sleep, but I shouldn't be here. I had no idea why he'd been here, or how he found me. I also had no idea why he'd left me here in this house.

Because he was a jerk.

He hadn't been acting like one last night. He'd been that

voice telling me things. He'd been comforting me, assuring me. But what I didn't understand was *why*, and my attempts to get up only made me lie back down. I had a massive headache. Probably from all the crying. I lay for a second with my face in the bedding, and the sharp scent caused me to sit up instantly.

It smelled like him, the bed. One side smelled like me, but the other smelled like Wolf.

Had he stayed here with me?

I didn't like the thought of it, and this time, I made myself get up. My phone was nearby, and I got that. I had no service, and a line being out due to the storm wouldn't surprise me.

Fuck.

I'd stayed in a foreign place. In fact, the exact place that had been the subject of a fight I may or may not have been a part of. I hadn't been throwing the punches, but my friend had.

Bru.

He was probably worried sick. I'd told him I'd find his sister and Bow, then ended up collapsed on the floor, weak.

Rushing, I left the room, trying to make calls on the way. Nothing went through, and something unusual was how quiet this house was. There was discarded trash on the floor, paper plates and cups, but no people. I hadn't been to a ton of parties since I'd gone to college, but typically, one would step over a body or two if one stayed late enough. That just came with the territory, but this place was empty.

Mostly.

Some light singing came from the kitchen, and my phone just about left my hands at the sight of Bow Reed. She was pulling toast out of a toaster, then buttering it.

Um...

I walked casually, slowly. This was very unusual, and I was so quiet I scared the shit out of Bow. She jumped, but when she realized I was the one creeping around, she laughed.

"Oh my gosh, Fawn. You scared me." She chuckled, still in her party clothes. Upon further observation, I was too. She placed down her knife. "Want some toast? It's about the only thing I can make."

My phone touched the counter. She was speaking to me like it wasn't unusual we were both here.

"It's also the only thing I could find in this house besides beer and hot dogs," she said, her cheeks rosy. She'd cleared a space on the counter to prepare her food, but the other areas were filled with trash. Again, discarded plates and stuff like they'd been abandoned. The punch bowl was still out.

I gripped my phone. "Why are we both still here?"

The million-dollar question. I knew why *I* was here, of course. I'd passed out, and Wolf had left my ass.

Wolf...

I couldn't think about him right now. Not without being confused, so I didn't. Even still, my throat thickened waiting for Bow's response, and she laughed again.

"Oh, right. This is probably weird. Seeing me." She placed her knife down, then took a bite of her toast. "I stayed here last night. We all did."

"All did?"

She nodded. "Me, Sloane, Wells, Thatcher, Dorian, and Ares."

Wolf.

"Bru didn't, but only so he could cover for us back at the house with our parents," Bow continued. "I don't know what excuse he made, but he was here at the cabin this morning when I woke up. Well, briefly. He said he was going for a walk, but he'd be back before everyone woke up."

My mouth parted. "Was he okay?" I didn't know after that fight.

I definitely feel like I dropped the ball when it came to him. I'd been so weak last night.

Bow's expression dropped upon me mentioning Bru. "He seemed to be, yeah, and crazy about that fight. Sloane and I didn't see it, but we obviously heard about it." She chewed her lip. "There was an ambulance."

I didn't get to see that part considering I'd been comatose on the floor.

Weak.

That voice in my head was so loud, but every time it rose, I heard another.

"You'll be okay... You're doing so good, baby..."

Chills hit my arms. Stupid chills that didn't make sense. I forced Wolf's voice out. It being there made just as much sense as his presence last night.

"Why were the guys here last night?" Really what I was asking was why was *Wolf* here? "Why are any of us here?"

"Well, the boys kind of commandeered the cabin after the fight, and that guy is okay. The one Bru hit?" Bow shook her head. "I heard what happened there too. He sounded like a jerk."

He had been one. I swallowed, and Bow continued on.

"Sounded like he just went to the hospital to get checked out, but word around the party was that he was fine. The EMTs checked him out."

That was good, and I'd never want Bru to get in trouble for helping me. "Why did the guys take over the cabin?" Why were they *here*?

Bow took a second with that question. She hitched a hip against the counter, nibbling on her toast before she answered. "It was, uh, Ares's idea actually."

"Wolf?"

She nodded. "He..." She played with her dark hair. "He wanted you to be able to sleep."

A voice elevated outside, one louder than the one

suddenly blaring in my head after what Bow said. Bow and I faced the kitchen window, the source of the voice.

"Good. You're here. Now, you can tell me *what the fuck* you were thinking," Wolf barked, charging toward something. He was shirtless, his constellation tattoo on full display in the bright sun. He wore nothing but a pair of joggers, his feet bare as he stalked toward Bru who had a couple grocery sacks in his hands.

Bow and I exchanged a glance for only moments before we left the kitchen and headed outside. We passed clothes-lines along the way, a couple sets of jeans and hoodies hanging on them. There were high-top sneakers below and dripping socks and hanging boxer briefs above them on another line.

Wolf had been wet last night.

He must have been out in the storm, but my thoughts had been limited that evening. I'd been lost in a sea of fear and confusion. The latter came from Wolf and a few things that were happening right now. Things like what Bow had said and Wolf suddenly stepping up to Bru. Wolf had his focus on him, but Bru glanced to Bow and me since we'd made it outside. Bru's head tilted. "Fawn?"

Wolf whipped around, scanning me. My flesh heated under his probing gaze. It was a physical reaction only, and I couldn't help taking inventory of him as well. I had no idea where he got his joggers, but they cinched in tight at his chiseled waist. Since they were so low, they exposed his flower tattoo on his hip. Just the top of it peeked out, and his hair was tousled and worked around like he'd been sleeping.

He also had bags under his eyes.

They were deep, dark circles like he hadn't slept, and Bru had a fair bit of darkness under his eyes as well. They weren't anything like Wolf's, but clearly, they'd both been up at least part of the night.

I forced myself not to care about the reasons behind Wolf's

lack of sleep as I headed toward both guys, and Bow was beside me. She was texting on her phone, and I had a feeling it was for reinforcements.

Bru started to cut around Wolf. I assumed because he didn't know what his brother's deal was, and he also had a bunch of stuff in his hands. They looked like groceries considering the bags, but Bru only got a step before Wolf entered his path. Bru sighed. "What are you talking about?"

"You're joking, right?" Wolf was snarling, *heated*. I had no idea what had his back up, but he was pissed. He shot a finger Bow's and my way. "You left her, bro. *Abandoned* her, Bow, and our sister last night."

I froze, and Bow did too. She looked at me, lowering her phone.

He said her *as in…*

Bru's attention cut to me, his expression a remorseful one. He obviously knew things had gotten out of hand last night, and I knew why he'd left. I'd told him to. He'd been really freaking amped up and needed to cool down. He did, and I understood that. He also shouldn't have stuck around in case the cops were called. He faced his brother. "I know. I…"

"You know." Wolf's laughter was manic as he fingered his hair. He really looked like he was losing his mind, and I didn't *get* it. I got him being pissed at Bru for leaving Sloane and Bow since he didn't know the whole story, but the other thing he said? The thing about me…

There was something I was missing here and misinterpreting. Had to be because this situation right here? Didn't make a goddamn lick of sense. "There was a fight last night."

Wolf looked at me, both boys did. I stood my ground in front of Wolf, though, and wouldn't let him yell at Bru since he didn't have all the facts. There had been a fight, and I wanted to emphasize that.

"We know about it," Wolf said, immediately separating his attention from me and returning it to Bru. Wolf put a finger out. "Regardless, you should have been there for them. Do you know what you've done? How I found her last night..."

My heart stopped, breath stopped.

Everything. Stopped.

It was like time had frozen, and Wolf used that word again. Her.

Me.

Bru scanned Wolf, his eyes narrowed. "What are you—"

"She's scared of storms, bro." Wolf was nearly nose to nose with Bru, his nostrils flaring. He wasn't speaking loud, but I heard him. I heard him speak my truth down to my bones. "She is, and I found her on the floor *in tears* by herself last night."

Bow glanced at me, and heat hit my face, shame. My weaknesses weren't something I advertised, and the humiliation was only made worse by the look Bru gave me. Sympathy wasn't the right word. It went deeper than that and made my stomach twist so bad.

Stop this.

The silent plea I couldn't voice. I was locked where I stood and reaching from my depths for Wolf to stop. Bru blinked. "What..."

"Yeah." Wolf nodded. He brought a curtain of his thick curls out of his face. "I mean, you know about her dad, right? What happened?"

I swallowed as Bru's attention hit me again. He did know about my dad, but he hadn't made the connection.

Bru's eyes closed. "Yeah."

Another curt nod from Wolf, and at this point, Bow stepped back.

"I'm going to go wake everyone. My texts are having issues going through," she said, slipping away. I supposed I was right about what she'd been doing, and I think we both knew how out of control this was getting.

Wolf's finger touched Bru's chest. "You should have known about that. *As her friend*, you should have known."

"Wolf, stop." I got my voice back, but only in time to watch Wolf's expression turn deadly. I'd never seen him so angry, and it was all directed at his brother.

"You talk about being her friend? Being there for her?" Wolf's head cocked. "Meanwhile, I was the one making sure she got down here okay. Mom and Dad said they didn't know she couldn't do cars until I—"

The words on his lips paused. Like he'd been in a stupor and finally came out of it. He faced me. "Fawn…"

I left and so damn fast. I didn't know what he was saying, what I was hearing.

"Fawn!"

Wolf called after me, chasing after me. He got in front of me since he was faster, but when he tried to touch me, I stiffened.

He lifted his hands. "I'm sorry. I shouldn't have said that stuff in front of everyone."

He was sorry. The first sorry I finally get from him, and it was about spilling my truths and not the myriad of other things he did. "What were you going to say?"

"What?"

"About the *cars*, Wolf? What were you—" I paused now, and I realized my heart was racing, slamming. "What were you going to tell Bru you did?"

Because it better not be what I thought. It better not be anything remotely close to what I was thinking. I didn't have the mental capacity to even wrap my thoughts around the possibility of him arranging those shuttles we had on the way here.

No, it wasn't possible.

Wolf was sifting through his hair again, and the longer he made me wait, the angrier I got. I couldn't channel my anger on one thing. I just knew that I was mad, and he was the source. He dropped his hand. "I made sure my parents had shuttles ready for you, and before you ask why, you know the reason."

It was like that day in the woods again where he was spewing nothing but confusing shit and rattling me. I swallowed. "Why would you do that for me?"

Why was he doing *any* of these things? Letting me sleep...

"Because you obviously weren't going to handle these things yourself." He scanned me, as if calculating a response, but all I had for him was more anger. He was literally confusing the fuck out of me right now.

"So, what? Is this some macho thing? A play? An agenda?" The latter accusations made complete sense. My mouth dried. "A way for you to look good in front of your family and make up for all the shit you did to me?"

He blanched as if I slapped him. As if this wasn't the complete truth and only further emphasized what an asshole he was. His mouth parted. "Fawn, that's not why I..."

I didn't care to hear it. His lies. This man had given me enough bullshit for a century, and I turned away only for him to grab me. I sneered. "Let go of me."

"That's not why I did it. Christ." He laced his fingers atop his head. Like I was frustrating him, which was laughable. "I knew you weren't going to speak to my parents yourself, and you obviously didn't tell my brother the issue."

The issue, meaning me. I laughed, and Wolf frowned.

"You didn't make accommodations for yourself, so I did," he said, his expression serious. "I did, and I don't fucking care what people think about that. I didn't do it for them."

And he expected me to believe he did it for me? Honestly, and without any agenda? I laughed again, shaking my head. "You wanted to look like the hero, Wolf, and as per usual, what a class fucking act you continue to be."

"What do you mean?"

"I mean, that shit you pulled during the storm," I shot,

and it took all I had not to lose my shit. He was still up to his fucking antics. Using me... "You came through last night like a hero. Being there when you knew what would happen when you found out about the party. Bru told me he texted Dorian we were going, and he clearly told you."

"Fawn—"

"Then you clearing the house so I could fucking sleep!" I called, raising and dropping my hands. "Bow told me that was your idea and what a hero you looked like then."

Wolf's mouth turned down, his head shaking. "Fawn..."

"And you dragged everyone here so they could see the Academy Award–winning production pan out—"

His hands hit the side of the house, his body crowding mine, caging me.

"I dragged *no one* here," he said, growled. "I came, and Dorian followed. Thatcher and Wells met us out here. They had the car, and they came so Dorian and I wouldn't have to head back into the storm on foot. They're also all my best friends and wanted to have my back."

Heat rolled off him, pouring into me. His smell hit me again, and I didn't like it.

It hurt.

It hurt so badly just like his arms around me last night and his comforting words. He knew exactly what to do last night. Exactly how to come through for the broken girl. My throat thickened, my eyes itchy, glassy. "You expect me to believe you walked in a fucking storm..."

"Ran actually," he said, pushing off the wall. "Five miles."

Five... miles.

Wolf's throat jumped. He blinked away, and I thought I would cry. "Why?"

I shoved him before he could answer, then hit his big stupid arms. He didn't move one inch, completely unaffected. He sighed. "Fawn..."

"*Why*, Wolf? Why would you ever—"

"Because I fucking love you, Fawn!"

I dropped my hands, gasping, reeling.

Wolf raised a hand. "Because I'm in love with you."

I'm in love with you.

I shook my head, stepping back, and Wolf followed. Between the dark circles under his eyes and the look he was giving me, he appeared physically pained. Like he was in pain to admit this.

Maybe he was. Maybe it hurt just as much as it did for me to hear it. "I don't understand."

It was like he was speaking a different language, one I didn't know and was too fucked up to understand. He was the one who fucked me up. Broke me.

Wolf's teeth clamped his lower lip, and eventually, my back touched the wall. He'd closed the distance.

And when he breathed me in...

His eyes closed, his forehead touching the space above my head. He was always so big, tall. "You were right about everything, and I know... *I know* I have no fucking right."

I was shaking at this point, and I felt that when he touched my cheek and placed so much warmth into my skin. When he made me feel things I didn't want to feel...

No... stop.

I didn't know if I was telling him or myself. I just knew this fucking hurt, and I hated it.

Wolf's hand was so big. It covered basically the whole side of my face, and he was shaking too, trembling. He placed his other hand on the cabin as if to stabilize himself.

"I'm so fucking sorry," he croaked out, his fingers pressing into my cheek and tangling in my hair. His voice had broken, the deep tone shattered like glass. His forehead touched mine. "I'm so fucking sorry, baby. What I did to you..."

I croaked out a sound now, my eyes so damn cloudy. I could barely see through the tears threatening to fall.

But for some reason, I allowed this to happen. I let Wolf

touch me and guide me to look up at him. His big hands caged my face, his dark eyes glassy and expression tortured. He shook his head. "I know I have no right. I know I have no right…"

He kept saying it. Over and over, he *kept saying* this, and I knew I'd hear those words for a long time. They'd be in my memories, deep and embedded for a lifetime.

I lost them when Wolf sealed our lips, when we both gasped, and I let him breathe out more words.

"I'm so sorry," he said, his tongue in my mouth. His forehead rubbed gently against mine. "I hate this. What I'm doing to you. What I did to us…"

The dam broke then. A rush of tears left my eyes in a single breath and coated both my cheeks and Wolf's.

"I need you," he rasped, his thumbs wiping away the hot trails. "I need you with everything in me, and I'm sorry. I'm so damn sorry, Fawn."

He was sorry.

I wasn't the only one finding it hard to breathe. Wolf was kissing me against the cabin wall, and for some reason, I wasn't stopping him.

Please, stop.

"Forgive me," he moved over my lips, and something inside me snapped. It snapped on, snapped to life. He could be as sorry as he wanted. He could need me too, but what about my need? I'd needed him once. I'd needed him so bad.

Wolf had ripped what we had away from us. He'd torn me *in half,* and I didn't forgive him, no.

I didn't know if I ever could.

Wolf had to have felt the sudden struggle in our kiss, me fighting both him and myself. There was a time when I'd wanted nothing more than for him to admit the truth about his feelings, but that time was long gone.

I knew that in my heart when I pushed him off me, breathless, and he was too. His big chest rose and fell with heavy breaths, and when he started to approach me, I raised a shaky hand.

"No." The single word left my lips strained, weak. I was so fucked up right now, and that was his fault. I blinked down more tears. "No."

I didn't know what I was saying no to exactly. I just knew this wasn't going to happen.

It couldn't happen.

Even still, I wasn't brave enough to see Wolf's response. I cut around him, but quickly discovered the pair of us weren't alone. Bru was there with his grocery bags, and he was the peak of a Legacy arrow. Dorian Prinze and Sloane were right behind him. They were in the distance, but they were there, and Bow, Thatcher, and Wells were directly behind them. It was like they'd all stopped at different points of their journeys, and I had no idea how long they'd been there. Maybe they'd all just gotten here.

Maybe they'd all been here the whole time.

Regardless, immediate shame hit. Shame that I'd allowed what happened to go on for as long as it had before cutting Wolf off. He worked around seeing my focus was on something else, and as soon as he saw his family, his attention transferred back to me. He took a step toward me, but Bru did as well. He frowned at Wolf and started to come in my direction, but I shook my head.

Bru stopped then, his eyes sad. It was in his nature to want to help me, save me, but he couldn't this time.

I didn't want him to.

This time, I was saving myself, and I did that when I walked away from the group on my own. I didn't know where I was headed, but I had a feeling it was far away from South Carolina.

CHAPTER
TWENTY-FIVE

Ares

"So, Brielle and I put Fawn on a plane back home this morning," my dad said, and I sat up. Bru did too. We exchanged a glance, but he appeared just as surprised by this news.

She left.

I knew this was a possibility. Fawn hadn't been here when all us kids got back to the Reeds'. We stayed to clean up the cabin and give the owner back his keys.

What an idea that had been, renting that place, and my swallow was hard as I studied my brother. He glanced away from me, and our parents focused on him. Everyone was in this room today. Sloane, Dorian, Thatcher, Wells, and Bow. The parents had basically accosted us when we got back, telling us there was going to be a group meeting.

The parents were here now too, each strategically placed between kids with the exception of Dorian and Sloane. Sloane sat on Bru's other side in a chair, while Dorian stayed behind her, his hands on her shoulders. Wherever she was, he was never far away. His parents, Royal and December, were on a couch nearby, and they didn't appear happy. None of the parents did.

The eyes came back to me when I arrived in this room today, and I supposed more than one set of parents believed I had something to do with Fawn's exit.

They'd be right.

In my gut, I'd known telling Fawn certain things would make everything worse, but I'd done it anyway. The root lay in selfishness, but not because I'd wanted to prove to her that I actually wanted to help her and not get in good with the others. My selfishness was my need *for her* and how I couldn't breathe whenever I thought about her. It was a pulse I couldn't fight, and I didn't want to.

I was tired.

It was physically exhausting fighting my need for her. All my insides ached, exhausted.

I stared at the floor, and ahead of me, one of my parents sighed.

"Fawn wanted us to let you know she'd call you, Bru, and that she's sorry for leaving so suddenly," Mom said to the kid, and my attention hit him again. He nodded, but he had something of his own kind of torture on his face, maybe guilt. In the end, she hadn't even let him help her. I think we'd all seen that when she'd shaken her head at him.

I hadn't wanted that *at all*, and though I'd had my back up about her friendship with my brother, I hadn't wanted her alone. By herself…

God, you're such a fuckup.

I felt physically ill in a room that probably should hold happiness. The Reeds' great room was decorated with a sixteen-foot Christmas tree, a slew of presents on the skirt beneath. I supposed, in a matter of days, we'd all be celebrating here, and Red would probably be on campus by herself.

"Which brings us to the reason why she left," Dad said, and I was so lost at that point. It was a combination of a lot of things, and I had my own guilt.

Heartache.

It hurt so fucking bad, and I sat there in the depths of it. My parents were asking what happened. They were asking why Fawn left as she hadn't given them a clear reason. They had apparently called us all here for the truth, but they were definitely looking at me while they asked the group. Maybe they were trying to be nice and not call me out, or maybe they wanted to put the pressure on me to fess up. They didn't have to do that, though, and I cut my dad off when his questions became more probing. I stood up and everything.

"She left because of me," I said, aware all eyes were on me, but I didn't fucking care. If I couldn't own my shit in front of Fawn, I'd do it without her. I pocketed my hands. "I told her I loved her, and she left."

This wasn't what my parents had expected me to say, nor did I think half the room. My buddies' mouths parted, and several parents blinked, my own included. Dorian, Thatcher, Wells, and even my sister had been gracious at the cabin regarding what happened there between Fawn and me.

I supposed they'd seen all they had to see.

The reality of what Fawn and I were had been right there in front of them, and they had left me alone in the aftermath of it. They'd cleaned the cabin with Bow, keeping their thoughts about the situation to themselves, and Bru had too. I had thought I'd hear it from the kid, but when I hadn't, there'd been no surprise there. I'd proven him right in the end.

They'd all been right.

"I see," my dad said, and his look of sympathy wasn't lost on me. I didn't deserve it, though, anyone feeling bad for me.

I stared at my friends and siblings. "They don't need to be here. This was all me."

The statement downplayed how much this all really was me. How much I'd fucked up when it came to everyone in this room.

And her...

The ache came back, and it stayed there as everyone filtered out of the room. My parents and I stayed, of course, but I was surprised to see Bru linger.

"I know this isn't a great time, but I need to tell you guys something," he said to Mom and Dad. Sloane was making her way out of the room with Dorian, but they both doubled back after he said that.

Bru faced her. "Sloane..."

"No, don't do that. Are you okay?" she asked him, and the probing was warranted.

The kid appeared sheet white. He legit looked like he himself would be ill today, and had I been paying attention to anyone else, I might have seen that. I stepped over, and his hands raised to me.

"Look. Don't do this. I..." He brought a hand through his hair. "I just have something to tell Mom and Dad."

"Well, if it's serious, Ares and I should be here," Sloane chimed in, and I didn't disagree. She frowned. "What's going on?"

Dad played referee in that moment. He shut down the talk with a pat to the air. "Let's all just be calm." He faced Bru. "Your mom and I can step out of the room with you, son, if that's what you need."

My brother was put on the spot in that moment, and his gaze fell on me last. With how the conversation had been going, I felt like this was the last place I'd be regarding the turn of events, but something told me my brother needed help in that moment.

It was the way he looked at me. There was a pleading behind his eyes, desperation, and that said something considering the argument we'd gotten into that morning. I should be the last person he'd go to for help, and that got my attention.

I glanced at Dorian who was still here, making my nod toward the door discreet. Something was definitely going on if the kid was bringing up something serious right now after I'd fucked up again.

I wanted to be part of the conversation, but I wouldn't be if Bru didn't feel I should be. I hadn't been respecting my brother lately, and Dorian got the hint. Dorian put a hand on Sloane's arm. "I'm going to go. You guys seem like you need this time."

I noticed he wasn't being a brute and trying to strongarm my sister into going. He wasn't because he knew that wasn't his place. Dorian Prinze, Thatcher Reed, and Wells Ambrose were three of the best guys I'd ever known.

Dorian did give me the eye, though, on the way out, and just because he was a good guy didn't mean he wasn't a nosy fucker. That eye definitely meant I'd be telling him exactly what happened in this room, but I'd have to get the play-by-play from someone else. I really did want to be here, but wanted to respect my brother. "I'll go too—"

"No. Sloane's right. You both should stay," Bru said, and he forced out a breath so hard my mom placed a hand on him. She asked him if he was okay, and all he did was breathe hard again.

This really was serious. He appeared just as frazzled as I'd been making him lately, which set off alarm bells. "Kid…"

"I'll explain, just." He paused, huffing out another breath. "Just sit. I'll explain."

He'll explain.

I did sit, confused as fuck, and Sloane took the seat beside me. Our parents chose to remain standing, but they gave Bru the floor.

"What's going on, son?" Dad repeated Sloane's earlier question, and all of us were wondering the same thing. The kid was pacing the floor now, and I thought he'd run a path into the hardwood.

He stopped on a dime.

"I got kicked out of school," he said, and my parents, Sloane, and I looked at each other. Bru swallowed. "I got kicked out for underground fighting."

CHAPTER
TWENTY-SIX

Bru

I felt like I was holding my breath before what I said, but the relief proved to be temporary. Within seconds, I felt as if I was drowning again, and the sensation only rattled worse the longer my family didn't respond. Their looks of stunned confusion managed to trump what Wolf had just said only moments before.

Which said something.

This announcement hadn't been the time. I fucking knew that, but it was eating away at me. Like I was being carved from the inside with a dull knife.

Like I had no control.

I couldn't even be there for Fawn this morning, my hands shaking now. She was on a plane flying over somewhere, and here I was unable to get my shit together. I was the best goddamn friend of the year and was just as crappy of a friend to my brother. He'd just made that announcement and was being completely vulnerable with everyone. He really had loved Fawn, and here I was making shit about me. Fuck.

Why can't I stop shaking?

Because I didn't have control, and I kept my shaking hands behind my back. I didn't want my family to see. Last night, I had to run through the woods to calm down following the fight. Meanwhile, Fawn, my sister, and Bow had been alone.

Why didn't I know she was afraid of storms?

Again, I was friend of the fucking year.

"What do you mean you were fighting, honey?" Mom asked that, Dad's arm around her. She squeezed my arm. "Underground fighting?"

It sounded foreign coming out of her mouth, and it had been to me until I'd started doing it.

It was the only thing that could curb the nightmares.

In the dead of the night, they'd come, visions of terror and brutality overtaking my mind.

Carnage.

A sea of rage and anger took hold of me. I started failing my classes because I couldn't sleep due to all the nightmares.

Memories.

Mom put her hands on both my arms, and Sloane was standing up. The only person still sitting was Wolf, and he appeared completely dumbstruck. He didn't understand what I'd said, and I probably wouldn't either. This was *me*, and though raising my fists in the past when I believed in something wasn't a foreign concept, the things I'd been doing during my nights while away at college had been. I'd beaten some dudes down almost to the point of death.

I always knew that point and didn't go that far. The fight would stop then, but it was never me to stop it. I'd always been in a haze and borderline blacked out.

"Fighting, yes, I..." I tried to focus on my mom's eyes and less on my siblings' stares. I wavered a little, though, and Dad guided me to sit.

Everyone was sitting then. Like they were the audience

and I was some fucked-up storyteller. Dad raised a hand. "Let's back up. You were fighting? Did you need money, son? Was it money you were fighting for?"

That would make sense, wouldn't it, and though I spent the money, I certainly hadn't needed it. My parents provided everything I needed while away at school.

The bulk of the money had gone back into training for my fights. I'd fought guys two and sometimes three times my size. The size hadn't mattered in the end. I trained hard, got big, and they always went down, always.

I shook my head, kind of ashamed it wasn't about the money. That would be a sane reason.

I put my face in my hands, and someone put their hand on my back, rubbing. I didn't want my family's sympathy.

"Why were you fighting, then?" Mom asked, and when I glanced up, she had her eyes on Dad. My siblings' focus was glued to me. Mom cocked her head. "And you got kicked out of school for it?"

I'd come to find out my university had a zero-tolerance policy for that shit. Illegal betting. Fighting.

Sure didn't stop me.

Again, it was the only thing that could distract me from the visions in my head. Whenever I closed my eyes at night, I saw suffering and an old man's pleas. I saw the whites of his eyes before I pulled the trigger and unloaded a gun in his old fucking chest. He was the man who hurt my sister and nearly destroyed all our lives.

A man I'd called a friend.

I had allowed a nightmare into my sister's and my life back in high school. He'd been responsible for taking her away from her true family, the Mallicks, when she'd been a baby. The fucker would have hurt her more had I not stopped it, and I didn't regret what I'd done. I would have done it ten times over.

Killed him.

"Yeah, I got kicked out. School had a zero-tolerance policy for fighting and illegal betting," I explained, suddenly feeling crowded. I got up so I could breathe, and the rustling around me let me know my family was getting up too.

"Bru, we don't understand."

That was my sister's voice, and it physically pained me to hear the concern. Concern for me. She finally got her perfect life, and I didn't want to ruin it with my shit.

I turned to find she'd been directly behind me, and our parents were behind her. They were all waiting for answers, and though Wolf clearly was too, he stayed back. His fingers clenched like he was at war.

Wolf's jaw moved. "Was it because of me? Me and everything that happened last year with my cancer?"

Everyone looked at him and appeared even more confused. Maybe because they didn't get why my brother falling ill would ever be the reason I started fighting. Their brains *literally* didn't think to go that route, but Ares's did.

This didn't surprise me. I'd gotten to know my brother and, hell, our friends a lot since they'd come into my life. Thatcher, Dorian, Wells, and Wolf all tended to deal with their problems in anger.

Violence.

They didn't deal with their feelings. They avoided. It was a bond I hadn't been sure I shared until I had gone away, but the desire to deal with shit that way hadn't always been there. I hadn't always been fucked up.

Death. Carnage.

I closed my eyes and couldn't even look at my brother, ashamed. I shook my head. "Nah, Wolf," I said, then faced our parents, and I swallowed. "And I fought people... hurt them because I liked it."

Ares

. . .

The kid walked off after he said it. He left the room, and right away, our parents and Sloane started after him. Right away, they started freaking out, but before they could go full-blown crazy, I stepped in. I ended up cutting off the group at the door and got more than one look.

"Let me go," I said, and unlike everyone else, I wasn't freaking out. What the kid had said had been alarming, but I wasn't freaking out.

I probably should be like the rest of them, but for some reason, I shut down all those feelings. I was completely one hundred percent concerned for the kid. Especially after the guys and I did hear about that fight last night. It'd been brutal from our understanding and resulted in a dude being taken away in an ambulance.

This was all concerning, and I was concerned, but I also related. I got anger. I got rage, and I needed to be there for my brother in ways I clearly hadn't been lately. I had no idea he'd been going through so much stuff.

No one had.

I saw that on all of our family members' faces. My parents and Sloane seemed to swap confusion and dismay, and Dad shook his head. "Ares…"

"Let me go, Dad. I'll bring him back." I doubted Bru went far and probably just needed some space. All of his family going after him wouldn't help anyway. "I'll bring him right back. I swear."

My parents consulted each other with a look, but in the end, they did nod. I started to go, but Sloane grabbed my arm. She had her necklace on. It was identical to mine, and it was rare either one of us took them off. It was our thing, a twin thing.

My sister and I had been so disconnected lately. This had

been my fault, and I didn't blame her. I put her through a lot of shit and was about to put her through more.

I kept that to myself, nothing else priority now but the kid. I missed my sister, and I was sure she missed me just as much. Back at the cabin, we hadn't really talked, but I didn't think that was because she was mad at me anymore. If anything, she probably felt sorry for me, which was why no one had talked to me. They'd all given me my space, and I assumed it was because of that same reason.

"Are you sure it should be you?" She spoke the words under her breath, and the kid and I did have a fight this morning. "I don't know if it's a good idea."

Hell, I didn't either, but I was going to try. Like stated, I hadn't done right by my brother. "Just trust me. I'll bring him back."

I was pretty sure I could after I talked to him, and before I left, Sloane squeezed my hand. It said a lot, and I was starting to feel like we'd gotten over our hump. I was glad. I didn't like her mad at me, and that went for any of the people I cared about.

"So how freaked out is everyone?"

The kid was out back behind the house, a blunt between his lips.

I strode over to him following what he said, my hands in my pockets. He leaned back against the house, his arms crossed over his beefy chest. I supposed now I knew why he'd come home jacked. He'd been fighting. I folded my arms. "I'm sure as well as you can imagine."

Bru shook his head. He pulled the blunt from his lips, then immediately pressed palms to his eyes. "Shit, how did everything get so fucked?"

I knew the feeling. God, did I know it. "What happened?"

He removed his hands from his eyes, frowning. "I think you've got enough to worry about."

He didn't sound angry when he said it, or even sarcastic.

If anything, it accompanied a look all my friends had given me back at the cabin today. It'd been looks of sympathy.

Sadness.

The people in my life definitely felt sorry for me. They saw me bleed my heart out, and they felt sorry, but they shouldn't. I deserved every bit of what happened at that cabin today between Fawn and me.

No matter how shitty it felt.

I fucked that girl over so bad, and my latest sin had been telling her the truth. I swallowed. "I'm asking about you."

"Of course, you are," he said, being sarcastic now. He took a hit off his blunt before forcing the smoke through his nose. "Better than dealing with everything that happened and your own feelings."

It was kind of crazy that I didn't always know this guy. Because he was getting me in ways just like the guys did.

Bru sat on the ground, and I did too, right next to him.

"So how long you been kicked out?" I asked him. Like he said, it was easier than dealing with my own stuff.

"Right before break." He smirked, but it didn't look like he found anything funny. "I was on a hot streak, and I think some people were losing too much money. I'm assuming somebody found out I was in school and called it in."

"But you weren't doing it for money?"

"No, Ares. I wasn't." He appeared frustrated, terse. He brought his palms to his eyes again. "You probably think I'm crazy."

I didn't, but I did want to understand. "You said you liked it?"

Something akin to shame hit my brother's eyes when he drew his palms away. He stamped his blunt out, then brought his arms around his legs. "It kept me distracted. Whenever I closed my eyes, I got nightmares and shit." He faced me. "Nightmares about everything that happened in high school. What I did?"

I lost his gaze before I could respond to that, his lips turned down.

"Fighting gives me a high. A rush." He rubbed his arms. "It just feels... good."

He didn't look at me and more of that shame hit his eyes. He cringed, but I didn't. Again, I was listening.

"You know, I don't regret what I did," he said, finally looking at me. His eyes were red, his face the same. He shook his head. "I don't regret one bit removing the guy from the world who hurt our sister."

Chills hit me, but not because of what he said. Our sibling's kidnapper needed to die.

I just hated that Bru had to be the one to do it.

What happened in high school wasn't so distant. I mean, it was my senior year, which wasn't that long ago. My family found out who was responsible for taking Sloane from us. Once they had, they aimed for action, but the kid had just been faster. He was closer to the party who was responsible and saw an opportunity. He took the fucker out, doing what any of us would have found difficulty doing. That included myself. I would have done it too, but it would have been hard. Bruno Sloane-Mallick had taken a life that night.

And he was clearly still having a hard time dealing with it.

I supposed we'd never worried about him, again, myself included, and I recalled my parents advising counseling for him back then. He'd refused, saying he was fine.

How was I not blood-related to this kid, but we were so similar?

"What do you think Mom and Dad will do?" Bru asked me, swallowing. "They have to think I'm nuts."

He wasn't, and I didn't like him saying that about himself. "You're not crazy, and you forget they had to deal with me."

And they did for a long time. I had my own troubles in high school, and even though they were before Sloane and Bru came into our family, they were there. I didn't talk about the issues of my past much, but I was sure he'd heard. Things had gotten dark back then.

Bru faced me. "How did you deal with all that?"

I found a reason to push on for starters, and that started with a night and a party.

A girl…

Swallowing, I looked at my brother. "I did see someone. Aka lots of therapy." And still did from time to time. Not lately, though. Not lately. I bumped his leg. "I had to deal with all that anger going on inside me. Lots of anger. Guilt."

Something told me he could relate to what I said when his head hung. I was sure he had his own reasons for any anger or guilt he felt, and I hated he could relate at all. That shit truly sucked, and I hated if any of that was affecting him.

"But I did have to deal with it," I continued. "If you don't, that shit just bottles up. It explodes and usually in shit ways."

I had a feeling he knew exactly what I was talking about. He nodded, and we both stared at the sky.

"Will you come with me? If I asked them about seeing someone, talking to someone…" Bru studied the ground. "Will you come?"

I answered him in a way I was sure surprised him. I'd been very guarded lately. Had to be, but I hugged the shit out of the kid in that moment. I think we both needed it.

Though, obviously in different ways.

Bru held on too, held on to me, and we just sat there in the hug. We were two guys with a bunch of fucked-up problems.

So many problems.

I closed my eyes, and I wasn't the first one to let go. In fact, I didn't let go.

"Ares?" The kid was patting my arm, supporting me when I was supposed to be supporting him. "Ares, you should talk to her. Go after her."

My eyes shut tighter.

Fawn.

I had talked to her, and he saw what that got me. And anyway, it was divine intervention. The universe knew the scenario of her leaving was the only way. It was the only thing to keep her out of my life and preserve things the way they were for her. She'd have a happy life away from me. She'd have no more hurt. No more *pain.*

"Ares?" The kid was facing me now, but he didn't let go. "Ares, you love her."

There was no question there, and I did let go. I eased away, staring at the ground and closing off.

Bru sighed. "I don't know why you hid that, but you should go to her."

He didn't know what he was saying, and Red was definitely worse off if I did. "I don't want to hurt her anymore, kid."

"Can't do any more damage than what I just did when it came to her." He shook his head. "I should have put two and two together about the storms. And the cars?" He sighed again. "I feel terrible. I should have known about all that."

It was amazing that I did.

She trusted you.

And I'd stomped all over that trust. I did, and that would only continue if I made myself a permanent fixture in her life. It was inevitable.

Destiny.

There was no world in which Fawn and I had a future. Too much had happened. *I'd done* too many things when it came to her.

"But you did know that, Ares." Bru cocked his head. "You know, Fawn and I were pretty good friends before she switched schools, and never once did she tell me any of what she told you. She loves you. I've seen it."

I gripped my legs, but something he said gave me pause. I looked at him. "You said she switched schools?"

"Yeah, there was this fight," he said, and my mouth

parted. He frowned. "Some girl was bullying her pretty bad. Fawn got in a fight with her and left after that. She left town and went to a different school."

She left.

So Bru… *my brother* was the guy from the story she told me. The one where she said she had a connection with a guy, but this bitchy girl got in the way of it. The girl *locked Fawn in a car* because the girl herself liked the guy.

That guy was my brother.

I didn't know how to feel about that, and before I could voice thoughts about it, Bru spoke.

"I thought once upon a time, Fawn and I were cheated out of something because of that. That there may have been something between us before she switched schools," Bru continued, and my heart raced. Again, I didn't know how to feel. He smiled. "That turned out to not be the case, and in a weird way, I'm glad she left. Not the circumstances, of course, but I am glad she left, and that chapter between us was closed."

I didn't know what to say but decided to listen. Listening felt best right now. "Why?"

My brother put a hand on my shoulder, and there was so much in his eyes. I couldn't read any of it. There was just so much. "Because I'm not the one, Ares. For her, I'm not it. I don't think I ever was, and I wasn't supposed to be."

He squeezed my shoulder, and my throat thickened.

"Recently, she and I had a conversation, and I told her I wanted her to be happy," he said, letting go. "And I know, despite everything you've done, what's inside you. I know what you're capable of and loving her is unquestionable. There's few who can match that kind of love."

My nostrils flared, my throat thicker, tighter.

"You can make her happy, Ares." My brother's smile lifted. "Now, you just have to believe it."

CHAPTER
TWENTY-SEVEN

Fawn

I nearly forgot about Christmas, and I did forget New Year's Day when it eventually rolled around. The only reason I didn't forget the former was because my mom and stepdad texted that day. Mom texted Merry Christmas and hoped I wasn't working too hard. She and Anton also sent lenses to my dorm. Brand-new ones for Christmas.

I opened them by myself that day, my tree a bookshelf. At least, I celebrated that day. On New Year's Eve and Day, I just slept because in sleep, I didn't have to think about anything. I could just rest in a dream world where things didn't have to make sense, and I could be at peace.

Wolf: I'm at the party.

Wolf: It's storming, and I needed to make sure you're okay.

Wolf: Please answer if you can. I just want to help.

Wolf's texts eventually did come. I wasn't sure when I'd gotten them, but I read them long after he'd sent them.

I deleted them just as fast.

His brother was the only one to hear from me after I got home outside of my mom and stepdad. I was still worried about him and wanted to make sure he was okay.

Me: I got home fine. Hope you're okay. I'll call when I can.

Bru: Good. Glad to hear it. And I could be better, but I think I'm headed toward there. I'll tell you all about it when I talk to you next. I'll be waiting on your call, but no rush. You take care of you.

Me: You too.

I'd like to say that call came quick to my friend, but it didn't. I'd like to say I didn't hermit and left my dorm, but I only left to get my books for spring classes and food. I literally stayed in my hole and didn't leave until it was time to go back into the world. My college friends thought I'd died, and that was what they joked about the first week of classes when they did finally come. Nearly all had sent me texts wishing me happy holidays, but I hadn't responded. I fucked up and closed in on myself. I wallowed in self-pity, and once again, let someone into my head.

I'm at the party.

It's storming, and I needed to make sure you're okay.

Please answer if you can. I just want to help.

It didn't matter that I'd deleted Wolf's texts because they reserved permanent space in my head. They lived there rent-free just like the other shit he did, said.

I need you with everything in me.

I hated him for saying that. I hated him for breaking my heart, then doing it again with his confession. I hated even more that there was a time I needed him and still felt that need deep in my soul. I hated him for making me hate him.

And I hated me for loving him.

There were times in my life where I felt deep anger, but what Ares Mallick had put me through in the past few months challenged some of my worst. He made ugly appear inside of me. It latched on to my soul and did make me hateful. Angry.

I remember the day I first saw him on my bus route. It was the first week of classes, and I noticed because, well, everyone noticed. Ares Mallick was on my bus route.

Ares Mallick was riding the bus.

I froze at the top of the steps when I saw him. He was sitting there, right in the front, but he didn't look at me. He had his earbuds in, his head down while he wrote in a notebook. In fact, he was so engrossed in the task that he didn't notice me when I basically rushed past him. I was completely out of breath by the time I got to the back of the bus, and I must have been holding my breath because I was dizzy when I sat down.

Why is he here?

That'd been my thought because Ares didn't ride the bus. I knew that for a fact because he had a nice-ass Hummer he'd all but tried to shove me into before he'd found out I didn't do cars or even trucks.

I stirred in my seat after I saw him, hunkered down, and though Ares glanced up after I passed him, he didn't turn. He just eyed the space I'd passed beside him. Like he was observing nothing but the air before going back to whatever he was doing in his notebook. I knew that too because he put his head down, his attention redirected.

I watched him like a hawk that day and continued until he finally got to his stop and left the bus. He'd gathered his stuff, tugged his hoodie's hood up, then exited. He left.

That was the first day.

The second he was wearing a hat. It was on backward, and his rogue curls pushed out of the front. He was facing the aisle, and he took up so much of the bus seat I had no idea how he'd folded himself in. He'd managed, though, his head back to the window and his foot on the seat. He appeared to be sleeping this time, but his head was rocking like he was listening to music. He also had his earbuds in again, so that was a possibility.

Gratefully, I didn't have to pass him that time. He was in one of the very last seats at the back of the bus, so I took the first one, hoping and praying he didn't see me.

That didn't stop me from taking a peek back at him on occasion, and each glance concluded with the same result. He didn't move outside of his head bobbing, and he didn't open his eyes either. He was just *there* until, well, he wasn't. He once again got off first, and though I hunkered down in my seat, made myself small, he didn't look at me. He just left.

And that was the second day.

By the third day of him sitting there, I had enough. It'd been a full week of this shit. A week where I'd seen him and been forced to ignore his large presence. Since this was the third spotting, I noticed no one on the bus was aware of him but me. They must have gotten used to his presence because there were no more whispers about the Legacy guy who was taking the bus when he definitely had a nice truck. Even if he didn't, I was sure he could hire a chauffeur to take him to his classes. He had money like that.

I angled around to look at him at the back of the bus that day, refusing to make myself feel small. I was *tired* of playing small when it came to this guy.

I was tired of him tormenting me.

He was every day he was there, and he had to know that.

I need you with everything in me.

One of the last things he said to me played suddenly in my head, and I certainly didn't need him. What I *needed* was for him to stay away and utilize the size of this campus. The two of us didn't need to see each other. We were different majors in different departments. There was absolutely no reason for the two of us to run into each other.

I got up that third day. I stalked over, and even though I felt sick with wobbly legs, I approached him. His hood was up, his head down, and he had his notebook out again. He'd been so engrossed in his task again he didn't look up at me, and what he was doodling gave me pause.

Flowers.

There were flowers in the corner spaces of his notebook, beautiful flowers of black and gray, and though they didn't take up much space, they drew my attention. They were on a page of notes, I assumed, he took for a class he had. The notes took up the majority of the space, but again, the flowers drew me in the most. They looked like the tattoo on his hip, the same flower over and over.

Making myself look away, I stood tall. "What do you think you're doing?"

He didn't hear me at first. Or at least acted like he didn't. He glanced over a moment or two after I spoke, but once he did, he instantly tugged his hood down. His wild curls spilled out of it, and when he pushed them back, I spotted an earbud in his ear. He took it out. "Hey."

I almost wanted to laugh. He greeted me like an old friend. Like casual conversation between us was normal.

Like he wasn't a son of a bitch who continued to torment me.

I swallowed. "Why are you here on this bus?"

He eyed the space around him, and his eyebrows knitted together. Like my question confused him, and I took inventory of the darkness under his eyes. It appeared he wasn't sleeping, which reminded me of that day at the cabin.

A block of ice formed around my heart, and I made myself forget those memories. If Ares Mallick could or couldn't sleep, it was none of my concern, and even with the darkness, he was still the most handsome guy I'd ever seen. He was steal-your-breath handsome, beautiful, and the thought in my

head made me hate him even more. He shook his head.
"What do you mean?"

"I mean, why are you taking this bus?" I wouldn't back off
from this. It was weird he was taking the bus, and I wouldn't
let him make me look crazy. "You don't ride the bus. You
have a truck."

"I do."

"So why are you taking the bus?" He was making me feel
like a fool.

And my voice was shaky. I was nervous because he was
beautiful and being around him did steal my breath. I wished
it was just because he was attractive. I wished desperately it
was only that. I could pass off attraction.

I could pass it off.

Coming back here was a bad idea, and I wanted to
backpedal. I couldn't now that I was standing in front of him,
and when he pulled his curls away again, he sighed. His
nostrils flared, his shiny nose piercings glinting off the light in
the bus. Reaching up, he used his long wingspan to tug the
cord to make the bus stop. Most people had to stand to do
that, but Ares Mallick didn't.

"I'm taking the bus because it's more economical than my
truck," he said, and my mouth parted. He spoke casually, a
reasonable answer.

Things weren't so simple with him, and as the bus cruised
to a stop, Wolf got up. He took his time, gathering his things
slowly. Once he was done, he towered over me, but I didn't
back down. No matter how good he smelled or how shitty it
felt to be this close to him, I didn't move.

It did feel shitty. It did fucking hurt, but I refused to
waver. I stared him right in the eyes, and he did the same for
several moments before wetting his lips.

"See you around, okay?" he stated, then eased past me.

See me around.

Again, he said this casually. Like he actually would see me

around, which he wouldn't. I wanted to laugh, but I was too pissed off.

I ended up sitting down in his seat. Mostly because I was stunned, and I wished I hadn't sat there. I had to continue to smell him all the way to my stop.

And I nearly missed it because of it.

CHAPTER
TWENTY-EIGHT

Fawn

"Can you tell your brother to back off?"

Noa Sloane-Mallick whipped around after what I said, her chocolate-brown locks going with her. As it turned out, it was very easy to find members of Legacy. At least, their classes. I just asked around, and people told me exactly where to go to find Sloane at this hour.

I'd surprised her, clearly. She'd been unloading a sketchpad onto the table, and no doubt mirrored the look I had when she had dropped in on me. It was kind of crazy how I was doing that now.

I didn't feel like I had a choice.

I'd seen Wolf again. He'd been right there on the bus this morning, a new week but yet another sighting. Apparently, he'd made good on his promise about seeing me, and even though he stayed at the back of the bus, that didn't matter. I was still aware of his presence.

I was still aware of him.

I'd stayed up front, but just him being there frustrated me

so bad I'd skipped my next class entirely. I'd gotten off my stop early, then asked around where I could find Sloane. She had an art class, and so, here I was.

She sighed in my direction. "What did he do?"

The fact that I didn't have to elaborate Wolf was up to something at all was exactly why I was here. She knew how terrible he'd been to me, our history. I folded my arms. "He was on my bus this morning. Just riding it. But he was there, and I saw him three times last week."

He didn't take my fucking bus. He just didn't take the bus, and upon hearing this news, Sloane shook her head.

"So now I know why he was late for all his classes last week. At least the ones he shares with me," she said, and my mouth parted. Her eyebrows narrowed. "What happened? Did he say anything to you?"

I was still wrapping my head around the fact that he was making himself late for classes. And for what? To see me?

You know that answer.

I didn't want to know that fucking answer. I didn't want him *doing* this. My jaw moved. "I need him to back off. It's just making things worse, and it's... It's not fair."

I couldn't stand that my voice cracked, and when my throat got thick, I stared forward. I didn't trust myself not to cry again. I was always *fucking crying* lately when I didn't even really cry.

That was before.

That was before Wolf and all his frickin' antics.

I started to get up, but Sloane touched my shoulder. I faced her, and she was frowning, the expression deep.

"Fawn, I get your anger," she said, but stopped and bit her lip. Like she was debating her next words, and maybe she was. I was sure she and her entire family got my anger, and they had a fair bit themselves. Wolf had ruined the holidays for everyone. Not just me. She sighed again. "I get it, and it's completely warranted. Nothing justifies what Ares did to you."

She was right. Nothing did.

I felt a *but* coming on, but it didn't come. Sloane ended up facing forward. Again, like she wasn't sure what to say.

In the absence of her words, I eased out of my chair. I swallowed. "Just tell him to stop."

I didn't feel like there was anything else to say, and I didn't think there was. Even she didn't have anything for me. There was no *but* after all the things Ares had done to me.

And even his twin knew that.

———

"Hey, you. I was hoping you'd reach out."

It was good to hear Bru's voice, real good.

I didn't know why I called him after I got home. Following the talk with his sister, I'd just been out of sorts. In fact, I hadn't focused very well on the rest of my day. I had a couple more classes, but my brain had just been other places. That hadn't been Sloane's fault. Addressing everything with Wolf had just gotten to me. It put me back in my head, and I...

Anyway, I needed a friend, and even though I had them here, I wanted to talk to Bru. I also said I'd check in with him and wanted to be a better friend. "Do you hate me for ghosting you?"

It hadn't been intentional, and I was sure he knew why I just up and skipped town.

Of course, he knew. *All* of Legacy knew why I'd left. They'd been there after all.

I was feeling sick again and questioning if I was ready to call Bru at all. I hated it, but talking to him just brought it all back. It was so fresh.

"You really think I'd be mad at you for taking some time

to deal with things?" He laughed a little into the line. "I think you know me better than that. We may not have been friends for a while, Fawn, but I think you know better."

I did, but I couldn't help being uneasy. I mean, I had ghosted him.

"Are you doing okay?"

Okay, so we'd both asked that at the same time and did start laughing. That felt good to laugh. I was all bottled up lately, so yeah it felt good.

"Really, though. How are you?" he asked, and I wasn't sure I wanted to say. This was still his brother I was dealing with. "How was your Christmas?"

Lonely, but I didn't want to tell him that either. It just sounded pathetic. "Talked to my mom a little. She sent me some new lenses since I was on campus."

"I'm assuming you spent the holidays alone."

Leave it to Bru to call me out. "Yes, but don't feel bad about that."

"Can't help that, and I double, hell, I triple feel terrible for not knowing about the cars and the storms," he said, and I pulled in a breath. "I'm sorry I didn't pick up on that."

"It wasn't your job to pick up on it."

"Yeah, but still. I dropped the ball, and I'm sorry. Truly."

He had nothing to feel sorry for. "Please don't let this conversation turn into that. You feeling sorry for me?" I shook my head. "That's not what I want, okay? I want the opposite."

His sympathy just made me feel weak, and I wasn't some weak bitch. I was stronger than this and knew I was.

I am.

These days, I was having to coach the thoughts into myself, but it was the only thing I had. I *had* to believe it. I had to be it. The alternative would be me breaking, and I wouldn't. I refused.

"Okay, I won't. And we don't have to talk about that," he

said, and it was a relief. I knew it was a cop-out. Not talking, but I wasn't ready right now. Bru breathed harshly into the line. "I do have my own apologies, though. There was a reason I didn't push you to connect with me right away and definitely did my own version of ghosting. I did, and I'm sorry about that."

I sat up. "Are you alright?"

I realized now he'd never answered me before when I asked if he was okay, and his text messages had said he wanted to tell me something. I'd been so fucked up myself I hadn't been able to reach out.

God, I'm a terrible friend.

I certainly wasn't there for him, and dealing with my own crap or not, I should have been better about checking in with him.

"I could be better," he said, which made the guilt hit me more. He'd said the same thing the last time we'd texted. "But I do think I'm headed there. In fact, I'm really hopeful for that, which has been a relief."

I brought my legs up. "What's going on?"

My thoughts immediately went to the fight. Maybe his parents found out and hadn't been happy.

"Got your popcorn?" he questioned, but laughed a little. He didn't sound tense, which was good, but still. "Might as well settle in because what I'm about to tell you is a doozy."

And a doozy it turned out to be when he really got into it. I sat back against my headboard and just listened, my jaw slacked. Bru got kicked out of school?

And for... fighting?

The Bru I knew once upon a time wouldn't even look at someone funny. Let alone fight them. But then again, there *had* been that fight at the frat party. He'd punched that guy within an inch of his life, and that'd been shocking. Alarming. I'd been scared, but not for myself. It'd just been so out of character for him.

"How did your parents react to everything?" I asked, finding an appropriate place in the conversation to speak. I hadn't wanted to interrupt him. I definitely realized that lately a lot of our friendship had been about me.

"Well, they were shocked. Especially when they realized why I was fighting. There was an incident I had in high school surrounding violence. It wasn't good, and I still hadn't dealt with it."

I had no idea. "Bru... wow. I mean, wow. I didn't know."

"Surprised you're not the only one with secrets?" The familiar smile I'd come to know and love returned to his voice, which made me smile. "You don't need to feel guilty or ashamed for things you're going through. I'm learning that myself. I started seeing someone here in Maywood Heights, a therapist. It's new, but it's already helping just talking about stuff. I trust him and my family does. It just feels good to talk."

I knew all about talking. Back when I was in the rough of everything surrounding my dad, I'd seen a cocktail of therapists. I hadn't really had my turnaround until I'd gone to rehab, though. That was how bad things had gotten. I'd gotten really into the party scene and things had gotten dark.

They weren't as dark now, but I was still going through things. Clearly. "I'm glad you're talking to someone. So, you're taking a break from school, then?"

"Yeah, until I work some stuff out. But hey, you never know. You may eventually see me at Pembroke. I mean, my friends and family go there, so you never know."

That'd be nice to see him. It'd be more than nice.

The line went silent, and in that silence, I worried. I wasn't sure what he was going to say, and I didn't want to field any questions about certain topics. There weren't many, but there were some.

"Did he talk to you?" he asked, and my stomach launched into my throat.

Did. He. Talk. To. You.

And there it was. Basically, it was confirmation that I'd probably been discussed at some point, and I wasn't surprised.

They were brothers.

Even still, these were waters I couldn't wade into. I couldn't tread the fucking water without drowning. I swallowed. "Bru, I don't want to talk to him, and you know why."

He should understand why. He was there just like everyone else that day.

That day...

Again, I couldn't tread the water and didn't want to. No.

More of that silence filled the line, and that reminded me of Sloane. She hadn't had much to say because there really wasn't anything to say. "Fawn, I get it, and I won't ask you any more about it. I just want you to be okay. I want him to be okay too."

Him.

"I care about you both. Love you both." He sighed. "So, yeah. Anyway, tell me about your semester. I'd love to hear about it. I'm going stir-crazy being here at the house."

I could do that topic, and it was certainly easier. There was only one way for me to be okay, and it wasn't talking about Wolf Mallick.

It was making myself believe he and what we had never existed.

CHAPTER
TWENTY-NINE

Fawn

I made myself sick. I literally woke up with a fever, chills, and my entire body aching. As it turned out, I had some bug that was going around. It hit me like a son of a bitch, and I could barely leave my bed.

I did this to myself.

I knew I had. My immune system just couldn't handle all the stress I was carrying in my body. Of course, that was my own theory.

Me: I feel like death. Can you bring me food?

I was forced to ask for help around day three. I'd run out of basic things to keep me alive, so I had no choice.

Heath: Sure. Saw your status about being sick. Do you need anything else?

It wasn't often I went to social media to gripe, but I did that week. I was glad I did, and I was triple glad when my former roommate, Heath, did pull through. He brought me meds on top of food the night I asked, and I was surprised to see that wasn't where his help ended. The next day, a light tap hit my door, and when I opened it, I was surprised to find a bagel with avocado spread. I often got those on campus, which was why I was surprised.

There was no Heath in sight, but there hadn't been the previous night either. I figured he hadn't wanted to catch my germs and left.

I received the bagel quickly that day, and that was when I noticed the notebook underneath. It was filled with notes from the previous day's classes. Heath and I were pretty much in all the same classes, but I was still surprised he helped me out by doing that. I certainly hadn't asked him to.

Thanks for the grub and helping me out, I texted him, and his response was quick.

Heath: No problem. Feel better.

Heath and I had always been cool, and I did consider us friends. I mean, we'd been roommates, but I always did hold him at arm's length. It was nothing he did. I held everyone at arm's length.

Because I'm guarded as fuck.

It was hard with emotions for me. I felt things hard when I felt them, and after losing my dad, I just put up a brick wall. My school friends picked up on that after a while, and though we were all cordial and hung out, I didn't really have strong connections with them. At least, not outside of the basic sense. I had friends, but I never let them in. Not really.

Days of coughing, fever, and me filling up trash bags with tissues befell me over the next few days. I still was having a hard time getting up due to my body aching and just, well, the overall feeling of death. It really fucking sucked, but the bright light was Heath's supplies. For some reason, they didn't stop after the bagel day, but I certainly didn't turn them away. It was a nice contrast to a day filled with coughing fits and blowing my nose out, and I knew his reinforcements were there by the short tap at the door. Sometimes I didn't answer right away. Actually, I never answered right away. Again, I felt like death, but he was long gone by the time I answered anyway. He always brought me food, typically groceries or something I could microwave, and a set of notes accompanied whatever he delivered. They'd be from the previous day's classes, which I was grateful for.

Heath really was going out of his way. The notes were always handwritten, and because of that, I made sure not to sneeze all over them. I figured he'd want them back eventually.

I felt bad but I barely did look at the notes. I spent more time on the couch aching and wallowing in my feelings. Bru and my mom and stepdad checked on me from time to time upon seeing my social media status too, and I finally did start to feel better the following week.

I was fucking grateful, and when Heath knocked on the door that week, I finally had the energy to answer. Honestly, I kind of wanted to catch him in the act since he'd been so stealthy about his deliveries. I also wanted to thank him and intended to when I opened the door that day.

Except I didn't catch *him* at my door.

"Sloane?" I angled out of my dorm, staring at the back of a tall girl in a thigh-length hoodie. It was so long because it was big on her. She always wore big hoodies. My mouth parted as I closed the door. "What are you doing?"

I was only seventy-five percent sure it was her. She didn't stop right away, but when she pivoted, I saw clear as day I'd been right. She had her hair up, and the words *Pembroke Football* were stamped on her hoodie. She was obviously wearing her boyfriend's stuff. She came back slowly. "Hey."

"Hi," I returned. She stopped in the middle of the hallway and glanced down.

I did too, seeing a brown bag. It had what I assumed were groceries inside. They always came in the same bag, but I saw no Heath in sight. I mean, I never did see him, but that was how he left things. A notebook was even beneath the bag like always. Notes...

I didn't understand what was happening here, and Sloane only came so far. She might believe I was still sick, but how *did she* know? "Sloane—"

"You weren't supposed to see me doing this," she said, her knuckles tapping together. She appeared anxious, worried. "I should go."

No, she shouldn't actually, and she did stop when I called her. I wanted her to explain why she was here and sneaking stuff in front of my door. "You brought these things?"

She'd already confirmed, but again, this didn't make sense.

She angled around slowly, but didn't come back. She stayed there. "Yeah, and please don't be mad. He..." She played with her hair. "He didn't mean any harm."

He didn't. Mean. Any. Harm.

Alarm bells went off, and they were so freaking familiar. I raised a hand. "Are you saying Ares asked you to bring this stuff?"

I heard the words coming out of my mouth, but even still, they felt weird. They felt *ridiculous.* Especially because I asked her to *ask him* to back off. He shouldn't even know I was sick. Let alone be helping me...

Reality started to hit around the time Sloane came closer. I started to walk away, not wanting to hear it.

"He asked me to bring things today, but he stopped by on the other days."

What she said gave me pause, and alarm bells sounded again. I didn't know what to feel. Anger. Frustration...

Pain.

I think I was feeling it all by the time my hand touched the doorknob, and I was so freaking tired of it. I was tired of everything when it came to this guy, and it quite literally made me sick. My forehead touched the door. "What are you talking about?"

Because all of this should have been Heath. *Heath* was the one bringing me all these things and helping me out.

"You didn't make accommodations for yourself, so I did…"

I gripped the doorknob, hearing Ares's voice in my head. He was always, *always* making accommodations for me. He did and long before that last day at the cabin.

Why does he hurt me like this?

He was killing me. Every day he did this shit, he was killing me. I placed my hands on the door, and Sloane eased closer behind me. I didn't know how close, but I couldn't face her. I didn't know what I'd do about this situation. If I'd freak out, or even cry. I was so tired of crying too.

"He's been missing classes, Fawn," she said, my fingers knuckling against the door. "He's missed too many, so he asked me to bring you everything today."

I almost asked her to elaborate, but then I thought, why bother? I had notes… pages and *pages* of notes from my classes, and they were all handwritten. They were in his handwriting. I sighed against the door. "He's been attending my classes for me, hasn't it? Getting me notes?"

I knew the answer before I even turned around. Sloane was there, and like before, she did keep her distance. She really did know I'd been sick. She played with her hands. "Like I said, he didn't mean any harm. He was just trying to help you out."

"But how did he know to help me out. How did he…" I was shaking, my hands knuckling. "Why does he keep helping me out?"

She had no answers for me, but she didn't have to have any, did she?

"I need you with everything in me…"

I was crying now. Replaying those words he'd said in my head made me cry. Steady tears blinked down my cheeks because I needed him too. I maybe needed him more than he needed me, and maybe that was where the real source of my hate came from. That my need outweighed his, and he'd *made me do that*. He'd made me love him with everything in me.

I couldn't help my love. It came so hot and so fast. I wanted the feelings I had for him to just be lust. I wanted it so desperately but it wasn't. I loved Ares Mallick.

I more than loved him.

The reality of that made me shake, and I audibly heard Sloane swallow in that hallway.

"He ran into your friend Heath," she explained. "He asked him how bad you were. He saw your social media status."

Of course he did.

"I need you with everything in me…"

I closed my eyes, my palms wet. I was freaking ugly crying at this point, and Sloane took the wall beside me. Again, she kept her distance.

"Fawn," she started, but then paused. Once more, it was like she was choosing her words carefully. "Fawn, I think you're both suffering."

I was breaking down, shattering. I braced my arms. "He broke me."

The words came out in a whisper, a weak, blubbering mess, and I hated it. I gazed up to see Sloane nodding, her expression terribly sad, and that made me feel even weaker. It made me feel more ashamed. She bit her lip. "I know a thing or two about that. Dorian and I had our ups and downs."

I ran a sleeve under my eye. "Yeah?"

"Oh, yeah." She smiled. "He's not perfect. Neither is my brother, and I'm not either."

Nor was I. I was the opposite of perfect.

He made you better.

In so many ways, he had, and I hated to admit that too. I had been getting better. I was talking to my mom and stepdad... I had been getting better, and I wasn't shutting people out. It was like I wasn't making myself suffer anymore for my dad's accident. I was trying to live and have the life I knew he would want for me. One without guilt or hurt. I always distanced myself from my family because *I* couldn't move on. I had too much guilt surrounding the accident, too much pain, and Wolf had told me that wasn't what my dad would want for me. He'd told me to live and taught me how to love myself again.

He'd taught me how to *be* loved.

CHAPTER
THIRTY

Ares

"Ares, it's time. We need to take action before this thing starts to get away from us."

I stared out the window of the local hospital. Queenstown Village had fresh snow. It was nothing like it'd been during the holidays. After my family and I had gotten back from South Carolina, I'd thought my nuts would freeze off in my hometown. No, the snow here back on campus wasn't like it was there. It was better, light.

It was still snow, though. It was cold, and the air was extremely bitter. It was like the world was just dying all around me, and in a way, it was. It was dead during the winter, but it would always come back.

Dr. Easton sat in front of me. He normally operated out of Johns Hopkins, but when he saw me in person, he came to the local hospital. He arrived a couple months ago and hadn't left. He'd been here for me. He sighed. "The clinical trial isn't working. I'm advising we start a standard course of treatment. We need to do that before this becomes something there's no going back from."

But the thing was, it was working. At least, it had been. The tumor hadn't gotten any worse. It was stable, but I guess that wasn't the endgame. It never had been.

I wet my lips. "A standard course of treatment?"

"Chemotherapy."

It was like a curse word to me. It represented that my life was going to change, and that my world was going to change. I couldn't hide chemo from my family.

I could hide *this* from my family.

"You're going to need to make a decision." Dr. Easton leaned forward. He was on the younger side, but I trusted him. I was sure when my grandpa had given me the referral for another doctor, he'd never thought I'd be using it as a way to keep information from my family. If he had, he wouldn't have given me the referral.

I stared out the window. "Okay."

"Okay?"

I closed my eyes. "Fine. I will. I'll make a decision."

It seemed I didn't have a choice. It was start a standard course of treatment or let this *thing* take me. It was something I'd barely had to battle before. It'd been so easy. A surgery, some recovery, then I was back on my feet. I'd strong-armed that shit the first time, and there hadn't been time for the people in my life to truly be scared. I'd handled it back then. I'd beaten it.

And I'd beat it again.

My phone buzzed outside of the hospital, and I was surprised to get the text.

Bru: I'm in town. Want to get coffee?

I didn't know why he was in town. He was supposed to be at home and taking things easy. He'd worried the fuck out of everyone back at Christmas, but I'd never been prouder of both him and our family. My parents had let Bru talk, and once he had, they embraced what he was going through just like they had me. I'd had a really dark period of my life, but my parents hadn't freaked out back then. They'd been sad, but they had gotten me through it. They came at the situation with Bru in the same way, and Sloane and our friends had been just as supportive. My buddies had found out shortly after my family's discussion, and we all had been there for the kid. That was what we did for each other.

Swallowing, I asked Bru why he was here, and he texted back quickly.

Bru: Sloane's been bugging me to come visit. Says it might help since I've been stir-crazy lately.

The kid had been working on himself back at home, but I could imagine being back with just that and nothing else to do was making him antsy.

Bru: Saw her and the guys. They said you were at your doctor's appointment.

I had been, so I texted that in confirmation. He restated he wanted to see me, and of course, I wanted to see him too. I started to say we could meet up, but he texted me back first.

Bru: Also came to see Fawn today. Just left seeing her actually.

I was sure he had. They were friends after all, and I was glad she had that. A friend.

My thumbs hovered over my phone. It'd been over a week since Sloane had told me Fawn caught her in her dorm's hallway. It'd been over a week since I'd basically gotten found out, and from how it sounded, Red hadn't been happy.

My sister had told me she'd cried.

I was always making that girl cry, and I did back off this time. I stayed off her bus route and rerouted my attention. It was better I stayed away.

"You're going to need to make a decision."

Ignoring Dr. Easton's voice, I texted my brother where we could meet for coffee. I probably could get some today since I wasn't on a special diet anymore. The clinical trial the doctor had me in required it. There obviously wasn't a point to keep doing that now.

I slammed my Hummer's door shut in the hospital's parking lot, and I was proud of myself.

I only punched the wheel once before pulling away.

———

"Ouch. You alright?" Bru pointed to my bruised knuckles. I'd fucked them up pretty good when I'd punched the steering wheel, but I'd barely noticed. My hands were numb half the time and tingling the rest.

I shrugged, then shoved both hands into the front of my hoodie. The kid and I had been chatting for a few minutes over our coffees. We just had some general back-and-forth about how he'd been doing, which was well. He was still seeing his therapist back home, and he'd been helping Mom out at her office to stay busy. Our mother was the mayor of the city.

During the short chat, I must have forgotten about my hand. I flexed my fingers. "Got it caught in the truck door on the way here."

I mean, what was another lie anyway? I'd dug myself so deep, so why not just lie again? Lie forever?

Because it's not possible.

I would if I could. *I'd handle this shit* all on my own so my family would never ever have to deal with it. The amount of trauma in my family could make headlines, and it had.

"Damn." Bru gestured for me to show him my hand, and I did to humor him. He might have a future in medicine with the way he was looking at it. "Make sure to ice it when you get back to your dorm."

"I will."

Bru nodded. "So, you're not going to ask?"

"About what?"

The look my brother gave me made me think I'd asked something crazy. He lifted his hand. "About Fawn. You're not going to ask how she is? I told you I saw her today."

I didn't see the point. Not anymore and especially after today. It just made shit so much worse and added to the tension in my chest. My heart. "You know there isn't a point to that."

And he also knew how shit had gone down recently. Everyone knew that my attempts to be near Fawn hadn't ended well. And that was all I'd wanted. To be around her, near her...

It'd been pathetic really. I thought if I just waited and *was there* that maybe she'd want to see me or be around me. I'd let my brother convince me at Christmas there was a point to reaching out. That there was a point to putting myself in a position *to be* around her, but today taught me differently. Fawn didn't need me in her life right now. There was already about to be so much collateral damage and...

My hands flexed again, my body shifting, back straightening. Sitting in chairs was an effort these days, and the same went for lying down or even walking. I didn't know when my body would betray me and have a bad day. Some days it was cool, and there was minimal discomfort. Others not so much.

"You know you two are incredibly frustrating," my brother said, laughing a little. His awareness of my physical woes was the same as everyone else in my life. It was nonexistent, and that was intentional. I'd been good at hiding it, great at hiding it, and for months.

So many months.

Bru's head tilted. "I wasn't exactly honest when I said I came out to see Sloane and you guys. I mean, Sloane's been bugging me, but I got in the car today because Fawn called me."

That got my attention, and my focus dashed back to him. The kid slid something across the table, and when I looked at it, I realized it was a wedding invitation. My brow jerked up. "What's this?"

"It's a wedding invitation."

"I got that, but why are you showing it to me?" And why had Fawn called him?

Bru smiled again. "That's why Fawn called me. Apparently, she's taking pictures at it. It's this Saturday."

"Okay."

"Well, she needs an assistant. She's taking pictures as a favor for a friend she has. Says his name is Heath?" he stated, and as I was aware of her friend, I nodded. "Anyway, he's in the wedding, so he can't take photos for the bride and groom. The groom is his cousin and asked if Heath knew anyone who could do photography. Their other photographer bailed out on them."

I still didn't understand, and all Bru's grin did was lift.

"Bro, she needs an assistant, and she asked me *to ask you* to do the job," he said, and I blinked, twitched. He laughed. "She wants you to help her. She knows you're into art and stuff."

Yeah, but I couldn't take pictures for shit. That wasn't my fucking medium at all, and why would she ask him to ask me? I shook my head. "Why would she want me to help?"

Bru gave me a look like it was obvious, but it wasn't. Not to me. He leaned forward. "She wants to see you, Ares," he said, and my mouth opened. "She's obviously using this as a reason to. I think she feels like she needs an excuse."

What he said gave me more hope than it should. I shouldn't hope for this or want her to see me. I shouldn't want to see her. After today, I shouldn't want to.

But I did.

I was fucking desperate for that, my chest tight and aching for it. There may not be a reality in which she and I could ever be, but at least, I could be around her for a little while. I could be near her and tell her the truth she deserved.

I could say goodbye.

CHAPTER
THIRTY-ONE

Fawn

"You're a godsend for doing this, you know." My friend Heath was in a suit and appeared rather dashing. His personal style was more scholarly, but today, he wore a formal gray three-piece suit since he was in the wedding. He grinned. "I know how you hate weddings."

I didn't *hate* weddings. I just hated shooting them. The days were long, tiring, and required an obscene amount of my mental capacity.

It was a capacity I unfortunately didn't have as I scanned the hotel's atrium. Heath's cousin was getting married in one of the hotel's ballrooms, and the reception was going to be in another. Anyway, my gaze zoomed over the atrium in a frenzy, and Heath noticed.

"You nervous or something? You always do well at these." Heath was tinkering with his camera. He was loaning me a spare since I'd have an assistant today.

God, why had I asked Wolf to do this?

He wasn't here yet, and I felt like I was going to be sick.

I'd asked Bru to ask him to be here, and Bru had texted that Wolf would. Even still, I didn't know what I was going to say.

I was feeling very ill, and even though the sensation wasn't like my cold, it still sucked. My stomach was basically in my throat, and I was glad I'd already gotten pictures of the bridal party out of the way. Those had been early this morning, and my focus was shot. I scanned the atrium filled with people waiting for the ceremony to begin. I glanced at Heath. "Not exactly."

I wasn't nervous to take pictures. Pictures I was good at. What I wasn't good at was Wolf and how he made me feel. He got me so in my head, and I...

"Hey, I'm not late, am I?"

I swiveled around, and in front of me stood a Big Bad Wolf. Ares had his hands in his pockets, and he was wearing all black like I'd requested. His dress pants hugged his chiseled legs like sin, and the same went for the button-up he had rolled at the sleeves. It exposed the corded muscle of his arms, and his hair was up and out of his face. I'd seen many guys dressed in full suits today, but Ares Mallick in a black dress shirt and trousers managed to outshine them all. It was the way he carried himself, I think.

Or maybe I just noticed that.

No, I wasn't the only one to notice. Wolf had more than one set of eyes on him from both the male and female population. One set was Heath's, but I think that was just pure shock. I hadn't told him who my assistant would be today, but that was due to fear. I was scared that I'd asked Wolf to come meet me.

I was terrified.

Of what, I wasn't so sure. Things had seemed so much simpler when I'd called his brother. Bru had asked my thoughts behind the request, and my reasons surrounded answers. I needed answers from Wolf. There were things that had happened between us that required them, but at the present, I wasn't thinking about any of it. People were looking at Wolf, but he was only looking at me.

He was smiling.

He had a nice one of those when he wasn't using it against you, and I found it so hard to forget that. He had used it against me.

"No, you're not," I managed to say to him, and it was an honest question he'd asked. I mean, people were moving around like things had already gotten started, and I had taken pictures already without him. Again, it was due to fear, being around him... "The ceremony is about to start in a little bit."

I felt like I was having an out-of-body experience standing in front of him. Especially when I had to explain to Heath that Wolf was my assistant. Needless to say, that surprised the fuck out of him. At one point, he and our other friends hadn't even been able to mention Wolf's name around me.

That was how bad it had gotten, but I forced bravery into myself today. Again, I wanted answers, and that was why Wolf was here.

This was what I told myself when I watched Heath greet Wolf, and something that surprised the fuck *out of me* was when Wolf brought Heath into a handshake-hug combination. Dudes greeted each other like that, but Wolf hadn't been Heath's biggest fan. He'd expressed jealousy of my former roommate on more than one occasion.

That didn't seem to be the case today, and my stomach flipped for some reason watching the exchange. I was unsure of the source, but the flipping only turned into a somersault when Wolf explained he'd do his best to help get great pictures today. I had no intention of actually letting him shoot, and the spare camera really was for me. Heath had a great camera too, and I aimed to swap them out from time to time.

Wolf didn't know that, but even still, he wanted to assure Heath he'd do his best. Heath appeared grateful for that, and after thanking us both for the favor, he left us to go find his cousin, the groom.

He left us.

I hadn't been alone with Wolf since the cabin, but even that day, we hadn't been truly alone. Like when I'd talked to him on the bus, we'd had an audience, but for a short time, it had felt like it was just the two of us. It'd been just as terrifying as it was now, and a flash of panic hit me. I forgot everything I intended for today, and my focus was going to the camera in his hands. Heath had handed his off to Wolf before he left, and I nodded at it. "I don't expect you to take any photos. I'll be swapping my camera out for Heath's from time to time."

It was brave of me to do this, to trust and let him hold my dad's camera, but I would.

I should question that trust, but I wasn't. I knew I didn't have to because I knew he'd take care of my dad's camera.

I knew he'd take care of me.

This terrified me too, because it was in direct conflict with what I wanted to do in this moment. I wanted to yell at him, scream, and demand why he hid his feelings. I wanted to ask him why he'd hurt me and chastise him for all the pain he'd brought me. I was still so angry at him, and that was where my conflict lay. I knew he would take care of me, and I both hated and loved him for that.

Love...

Wolf's nod was curt, and that easy smile of his made my stomach flip again. He rubbed his neck. "I have to say, I'm relieved. I kind of suck at taking photos."

I'd laugh if I wasn't so terrified. Terrified of *him* and all this.

Brave the fuck up.

"Where do you want me, Red?"

My eyes flashed. "What?"

He laughed a little, and when he approached, my stomach

was basically in my mouth. It was too hard to avoid him this close. His draw. He gazed down at me. "Where do you want me today? What do you need from me?"

There felt like there was a question behind the questions, but that could have been in my head too. I wasn't listening to my head these days. If I did, I would have opened the floor in that moment. I had so much to say to him, but in the end, I just gave him my extra gear. I went into work mode and told him to follow me as I headed into the ballroom. I was more intent on capturing this wedding than actually talking to him. I was *avoiding* when I did want to talk to Wolf.

I just didn't know how.

————

I gave in to cowardice that Saturday. Instead of talking to Wolf (like I wanted to), I buried myself in the job and did everything I could *not* to talk to him. He was there for the ride, of course. He held my gear and did everything I asked him. He never asked me for anything or asked anything of me. He was just there.

He helped.

The real cop-out was that I even staggered our breaks. I let him have one, or I took one and gave him the camera. I never obligated him to take photos or anything, but I wanted him to be available if I was out of the room. This went on all day, and it was easy because this was a wedding. It wasn't about me, and it wasn't about him.

It was easy.

The day faded into night. The champagne toasts were over, and the cake was cut. Half the guests were gone at this point, and Wolf and I lingered in the room glowing in lime-colored lighting. It was one of the bride and groom's wedding colors, and it was everywhere. It highlighted the walls and flashed on the dance floor. Even my dark clothes had a subtle tint.

And it highlighted Wolf too.

Everyone's focus was on the bride and groom and the remaining guests on the dance floor, but I watched Wolf. He had his back to the wall and watched on while people slow danced to a song about falling in love. I probably should be out there, taking more pictures, but I found my focus in Wolf's direction. I had my camera on him, but I wasn't taking pictures. I just observed him, following that sharp bone structure while we all listened to lyrics about finding the right person. *Our* person.

Wolf noticed. His attention casually drifted in my direction, and I remained frozen. I didn't lower the camera. I didn't do anything. I was lost in those dark eyes that stared a hole through me on the other side of my lens. Wolf didn't move either, but that classic, handsome smile of his quirked right. He caught me, but he didn't do anything about it.

At least, not at first.

Eventually, he came over, and I was forced to lower my camera. We'd both worked a full day, and even though I took all the pictures, he'd done his fair share of running. I felt like I had him everywhere grabbing me things, and he never once complained. He just did everything I asked. Even if that required him to be on the other side of the room. He kept his distance when I wanted him to and never pressured me to talk. He had to know it was unusual that I asked him here, but he didn't push me.

He waited.

He didn't seem to be now when he came over, and my lungs immediately got tight. He stopped right in front of me, pocketing his hands. "You, uh, you wouldn't want to dance with me, would you, Red?"

I was shocked that he asked, but was astounded even more that I wanted to. I told myself it'd be a great place to talk to him. We'd be close, and that was my thought when I shifted my dad's camera to my back. Wolf did the same with Heath's, and I followed him out to the dance floor.

That was the last thing he let me do on my own, because once we were on the floor, I was in his arms. I was there in a familiar place, and I think I died a little. He left no inch of space between us when his arm looped around me. He managed to do so despite my camera potentially being in the way, and I was forced to hug him close right back.

I was forced to feel.

It came in a wash over me, and overwhelmed me so much that I distracted myself and pressed my cheek to his chest. I couldn't look at him directly, closing my eyes. "Thanks for helping me today."

It was the only thing I could get out, another distraction, and I felt his finger loop around my hair. He got the frizzy strand around his lengthy digit, my hair all over the place from the busy day.

"Of course," he said, his finger in my hair grazing my cheek. I felt that touch through my entire body and it made me uncomfortable enough that I pulled away. The fact of the matter was there was too much comfort in that touch. It felt so good, too good.

I ended up off the dance floor and back to our wall. Wolf followed me into a shadowed corner, and as soon as we both came to a stop, I turned. "Why now, Wolf? Why now after... *everything*?"

My question gave him pause, his mouth opening. His gaze bored into me, and though there was silence, he knew exactly what I meant. He'd broken my heart, and I'd accused him months ago of having more feelings. He'd said at the cabin I was right about everything, which meant he'd lied.

I just didn't understand why.

I didn't understand the point of the lie. I mean, why hurt someone you claim to love? Emotion thickened my throat, but

I pushed through it. "Why now, huh? I mean, was it Bru? Did you feel threatened by our friendship—"

"Fawn, you should literally be with anyone else but me."

Completely thrown, I blinked, and Wolf's gaze hit the air. Like he was deep in thought, contemplation, and when he came back, he just looked sad. That was how he looked at the cabin too. He shook his head. "I'm fucked up, Fawn. I was when we met, and I am now."

I didn't understand the *when we met*. He was obviously referring to the stadium fight day, but I didn't get why he was bringing it up.

No, I didn't understand, and he gave *me* pause when he approached. He put his hands on my arms, and I absorbed the touch just as deeply as when he'd played with my hair.

"It may be in a different way, but I am," he said, scanning my face, my eyes. "Truth be told, you should probably be with someone like my brother. He'd never do the things I've done to you. Doing to you…"

I assumed he said this because he was still hurting me, which he was. He was playing volleyball with my heart right now, and I didn't get that. I didn't get why he kept *doing* this.

"Fuck, Red." The words sounded terse, frustrated. I didn't know if he was angry with himself, or what. He swallowed. "I've hurt you, and if you let me, I'll *still* hurt you. I will because I'm fucked up, and I don't want to do that to you anymore, Red. You deserve so much better than that, and I *can't* hurt you. Not anymore."

His voice broke, and he was breaking me too. He was acting like he couldn't help hurting me. Like he was broken, damaged goods, and I could relate. I wish I couldn't, but I could.

He's not perfect. Neither is my brother, and I'm not either.

I thought about his sister's words, and how I knew a thing or two about being broken too. It seemed we were all hot messes, and Wolf was falling on the sword to his vices. He wasn't fighting, and that wasn't the Wolf I knew. "Then don't hurt me anymore."

His laughter was dry. Like he was physically in pain, and maybe he was. Again, I could relate. He cupped my cheeks. "It's inevitable, I'm afraid." His thumb brushed my cheek, and my stomach locked up so tight. Something felt so final about what he was saying, and that wasn't fair. He wasn't giving me an option at all in this and completely taking decision power away. He wasn't allowing me to make any kind of choice for us, and that wasn't fucking fair. "You asked me why now? There is no *now*, Red, because we are fucking *always*. You are it for me, Fawn Greenfield. End. Fucking. Game. The only reason you know about it all now is because I'm weak as shit and couldn't keep it from you."

It all came out rushed, but I didn't miss a word.

Always?

I wasn't even sure if it'd been always for me. In fact, I was pretty sure I spent more time hating Wolf than loving him.

Always...

Wolf let go and faced away like he couldn't look at me anymore. He wet his lips. "Fawn, I—"

It wasn't professional what I did next. I mean, we were still working this wedding, but I didn't fucking care. I wanted a choice in all this.

And I was deciding us.

I was deciding to fight, and when I kissed Wolf, I put all that out there. He may want to fall on the sword, protect me, but I wasn't letting him. Hell, I wasn't letting me do that either. It'd be so easy to run away from all this, but for once, I was choosing the other path. I was choosing us.

I was choosing him.

Wolf fought back in the shadows. His hands were on my arms, but his mouth wasn't stopping. He didn't want this to end either, his tongue in my mouth.

"Fawn, I can't." His hands gripped my arms tight, but he

kissed deeper, stronger. "Fawn, you don't know everything. I'm so fucked up. Things are so fucked up."

I may not understand the brevity of who he was, but I was getting a choice in all this. He needed to let me fight and not be a fucking dude for once. I didn't need protecting. I could protect myself.

"Please. *Please* let me end this." He brought my hair out of my face, and I basically had him pinned to the wall. I was being the aggressor here, but he wasn't doing much fighting. When I kissed deep, he went deeper still, and the groan left his mouth. "Let me end this for you. It won't work. We—"

"Shut the fuck up." He wasn't ending this without giving me a say, and this was me saying it. I was choosing to fight for us, and I wanted him to fight too. I was letting him know it was okay to have us and have this. I was giving him permission, and he may have flaws, but I did too. They were deep wounds that still needed healing, but they'd gotten so much better since he came into my life. I made so many strides, and even though I resisted those changes, it didn't stop them from being true. When I'd met Wolf, he was nothing but a vicious, vengeful prick, but I hadn't seen that guy in a long time. He did his own fair bit of changing too, but that wasn't because of me.

It was because of us.

CHAPTER
THIRTY-TWO

Fawn

Wolf wasn't resisting anymore by the time we booked a hotel room. We were in a hotel, so it was easy to do after things wrapped up with the wedding. I gave him no time to think, and he gave me no time to think with his mouth on me. His lips sealed over mine shortly after we entered the suite, and with their taste, I instantly consumed myself in the kiss. I was so hungry for him.

I was so hungry.

I'd fought all this between us for so long and so hard, and the moment I gave myself an inch, I lost myself. I lost myself in him and in us, and Wolf picked up on the rush right away. He got my hands, his mouth slowing mine down.

"Slow," he said, his lips enforcing the intent. They eased over to my cheek, then down my neck. "Slower, Red. Let me taste you."

He teased me, his mouth parting on my jaw as he unbuttoned my shirt. This *wasn't* Wolf Mallick. He was always so hot, so fast. We both were.

But that wasn't the case now. His hand eased into my top and covered my back. I ached for more, but I waited. He guided me into the bedroom of the suite and shed my top along the way. He kissed a line between my breasts and completely bypassed my tits, which surprised me. He always manhandled them, but he left my bra on when he sat on the bed. He undid my pants and pulled my underwear down with them. Soon, I was stripped from the waist down, and he sat in front of me.

"Slow," he repeated, kissing my stomach and a noise left my mouth. He had me in such a vulnerable way, pretty much naked with my tiny curls in his face. He moved to that area when he got on his knees, and again, he did this agonizingly slow.

"Oh, God." I had my hands on his shoulders as he kissed me there, Wolf Mallick on his knees *for me*. I recalled a time he'd made me do that for him. It'd been humiliating and a way for him to teach me a lesson. He'd wanted power over me back then.

But that'd been then. *Now* I had him below me, a damn near seven-foot *god* making me moan as he kissed my folds apart. His tongue entered and swirled around my clit so deliciously I thought I'd get off right there on his mouth. I tried to move my sex away, but all Wolf did was fist my ass.

"No. Let everyone in this fucking hotel know what I'm doing to you," he said, feasting between my legs. He gripped my ass, then positioned my foot on the bed. His tongue started doing a darting motion, fucking me swift and direct before swiping across my bud. He was teasing me again, and I was going to come.

"I can't. I…" I fought my scream, gripping his hair. It was all I could do not to go over the edge. "Wolf, I'm going to come."

"Then fucking come." He gazed up at me while he feasted, and those dark eyes did take me over the edge. The sound that left my throat could definitely be heard on the other side of these walls, which was obviously his intent.

Wolf groaned as I gushed into his mouth, my body twitching, convulsing. His gaze didn't let up. Like he wouldn't let me flee or turn away from him.

"God..." I palmed my breasts, jerking against his face. He didn't stop licking me until I finished, and when he rose, he grabbed the back of my head. He bruised my lips in a passionate kiss, and I wavered on unsteady legs.

"Get on the bed," he said, unfastening my bra. Once it was gone, he tweaked my nipples, making me ache more. "In the center. Legs apart."

The command sent a buzz between my legs again. I wasn't sure I could come again so fast, but I did what he said. I got on the bed even though I did feel vulnerable. I prided myself on my confidence when it came to my body. I was aware I wasn't the tiniest girl, but that was other people's problem. Not mine.

Even still, this was Wolf Mallick. The football player. The god. I was sure there wasn't a girl on campus who didn't want to fuck him, and a healthy number of guys too.

But he wasn't fucking them. He was here with me in a room ambient with warm light. He undressed in front of me, his shirt buttons flicking open and revealing his necklace and golden chest. I'd found out he was a combination of races, cultures. Casual conversations between his friends and family during the holidays mentioned he was Middle Eastern, Latinx, and white. His tanned skin flushed down to his abs, but he only gave me a peek. He stopped unbuttoning and focused on me. "I said legs open, Red. I want you ready to take me."

My legs had fallen closed, too focused on him. I widened them, and Wolf's already dusky eyes darkened. He continued to remove his clothing, but he did so achingly slow. Each move was calculated, and I couldn't help my fingers going in between my legs. I flicked my clit as he revealed his shoulders, then fucked myself when he was down to his boxer briefs. A noise rolled from his chest upon seeing what I was doing, but he didn't rush to come over to me. Grabbing his cock, he watched me fuck myself but stayed on the other end of the bed. He fisted his thick length through his boxers, wetting his lips.

"Tell me you don't want anything between us," he said, pulling himself out. He moved up and down that long length, his thumb gliding over a drop of pre-cum at the tip. "Tell me you want to feel me as bad as I want to feel you."

I recalled him using a condom the last time we'd been together, and it made me wonder if he'd been trying to respect me. He'd always taken what he wanted from me, but he hadn't toward the end.

He was asking for permission.

He really had changed, but there were parts of him I never wanted to lose. There were parts I needed and wanted to consume me.

"Please," I said, and he was on the bed. He removed his boxers, and he was just as naked as me on the sheets. The flower tattoo on his hip moved as he shifted close.

"Red..." Wolf hugged me into him, on his side when he slid himself inside me. I called out, and he pivoted to his back. "Ride me."

His eyes closed, gently rocking me into him and fisting my hips so tight. It felt like he was holding back, and he winced like maybe I was hurting him. Concerned, I didn't ride him like I normally would have, but then, he was kissing me.

He was drowning me.

I was so consumed by him, and without warning, he brought me to my back. He laced our fingers, holding on just as tight as he had my hips.

"I love you," he gritted out, his forehead rubbing against

mine. His teeth sunk into his bottom lip, his thrusts deep, controlled. "I love you so much."

I loved him too, and I nudged his curls away from his face with my nose. He had some loose from his bun, and I wanted to see him. I touched my mouth to his cheek. "I love you too."

He shuddered above me, his hands so tight in mine. His arms were shaking, his thrusts so controlled, and I wasn't sure why he was holding back the way he was. It made me scared because of what he'd said before. He'd been resistant downstairs, hesitant to us and continuing this.

He brought me to my side, and when he did, he stayed behind me. He hugged me close while he fucked me, his mouth touching my shoulder.

"You're everything to me, Red," he said, his hips picking up. He hit me so full, so *deep*. "Fucking everything."

Something about the words tumbled me over that high cliff again. A wash of heat exploded inside my core so intensely my toes curled, and Wolf's teeth sunk down into my shoulder. The pain caused me to call out, and when Wolf's hips stiffened, I assumed he met that same high. His roar into the room challenged my earlier scream, and my shoulder barely muffled the sound. I held on while he released, his seed filling me up and his dick vibrating inside me. I felt so full and didn't let him go afterward.

I didn't want to.

I think a part of me was still scared that he'd clearly been holding back while we made love. It made me worried that he wouldn't let himself go there. I knew he'd said he loved me, but I still worried.

I ran my fingers across the hairs on his arm. "Wolf?"

He either didn't hear me, or was sleeping because he didn't answer me. I ended up closing my eyes, just lying there. I didn't think I could sleep.

Again, I was too worried.

CHAPTER
THIRTY-THREE

Fawn

"How about a bath?" Wolf must have been aware I wasn't sleeping. I felt like I'd barely closed my eyes before his lips landed on my shoulder. He squeezed me into him. "What do you say?"

It sounded nice, really nice. I turned in his arms, and his dark irises were on me. I'd worried before I'd closed my eyes, but maybe I didn't have anything to worry about. I nodded, and his mouth touched my forehead.

"I'll get it started. You stay here," he said, and I opened my eyes again after he left the bed. He'd already put his boxers on, and I studied his strong back and that striking tattoo that traveled down the length of his spine before he disappeared into the bathroom.

Maybe I'm paranoid.

I thought I'd felt some resistance on his end while we'd been making love, but maybe I hadn't. Maybe I was just scared of all this myself, and I'd channeled my own fears into the evening. I wanted this to work with Wolf. I wanted to get out of my own way and make this work.

I ended up not waiting in the bed for him to come back. I pulled the sheet off the bed, and after wrapping myself in it, I followed after him.

The air was warm in the bathroom and thick with floral aroma. Wolf himself was sitting on the edge of a whirlpool tub. He poured bubble bath in, and I studied him working his broad shoulders while he did it. Eventually, he put the bubble bath down and slid his hand along his lower back. He massaged there, doing so for several moments before he glanced over his shoulder and caught me looking at him. He turned off the water, then smiled at me. "Impatient much, Red?"

I guessed I could say so, but I was wondering now if he'd done something to his back with the way he'd been rubbing it. "Your back okay?"

I'd had him do a lot of things today. No heavy lifting or anything like that, but he'd often had to carry my gear on his shoulders.

My question gave him pause. Like he didn't know what I was talking about considering the way he looked at me. I came over. "You were rubbing your back. Are you okay?"

It made me really wonder now and worry in a different way. I noticed he'd been stiff while we were having sex.

Had I pushed him too hard?

Something tight settled in my stomach. That I had accidentally hurt him today with all the work I'd had him do. He'd had issues with his back in the past, and I should have thought about that.

I must have looked like I was silently chastising myself, because Wolf grabbed my hand. He kissed it before kissing me, and my mind instantly went blank.

His kisses had a way of doing that.

It was like a warm remedy, all the worries in my mind

fading away. He was on his feet as his hands folded over my shoulders, and soon, he was stripping me bare.

I moaned at the feel of his hands gliding down my hips, and I shivered when his mouth brushed my ear. "I love how you worry about me. How much you care," he said, his nose nuzzling my ear. The chills went deep, and I laughed when his lips touched my neck. "Now, into the bath. It's getting cold."

He guided me in, and I was on full display for him. Normally, I'd have thoughts about being so vulnerable, but Wolf's hungry eyes roved over me, and I didn't have time to be self-conscious. I felt desired.

I felt loved.

He had said he loved me, and when I got into the bath, I made room for him.

"No. This is for you," he said, then remained on the edge of the tub. His hands framed my face, and his smile was incredibly warm when his thumb guided some hair off my cheek. "Let me take care of you."

That sounded nice too and reminded me of earlier when we'd made love. He had wanted to take care of me then too.

I gave him my back, and he put my hair up. He used the hair tie he'd been wearing and something felt so intimate about that. Like he really was trying to take care of me. I think I could safely say no guy had ever *put my hair up*. He obviously knew how because of his own thick locks, and again, it made me feel cared for. He kept some of it out in the front, a few wavy strands framing my face.

"Are you sure you're okay?" I asked, as he guided water over my shoulders. He was using his hands and bath gel to wash me, then rinsing the suds off. "I didn't have you doing too much today, did I? I know you've had problems with your back in the past."

I knew he was okay now. He'd said his cancer was a thing of the past, but one never knew. He might still have off days even though he'd shown me nothing but the opposite on more than one occasion. I mean, the guy had picked me up off my actual feet before, and I wasn't a small girl.

Regardless, I probably should have checked in before assuming he never did have those bad days. Wolf's hand cupped my shoulder, and when he didn't say anything, I gazed back. No words were exchanged between us as he glided his fingers down my arm. He followed the trail of my tattooed flowers, his lengthy digits creating goose bumps on my skin.

"Wolf?" I didn't know why he wasn't answering me. Had I pushed him too hard today?

"This isn't going to work, Red," he said, and my body instantly locked up. It became rigid and gut-wrenchingly tight. His finger outlined one of my flowers. "I want it to. God, how I want it to, but too much has happened. Too much is happening."

My mind was in a whirl. I was so confused. "What do you mean?"

But in the back of my mind, I knew. He had tried to end this downstairs, and I'd been so worried when we'd been making love. He had been holding back.

I just didn't get *why*?

I was so confused why he wasn't fighting for this to work between us. *He* was the one who'd hurt *me*, but I was willing to fight.

I was thrown for a loop when Wolf brought me close. He got my shoulders and everything and was inches away.

"I have cancer, Red," he stated, and my breath escaped. It was short wisps, gasps. He nodded. "I do, and I've had it for months."

I've had it for months.

The words didn't compute. My body was shaking, my head shaking. "What do you mean you have... cancer? You said you had a surgery. You said..."

The sentence refused to continue.

Cancer.

The word in my mind sounded like another language, and it still didn't resonate. He had to be joking. He was messing with me. He had to be...

Wolf's head lowered, his gaze hitting bubbly water. He wasn't making eye contact with me, and the longer he wasn't, my body wouldn't take in air. My lungs squeezed, and it felt like someone had reached into my chest and was suffocating me from the inside. Like I'd been bucked by a horse and hit by a semi at the same time.

Cancer.

Wolf's tongue eased over his lips. He was squeezing me now, my shoulders in a firm grip in his hands. "It came back, Red."

It. Came. Back. Red.

I think I was only above water because he was holding me now, and if he let go, I would have fallen. He said he had cancer. And for months? I faced him. "Did it happen after us?"

I didn't know why I asked that. I think it was shock and wondering how long he'd actually known. If all this had *happened*, and he'd kept quiet about it during the holidays.

If he'd kept me in the dark that long.

No sooner had I asked the question than Wolf gazed away. His hands slid up and down my freckled arms, and the air puffed out in gasps again. "Wolf—"

"It was before us," he said, cringing, and my mouth dried. My throat *dried*. His jaw moved. "I found out shortly before."

I really didn't understand now. I didn't fucking understand. I shook my head. "So the fake relationship? Helping your family?" My words quivered, my throat thick. "This really was for them?"

I didn't understand in what way, but it had to have been. He'd said back then that he wanted the relationship to help them, and he hadn't been talking during that time like they knew.

They didn't know.

No, they couldn't possibly have. I'd been with his family and friends only weeks ago. I'd *seen* them, and they'd only laughed during the holidays. They'd been joyful, and the few times there had been tension surrounded when they'd found out about the fake relationship and what Wolf had done to me.

They didn't know.

There was no way he'd told them about all this. If he had, I would have seen it. I'd never been around a family before when someone had a serious illness, but that topic would have come up. They would have asked about Wolf and made sure he was okay and doing well.

Why hasn't he told them?

Why hadn't he told *me* and what was all this? Wolf swallowed. "I knew things were about to change, yes, and I guess I was buying time." He scanned away. "They needed a distraction."

A distraction.

My heart broke again, and at this point, the pieces couldn't be swept up. They were too fine, microscopic.

I was the distraction.

What was crazy was I couldn't even be mad at him. I wanted to be. God, how I did, but who could have known this would have happened between us? Who could have known *us* could have happened?

God.

I rubbed at my chest. Something had happened between us. Something so deep. I scanned his eyes. "How much pain are you in?"

We'd made love tonight. We'd made *fucking* love, and let's not even talk about all the things I'd had him doing tonight. He'd been carrying my stuff, and I'd been commanding him around. He'd taken every direction and hadn't said a fucking thing, and then there were all the times we'd been intimate before tonight. He hadn't looked stiff back then, but he had tonight.

He had tonight.

I felt so fucking ill. Like someone was carving me with a dull knife, and as if Wolf knew all the thoughts whirling around in my head, he made me focus on him. His hand went to my cheek, which was apparently wet. I knew because his thumb slid down a trail of tears.

"I don't want you to concern yourself with that, okay?" he stated, and a sound left my lips. It was something between a croak and a cry. He was in pain. He had to be.

I wondered for how long.

I wondered how long he'd suffered. Had it been way back when he'd first found out? Maybe it had been to some degree, and if there had been pain, he'd clearly been hiding it back then like he was now.

"How bad is it?" I didn't know how I managed to ask the question. My insides were breaking so fucking bad. "Wolf, how bad is your condition?"

He didn't look like he wanted to answer the question and didn't at first. No, he wasn't running away from this. He couldn't. Fucking *no*.

"Ares, how bad is it goddamnit!" My voice shook the walls, the only sound in this room besides my labored breathing. I was trying so hard to keep it together, but I was failing.

Wolf's face filled with a charged red color, and normally, that was me. Normally, I showed what I was feeling in that way, and that was the only indicator he was feeling anything. He was holding it all in so well. His thumbs brushed the loose hairs framing my face. "Pretty bad, Red."

My eyes closed, my fists in a tight squeeze. "How *bad*?"

I was going to lose it worse than I was already. The only

thing that could come next was harsh vomiting, but I was holding it back. I had to.

Wolf's sigh left his full lips. "It's a tumor, and it's not in a great place. It's in my back again, but any kind of surgery is high risk. It's too big this time and removal could leave me paralyzed or worse."

I swear to God the only thing keeping me together at this point was information. It was the only way I was holding on, the need for it too great. "What can be done?"

Again, his silence was sending me over the edge. He scanned my eyes, and his mouth opened. It did, but he wouldn't speak.

"Please." I was begging him to talk to me. To give me some kind of hope.

His gaze hit the water once more. He stared at it like there were a million thoughts behind his eyes, but the question was simple. "My doctor started me in a clinical trial last semester, and I was willing to try it since they've seen success with cases like mine. I wasn't feeling many symptoms from the tumor when we started. Mostly tingling and some numbness, but the tumor was growing really fast, and I had to act fast. I thought I could handle treatment on the low and not worry my family."

Hence the need for a distraction.

I bit deep into my lip. "Did it help?"

"It stopped growing," he said, and my heart lifted. "It did, and I had to go on a special diet. I lost weight."

He lost weight.

Of course, he had. Of course, he *did*. Hindsight was something else. Hindsight was a fucking jerk.

"But there haven't been any changes in a while," Wolf continued, and my heart sunk again. "It's not getting worse, but it's not getting better either. My doctor wants to start a more aggressive form of treatment. He wants to get ahead of it before it becomes something we can't deal with. He's afraid it will start growing again, and if that happens, the odds of a successful removal are slim. The way it looks right now no doctor will touch it. Believe me. I've looked."

An aggression hit his voice, but mine only remained with him and the situation. I was frustrated with him for dealing with this all by himself, and he still clearly was. Again, I would have seen if his family knew about everything since I'd been around them.

He also hadn't told me.

He hadn't at first, and that hurt in ways that cut so harshly. It didn't matter how much his condition... his situation wasn't about me. I was hurt he hadn't told me, and I also had frustrations with myself. I was frustrated I hadn't seen the signs, and there'd been so many.

"Why did you let me run you around all day today, huh? You had to have been hurting." I blinked down tears. Again, those frustrations. I should have fucking known. I should have *seen* it. "Why did you do that, and why did you make love to me tonight? I saw how stiff you were. Why would you do these things? Why would you..."

I was shaking because I was so, so scared. I was scared for his life. I was terrified, and if I in any way added to his pain, I'd never forgive myself.

"Hey." Wolf's hands never left me, but now, they were focusing me. He made me look at him, his hands firm on my cheeks. "Today was one of the best days of my life," he admitted, and I instantly started trembling. The dam broke and the tears finally came down my cheeks in a steady stream. Wolf kissed one cheek, then the other. "Being with you has been some of the best days of my life."

He was talking so finally. Like he really was dying.

My hands locked on to his wrists, my grip strong. "Why didn't you tell me? You knew this whole time, and you didn't tell me."

It didn't even come out in a scold. I was too terrified. I was in too much pain, and I unfortunately knew pain like this. It was something I never wanted to experience again after my dad had died.

And here we were again. I was deep in the influx of it, and it was so severe. A part of me died that day my father passed, and it was happening once more.

It was *ending* me.

Wolf guided me to refocus on him, and he was blinking profusely. Like he was fighting with all he had to keep it together for me when he shouldn't have to. He was the one this was happening to. Not me. "I didn't because I'm not your problem, Red. You hear me? *I'm. Not. Your. Problem.* I'm a shit person, Red. I hurt you, and I *used* you. You understand me?"

I did understand, but what he didn't was that he was my problem.

Because I loved him.

I fell in love with him, and neither one of us planned for that, but that was what had happened. It had, and he couldn't take that away. He couldn't do it any more than he could for himself.

You are it for me, he'd said to me downstairs, and suddenly, all that time we were apart made sense. He'd said he always loved me, but maybe for a while, he couldn't. Maybe he put it away. Locked it up.

"And even if I hadn't, I won't be your problem," he said now, and this was the first time I heard something in his voice. I'd been the one who was a mess this whole time, but his deep tone definitely cracked in that moment. It wavered, strained. His forehead touched mine. "I want you to live your life and not worry about me."

He really was doing this, *again,* he was doing this. "Why don't you let me decide that?"

It wasn't fair what he was doing, and he was making me want to hate him again. It was impossible, because even without his cancer, I couldn't hate him. He'd made me love him too hard, too deep.

"Because if I can do one thing for you, it's to keep you out of this," he said, my heart shattering all over again. His eyes closed. "You never should have been a part of it, and for that, Fawn, I'm sorry."

My shoulders shook, my body racked with sobs. I wasn't even holding it back anymore, and Wolf was barely keeping it together himself. His eyes clenched tight, his hands bracing me. "I wronged you so badly, Fawn Greenfield. You never should have been a part of my life. I brought you in selfishly, and now, fucking now…" He kissed my forehead. "Now, I'm saving you from this. The next few months of my life are going to be fucked, and I can't have you be a part of it. I fucking *can't*."

He didn't need to save me. I was strong, and he knew that. He knew that.

Even still, he wasn't giving me the option. He got up from the tub, and I saw how agonizingly slow he did this. Slow like he was truly in pain.

So slow.

I really should have known, but none of us knew. He did it too well. Fooled us *all*. "Why doesn't your family know yet?"

This was a guess, but the signs of that were there too. *It was true*, and he couldn't possibly do whatever was next on his own, by himself?

Wolf stopped walking, but he didn't face me. He simply gripped the doorframe. His back was on display as well as that beautiful art. He probably didn't do much of his art anymore. He'd said his cancer had messed up his hands in the past.

It made my heart rip apart in new ways. How much he'd lost. How much he was *losing…*

"Just be happy, okay? Do that for me. *Be happy*," he said,

and that strain in his voice made me grab my mouth. I would have audibly sobbed if I didn't. I would have broken down worse than I already was. Instead, I waited until he left the room.

I couldn't remember when I stopped.

CHAPTER
THIRTY-FOUR

Ares

"Eh, Wolf?"

I turned on the couch, Thatcher's voice behind me. He came over with Wells to play video games with Dorian and me at our dorm. They did this all the time. I mean, they lived across the hall, so we were always in and out of each other's dorms. Eventually, we all planned to get a house together.

That'd been the plan.

Plans were different these days for me. In fact, there was no plan. There was reality and how I aimed to handle it. There was death and there was life.

There was life and then there was death.

I'd made a choice a long time ago that I'd do anything I could to make my family happy. That I'd take on any burden so they wouldn't have to. This became especially important after everything I'd put my family through in the past. I'd get stronger, braver, and I'd done that every day since I'd decided. I *wasn't weak*, and I handled my own shit. I wasn't anyone's burden and refused to be.

Refused.

Today, I was supposed to break that promise. I asked the guys over to talk to them. This would be the icebreaker that would lead into discussing everything regarding my health with everyone. I needed my boys and had even left my sister out of this. I'd made sure she wasn't here today when I asked them over, not ready...

I needed the guys' strength and *their bravery* today, but here I sat on the couch. I wasn't even playing videos games. I just watched.

I was weak.

My strength had left me after speaking to Red. That shit *broke me* and severely. I had nothing left after that. All that fight I had in me... the wolf persona I'd fought so hard to create had shattered after only one day with Fawn Greenfield. Being with her had destroyed it all and annihilated the last strength I had to talk to the guys. I'd had to hurt her again and that shit *ruined* me.

And wrecked her.

I wondered if it was possible to be whole again after that. If she'd be whole, but the only way she had a chance was far away from me. I'd told her what she needed to know. I'd used her and let her know that.

I'd used her.

I had in so many ways but refused to drive the dagger more than I should when it came to her.

I really was weak.

I was, but I wouldn't hurt Red more than I already had. That girl had gone through shit because of me. She'd had enough of me for a lifetime.

She'd had enough.

I think we both had, but I was leaving myself out of this. I'd suffer a million times over so she wouldn't have to.

I felt comatose as I faced Thatcher who was still behind the couch. He had his hands together, and the door was cracked behind him. He pointed toward it. "Hey, uh. Guess who's at the door."

I didn't have the energy for games, facing forward. Dorian and Wells continued to button-mash their controllers in front of me. We'd all been sitting here for hours. It was a Sunday, and they'd given up on trying to talk to me. They knew I'd gotten in last night, but they assumed the worst when I'd said I didn't want to talk about what had happened with Red.

It had been the worst.

My sister had been here too at one point. She'd ended up bowing out to get some studio time in at one of the spaces reserved for students on campus. She'd said she had a deadline for a class, but I knew it was just to give me my space. Normally, Dorian would have gone with her, but he'd stayed behind because of me. He didn't say it, but he had. I'd come in moody as fuck last night, and he saw that. Since he had stayed here, I'd decided to use that as an opportunity to call all my friends over. *To talk.*

That was until I'd gotten weak.

I literally had nothing left after that conversation with Red, and it took me a second to realize her name had been mentioned. Thatcher had said it, and I turned toward the door. It was still cracked, and I couldn't see out of it.

"She's, um, here, my dude," he said, smiling. In fact, he was grinning so big. He braced his large hands. "She said she wants to see you."

Thatcher had to have been mistaken. *I'd ended* this, but no sooner had he said the words, and I was off the couch. Normally, I'd be intentional about such maneuvers. I was often stiff if I sat too long and didn't need the guys seeing all that. I must have had some adrenaline backing me because I ignored my tight muscles and shot toward the door.

I was sure I'd be regretting that later, but at the present, I didn't care. I passed Thatcher who was still grinning along the way, and in the far-off spaces of my mind, I knew the others were watching. There were no more game sounds behind me.

But I forgot about all that with her in front of me.

Red's head darted up when the door widened, her face filled with an intense flush. She had her ripped jeans on even though it was barely above freezing outside, as well as that puffer coat *I hated* because it always hid her sexy curves. She had it open today, though, and her crop top revealed her freckled waist. It looked so soft, always so soft.

Who wears mittens, Red?

My Red did, and her hands were gripping like crazy inside them. She had those on and a little hat with a pom-pom on it. She basically looked like a sexy little Christmas elf, and I was well aware of what I'd internally called her.

Mine.

I knew it wasn't right to associate her in that way. Even in my mind, it wasn't all right, but I'd done it anyway.

And the guys were behind me.

I didn't turn to see them, but I could certainly feel their presence. I also noticed Red gazed over my shoulder before focusing on me. She lifted a mitten. "Hi."

The wash of dopamine that hit me when she said that literally loosened my stiff muscles. This girl was like a healing agent.

If only she could be.

If only she was the solution to everything that was going wrong, and she was to an extent. She fixed things in almost every way I needed. My hand gripped the door. "Hey. What are you—"

"Is your truck here?"

Uhh...

I must have not spoken fast enough because Red was scanning around the hallway. She was also shifting on her sneakers, and she huffed out a breath before looking at me. "Your Hummer. Is it outside?"

It was, but I was unsure why she was asking about it. I eased out into the hallway, closing the door. "Yes…"

"Can you get your keys and meet me outside with it, then? Out back?" she questioned and started backing away. She was also gazing around the hall, and I didn't know if it was because of nerves or because she was looking for someone.

Suddenly alarmed, I started to ask, but then, Red was gone. She headed down the hallway, and I was so thrown I headed after her. I already had my keys and my phone, but I failed to get a coat.

I didn't care, and I lost Red when some traffic in the hallway hit. Some study group or some shit literally had all their stuff spread out in the hallway. I scanned above them. "Red—"

I lost her when she cut a corner, and by the time I did get through the traffic, she was gone.

Fuck.

My next move was to head outside. To get my truck and drive it around back like she'd said. I didn't know what was going on and couldn't move as fast as I wanted, but I got my Hummer as soon as I could. I got it around the back of the building quick, and when I did, I noticed only one person out there. Red had her coat zipped up, and she was standing in an empty part of the lot.

What the fuck?

She didn't seem like she was in trouble or anything. She was just standing there, but her awareness spiked when I pulled my Hummer in front of her. A noticeable stiffness grabbed a hold of her, and I internally cursed myself for driving up on her so fast. She was scared of cars, so I quickly shut it off.

"What's going on?" I rounded my truck, the cold shooting a laser through my body. I managed to grab a hoodie I kept in the back of my ride and put it on, but it was still cold as fuck out here. It was even worse because I was stiff. "You all right?"

She wasn't acting like it, shifting. She kept transferring her focus from me to the truck, and I did something I probably shouldn't have.

I focused her attention. I did when I put my hands on her shoulders. I started rubbing, and right away, she came back to me.

She came back.

Her awareness returned her, and I saw it well. I observed how the resistance left her body, and suddenly, I was the only thing in front of her. I became her sole focus, and that grappled me in ways that *socked me*. I loved being this girl's center.

Which was stupid of me.

It was so stupid, and once I realized she was grounded, I let her go. I didn't get a whole lot of feeling in my hands some days, but I still felt the heat of her. It vibrated through me, as well as that floral scent of hers. It was in the air and completely around me. *She* was around me. Everywhere.

"I want to drive your Hummer."

She pulled me out of my tortured thoughts. She did when she started talking crazy. My mouth parted. "What?"

"I said I want to drive your Hummer, Ares," she husked out. She was still focused on me, but then she glanced over to my ride. "If you'll let me, I'd like to drive it."

She was still talking crazy talk, and I shook my head. "What are you talking about?"

Instead of answering, she stepped over to my Hummer. The thing made her look like a little kid it was so big, and that was why I'd gotten it. I liked big cars, and there was plenty of space for the guys and me.

It made Red appear so small, though, and despite stepping cautiously, she did move toward it. She gripped the handle, and the next thing I knew, she was getting inside it.

What the hell!

Again, I darted. My body was going to kick my ass in the morning, but I didn't care. The last time this girl got in a car she'd told me she'd blacked out. Her phobia of cars was real, but for some reason, she was in my truck right now and behind the wheel. I reached for the handle to help her get out, but she locked the door.

Holy fucking shit.

I didn't know if Fawn was losing her mind or what, and behind the wheel, she just sat there. Her hands were above her in tight fists, and I tugged crazy at the door. "Red, open the door."

She didn't. She just sat there, her hands up, her fists tight. She closed her eyes, and her mouth was moving. She looked like she was saying something, and instead of trying the door again, I headed around to the passenger side. I noticed she'd manually locked her door, and the passenger side was unlocked when I got there.

I got in, got next to her. I shut the door off from the cold, and right away, I saw what she was doing.

She was... counting.

She did one through ten, then repeated the sequence over. She did this with tight fists, and I watched her.

I couldn't do anything else.

I just sat there, awed, and she continued to count, and I recognized the breathing she was doing. I also did breathing exercises when I'd had bouts of anxiety in the past.

I stayed silent. I didn't want to panic her, and again, I was awed. She was in here just doing her thing, and I couldn't help it. I was truly in awe of her.

Especially when she released her fists.

Incredibly flushed, Fawn's eyes opened, and when they did, she placed her hands on the wheel. She touched down, rubbing, and that was when I leaned forward. "Red?"

Once more, she ignored me. She just kept rubbing the

wheel. Like she was focusing herself or calming down. "What's next?"

Her statement added to the confusion of that moment. "What do you mean?"

She glanced over to me for the first time, and how calm and collected she really was. This was one of her greatest fears, but here she was doing it in my monster truck. She wet her lips. "What's next for me to drive?"

I didn't understand all this, or what her motivation was. Again, she was acting crazy, and because I didn't know what was going on, I handed her my keys. That was basically what she'd asked for, and I realized now I could have gotten into my truck this whole time. I could have stopped her from doing this, but for some reason, I was handing her the key to start this thing.

Because I'd give her anything.

She had no idea how hard it was for me to let go of her again. It actually had broken me, and I'd been vacant just this morning. I'd left my body like the life had been drained out, but now, it was back.

It was back.

The girl fucking healed me so much. She made the mental shit hurt less, and the reality of that caused a harsh ache inside. It *killed*, because I knew I couldn't keep it. I wasn't worth keeping it. I wasn't worthy of being hers in a thousand lifetimes. Not after what I'd done. Tried to do…

I had used her and tried to do right by her. Even still, she was *here* and making this shit so much harder.

"I don't have a license," she said, once more rubbing the wheel. She hadn't started the truck, but the key was in the ignition. She gripped the wheel. "But I can drive. I haven't forgotten how."

I believed her, and because I'd apparently do anything she wanted, I strapped in. She did too, and I watched in complete fascination when she did start my ride. It hummed to life like a cave monster beneath her, and though it did give her pause, she just counted again. She breathed. She pushed through.

And then…

Well, then a miracle happened. *She* happened when she put the truck into drive and took off. She didn't go flying or anything. We were moving slowly, but we moved.

She allowed us to move.

Red's hands were ghost white on the wheel, and once more, I watched her. I stayed there in pure fascination.

Adoration.

Red had to be *terrified*, but here she was driving us around the parking lot. We circled our own little corner of the lot, and Fawn guided us. I didn't move an inch. I really didn't want to scare her or break her concentration, but not once did I question if she'd keep us safe. I trusted this girl with my very life.

I always had.

She'd had that trust for longer than she knew. Fawn Greenfield was *my* center, and she'd been that for so long. I honestly didn't know when she wasn't.

Swallowing, I brought the focus off myself and stayed on Red. Her breathing was rapid beside me, her hands still locked on the wheel, and I finally did reach over. I couldn't help it. Squeezing her shoulder, I wanted her to know I was here and supported her. I smiled. "You're doing great."

This was an understatement. She was doing amazing, and she needed no motivation or validation from me. She knew what a badass she was by conquering this fear right now.

Because she smiled.

It was big and bright, and I knew it had nothing to do with me. Deep in my gut I just felt that, and I loved that for her. She knew this was her demon to slay and she was doing it. She did it.

And we went faster. The truck kept steadily increasing in acceleration, and no way did I stop her. I just let her drive, and eventually, she did stop. She parked, and when she did, she dared to do so between a couple cars, which said something. Even I had issues parking this thing, but she did it.

Way to go, Red.

I realized now I never had to coddle her. I never had to do anything for her, because she could handle things herself. She could handle her life herself.

She doesn't need you.

Maybe she didn't, and I was happy for that. I loved that she didn't need me. I was grateful she didn't.

My gut clenched when she turned off the Hummer, and I didn't realize why until she faced me. She had conquered her demons, and now, she was about to leave again. Leave me.

Making myself be grateful for that too, I started to say, but Red unstrapped her seat belt and faced me full on. She put her hands together. "You see what I just did, right?"

I did see. How could I not? She was amazing. "Red—"

"You saw that, so you can *see* that I'm not weak," she stated, her voice suddenly quivering, and my lips parted. She squeezed her hands into fists. "I did that, and I'm not weak, Ares."

I didn't get why she was saying this, and I put my hand on her. I touched her face this time. Stupid, I knew. "I know that."

"Do you?" She was on the verge of crying again, her lashes fanning rapidly. Why could I not make this girl cry for a second? Just one goddamn second. She ran her sleeve under her eyes. "So you know what I'm capable of. I can handle this, Ares. I can be there for you and everything you're going through."

The words hit me so hard. Like I'd collided with a bullet train. She'd done this… for me?

Damn.

I'd made her think she was weak. That she had to prove something to me.

God, you're such a fuckup.

I kept fucking up when it came to her. I was *selfish* when it came to her, and I knew that when I brought her close. I evaporated all that space I needed to keep and pressed my forehead to hers. "Fawn, baby, you're not weak. If anything, you're the strong one."

She'd endured all I'd put her through, and I was the weak motherfucker. I just couldn't let go of this girl.

She wouldn't let me. Her arms looping around me, she fused herself to me, and my chest caved when she pressed her face into my chest. It felt good. So fucking good.

"Then why won't you let me be there for you?" she said, the words shaky, and her fingers curling into my back. She was doing it so softly. Like she didn't want to hurt me, and all of this was beginning already. She was holding on like she didn't want to break me, and that *destroyed* me. She sniffed back sobs. "Please let me be there for you."

I didn't want her to see me sick. I didn't want to *need her*.
You don't deserve her.

She'd never know how much I didn't, and that was me being weak again. I couldn't hurt this girl any more than I already had. I couldn't. I...

Fawn made me look at her. She eased both arms free, then pressed her hands to my face. She wouldn't allow me to run from her when all I wanted to do was leave, smoke on my heels. I was good at that, and she was too.

Apparently, she wasn't anymore. She really was the one with true strength. She fingered my hair. "Let me be there for you," she said, and then it was her forehead touching mine. She pressed her hands hard to my face, her head shaking. "*Please*, let me be there for you."

It was in that moment when it all broke. I shattered, and the next thing I knew, my arms were bracing around her head. I was rubbing my cheek into her hair. It was always so soft, and she was always so warm.

"I'm scared, Red," I said, and it was the first time I said

the words out loud. I was scared, but not of dying. Death didn't scare me, but the wake of my absence would. I was scared of what that absence would do to my family and friends. *That* was where my terror lay, and it radiated down to my fucking core.

I also feared losing this, this amazing girl in my arms. She'd conquered a fear today, and she'd done it for me. Fucking *me*. She'd done that for her monster and was now here trying to support him, save him.

Red.

I think I'd known when I answered the door I wasn't letting her go again. It wasn't possible, and I didn't care how selfish it was. I needed her.

And she was letting me.

CHAPTER
THIRTY-FIVE

Ares

I called my parents that night. I told them I'd come see them, but they ended up packing into the car and coming to see me. I told them briefly over the phone I wanted to talk to them about health concerns. I didn't want them to wonder for the two hours it'd take them to get here, and I also didn't want to blindside them either. That wasn't fair to them. They'd both been calm on the phone, and my dad had asked a single question.

"Is it back?" he'd asked, and that was when I'd glanced to Red. She was in my Hummer with me when I'd made the call.

And she'd taken my hand when I told him yes.

She was also there when I told the guys my parents were coming here. They were bringing Bru with them, and before they could ask too many questions, I called my sister. I told her she needed to come to my dorm, and she did right before my parents arrived. My parents did know the truth, but the guys and my sister didn't.

I wished I'd been brave enough to tell them before my

parents had arrived. I wish I'd done a lot of things different, but in that moment, I did what I had the mental ability to do. The guys and Sloane found out after my parents and Bru arrived, and it all spilled out. I gave them every detail and left out no iota of truth regarding my condition. I discussed every doctor's visit and even the secret trips I'd taken to Johns Hopkins. They'd been weekend trips and ones I hadn't told anyone about. No one had known about anything.

I'd hidden it all so well.

I didn't focus on their reactions. I didn't focus on anything but the truth, and I used Red as my center. She kept hold of my hand when I told everyone everything, and I doubt anyone even knew she was there at that point. She was silently in the background of all this, but that hadn't been the case when I'd first brought her today. Actually, the guys had been happy to see her. They'd been happy *for me* because they knew how miserable I was without her.

I'd failed a lot of people in this room. But the job I'd done on my friends, my brothers...

Dorian was too silent when I finally looked at him, and though my sister was on the cusp of crying after everything I said, she was asking questions. She got them in when my parents weren't asking them, and those had been hard. I told them how I'd found out I was sick at the beginning of fall semester.

I told them I'd been lying.

That was when the silence had started. At least from Dorian. Thatcher and Wells had been more vocal. They started yelling at me before Dad told them to take a walk. They didn't want to, but Mom advised that would be best, and Bru went with them. He wasn't as mad and also tended to be the peacekeeper in the family.

His exit let me know he needed to cool off as well, though. His face was incredibly red when he left the room with Wells and Thatch, and my stomach got so fucking tight. The guilt hit me in an avalanche, and it got worse watching Dorian.

It got so bad.

My friend wouldn't even look at me, and he was shaking. His big body was rocking back and forth while he rubbed his hands, and Sloane was massaging his arm as she was asking questions. She was taking care of him while dealing with this shit herself, and the guilt *of that* hurt so bad.

"You realize how bad this could have gotten?" my dad asked, bringing my focus back to him and Mom. Mom was silent too, but she had at least been speaking at some points in the conversation. She was scanning the floor. Like she was analyzing it with her brilliant mind, and that reminded me of myself. I looked for solutions even when I didn't have any or wasn't equipped *to have* any. I remained objective and tried to keep out the emotion.

But this was her son.

Make no mistake my mom was hurting, and I wanted to be sick because I knew how bad I was hurting her. She faced my dad. "That's the thing. We don't know how bad this is. We just know what he's told us."

It was like I wasn't in the room, and the voices inside my head were so loud. I wanted to end all this and stop this pain for everyone. Pain I'd caused. "Mom—"

"You're going to give us all the details of the doctor you've been seeing, and we're going to speak to him first thing tomorrow ourselves," Mom continued, her expression tight, serious. She was trying so hard to keep it together. I knew her MO. Again, it was like mine. She nodded. "We'll also call Dr. Sturm who should have *always* been in charge of your care."

I'd had to tell them about all that. I'd stopped seeing my old doctor because he was a link to my family I couldn't have. I'd known right away I was having symptoms again, and as soon as I had, the first thing I'd done was get another physician.

I'd hidden so much from them all.

"I also want the information of anyone else you've seen or had consultations with," Mom said, and I nodded. I'd do anything she wanted, anything they wanted. She shook her head. "God, Ares. What have you done? What did you do…"

Dad was rubbing Mom like Sloane was rubbing Dorian. Sloane was until she wasn't because in that moment my friend decided to get up. He *walked away*, and I watched as Sloane went after him.

Fuck.

Red, who was still beside me, squeezed my shoulder. She was checking her own emotions and had to be. A lot of this information I'd shared was new to her too, but the moment she noticed Dorian leave, she eyed me. It was like a silent exchange occurred between us. Especially when she nodded towards Dorian and Sloane's exit. She thought I should go after my friend.

How had I not always had this girl?

How had I fought the very thing I needed so badly? There was no way Red was okay right now, but here she was guiding me to go after Dorian.

I kissed her hand, thanking her so hard for that. Her response to that was a smile that made my heart tight.

God, how had I hurt everyone I cared about?

It was so bad, and though I did want to go after Dorian, I felt myself hesitate in front of my parents. I didn't want to leave them, but my dad, who'd obviously seen Dorian leave, gestured for me to go too. That right there let me know he too saw how unusual Dorian's reaction had been. My buddy had a tendency to either be explosive or calm, but not how he'd been when he left. It was like he was two seconds from breaking, cracking.

I went after him after kissing Red's cheek. I whispered to

her to look after my parents, and I hadn't had to explain her presence today. I think everyone could assume why she was here today. I mean, she'd held my hand the whole time.

I didn't deserve that girl, and that guilt only stacked on top of what I had reserved for my family. I headed quick down the hall after Dorian. He and I had upgraded into a bigger dorm fall semester, and he was in his room.

He was yelling.

"No, little fighter," he said, calling my sister by his nickname for her. "No, see that shit... That bullshit out here..."

His deep voice was strained behind the door, and I closed my eyes. Dorian didn't break. He got angry, but he didn't break.

"He really did play us all, didn't he? He said not a thing. Not a goddamn thing," he stated, and they'd all put together Fawn was a distraction. I'd definitely used her as an excuse to sneak away during that short time we'd been together. I'd had doctor's appointments they couldn't know about. Trips out of town.

I placed my hand on the door.

"He played us..." Dorian's voice cracked, and I knocked when I'd normally just open the door. I couldn't remember the last time either of us had had any kind of privacy. We'd pretty much revoked that from each other the moment we knew about the other's existence. Thatcher and Wells coming along only reaffirmed that none of us gave each other privacy. We were best friends and a pack of assholes.

I gave my friend his privacy today. It was the least I could do.

"If you're not Ramses or Brielle, fuck off," barked from the other side of the door, and I heard my sister trying to calm Dorian down. She was being super calm when she should be mad too. I was sure she was, but I think my cancer being on the table changed things. I was sure she was angry but defaulted into protector mode. She was looking out for everyone else in a time of need, and that didn't surprise me. If the roles were reversed, I'd probably be doing the same thing. I'd do anything so my family didn't have to feel pain.

This was so ironic. There was so much pain going on right now. I dampened my mouth. "It's me."

I expected an instant *fuck off* or something more colorful. I got neither, and eventually, the door opened. My sister came out, and though I gazed above her, I didn't see Dorian.

He was in there somewhere though, and my sister had on such a brave face. She appeared camera-ready like one would be for a press conference before giving bad news. She shook her head. "It's bad, Ares. He's bad."

I heard, my insides turning.

Sloane swallowed. "You should talk to him. I think it will help."

I nodded and started to go but stopped. I got her shoulder. "Why aren't you more mad, little?" She didn't have to put on a brave face for me. It was just us right now, and she could give me hell.

I almost wanted her to. I wanted her to do anything but guard her feelings right now. This was a lot, and it was bull-shit. She rubbed her arms. "I think I'm more scared, big," she said, nodding. She blinked before squeezing her eyes. "I am scared."

I brought her into my arms, and normally, she was the one doing that to me. I rubbed her back, and though she didn't cry, she gripped hold of my hoodie so hard.

I let her do that. I just held her and let her feel her emotions. I was scared too. Scared for everyone.

"You promise me you're going to fight," she said into my chest, and her voice was strained too. She gazed up at me with red eyes, but again, she didn't cry. She nodded. "You better fight and not leave us. I need you. I need both my little brothers."

She let a tear escape, and I rubbed it away.

"You only got me by five minutes, little," I joked, and she laughed, warming my heart. I squeezed her shoulder. "And you know me."

Me fighting went without saying, and she knew that. She hugged me, and I let her get it all out again. She was with me on all this, supported me, and it was so good to know. I didn't want to lose her either. I needed my big sister.

I told her that before letting her go, and that made us both laugh. It was very ironic considering our nicknames for each other, and I supposed that was the point.

Dorian didn't even gaze up when I opened the door, and my stomach soured. I knew I had a battle ahead of me with Wells and Thatcher. We were only separated by a year, but they took things way harder. They always had, and it'd always been Dorian to ground us.

That was why his reaction did worry me so much. He was leaning against his desk when I closed the door, and as soon as it clicked closed, he gripped the desk. That let me know right away he knew it was me in here and not my sister. He didn't even have to look at me.

He smirked. "So all that shit about you working on toning..." He shook his head, and his expression was cold as ice. "Changing your diet and staying out of the weight room. You said you wanted to tone. Do more cardio."

I'd had to tell them something since I knew I'd be losing weight. I started to speak, but Dorian raised a hand.

"Then the fact that none of us have been seeing you sketch lately. It was the cancer, right? Fucked up your hands?"

"D—"

"It was *the cancer*, right?" His voice was even while he gripped his arms, but make no mistake my friend was pissed. He looked pissed, was pissed. "Tell me the truth about that and your diet and the gym."

I pushed my hands in my hoodie's front pocket. "Yes, you're right about both. I obviously couldn't do the gym, and

I had to eat special for that clinical trial. It made me lose weight."

They knew about the trial. They all knew everything now since I'd just told them.

"Lying to us just like your secret fucking doctor's appointments." He rubbed his mouth. "So all those random classes you were missing last semester... Disappearing on weekends..."

"Doctor's appointments, yes," I confirmed, and he started laughing. The laughter was loud, charged, and the next thing I knew, he was in my face. He was grabbing my hoodie, and I think the only reason he didn't hit me was obvious.

He didn't want to hurt me. *No one* did, and I saw the same frustration on his face that Thatch and Wells had before they'd left. They'd been yelling, but they'd been so careful about it. They'd tiptoed around words when they never did. It was like they didn't want to hurt me or be insensitive when my friends never gave a fuck about that.

The situation was clearly causing them to hold back, but they were all furious at me. They were, but they were restraining that fury in their own ways.

This was D's way. He shook so bad before letting me go, but before he could get far, I reached for him.

He shouldered away, darting a finger at me. "Don't you fucking touch me, Ares."

I ignored him, getting his arm, and I could tell right away he didn't know how to fight me off. He had his hands up and got incredibly stiff, but I didn't fucking care.

"No. I said fucking *no*. Don't touch me, Ares," he gritted, but that went ignored too. I got my arms around him, as tight as I could go, and he locked up so bad. He cringed. "I said don't touch me. Don't fucking touch me. I swear to God..."

The words fell on deaf ears. I was making him deal with this. I was making him deal with me and wouldn't let him run.

"Don't touch me..." The strained words hit my ear the same time his hold came around me. He gripped my hoodie, his biceps shaking. "Don't touch me, you asshole. You fucking asshole."

Despite the words, he didn't let go. If anything, he braced me tighter.

"How come I didn't know? How come I didn't *fucking* know?" His voice shook worse than his hold, and I found more strength when I gripped him tighter. I pulled everything I had and put it into this because I got it now. Dorian wasn't mad at me, not really.

He was mad at himself.

He was mad at himself for not seeing, but this wasn't his fault. I closed my eyes. "I made sure you didn't, D."

I hadn't wanted anyone seeing, suffering. We'd all suffered so fucking much, and I'd wanted to handle this on my own. I'd wanted to protect them.

And I'd failed.

I'd failed so fucking much and made all this shit worse.

My words didn't help my friend. He just continued to shake, and when I looked up, I saw we weren't alone. Thatcher and Wells lingered by the door, but it was closed like they'd been standing there for a minute.

And how fucked up they looked.

Thatcher appeared almost worse than Dorian. He had his burly arms crossed tight, and he was barely able to keep eye contact with me. He kept looking away, his face red and splotchy. Wells didn't look much different, and that shit gut-punched me. They were the ones I couldn't get to shut the fuck up with their humor.

But not today.

Today, there were no jokes, laughs, and Dorian noticed they were there too. Normally, Dorian might try to hide his emotion, but he didn't when he reached for Thatcher.

Thatch resisted, shaking his head. He locked up just like

Dorian had, but D was persistent too. He got Thatch by the back of the neck and brought him over.

"You motherfucker," Thatcher ground out at me, but he didn't fight the hug I gave him. He got my hoodie. "You stupid fuck. What were you thinking keeping this shit from us?"

I was thinking I didn't want to hurt them. Stupid, and I knew that now.

I said nothing in the moment, though, because I didn't think he wanted an answer. He didn't any more than Dorian had.

Thatch squeezed his eyes. "You better not fucking die. You better not..."

Once his voice started to break, Wells joined us. He gripped Thatcher's arm, but I brought him into the circle. I got a *I fucking hate you* from him and other choice words that equally tightened my chest, but I knew he didn't mean any of it. I knew he just needed to feel this like the rest of us were, and we finally all were.

Because I let them in.

I needed my brothers. The only one missing was Bru, but I knew he was watching over our parents and Sloane so I wouldn't have to. I needed all the people I cared about in my life right now, and it took a girl driving my Hummer today to show me *my* strength. Red never had to prove herself to me, but I was glad she'd done what she had.

Because she showed me what I was capable of.

CHAPTER
THIRTY-SIX

Fawn

The next twenty-four hours happened quickly, but I was ready.

I'd told him I would be.

I'd made an unsaid promise to Ares in his Hummer, and it was the same promise I'd made to myself when I'd gotten in. I would put my own fears aside. I would be there for him, and *that* was what had gotten me in his truck that day. I'd made that promise to him, but the biggest promise had been to myself. I wouldn't allow myself to be held back by my fears, and this situation with Ares *terrified* me. I used to be so scared of loving him. In fact, I'd thought it may break me a time or two, but it never had. In actuality, I was made stronger by the love, and now, not loving him wasn't an option.

Neither was losing him.

Wolf had a lot of family come by in the next twenty-four hours. The majority of them I'd met. The Legacy parents had pretty much all made an appearance. They came to us in

Queenstown Village, and I got reacquainted with them all again. There'd been brave faces, sad faces, and new ones I hadn't seen. I hadn't met Wolf's grandparents, but a few of them showed up. One was his grandpa on his dad's side. The man had salt-and-pepper hair and bronze skin, and he was also the only one to insist he'd be inside the room when Wolf's doctors explained the brevity of his condition. I hadn't expected to be in that room in the hospital that day.

But I'd made a promise.

Again, it was unsaid, and when Ares took my hand and tugged me along with him into that room, I went. Not even his friends Dorian, Thatcher, and Wells were in there. They wanted to be. They'd argued to be, but their parents (who were also at Wolf's appointment) told them they should wait. They didn't want to crowd the room, and the room was crowded. Besides Wolf's grandpa, his parents were there, and of course, his siblings. His sister, Sloane, was on Wolf's other side while Bru was on mine.

I'd done what I could to support Bru too in the past twenty-four hours. I gave my friend reassuring smiles and glances when I was just as terrified as I was sure everyone in this room was. Wolf had a couple doctors. Apparently, he'd stopped seeing one of them for the other, but they were both there, and they must have had recent contact with each other because they both broke down what was going on with Wolf together. They told everyone in this room everything, and even through it frightened me, I remained still. I remained calm.

I remained.

I got Wolf's hand during the worst parts. He knew all this information, but he wasn't dealing with his family's reactions well. He kept looking around and cringing whenever a part of the news negatively affected the room. An example of this was when one of Wolf's doctors explained the tumor in his back wasn't able to be operated on in its current state. They said it had grown too large and its location was difficult. They used words like *paralyzed* and *death*, and Wolf's mom finally accepted a tissue then. She hadn't cried, but she'd been offered some just in case.

She accepted one this time, though. She dabbed lightly beneath her dark eyes, and Wolf looked so tortured upon seeing this, pained. He gripped his leg, but I took his other hand, claiming both. I supported him the whole time and especially when the conversation moved to talks of chemo and other treatments. Both the doctors agreed that chemo-therapy was the way to go in order to get the thing smaller so it *would be* able to be operated on. Wolf hadn't lied about how bad this was.

It was so bad.

Even still, I didn't let myself break. I couldn't. I was *dying* inside, but on the outside, I made myself appear the opposite. Wolf's grandpa shed emotion too at one point in the conver-sation. He had a handkerchief out and hadn't tried to hide that. Upon seeing that, Wolf's dad rubbed the man's shoulder.

"I'm so sorry, son," I heard the older man whisper to Mr. Mallick, and I supposed they were both Mr. Mallick. They themselves were father and son. Wolf's grandpa closed his eyes. "I had no idea he was hiding his treatment from you. I never would have given him the referral for another doctor had I known. I never would have…"

Wolf's dad reassured the older man it was okay, and I did know what they were talking about. Wolf had hidden his treatment from everyone by using another doctor his grandpa had given him, and I'd heard about that. There were whispers amongst his friends, family.

He really had been trying to do this on his own.

Wolf witnessed the exchange between his dad and grandpa, and that torture radiated across his handsome face. His chiseled jawline clenched, and he asked to excuse himself in that moment. He said he just needed a few moments.

He left before that permission was granted, and more than one person in the room moved to go after him. Two were his parents, but they needed to be in this room. They were needed for Wolf's siblings who also attempted to go after him. These people were hurting so bad, and they needed to worry about each other.

"I'll bring him back," I said, hoping they'd let me. I mean, I wasn't family, but hoped they would. No one asked me directly about my presence here, but Wolf's hand pretty much hadn't left mine. They knew we were together again.

Even still, this was a bold ask, and I was grateful when I got a nod from Wolf's parents. Bru smiled at me a little too, and that made me feel good that he supported me going as well.

Wolf hadn't made it far.

The large guy sat in a chair in the middle of the hallway, his head down, his fingers in his hair. I noticed he hadn't made it as far as his friends and his other family. I knew them to all be waiting out in the hospital's waiting room down the hall.

I stepped lightly. Wolf did have a lot of friends and family here. He did have a lot of love, and he probably didn't need me. Regardless, I allowed myself to be available, and when I sat down, he didn't move. I assumed he didn't know I was there, so I opened my mouth to announce my presence.

That was until he pivoted.

Wolf lifted his head, and the next thing I knew, it settled on my chest. His dark curls landed in my face, his musky aroma swirling around me.

He does need you.

It made me feel warm. Especially when he drew his long wingspan around my waist. He brought me close, only the armrest between us, and I buried my fingers deep in his curls.

I hadn't said a word when I'd come over, but somehow, he knew it was me.

My mouth touched his hair, and he sighed beneath my hands. He was like a large animal in a cave, dormant yet completely alive. He shook his head. "I fucked up so bad."

I didn't know if he wanted a response, and I smiled before giving one. "Yeah, you did."

His head lifted, but upon seeing my smile, he gave one right back. It was nice to see. He had a great one of those.

"Ah, Red," he said, taking my face in his hands. He ran thumbs across my cheeks. "You know what you're in for, right? What things are about to look like real soon? It's not going to be pretty. It's going to be fucking terrible."

I assumed he meant his condition, and the doctors did say he'd be sick. Real sick.

He hugged his arms around me. "You're going to see me at my worst and..." His mouth touched my neck. "It's going to be hard for everyone, and I don't want you to see me like that."

I knew he didn't. I nodded. "I understand."

"Do you?" He lifted his head, and his hands returned to my face. He scanned my eyes. "You can walk away right now, and there'd be no harm, no foul. I swear you wouldn't hurt me. If you walk away..."

I kissed him, so done with that *talk*. He knew I wasn't leaving. He knew I was in this, so he needed to stop with this.

He braced my cheeks, bruising my lips, and maybe even harder than I was bruising his. He needed me right now, and I wanted to be needed. I was here for him. I *got* him and had his back.

Because I loved him.

My eyes were wet when he lifted his head, and I was well aware I cried at the drop of a hat lately. I actually loved that I did. I used to hide my emotions, and that was another thing

I'd let go by being with him. I wasn't afraid to feel vulnerability, to show it.

His thumb brushed my cheek. "I'm always making you cry."

He was, but this time, it wasn't his fault. I nodded with a smile, gripping his wrist. "I know what I signed up for. I'm with you on this. I'm not leaving."

And he couldn't make me. He could try, but I'd always be in the background. I'd always be around and willing to help, and he couldn't stop that.

His handsome smile returned before he pressed his mouth against mine again. "Always saving my life," he said during the kiss, and I warmed inside.

Because he saved mine too.

CHAPTER
THIRTY-SEVEN

SPRING

CHAPTER
THIRTY-EIGHT

SUMMER

FALL

CHAPTER
FORTY

WINTER

Fawn – the present

Wolf shifted next to me, restless. His parents were here at this doctor's visit today, so that probably only added to his anxiety. He wanted them to have good news.

And we wanted him to have good news.

The last year had its struggles. Ups and downs included watching my boyfriend get extremely sick and going through what had to be the toughest year of his life. It included sacrifices on all sides. Personally, I delayed my internship with the *New York Times*, but my own sacrifices were nothing compared to Wolf's. He lost yet another year of his life.

But the trade-off gained him his life back.

Looking at him it was like no time had passed. Well, except the obvious. His hair was shorter now but give him until summer and I was sure those curls would be right back down to his shoulders. He'd cut it proactively before undergoing chemotherapy last year, but now, it was back and just as full as it'd been, vibrant. Other changes included him nearly matching the size he'd been prior to all his treatments, and that both pleased and frustrated the hell out of everyone. Myself included. Once his doctors cleared him, he'd been right back in the gym. He'd probably end up being bigger than he'd been before all this just to prove a point to all of us, but he didn't have to. We knew how strong he was.

He showed that strength now, that restraint. He no doubt wanted to blast his doctor with questions but sat patiently beside me. It still felt weird being here for these doctor's appointments, but no one made me feel that way. Least of all Wolf.

He had his arm around me, squeezing my shoulders. "So, what you got for me, Doc? Good news?"

My boyfriend wanted to jump out of his skin, and I did too. He got his bloodwork and scan results today, and those days were always unnerving. None of us knew if bad news would come, and again, Wolf's parents were here.

He faced them, and I knew for a fact the majority of his restlessness came because they were here. He wanted them to be okay first and foremost because that was the kind of guy he was. I was learning that was typical amongst Legacy in general, and the only reason his friends and siblings weren't here was because Wolf didn't allow them. Very early in this whole journey, Wolf had put his foot down when it came to his appointments. His condition was already disrupting his family's life, so he told Dorian, Sloane, and the rest of them that he wanted as few people at his appointments as possible. They didn't always agree with that, and sometimes Wolf was hard-pressed to keep them out, but the majority of the time, they respected his wishes. They did under the caveat that he'd relay any and all information.

He always did, and as I sat next to him, I sometimes wondered why he allowed me to be there. I did until he'd lace his fingers with mine, and I'd squeeze his hand right back. He'd always relax after. His big body would settle into his chair, and something inside me would settle too. He made me at peace.

Apparently, I did that for him too.

I rubbed his arm as he squeezed my hand today. The other remained around me, and we held steadfast on to each other. His parents sat next to Wolf in a similar state. Wolf's mom had his leg, but her other hand was with Wolf's dad. His father, Ramses, squeezed his wife's shoulder. I think we all waited with bated breath for another crop of results.

"I don't know what to tell you, Ares," Dr. Sturm said. He was Wolf's primary doctor again. His other doctor had gone back to Johns Hopkins.

He was no longer needed after Wolf had had his surgery.

I think we'd all thought Wolf's chemotherapy would be difficult, and it had been. Watching him suffer, lose weight… hadn't been easy, and even worse since we didn't know if it'd work enough for Wolf to be able to qualify for surgery. That part had certainly been difficult, but once Wolf had been cleared to remove his tumor, the true difficulty had begun. There'd been a period where reality had set in and none of us knew what kind of state Wolf would be in after he had his operation. We didn't know if he'd be paralyzed or…

I didn't wrap my head around the worst. During that time, I hadn't let myself because I couldn't break, and I couldn't let him see me break either. Wolf needed me in those moments. He needed me during that trauma, and I was there when he ultimately did come out of that hospital room. I was there during recovery, and I was there when he did take his first steps again.

We all were.

I'd bonded with this family, Wolf's family and friends, in

ways I didn't believe was possible for someone like me. I was too beat up, too broken after everything with my dad, but being around all that family and love *gave me* strength. We all got stronger after everything, and my strides hadn't stopped there. I spoke to my mother and stepfather weekly now. They couldn't shut me up on the phone.

I couldn't be the only one whose heart leapt after what Dr. Sturm said, but his warm smile eased that away. He only smiled when he had good news. He cocked his head. "You continue to make my job very easy. Your scans and bloodwork look amazing. Nothing out of the ordinary is showing up. Everything looks good and perfect as it has been."

I squeezed Wolf's hand so tight, and at the same time, his parents released a breath. It was like oxygen was pushed into the room, and we were finally allowed to breathe it.

"So, he's good, then?" Wolf's dad asked even though he'd heard the news, and Wolf faced him. So much hope was in Ares's eyes, and I knew it wasn't for himself. He wanted his family to be okay above all else. Ramses rubbed Brielle's hand. "He's still good?"

"He is, Ramses," Dr. Sturm said. He lounged back against his desk and turned, tossing a file on it. I assumed that was Wolf's file, and when the man turned around, he was grinning. "And honestly, your son's case has been one of the highlights of my career. To tackle all this *twice* and with the odds stacked against him in the way they were that second time?" Dr. Sturm shook his head. "A true highlight. I'm sure many of us in the medical community will be talking about this case for years to come."

Because he had more years, plenty of years, and Wolf was seeing that too. His mouth parted like he was letting it hit him, and it was hitting me too so hard.

He's okay.

He really would be, and *I* could breathe again. I think the reality of that collided with us the same time it did Wolf's parents. His mom reached over, hugging him.

"He is a fighter. My baby," she said, pulling back to look at him. She had her hands on his face, and he never fought her on such affection. He always let his family in, always.

How much he'd changed in the last year, and I got to witness that firsthand when his dad brought him and his mother into a hug. They squeezed the shit out of each other, and I wanted to cry.

Especially when Wolf grabbed me.

He brought me right into the circle. He *never* forgot about me, never, and his parents opened up that big hug. His dad gripped us all in that mighty embrace, but even after it released, Wolf didn't let me go far.

"We did it, Red," he said, his forehead on my temple. He rubbed against it. "We did it."

He did it, and I folded my arms around his neck. "You did it."

It all started with him, and his ability to let us all in. He'd broken down many walls this year, and I had no words for what he'd done for mine. We made each other so much better.

I felt like Wolf and I were in that moment for so long, and his parents were smiling at us when we ultimately let go of each other. This family had really allowed me to become a part of theirs.

Wolf's mom squeezed my leg, and I got nothing but a warm expression from Wolf's father. Ramses was probably one of the kindest people I'd ever met, and Wolf may argue that he might not be this man's son, but I did see some of that in him. Wolf was giving and took care of others even when they didn't know they needed it.

Even when I didn't know I needed it.

Wolf laced our fingers once more. He kissed the back of my hand, and Dr. Sturm smiled largely in front of us all. I was sure he was used to all this. There was a lot of familial joy in this room over the course of the last year. Every time Wolf beat a hurdle or eliminated an obstacle there was joy.

"So I guess now we just continue what we're doing," Dr. Sturm continued. "We monitor you and make sure things continue to be this smooth. I'm hopeful for you, though. I think you've shown us all a miracle or two in these past couple years."

Wolf was grinning at me while he squeezed my hand. "So I can go back to school, then?" he asked his doctor, and I knew he wanted to badly. He'd done a couple online classes last semester while he'd been home, but I was sure if he'd had his way, he would have taken a full course load. His parents had advised against that, though, and his doctors had too. Wolf had also been doing well then, but no one wanted him overwhelmed.

"I can't see why you can't attend in-person classes this spring or even a hybrid situation with some in-person classes and some online." Dr. Sturm nodded. "The world appears to be your oyster right now."

"But whatever he decides to do he will be attending his doctor's appointments and reporting everything to us as it happens," Wolf's mom said, eyeing him, and Wolf was quick to nod in agreement.

"I will," he confirmed, taking his mom's hand. "You won't have to worry about that. I'll do everything I need to do."

It was crazy watching him with his parents. It was crazy watching him with any of his family. Whenever they asked him something or needed something of him, he didn't push them away. He truly did let them in, and that inspired me so much. I too had had that issue in the past, but not anymore.

Again, Wolf created miracles.

―――

"Red, I won't tell you again. Now, shut the fuck up and sit on my face like a good girl. *Now.*"

Wolf grinned after he said it, that handsome one that never ceased to send a sharp pulse directly into my pussy.

God… dammit.

The urge to defy outweighed the sensation. That and not wanting to do anything that may fuck up his spine. I stayed by the door, rubbing my thighs together. "What if I hurt you?"

I mean, it was a real fucking fear, and I'd be lying if I said this hadn't come up before. Wolf's doctors had cleared him for sex a while ago. This had obviously been spoken about outside of the appointments with his parents, and though we'd been having sex since, I came at it with a strategy. I didn't let him do anything that would overexert him, and I definitely didn't *sit on his face*. His tumor may have been in his back, but all that shit was connected.

Wolf growled after what I said and basically appeared godlike in the center of the bed. The comforter draped lazily over his muscled torso, leaving one of his chiseled legs exposed. His curly hair was tousled and run through, the job I'd done on it since we couldn't keep our hands off each other after his appointment today. We'd gotten some good news, and I guessed we'd been… excited. Reality set in quick, though, when he tried to *get me on his face*. I ended up saying I had to go to the bathroom and bolted. A reminder of why I had was on the side of his chest.

Wolf's chemo scar told us all of the journey he'd been through. It was a representation of what he'd overcome. He'd climbed that hurdle, so strong, but he was also human, and I'd never forgive myself if I did something to hurt him. He frowned. "You won't hurt me, and you're being silly."

I wasn't, not really. He'd obviously had real issues with his back. He may be good now, but he had, and I personally had gained a few pounds since last year. I normally was very active with my photography, but lately, I hadn't been able to get out as much. I'd easily gained two dress sizes and was so not trying to get on this guy's face right now. I crossed my arms. "You could die."

Well, not *die*, but I could fucking hurt him.

Wolf's response to this was to lift his eyes to the ceiling, and I was starting to regret how handsy we'd both gotten after leaving his parents. They'd driven back home to Wolf's hometown, and Wolf and I had ended up at the place he shared with his brothers. Dorian, Thatcher, Wells, and Bru had gotten a place together at the start of the semester and kept a room available for Wolf when they got it. The majority of Wolf's treatment he'd spent with his parents, but following his recovery he'd moved in with his brothers. The room they kept for him was always intended to be his when he returned to school, and Bru's room was across from Wolf's. He'd started at Pembroke in the fall, along with Thatcher's sister, Bow.

So many things had changed, and though time had stopped for all of us in ways, it moved on too. I'd continued school as well during Wolf's treatment and recovery, and it was only a matter of time before Wolf caught up. He was just stubborn like that, driven. Honestly, I wouldn't put it past him to graduate with Dorian and Sloane when it was time.

There was no stopping him now that he'd gotten his life back.

I really was so proud of him, but that drive of his certainly wasn't in my favor today. Ares threw the blanket off his lap, exposing his thick cock, and distracted by that, I failed to register the two strides it took him to meet me at the door. He immediately grabbed my bare pussy. My panties had been the first thing to go, along with my leggings.

"Then I die," he said, catching my moan in his mouth. He dueled his tongue with mine, reaching beneath my sweatshirt and fisting my breast. It was a wonder I had on any clothes at all with the way we'd been all over each other the moment we entered his room.

"God, I fucking hate you," I said, a complete lie, but he did frustrate the fuck out of me. "I don't want to hurt you."

His response was to back us toward the bed. He filled his hands with my ass cheeks, then tumbled us onto the mattress, and the shriek I let out could probably be heard by the entire house. He'd surprised me, yeah, but he had no business pulling such a maneuver.

"Red, you on top of my face would *not* hurt me," he said, and as if to emphasize his point, he pulled me on top of him. He pushed my sweatshirt above my sex before guiding me on the journey up to his face. I hovered above his mouth, and his eyes darkened below. "*Sit.* Full weight."

Gripping my thighs, he made me, and his groan over my sex made my entire body buzz. I gave him my full weight and as soon as his tongue parted my folds...

"Fuck..." The word released from my lips involuntary. I bit my knuckles, grinding into his face, and his fingers bit into my thighs so bad I thought he'd draw blood.

"That's it, Red. Fucking smother me," he gritted, making permanent marks on my freckled, tatted skin. I eased my sweatshirt up, watching him lave my folds. He appeared like a man drunk. He groaned. "So good. So fucking good, Red."

I removed my sweatshirt just to watch him, and as soon as it was gone, he unfastened my bra. I worked it off, and he filled his hand with my breast. My creamy flesh spilled between the spaces of his fingers and his feasting became a frenzy. He held my sex tight to his mouth, swirling his tongue over my sensitive clit.

"Wolf, I'm not going to last. Wolf—" I convulsed over his face, coming that *quick.* Twitching, I tried to be mindful of my weight as I came down from the high.

Wolf noticed.

With a firm hand, he forced me to bear down, then drank

from me like a sweet beverage. He took down every drop, and even after I was done, he didn't stop. He started kissing then. He kissed me *down there.*

"*Never* think about hurting me. You understand?" he growled, his kisses suddenly aggressive. It was like he was trying to make a point, prove one. "I know my limits, and you aren't it. Not by a long shot, Red."

His kisses started getting softer then, and I pulled back my hair to watch him. He pulled one of my lower lips into his mouth, sucking so softly before guiding me off him and onto my back. His cock hung weighted between his muscled thighs, and he used it to tease at my center. He didn't enter me, just played.

"You're what makes me strong," he stated, easing inside, and I didn't think I was ready to come again so fast. I figured I wasn't, but the moment he was inside, stretching me, I bore down. A moan escaped from my lips, and he kissed it silent. "You're perfect. So perfect for me."

He was making me emotional when he laced our fingers. When he kissed my mouth open and thrust so deep and full. It was like he was trying to prove a point then too, and I was going to let him. I was done fighting.

"I love you," I said, making him kiss me harder. He was so very perfect for me too. This year, I think, taught us both something. It showed me what my own limits were. It showed me my strengths and what I was able to endure. There had been some hard times. Watching him sick and suffering had been hard, but not once, did it break me. I stayed strong, but most importantly, he allowed me to be there for him.

Wolf had let everyone into his life. He didn't fight alone, and we'd all made him stronger. Not just me. His brothers, siblings, parents, and extended family had all been there for him this past year, and I'd never seen him so strong. His strength came from those he loved.

The fact he considered me in that number made me fuck him harder, and he groaned from above me. He gathered my thighs under a firm arm, placing my ankles on his shoulder, then watched where he disappeared and I began. He fucked me raw and good and exploded inside me with several hard thrusts.

He bit my leg while he did, and that sent me over the edge as well.

"Fuck, baby. Fuck," he said, his bites turning into kisses on my rosy skin. "Fuck, you don't know how much I love you."

I think I had an idea and found myself coming down as he did. He parted my legs and stayed inside me while he kissed me from above.

"I love you, Red," he said, warming my cheek with his mouth, my neck. "I love you so much, Fawn."

Warmth exploded inside me, and I hugged him so close. He had no idea how much I loved him either, and something emotional hit me just then. Suddenly, I wasn't counting weeks or months with him. I wasn't counting days. I suddenly saw myself counting on forever with him.

And how I got to keep him.

CHAPTER
FORTY-ONE

Ares

"I like what you did with that," I said, closing the bedroom door behind Red and me. She had her camera in her hands, but on the strap was something I'd given her.

I had no use for my old Court ring from high school, but seeing it attached to Red's camera, something that meant so much to her... yeah, that shit hit me hard, and I got the idea to give it to her from Dorian. He'd given his to Sloane before college, and she wore it around her neck. Red had fashioned hers into a charm of sorts, and it hung off her camera strap. I'd given it to her before my first round of chemo.

Looking back, I hadn't been sure why I had. All that Court stuff hadn't really meant too much to me and was something I'd done with my friends just to be a part of the community. Our dads ran the Court, so it kind of went without saying that we'd be a part of it. It was an old society, and one that'd been in our hometown since its beginnings. Even still, I hadn't given two shits about it. Joining up had just been something to do, but the moment I gave Fawn that ring and saw what she did with it? It meant something to me, and suddenly, I got why Dorian gave his to Sloane and why both our dads had given theirs to our moms.

It was like I'd shared a part of myself with Fawn that day, and the action bound me to her in ways I hadn't expected. I didn't think the two of us could get any closer. I mean, her saying she wanted to be around for me…

Yeah, I didn't think we could get any closer, but her accepting my ring had taken us to a new level. It was the fact that she'd accepted it. She'd chosen it.

She chose me.

I'd placed many claims on Fawn in the past, but it wasn't until she'd accepted my ring that I realized those claims were false. They meant nothing, shit without her wanting me too.

Her taking the ring had told me she did want me and made a declaration I hadn't known I needed. It told me she accepted me and felt I was worthy of her.

And that I could have her.

Fawn was distracted while tinkering with her camera. After we'd fucked, she'd told me she wanted to get out and get some shooting done. I had a bunch of her photos up in my room. She liked to take candids of people doing kind things. Random shit like people opening the door for others or even just letting others pass them on the street. She liked to do things like that. Show people at their best, and she had a few of my sketches too.

They were mostly of her naked.

Of course, those were for my eyes only, and the moment I addressed her, mentioned the ring, she glanced up with those big hazel eyes and a smile that hit me in the chest just as hard as it stiffened my cock. I'd gotten those freckled lips around me before we'd left my room, and I wanted them right back. She lowered her camera. She allowed it to rest on her chest since she wore the camera strap around her neck. "Thanks for giving it to me."

She could have anything she wanted from me, this girl, and she fucking knew it.

Getting her by the ass, I pressed my mouth to hers, regretting leaving my room at all, but I owed my family a conversation about what had happened today at my appointment. Red and I'd been a little excited about the events that had occurred, and I'd failed to text any of them after getting the good news.

"Look at that. He finally came up for air."

Well, Dorian noticed he hadn't gotten a text, and I groaned when I had to physically separate myself from Red. We made it into the living room of the house I shared with the guys, and when I glanced up, Dorian was snarling at me. He sat on the couch with my sister, all puffed up and looking pissed.

He glared. "It's a good thing none of us were wondering how your appointment went today. Otherwise, we'd all be a little pissed you didn't text or call right away."

The sarcasm not lost on me, I released Red to face my friend. "Sorry. Didn't mean to make you wonder about it."

Guilt started to catch up with me now that I didn't have my face filled with my girlfriend. Even worse because I had taken my time with Red after she'd been so resistant to sitting on my face. It'd come up more than once, and every time it did, I spent as many moments as I could reassuring her that my favorite thing in literally the goddamn world wouldn't kill me. Every inch of that girl I needed on top of me, spoiled by it.

The urge hit now as I filled my hands with her generous hips, even fuller these days, and my buddy's glare worsened, deepened.

Sloane placed her hand on Dorian's chest. "Hey, it's okay. I'm sure things are fine. Otherwise, he would have texted right away." Sloane cocked her head at me, my twin more logical but equally pissed.

I wet my lips. "Really, I am sorry."

"Yeah," she said, her expression chilly as fuck, but it warmed in Red's direction. The two had bonded like crazy during the last year, which I loved. Sloane had been playing warrior for everyone. She wanted to be strong for everyone else. Red definitely had some of that going on too, and they both helped each other when they needed breaks. It didn't matter how much Dorian or I pushed them to go take some time to just have a coffee or think about something else besides my health. Neither listened, but when one pushed the other, they did. Again, they'd bonded. Fawn did that for Sloane and Sloane did that for her too.

Thatcher's sister, Bow, had been helpful too for that. Especially when Bow started at Pembroke this past semester. The girls got to go out and just be girls. I wasn't entirely sure what that meant or what they did when they were out, but they always came back with smiles on their faces. As far as I was concerned, that was enough for me regarding how helpful they'd been for one another.

"Oh, nice. The asshole is here," Thatcher grumbled, sweeping into the room. My eyes lifted, and Thatcher cocked his head of spiky hair at me before dropping into one of our La-Z-Boys. The setup we had here on campus was pretty sweet, and it was quickly becoming the party spot here at Pembroke U. It overlooked a valley of lush hills and had about half a dozen rooms. The recliner labored under Thatch's weight. "So, you gonna give us an update or what?"

I opened my mouth to start, but Wells and Bru entered the room. They might have been gaming or studying. The studying part was probably more so the kid than Wells. Wells didn't study for shit unless it directly involved him in the kitchen. Something told us all he'd be heading down the same track as his grandmas, who happened to be celebrity chefs, and Bru was already caught up after the semester he'd lost. I was proud of the kid. We all were. He'd been working on himself and was so much happier for it. It was nice to see, and we all loved that.

Wells knocked my foot with his boot, and if I didn't have my limbs wrapped around Red, I would have gone for him. Actually, I tried to, bringing her with me, but she refocused my attention to her hips instead, rocking into my hands. She did this on purpose for sure, but I didn't fight her on keeping the peace.

I mean, I got to keep on holding her hips.

God, this girl had me gone, but I didn't mind.

"Nice of you to show your face, Wolfy," Wells chimed, plopping near Thatcher on the other La-Z-Boy, and Bru got Red's hand.

"What's up, brosef?" Bru announced before he and my girlfriend immediately went into their *bro* thing. They had a handshake and everything, and when the two let go, Bru snapped. "I see my brother let you up for air."

"Exactly what I said," Dorian called out, and suddenly, he wasn't so pissed but smirking. I grimaced at them both but found myself suddenly calm when Red rubbed my chest. I used to laugh about that shit when Sloane did it to Dorian to calm his ass down.

I had to remind myself to apologize to my friend for the hard time. Whenever this girl's hand was on me, it did make shit better.

"Nothing much, broskee," Fawn said to my brother, and that was something interesting to get used to. The two were a couple of bros like I was with mine, so yeah, it was interesting.

And then that whole kiss thing…

They'd told me about all that together. Sat me down not long after Fawn and I had become official. They had said they hadn't wanted it to be a thing because it wasn't one. Even still, they had looked nervous as they'd explained what had happened and when and how it had established they were only friends. I think they'd been worried about my reaction, but I didn't give them much of one that day. In fact, after they'd told me, I just took Fawn's hand and we all watched a movie with the others that night.

I mean, what reason did I have to worry?

I didn't, and I'd known that then as I did now. The two were friends, and I was glad Fawn had that. She needed something outside of what we had, and I was so happy she was letting herself have that.

Even still, I liked to remind the kid what was what and wrapped my arms around Fawn's waist. I tucked her into me. "Hey, kid, how's single life? You been seeing anyone recently?"

He was worse than me when it came to that shit. I didn't date, but at least I fucked before Fawn, but the kid didn't even do that. He was always studying or hanging out with us or Bow. Bow probably saw him more than the rest of us since all the two did was study. Bow was no doubt in the library now since she had winter classes. She didn't have to, smart as hell like Thatch, but she filled her break with them. I was serious about school, but she and the kid were on another level.

Knowing exactly what I was doing (and noticing how my hands were curiously moving towards Fawn's *ass*), the kid lifted his eyes. Their history wasn't a thing for me, but I liked to throw shit in his face to tease him when I could. Especially about that coming-up-for-air comment.

"Anyway," the kid said, taking another couch in the room. He opened his hands. "You going to tell us about how everything went?"

I did after that, not hesitating, and the tone of the room lifted right away. I got a few fist bumps and a hug from my sister, and I welcomed them all. Things were really starting to feel perfect again.

It was perfect.

Fawn and I were on the couch now, and I really couldn't believe how far we'd come. I couldn't believe she was here, and this all was starting to feel like a dream.

"You didn't tell them the best part," she said, rubbing my leg. She faced the room. "Dr. Sturm says he can go back to school in the spring."

The room exploded then, the guys and Sloane up on their feet. The guys basically dog-piled my ass. Well, everyone but Thatcher, and I was surprised when he barked for us all to settle down.

"Don't want to break the dude. Jesus," he said, but he was grinning too. His spiked earring danced when he lifted out of the chair and reached for my hand. He released it with a snap. "So you're really cleared for everything?"

"Yeah, dude," I stated, grinning myself. I faced Red. "It seems everything's getting back to normal."

"So that means you can go on the trip?" Wells popped up. He flashed me teeth. "Our ski trip. You can go?"

The topic of a short trip to the slopes upstate came up over Christmas. I wanted to go, but I wouldn't without clearance from my doctor as well as my parents. I didn't want to do anything that would worry my folks.

"Now, I don't know about all that," Thatcher said, again surprising me. He faced the room with a shrug. "Bro could hurt himself."

"Actually, I've been cleared for that too," I stated, knowing I'd gotten that before the end of my appointment. I'd specifically asked Dr. Sturm about the trip and did so in front of my parents too toward the end of the appointment. I nodded. "Dr. Sturm says it's cool. Though, he advised I stay on some of the lighter slopes. My parents are good with it too. They just asked I don't overdo anything."

I probably wasn't going to ski at all and really planned to use the trip to explore the ins and outs of Fawn Greenfield. She was going to go too if I did, and I had zero plans of leaving our room. It was a girls-and-guys trip, and my sister was going too. Bow, Thatch's sis, would be as well but couldn't since she had those winter classes.

I really was looking forward to just doing something fun with my family and one hundred percent with my girlfriend. From what I heard, the guys rented a pretty kick-ass cabin, and I wouldn't mind wrapping myself up with Red in front of a fireplace.

Thinking about that now, it took me a moment to realize Thatch had raised his voice. Actually, he was barking at Dorian who had his hands lifted.

"Thatch, his doctor cleared him," Dorian explained, but Thatcher was all red. He was also shaking his head adamantly, and I frowned.

"Doesn't make it smart," Thatcher said, getting up. "Anyway, whatever. I'm going to go pack for the trip."

Before I knew it, he was out of the room, and Wells was going after him. Wells stopped just before, though, facing the room.

"I'll go talk to him," he said, then came over and tapped my fist. "Congrats, my dude. Wolfy's back, baby, and hell-fucking-yeah to that."

I laughed but could only do so a little. I stared in the direction of Thatcher and Wells's exit, but my attention redirected to Dorian and Sloane when they stood.

"You should talk to him too," D said before slapping my hand and giving me the same congratulations. After he did, Sloane hugged me. It was hard and just as strong as she was. She told me congrats too, and the kid did as well before leaving. They all went to pack for the trip, stating so before they left, and even though I should now too, I stayed on the couch with Red for a beat.

She rubbed my leg. "You okay?"

She could obviously see I was bothered about what had just happened, but because she was wonderful, she didn't directly ask me about it. She should, though. I'd tell her everything.

Which was crazy. Not so long ago I'd shut down multiple times in front of this girl. Now, I found myself doing anything I could to keep her in my life. There was a time I'd been willing to punish myself so she could live one free of me. I hadn't deserved her and still didn't think I did.

But I needed her. Fuck did I need her, and I was willing to be selfish to have her. I touched my forehead to hers. "Yeah, I'm good. Thatcher's not, though. He doesn't do good with people suffering around him, and he's channeling some stuff on me."

That was the reason for his outburst, and I knew because I did know his life.

Red's eyebrows were narrowed when I lifted my head, and of course, she didn't know. Us guys were so tightly wound, and Thatcher was no exception when it came to his business. I drew a thumb down Red's cheek. "It's his grandma. She's been sick off and on for years, but lately it's some new stuff." It was bad, real bad, and I felt for the guy. I sighed. "It's not looking good for her, and it's been rough on him."

Though, he definitely tried to hide it, my friend. Again, he kept that shit locked down, but his boys knew. We all knew each other so much.

Fawn's face fell upon hearing what I said. She hugged her arms. "Damn."

"Yeah." I released another breath, rubbing my hand down Red's back. "It's been tough. He's had to deal with her being sick before that, and then everything going on with me and the cancer?" I shook my head. "My buddy's strong, but he's going through it."

Again, I felt for him. I couldn't imagine.

"So he doesn't want you to go on this trip and risk hurting yourself," Fawn concluded, and I nodded. She took off her camera, then pushed her arms around me, and it was like heaven opened up its gates. It felt that way every time I was with her, and once more, I didn't care if I deserved it. I didn't deserve it, but I wasn't willing to entertain a life without her.

I wasn't strong enough.

I needed Fawn like I needed air or water, and if that made me a selfish bastard, so fucking be it. I was going to have this. I couldn't *not* have this.

I held her close. "He doesn't, but I'll talk to him. He'll be okay, and I'll take it easy."

"You better." She placed those hazel irises on me, so much love deeply rooted there. She looked at me every day like that. Every fucking day like I was her everything. Like she couldn't live without me either, but I knew the truth. She could live without me.

And if she knew better, she would.

CHAPTER
FORTY-TWO

Ares

"Hey, Thatch, can I talk to you a sec?" I asked him. He and Wells deposited like five bags of food on the counter. We'd just checked into our cabin a couple hours ago, and the first thing they'd done was hit up a grocery store. They wanted to beat the snowstorm that was coming in and just barely did considering all the snow on their jackets.

Thatch shook some of it off his big shoulders. "I don't know. Can you?" He smirked, being a dick. He defaulted with humor for sure because every time I had seen him since we'd left campus, he'd grunted at me. He had basically ignored me while we'd packed up the cars and wasn't shy regarding his position when it came to me coming on this trip.

Dorian eyed him. "Don't be a dick," he said, voicing my thoughts. The two of us had been sitting at the counter in the kitchen before the others had come in. The girls and Bru were unpacking somewhere in the cabin, and Dorian and I had taken the time to talk amongst ourselves. It'd been mostly about Thatch and what I would say to him when he and Wells came back.

All Dorian's chide did was make Thatcher grunt again, and after he did, Dorian set his eyes on Wells. It was a strong look and the head-jerk he made toward the door right after let Wells know Dorian didn't want him in the kitchen right now. Dorian got off his barstool and left the room himself after the gesture, and eventually, Wells followed him.

"I'm going to go help D start the fireplace. Get this place warmed up a bit," Wells said, even though Thatcher and I both knew Dorian hadn't said shit about starting a fire before he'd left.

Thatcher smirked, a couple twelve-packs of beer under his burly arms. It seemed he and Wells were putting those fake IDs to good use. He opened the fridge with his shoulder. "Say what you have to say so I can go take off all this soggy shit and relax and enjoy my vacation."

My friend certainly had his back up today, but I got it. I hated that I did because he was going through shit. I laced my hands. "Do you want to talk?"

I knew he didn't. He was like the rest of us when it came to bottling up shit, but I thought I'd ask anyway just in case. There was a time when I think I'd wanted to be pushed on my issues, but no one ever had. If someone had back then, I might not have gotten so caught up in my lies.

There was an iota of a moment when I thought Thatcher may talk to me. He paused after putting those beers away, then just as quickly he mumbled out something and closed the fridge.

I sighed. "Come on, bro—"

"Fucking *what*?"

"You know what." My lips turned down. "Now, you can keep with the attitude shit, or you can fucking talk. You can deal."

I knew what it was like to hide all that shit, and it didn't feel good.

Thatcher shook his head. "You're one to talk, bro." He said the words under his breath, frowning hard, but I heard them. He shrugged. "What the fuck do you want from me?"

Nothing really, and when I didn't say anything, he started to pass me. He had to get through me first, though, and I'd picked up speed since recovery. I'd picked up strength, and I gave him some when I hugged him. I didn't say a word because I didn't think the occasion called for any.

The big asshole didn't move, but I noticed he didn't pull me off him either. He just stood there taking it, so I hugged him harder.

"Just," he started, and I heard something clear in his voice. Emotion made it thicker, hoarse. He released a breath. "Promise me you won't do something stupid this weekend. That you'll take it easy and just not be stupid."

That'd been the plan from the jump as I was done doing stupid things. I nodded. "I promise."

"Okay."

I let him go, and though he moved away, taking his space, he didn't leave the kitchen. He scrubbed into his inky hair. "You do that, and I guess we're cool."

"Cool." I smiled. "And that offer still stands if you want to talk. Or even if you don't. That's okay too." I braced my arms. "You can talk to any of us. We'll listen."

It was something he knew, of course. He didn't have to hide things, and he'd only feel better if he didn't.

It was crazy this was coming from me of all people, and I knew that had to do with a girl somewhere in this cabin. She was a girl I didn't deserve but was too selfish to let go of.

Thatcher nodded, and his mumbled *thanks* made me smile again. He had his own pace when it came to things too, and that was all right. It was cool with me as long as he knew the door was open. It was with any of us, like I said.

The guy still didn't move, and I didn't either. He had his hands in his pockets like maybe he wanted to say something, but his head jerked up when an amplified roar radiated through the cabin. It hit me deep in my bones and sent both Thatcher and me running in its direction.

We both ended up in the living room, nearly piled on top of each other. The fire in the fireplace was untamed and in front of it was Wells. Dorian was nowhere in sight, and Wells was on his knees. He cowered, shaking, and when Thatcher and I came around him, we could see why.

Wells had his hands out...

And the flesh was falling off his fingers.

CHAPTER
FORTY-THREE

Fawn

"Who the fuck lights a gas fireplace with fucking lighter fluid?" Dorian Prinze had his hands braced. He breathed a harsh breath into them before grinding his teeth. He gazed up. "Huh? Who the fuck does that?"

The answer was Wells Ambrose, but no one said this. Sloane's response to the question was to rub Dorian's leg, and Wolf, Thatcher, and Bru remained silent. Thatcher was the only one standing. He gazed at the set of double doors in the hospital's emergency room and had been doing that since Wells had walked through them. We'd all been sitting here over an hour.

This whole situation was a nightmare, and Dorian was right that Wells had done that. We'd all seen him before a nurse had taken him back, and his hand hadn't looked good. I hadn't gotten to see much of it since I'd driven over in a separate car. The guys had rushed him off to the hospital and Sloane and I had arrived second. Everything had moved really fast.

I had seen his hand a little bit, though, the skin bubbled up and... It'd been gnarly, and it was by the grace of God he'd only managed to burn one of them. Sloane and I had seen that fire before we'd left the cabin, and it'd been bad. It had certainly taken effort to put it out, which was what we'd done since the guys were tending to Wells. Sloane and I hadn't gotten to see him long before the guys had swept him off to the hospital, and when we'd gotten here, he hadn't appeared to be in too much pain considering the state of his hand.

I assumed that had been an act, though, a way to appear strong in front of everyone. I'd tried not to stare before he left, but had noticed he'd winced between interactions with his friends. I gathered he hadn't realized anyone was looking at him.

Dorian's jaw clenched. "I swear to God I leave the room for a fucking second. Can't even take a fucking piss without shit hitting the fan."

"D." This came from my boyfriend. Wolf had his long reach around me, and he was playing cool about being calm too, but I knew better. His fingers kept tapping against my arm, which was something he did at his doctor's appointments too. Wolf already didn't like hospitals. I didn't think any of us did since we'd been inside them so much in the past year. The situation now was only making my boyfriend's nerves about them worse.

I rubbed his leg, getting calm myself when the rhythm of his fingers slowed. His restless digits ended up gently squeezing my arm, and I warmed inside. I didn't like him uneasy, and Dorian Prinze didn't like being told what to do. He started to say something to Wolf, but Thatcher shot off the wall.

Dorian followed him with his gaze. "Where are you—"

"Need some air and a smoke," Thatcher grunted before stalking off, and Dorian scrubbed his face. I could imagine this whole thing wasn't sitting well with Thatcher. I mean, it wasn't with any of the guys, but Wolf had told me Thatcher was already going through some stuff.

Like everyone else when Wells had been there, Thatcher had played off that he'd been okay. He'd sat beside Wells and kept asking him questions. It was like he was trying to keep him busy and not focusing on his hand, but Thatcher had rocked during every question. He was restless too and hadn't sat since the nurse had taken Wells.

Thatcher's big body disappeared through the ER's double doors, and with a sigh, Dorian glanced over at Wolf. Dorian frowned. "I'd go, but I don't know what I'd say. I might make it worse right now."

Meaning he wanted Wolf to go after Thatcher. Wolf faced that way, but not before squeezing my arm.

I wanted him to go. His friends needed him, and I wanted him to help them in whatever way he could.

Wolf and I had developed something of a code in the past year. It was a set of exchanged looks, and it was necessary in front of his parents and others in his life. It was a way for us to check in with each other, like our own secret language. Today, I gave him the look that said it was fine for him to leave me, and without question, he kissed my cheek.

"I'll be back," he said, his lips lingering. The warm heat ran down to my soul, and he didn't let go of me without another gentle squeeze to my arm.

I followed his back with my gaze as he got up, and when I returned my focus to the others, I spotted Bru smiling in my direction. He and Wolf both liked to mess with each other. Bru would get on Wolf for being all over me all the time, and Wolf would tease Bru because of *the kiss*. I still cringed thinking about the day Bru and I had told Wolf about that, but telling him had been necessary. I didn't want anything between Wolf and me. Anything.

The two of us had come such a long way, and we didn't do secrets anymore. We were honest with each other, so telling him about everything with Bru had been important to me. Anyway, Wolf hadn't been mad, but since then, he always rubbed the fact we were together in Bru's face. He thought I didn't notice when he got all territorial, and I only let him get away with it because Bru always called him out about it. Bru was the first to let the room know when Wolf was being his wolfy self. Wolf was possessive and a complete caveman.

Secretly knowing I liked that, I sat with the thought, but would never *ever* tell him that. My boyfriend already had an ego for days, lifetimes.

"Well, I need a stiff drink," Bru announced before rising on his feet. He sighed. "But since we can't have that right now, who wants coffee? I saw a machine when I hit up the bathroom, and I'm sure it's got the best crappy hospital coffee money can buy."

He was obviously trying to keep the mood light for the remainder of us, but Dorian was still stewing. He was rocking now as he rubbed his arms, and Sloane was tending to him. She smiled at Bru. "Sure, loser. I'll take cream. No sugar."

"Black," Dorian said, and Bru gave a curt nod.

"I'll help." I was on my feet right behind my friend, and the moment we were out of the busy ER felt so nice. It was like a blanket lifted, and I think Bru felt that too when he released a breath.

"Well, this whole thing is a dumpster fire," he said once we got to the coffee machine. He swiped his card on the machine. "No pun intended."

I'd laugh if it felt appropriate. "This is no time for humor."

"Actually, it's the perfect time," he said, before attempting to press a button on the machine. He was frazzled, though, and didn't seem to know what he was doing. "Fuck, what did Sloane say she wanted?"

This really was affecting them all in different ways, and I took the initiative and pressed in the order for him.

"Thanks," he said, the button literally in front of him. He

shook his head. "Don't know how I missed that."

"It's cool."

He nodded as a cup came down, and the thing started to fill with coffee. He stared at it, appearing lost, and maybe he was a little. I rubbed his arm. "Wells is going to be fine. We all saw him before he left. He seemed good."

In fact, Wells's attention had seemed to focus less on his injury and more on the male nurse who had taken him back. The tall blond had definitely gotten a full stare of the nurse's ass before the guy had guided Wells away.

I mentioned that, and Bru smirked. He shook his head again. "Yeah, the guy's nothing but a ho," he said. The coffee finished, and he took it out. "He is probably fine while we're all out here fucking worrying."

He jammed his fingers against the machine for the second order. I think he only stopped because of the high-pitched voice that chirped down the hallway.

"Excuse me. I'm looking for Wells Ambrose. Do you know what room he's in or—"

"Bow?"

Bow, Thatcher's sister, whipped around after Bru called her, and I blinked that she was, well, here. Bundled up to her neck, Bow rushed over in a wool coat and snow boots. She waved a hand, the pom-poms on her gloves matching her earmuffs. "Bru! Fawn! Thank God."

The pair of us met her halfway, and she was out of breath by the time she got to us. She may have been out of breath *before* she got to us, and she was rushing so bad she nearly tripped and fell on Bru.

He stabilized her. "Bow... What..." He gazed around. "I thought you had classes."

I thought she did too, which was why she hadn't come with us on this trip.

The coffee forgotten about, Bru got Bow out of the fray, and I took the one he had from him. Bow was panicking like… crazy. Her cheeks were beet red, and she had so much snow on her it appeared she'd tobogganed her way here. Her dark hair was coated in snowflakes, the strands curling at the ends.

"I was, but Sloane texted me. She said Wells burned himself?" She said it all in one breath, gazing around the hospital like she'd see him. "Is he okay? What happened?"

Bru explained briefly, quickly, and Bow's blue eyes turned into saucers. She appeared horror-struck. Especially when he got to the part about Wells's skin looking melted. The flesh was more bubbled up than anything, but yeah.

"Oh, God." She covered her mouth, looking sick. "Is he going to be okay?"

"He should be, yeah," Bru continued. "I mean, I don't know for sure, but we were all with him up until he went back to see a doctor. He seemed fine, but he looked like he was in a lot of pain."

Bow's breath came out in short wisps, and Bru patted the air as if to calm her. Bow was really panicking here, and I guess I wasn't surprised. Legacy was a tight unit, and anyone around them could see that.

"Come on. I'll take you back to the others," Bru suggested. "They're all waiting for him in the ER."

I followed along after the pair, the three of us pushing through the double doors back to the emergency room. We headed in the direction of the waiting room but stopped when someone called Bow's name.

"The fuck you doing here, squeak?" Wells Ambrose strode down the hallway, looking angry for some reason. His coat hung limply off one of his broad shoulders, and that probably had something to do with the fact that his hand was bandaged up to his forearm. His jaw clenched. "Did you drive here? Don't tell me you fucking drove in that snowstorm."

Bow blanched, and Bru and I stopped entirely. I think we

were all kind of shocked that Wells was here, and not in some burn unit, but once the shock wore off and Wells was glaring down at Bow, I think we all got our thoughts back. He towered over her, the height difference like Wolf and me, and that said something. My boyfriend was over six foot five, and I was nowhere near that. I might have gotten to five foot seven in heels. Bow frowned. "Sloane told me you burned yourself."

She was distracted by the injury. Her gaze settled on the bandage, but Wells's attention focused on nothing but her. He did look pissed, his face a hotter red than Bow's had been when she'd come into the hospital. The fact that he'd dyed his hair brighter than the snow melting on Bow's boots only emphasized the contrast. He bared his teeth. "So, you thought you'd take it upon yourself to drive all the way out here in the middle of a fucking snowstorm?" He fisted into his dark roots. "You could have fucking killed yourself—"

"Eh, Wells, lay off." Bru got between the pair. The two guys were similar in height and more easily matched. Bru's lips turned down. "She was obviously just worried about you. Take it down a couple notches."

"Fuck that, kid. She could have killed herself being stupid," he said, redirecting his snarl at Bru, but Bow pushed her way back into the conversation. She wiggled in between the guys like a little ninja and had clearly surprised them both when they blinked. Suddenly, they were gazing down at her instead of coming at each other, and Wells blanched when Bow shot a finger in his direction.

"I can't believe you," Bow snapped, stamping her boot. I'd yet to see this girl angry, so I did a little bit of a double take. She was like one of those Disney princesses who never raised their voice unless they were calling for their animal friends in the forest. She knuckled her fists. "I came all the way here… *drove* all the way here just for you to… to… Ugh!"

She stopped a person or two with her shout, then quickly

stalked off afterward. She blended into the hospital traffic, and Bru raised a hand at Wells.

"Really, bro?" he stated, and when Wells didn't do anything but stand there, Bru dropped his hand. He shook his head. "What's your problem?"

"She had no business driving out here, Bru," Wells grunted, and all Bru did was sigh. Bru faced me, and I nodded him along to go after her. I was fine, and Bow was currently headed in the wrong direction of her family. Probably because she didn't know where she was going.

That was also probably why Bru was picking up his pace down the hall, and since I had a cold coffee in my hand, I tossed it. When I turned back around, Wells was still there. I eyed his hand. "Are you okay?"

He barely paid attention to the injury. In fact, he wasn't paying attention to it at all as he glared in the direction of Bow and Bru's exit.

"Yeah, third-degree burns or something," he grumbled, and my mouth parted. He scrubbed into his hair with his good hand. "Do you know where the others are?"

I told him Sloane and Dorian were still in the waiting room, and Thatcher had gone out to smoke. I explained Wolf had left with Thatcher, and Wells's next move was toward the waiting room. All of his friends were in that direction, so I got that. I started to go that way too but noticed a familiar face down the hallway. I got closer and realized it was exactly who I thought it was. I lifted my hand. "Anton?"

My stepdad, Anton Weber, turned. He flanked a few doctors in white coats, but he stood out because he was in a suit. He always was for his job. He was a doctor, but more so a television personality like Dr. Drew. He tended to give his advice through media and interviews and was widely celebrated in the medical field.

He was also my stepfather and was very kind. Actually, kind was an understatement. He'd really been there for my mom and my family in general. After my dad had passed, he'd been a huge support system for us and had also helped me after that whole Cissy Armstrong thing. That could have been a huge legal issue since Cissy's family had money, but Anton had taken care of that.

He'd taken care of me.

It was something I hadn't thanked him for enough in the past, his help then. I wanted to, but I'd been dealing with so much. Fast-forward into the future, I closed myself off. I did from him, my mother, and everyone in my life.

At least, I used to.

My stepdad's smile quirked right when he saw me, an older man with dark features and salt-and-pepper hair. He raised a hand. "Fawn."

I was surprised to see him here and had just seen him and my mom at Christmas. I'd visited them both on the day and the days surrounding the holiday. The trip hadn't been a terribly long one, but I'd visited, and it'd been great to see them. My mom had cooked a roast, and it'd just been nice. It'd been normal and so good.

I was filled with warmth again by how so much had changed in the past year. How *I* changed. The only thing that would have made it perfect was if Wolf had been there, but I hadn't wanted to take him from his own family after such a trying year. He'd expressed concern for me going by myself, but I'd told him I'd be okay.

I really was okay.

I knew that as soon as I hugged my stepdad. It was how I had greeted him and my mom at the airport too. I hadn't been closed off, and it'd been wonderful.

"Fawn, what are you doing here?" he asked me, his accent thick. He was German, but he'd been in the United States for a while. His smile widened. "It's so good to see you, but I didn't expect to."

I hadn't either and laughed. "I could ask you the same."

He was certainly a long way from New York, which was where he and my mom lived. They weren't there a ton since they traveled a lot for fun and work, but they should have been there now.

"I suppose so," he returned, laughing too. His eyes warmed. "I'm here for work. A conference. I'll be doing a keynote."

Of course he was, an excellent speaker. That was probably why his work surrounded television and interviews now more than anything else. Anton used to be a surgeon in another life, and people respected his opinion.

"I hope everything is okay with you since you're here, though," he said, and I quickly explained why I was so he didn't worry. I told him about the ski trip and how I was here with friends. I also explained to him about Wells and his burn, but how he appeared to be okay. He nodded. "Well, that's good, and is your boyfriend here? Wolf?"

He was, and I wasn't surprised he asked about him. All Mom and him did was ask at Christmas, but they didn't have to probe much.

I couldn't stop talking about him.

I mean, I couldn't help it, and they knew what Wolf and I had been through. They knew about how he had cancer, but also how well things were going for him now.

I explained Wolf's latest development, how he was good and could go back to school, and Anton's smile widened.

"So wonderful to hear, honey," he said, his head tilted, and I asked if I could have a few moments of his time. That was if he had a few moments since he appeared to be busy.

"I'd love for you to meet him," I said, and really did. I always planned for Wolf to meet my family.

"Oh, that'd be wonderful. Let me just go excuse myself from the others," Anton returned, and my heart lifted. "You couldn't stop smiling in front of your mom and me at Christmas. It'd be nice to meet the one responsible for that."

CHAPTER
FORTY-FOUR

Ares

"Where's Fawn?" I asked Dorian and Sloane. Bru and Bow were with them in the ER's waiting room too, and for some reason, Bow had thought it was a good idea to drive like three hours in the middle of a snowstorm to get here. Wells had told Thatcher and I all about it after Wells made his way outside to find us. Wells had had a smoke while he spoke, and knowing our buddy was in physical pain, Thatch and I had stayed out there for a bit with him. The dude was lucky this hadn't happened in the middle of football season or something. That was some stupid shit he'd pulled, but I think Thatch and I were more relieved he still had a hand. I was pretty sure that was the only reason the pair of us hadn't given him a hard time while we were outside and had let Wells take his time with the smoke.

I really wanted to be back inside with my girlfriend after I found out my friend was okay, and the group in the waiting room glanced up following my question about her. Wells and Thatcher flanked me, and Wells had explained he'd already made a stop with Dorian and Sloane before coming outside to find us.

Even still, Dorian got up and asked Wells if he was okay. Wells nodded, and after he did, Sloane punched him on the shoulder for being stupid. He was stupid, but my focus really wasn't on that considering my girl was missing.

"She wasn't outside with you?" Bru asked, getting up. "I guess I just assumed she was since she wasn't in the waiting room when Bow and I got here."

The kid had gone after Bow. Apparently, Wells had given her a hard time about driving over here, and he'd mentioned that outside.

I watched in my periphery as Thatcher opened his hands and scolded his sister for that same thing. Bow crossed her little arms in response, facing away. Her face red, she told her older brother she didn't want to hear it, and as big as he was (and as small as she was), Thatch never really could control his sister. Rainbow Reed may be tiny and shy, but she was also a spitfire. That had to be the Legacy blood in her because she wasn't listening to Thatch at all until he sat beside her. He brought his voice down, and even though she called him a jerk for yelling at her, she didn't fight him when he put his burly arms around her. He asked her if she was okay, and she was smiling by the time he let go of her. Her big brother was obviously just worried, and I think Wells had been too when he'd told us. The guy wouldn't say that for shit, but he'd paced like a son of a bitch outside as he'd told us what she'd done to get here. Wells was always one to give Bow a hard time, but I tried to stay out of that drama unless he took it too far. He did sometimes.

Wells seemed to be okay now, as he studied Thatch and Bow. He was looking at his phone, but more of his attention appeared to be in that direction. My focus moved to my own phone.

"I'll text her," Bru said, but I was already doing that.

Me: Hey. Where are you? We're all in the waiting room. Wells is good.

I think she already knew that since Wells had told us he'd seen her too. In fact, he'd thought she'd been behind him before he left the ER.

Her text message bubble came up, her response quick.

Fawn: Hey! I'm by the bathrooms. You won't believe who I ran into.

Curious, a smile touched my lips. I told the others I'd be back, then texted her as I strode toward those very bathrooms.

Me: That was a very excited *hey*. Ha. Who did you see?

It had to have been someone she wanted to see since she appeared to be excited, and I spotted her once I left the ER. My girlfriend had her head down, her thumbs tapping her phone.

Fawn: He's just finishing up with some colleagues.

Fawn: We'll be along s

That was as much of the text message as she managed to send out since I scared her. I brought Fawn Greenfield against me, those soft curves of hers directly against my cock, and she squealed a little before realizing it was me. Immediately, she started hitting at my hands for freaking her out, but I didn't fucking care.

"*Wolf…*" she growled, but then my name turned into a sigh. I had my mouth on her neck, so I was sure that had something to do with it. "You're hopeless."

I was without her, and I didn't stop my pursuit until she told me she wanted me to meet someone. She said that someone was making their way toward us, which was why she eased herself away, but the only reason I let go of her was because I did make eye contact with someone. I'd never met the guy approaching us before. Never seen him.

But I knew him.

I knew him in a way that made dread hit me. Everything

solid became so fragile, weak and splintered. Everything *I had*
became vulnerable, and when Fawn stepped away to greet
the man, all I could see was the space between us.

So much space.

It was probably only a few feet, but it felt like miles...
leagues away from her in that moment. She grinned at the
man, and I knew she knew him well too. He was her stepfather, Dr. Anton Weber. He was renowned in the medical
community and probably because of his history with difficult
cases. He'd performed many surgeries when he had actively
practiced.

"Anton, this is my boyfriend, Ares Mallick. He goes by
Wolf," Fawn said.

She always referred to me as *Wolf* when speaking about
me to her family. I'd heard her call me that on calls and
spotted her doing the same in text messages. Whenever she
talked about me to her mom and stepdad, she always called
me *Wolf* and I never fought her.

I never did.

Fawn introduced her stepdad in the next moment. I heard
her in some far-off place, some distant land that separated her
from me. The sound, her voice, was murky like she was
underwater.

Or maybe that was me.

It had to be because the tightness in my chest indicated a
lack of air. Her stepdad, an older man, brought his gaze in
my direction, and I watched his expression change. His head
cocked, his eyes going curious, and for two seconds, I hoped
for something. I hoped that someone out there would
forgive me. That they'd let this one... my past and the deci-
sions I'd made go. They'd *spare me* and move on to someone
else.

That they'd spare her.

"Ares..." Anton said, and I knew in that moment my wish
had been denied. My sins would be upheld as well as the

repercussions that should have come long ago. I'd naïvely thought I had been spared.

As if a sinner wasn't always a sinner.

"Ares, this may seem like an odd question, but do I know you?" Her stepfather's question came innocently, and it was innocent. I probably was just a case file to him. One of many.

The heat that hit me surprised me, but I pushed that away to focus on Fawn. That space between us felt like continents now. Especially when her head tilted. She faced me with her own version of innocence, vulnerability. She had no idea what was going on, but in a way, she should.

After all, a monster didn't stop being a monster.

Fawn

Anton saying he knew Wolf didn't really make any sense.

I peered at Wolf, but he had his dark eyes on my stepfather. His nod was curt. "I suppose you do in a way, sir," he said, and my mouth parted. Wolf faced me, and a noticeable muscle fluttered in his jaw. His Adam's apple bobbed. "I submitted my case to you for treatment a while back."

He... what?

My eyes narrowed, not understanding. I started to speak, but Anton stepped forward.

"That's right. Your doctor... he sent it to me," my stepfather said, and though Anton was speaking to Wolf, Wolf's gaze didn't avert from me. That tight muscle feathered his jaw again, and he wasn't just squeezing my hand now.

He gripped it. He braced it as if afraid to let go.

My heart beat rapidly for some reason, not knowing why he was doing this or why he hadn't told me this information... my heart beat *rapid*. Words escaped from me, and Anton had his head cocked at us both.

"Yes, Ares Mallick," my stepdad stated, then suddenly, glanced directly at me. "Fawn, why didn't you tell me your boyfriend reached out about his case?"

Because I hadn't known, and Wolf was borderline cringing at me. He was as if he'd done something wrong, and the muscle inside my chest beat harder.

"I... I don't know," I said, swallowing hard. "I'm sorry. I..."

I didn't know what to say. I just knew my boyfriend was looking at me like he had done something wrong and the grip on his hand wouldn't let up. He held on like he was trying to fuse us together, and something behind his eyes caused my breath to stop. Wolf and I had gotten really good at speaking to each other without speaking to each other. We had to be in front of his family and friends. We never knew what kind of information the doctors would deliver at his appointments, and Wolf never wanted the people in his life to see his worry. He wanted his family and friends to know he was okay, but I knew the truth. I always knew when he was worried, restless.

Don't let go.

It was like I heard his voice in my head, his grip on me *so hard*, and Anton, as close as he was, wasn't a part of the conversation. Wolf and I were too good with our secrets. We were too good at appearing impartial and unaffected. We really did have a secret language, and he was forcing me to use it now for some reason. I didn't want my stepfather to see how shocked I was my boyfriend hadn't told me something.

My confusion was evident, but only to Wolf. His throat jumped once more, but before he could speak, Anton did.

"Yes, a difficult case indeed," Anton said, his hands in his pockets. He had his serious face on, the one he used on TV when speaking to people about anything medically related. He stood there with the look of a doctor. Meanwhile, I was trying not to let him see the truth, to hold on to Wolf and try to understand why he wouldn't tell me something so important. It wouldn't make sense that he'd withhold that information. My stepfather was a doctor and a very good one. It'd be natural if Wolf reached out, and he should have. Wolf's case had been very bad.

It'd been terrible.

It was in fact so terrible that my stepfather would have been the perfect doctor to reach out to. One of the reasons Anton was so well-known was because of the advances he'd made in the field of medicine. He was the one people went to *for* the difficult cases. The surgeries he'd performed even I knew about, and I didn't follow that stuff typically. People knew my stepdad.

Wolf knew my stepdad.

Obviously, not personally but he knew of him. He knew enough to know that he'd needed Anton.

My eyes scanned the ground, and all too quickly voices became background noise. I heard Anton speaking. I heard him, but…

"I'd like to speak to you more about your case, Ares," Anton continued, bleeding through my thoughts, so many thoughts. "Obviously, Fawn is here, um—"

"She can hear anything you have to say about my case," Wolf stated, breaking through as well. In fact, his deep voice shattered my thoughts. It broke them into a million pieces, and when our gazes collided, I saw nothing but guilt on his handsome face. Visual unrest took on a new definition with the way my boyfriend looked at me in that moment. His jaw moved. "She should know everything."

She should know everything…

I was shaking now. A distinct tremor was in my hands, and that was when Wolf acquired both. He held them both, held on to me.

Don't let go.

I saw that so hard in his eyes now, and I was two seconds away from letting it all crack. From losing *every* ounce of calm and stability I had in front of my stepfather. My boyfriend had lied to me. He'd *lied* about reaching out to one of few people who could help him. Why would he do that? He had no reason to do that.

Unless he did.

I was wavering, but Anton was still speaking. I wanted to run, flee from all this and whatever it was.

"I had my office follow up about your case, Ares, but I was told my services were no longer needed," Anton continued from somewhere. The location was unknown just like my physical body in that moment. I wouldn't feel a bucket of ice water if it hit me in the face just then.

Don't let go.

I think I tried to, but Wolf wouldn't allow it. The eye contact he made was just as unwavering as his hands fused with mine.

Don't let go.

"I was glad to hear it," Anton said, smiling. "I agreed with your doctor's course of action, which was why I rejected your case. You had options still and way better than the risk you would have had on my operating table."

Wolf grew so pale in front of me. Actual color left his tan skin, but I had to look worse.

"I used you. You understand me?"

I thought I had, but maybe all this... his lies went way darker than I ever could have imagined.

They had to be if he was still lying to me.

CHAPTER
FORTY-FIVE

Ares

Fawn and I drove back to the cabin together by ourselves. I'd arranged that. I'd felt fear in the past couple years of my life. I'd felt deep fear, but not once had it been for anything besides the people I loved. The people I cared about *meant everything* so no. I never feared death or dying. I never feared for anything involving myself or worried about feeling the fear of personal loss.

But I felt this.

I *felt* Fawn sitting beside me. I felt her locked up and every second of her not talking to me during our drive. She'd been doing that since we'd left her stepdad and the others at the hospital. Her stepfather had been kind and the complete opposite of how I'd thought he'd be. He wasn't the pompous asshole my mind wanted him to be. He was human, and he hadn't looked at me like a case file. He took me in like a *person* and even invited Fawn and me out for dinner. If things had been under any other circumstances, we might have. We would have had a meal, and I would have properly met one of the closest people in my girlfriend's life...

Girlfriend. The word felt so hollow, empty. The term was on shaky ground and had been from the jump. I hadn't earned that from Fawn, not really. The terms *girlfriend* and *boyfriend* meant something, and I'd taken that something and made it mine. I'd acquired it.

But I hadn't earned it.

A year had passed, and in that year, I'd been disillusioned. I actually let myself believe she was mine completely.

And not something I stole.

The fear settled in so thick as I turned off my Hummer outside the cabin. Fawn stared out the window, the snowflakes gentle now against the windshield. It was like the calm before yet another storm, a storm I knew was about to play out the moment we left the hospital, and she didn't want to immediately talk. She never said this. Again, she didn't speak, but the last time she had, it'd been in front of her step-father. She'd said she wasn't feeling well and I was going to take her back to the cabin. She hadn't spoken those words directly to me but insinuated that was what was going to happen next.

I hadn't argued. I just followed her and told the others we were leaving along the way. I said it would just be us, and I think they thought we wanted the alone time. That we'd do something with that and not what ended up happening. Fawn and I may have left together, but there was nothing but space between us, distance.

I sat back against my seat, my chest all fucked up and tight. Fawn sat pivoted against the door. She was curled up on it and tucked deep into her coat. I swallowed. "Fawn—"

"When did you ask him?"

A force slashed beneath my rib cage when she finally faced me.

Because she'd been crying.

Dry trails ran down both of her freckled cheeks. They were long dry like she'd cried when we'd first left but hadn't bothered doing it after that. I felt socked, physically ill, and the urge to reach out, bring her to me...

She wet her flushed lips. "When did you ask Anton to take your case?"

I wasn't surprised she was asking me this. My brain had had time to think of a lot of questions she'd ask, and this was one of them.

Either way, it wasn't easy to answer, and how I wanted to bring her to me. The physical need to comfort her burned my arms, but I fought it. "Shortly after I was diagnosed the second time."

In fact, it was right after. It was when I'd confirmed my life was going to change, and I couldn't do this by myself. I'd done my research. I knew Fawn's stepdad was the best, and if I had any chance of getting that *thing* out of me, it would have been with his help. I'd have survived because he was the best.

That hadn't been how it had happened. Dr. Weber had rejected my case, and now, I knew why. I actually thought back then he was some shallow fake fuck of a doctor who didn't truly care about patients anymore. That he cared more about being on TV than helping people. My case was fucked, but I'd seen the kinds of surgeries he'd performed. He could have done it.

At least, I'd thought he could have.

How wrong I'd been about him. He'd looked into me after everything, made sure I was good. I believed I'd been nothing but a case file to him, a distraction away from his TV appearances, but that hadn't been the case at all.

If I hadn't felt physically ill already, nauseous. The sickness only charged more violent with the way Fawn looked at me after what I said. She cringed like I struck her, and the bile rose in my throat. "Baby..."

The word only caused her to wince. Her body locked up, and I felt socked again.

"You said you used me," she said, shaking her head. "You weren't just talking about your family, were you?"

"Fawn—"

She rose up off the door, short puffs of breaths leaving her lips. It was getting so cold in the truck again. So very cold. "You asked me if I understood. You said you used me and asked if I understood." She swallowed. "It wasn't just for your family, was it? Us?" Her throat jumped. "Anton rejected your case and what? You thought I could help?"

Something like that. In fact, exactly like that.

My lack of words told her all the answers, and I watched the girl I love cringe again. She'd put it all together, so fucking smart, my girl.

I felt that slipping away too, her being mine, and I had to knuckle my hands not to touch her. My nails dug into my palms so hard I believed they'd bleed.

They might, and Fawn placed her own palms to her eyes.

"You said you wanted us to be friends," she stated, saying words I'd said, and at the time, I'd meant them. I had wanted to be her friend. She glanced up at me. "You wanted to get close to me, right? Close to me so I'd talk to him?"

Her voice broke, and with it, my resolve. I pushed off the door, and though she was still shaking her head, I put my hands on her cheeks. "Baby, I didn't..." I mean, what could I say? She'd figured it out. She truly knew how fucked up I was now, sick. I pressed my forehead to hers. "I didn't mean for things to be like this."

I had tried to end things between us. I'd tried to so many fucking times, but I was weak. Selfish.

She gasped in my arms. Her fists balled, and she pressed them into my chest. "Why didn't you tell me this last year? When you said you used me, why didn't you tell me this?"

Because that was more of my weakness. I'd tried to let

Fawn go initially when things had gone too far. When she'd told me she loved me...

I had tried to let her go then. I had, but I'd gotten weak and selfish again. I had taken her in more stolen moments, but I had sobered up. I'd told her I used her for my family, which had been true as well.

But it hadn't been the only reason.

Me almost using her for a connection to her stepdad had been a worse reason and one I'd known would break her. It would *hurt her* even worse than I was already hurting her the weekend she'd asked me to be her assistant. Back then, I hadn't seen the point in more hurt. Not when I was going to let go of her...

That hadn't been how it had played out, though. It hadn't been because she'd fought me. She had with her spirit and love, and *I* had broken. I couldn't hurt her for another reason.

And it had nothing to do with her.

I pushed my hands into her hair, looking at her. She appeared so fragile. Like she would break with my next words. "I didn't want to lose you."

The truth was sobering. It sobered me, and it most certainly sobered her. Her nostrils flared, and her tears fell in front of me.

"It's so fucked up," she said, hiding her face from me. The first place she'd gone was my coat, and that showed me the state of her resolve too. She probably wanted to be anywhere but here in my arms, but she wasn't letting go. She gasped into my coat. "And what's really fucked up is *I knew*. I knew something was off when you asked me to be your fake girlfriend. Like someone like you... who looks like you would ever..."

She didn't finish, but those words razored through me. She was wrong about that. She was fucking *wrong*, and I wouldn't let her think that.

I made Fawn look at me. Her whole body was shaking

now, but I made her. "You are everything to me. You understand?" I had no words to describe it. No fucking words. "You are the most wonderful... beautiful thing in the world to me."

I wish she knew how deep that went. How she was more beautiful than anything I'd ever seen, and I'd seen beauty. I was a fucking artist, and I'd seen it in a million different ways. So many beautiful versions, but none compared to her.

Fucking none.

It was like my words made things worse. It did when she pushed back. "What am I supposed to even do with that?" she questioned, cringing. "How do I get past that?"

I didn't know what she meant, but her wanting to get past anything having to do with us... me. I held on to her arms. "Fawn, please."

"How can I get past it, Ares?" she asked, blinking down tears. "How? Tell me."

I still didn't understand what she was asking me.

And I felt her slipping away.

It was like she was sand, and I was a broken hourglass. I brought her into me, holding her head. "What can I say? Please, baby, tell me what I can say? To fix this..."

I realized she'd asked me a question, but I was too fucked up to answer her. The possibility of her not wanting us anymore due to my fuckups was ending me.

She whimpered in my chest, and I cracked. My nostrils flared, and I saw nothing, my eyes blurry. I couldn't remember the last time I'd cried.

But I did upon thinking Fawn Greenfield no longer wanted me.

CHAPTER FORTY-SIX

Dear Fawn,

I thought it was important I reach out to you. You left so quickly, and I understand why you did. I fucking get it completely and don't blame you at all.

Something else I wanted to tell you before you left was that your opportunity with Kurt came from me. When I say that, I mean I got word to his office about your work and that you'd be a great candidate for his internship. I told him I didn't know you personally (which was true) and wanted to pass along work from a fellow student. I obviously ended up using that opportunity against you, and for that, you don't know how sorry I am. Hurting you every day... using you killed me in ways I didn't fully grasp until the day you told me you loved me. It was that day I realized nothing more could happen between us.

And how badly I'd doomed us.

Even still, I tried to hold on. I stole us, and I stole you. I tried to take something that was never fully mine and never could be. It couldn't with the foundation I started us on. I tried to escape it. Tried to run, but I suppose that stuff always catches up, doesn't it?

Always.

It's ironic that I once thought you owed me something. In fact, that was probably the biggest lie of all. You never owed me anything. In actuality, it was me who owed you. You saved me in so many ways I can't even count, and I've loved you for longer than I even let myself see.

I'm aware none of that matters now, but I wanted you to know that too. It's important, so goddamn important, Fawn. I'm not just in love with you. I'm in desperate, visceral need of you and want you like I've never wanted anything in my whole life. You truly are everything to me, and for that, I'm sorry too. I'm sorry I thought I could have you and felt worthy of you. I ended up breaking us both in the end,

and if I could sever a limb and take back what
I did to you, I would.
     I'd sever two limbs.

CHAPTER
FORTY-SEVEN

Fawn

Wolf didn't end his letter with his name. He only had two tattoos, and he ended the letter with a sketch of the one he had on his hip. He drew it in dark ink.

My finger moved over it, feeling the bump of the ink. I didn't know the last time I'd gotten a handwritten letter, and it came quick. I'd only been with my family in New York a couple of days. It was just Mom and me here. Anton was still traveling for work.

The period here felt like so much longer away from Wolf. He and the world of Legacy had been my entire life for so long. They'd become my family too in a way. How couldn't they with everything we'd all been through?

"I want you to know that your opportunity with Kurt came from me..."

The thing was, I wasn't even mad about that part of his letter. I should be, but I wasn't. I wasn't even upset that he'd used me. I'd forgiven him long ago for using me before, and this thing with Anton... Well, I couldn't find it in me to hate him for that either. Did the fact he'd done it stab me? Sure. No one wanted to be used, but I couldn't find hate in my heart for it. The raw truth of the matter was Wolf had thought he was going to die. He *was dying*, and he'd attempted to do anything he could to not make that happen. Had it been shitty what he'd done? Of course, but there was no hate in my heart for that. Maybe that was because I loved him or because I had forgiven him for hurting me before. I just knew I didn't feel the weight of that.

Not like I felt the weight of something else.

I'd asked him how I could get past another thing I'd realized. It was something that stabbed a million times worse than anything else he ever could have done. I could get past him using me to survive.

But accidentally falling in love with me...

That *killed* because I did feel like an accident. That he never did love me or never would have had it not been accidental. I fucking questioned his motives when all the fake-relationship stuff was going on. I had, and I'd never been a girl to be insecure about myself or my body, but that shit *hurt*. I didn't want to feel insecure, but I did. He made me feel that way because he hadn't wanted me from the beginning. Not really.

I'd been an accident.

I put the letter away, tinkering with my camera. I played with the ring Wolf had given me and was completely lost in thought. After Wolf and I had gotten to the cabin, I'd arranged to come back home to New York. There was still a little time left of break before school started, and I wanted to spend it with my own family. I hadn't known what else to do or what would happen when I got back to school. Would Wolf and I be together? *Could* I make it work after he'd admitted what he had? I didn't know. I just felt so goddamn vulnerable, hurt.

How can I get past it...

"Hey, sweetie, can you pass me that box?"

I'd nearly forgotten I was up in the attic with my mom. I'd come up here to help clean the dusty space of our brownstone townhouse with her but had ended up stuck in my head.

My mom was kind of adorable when she went all domestic. She had a handkerchief tied in her dark hair to keep the dust out of it like some 1950s housewife, but my mom was the exact opposite when it came to traditional gender roles. She was a woman of the world and very successful in her party-planning business. My stepdad did *really* well financially, but my mom had created a whole empire on her own. Actual celebrities called her for parties.

I got up, handing her the box she wanted. I apologized for spacing off, and she merely smiled at me before taking it.

"I'm just so happy I got to see you again so soon," she said, and she had sounded surprised on the phone when I'd called. I'd told her I wanted to stay for the rest of break if she'd have me.

She had.

So much time had passed with me pushing my mother away. I'd closed myself off after my dad had died, but she was here now and letting me be in her space like no time had passed. She waited for me. She waited for me to heal and get better.

And I loved her for that.

I hugged her, and her light laughter let me know that surprised her too. She patted my back, just letting me hold her.

"What was that for, huh?" she questioned after I let go. She touched my face, and warmth flooded my cheek.

I touched her hand. "I guess I'm just grateful you're letting me be here." I paused, chewing my lip. "For just letting me after I stayed away for so long."

She never pushed me to come home. She left that open, but never pushed. She was always around, waiting.

I blinked over cloudy eyes. "For waiting for me."

I think she knew exactly what I meant. I had closed myself off from her and Anton in the past. They'd done nothing wrong, but I'd just felt so guilty. Guilty for everything with my dad. I hadn't wanted to move on and be happy. My mom had found happiness after my dad. I loved that she had, but it'd been hard for me to allow myself to have that too.

I didn't feel I deserved it.

Mom's thumb brushed my cheek, her head cocked. "I knew you'd find your way, honey. Home to me and..." Her eyes crinkled warmly in the corners. "I'm just so proud of you. You've come such a long way. I mean, you're in college now. *Driving*." She shook my shoulders. "You're doing so good, and your dad would be so proud of you. He never wanted you to suffer after everything that happened."

My mom was there from the beginning of my struggles. She saw *everything* in its rawest form.

She got to see the growth too and had seen my gains. I'd called her after I had started driving again, and I did believe what she said about my dad. Someone else had told me the same thing and guided me to finally see that truth. Wolf had pushed me hard when it came to the responsibility I felt when it came to my father's accident. He hadn't let me run away and had helped address that guilt. He'd helped me *heal*.

My heart felt squeezed in that moment, choked. Regardless, I didn't allow my mom to see and actually helped her clean out the attic.

"I recall a time we weren't so sure you'd be able to go to college," Mom said, and I did too. I mean, how could I forget? My grades had been crap in high school. I'd barely gone, and when I had, I'd done a crap job. Honestly, it was by the grace of God I'd even gotten into Pembroke University. I certainly shouldn't have with my records. I'd been lucky that someone in admissions had taken a chance on me, and I never took that chance for granted. I was grateful for it every day. Mom smiled. "You've worked so hard for your sobriety."

It was something I'd worked for every day. Things had been so dark in high school. I had turned to drugs and alcohol after Dad had passed when I probably should have turned to my mom. Gotten help. "Thank you for getting me into treatment."

It'd been Mom to ultimately recognize I had a problem back then. I'd hid my disease well, but once she'd known about it, she'd gotten me the help I needed. She had without question or judgment.

I'd never be able to thank my mom enough for what she'd done for me back then. She'd been a great mom when she herself had been dealing with my father's passing. Mom put her arm around me. "I just made the call, and I wouldn't even have known there was a problem at all if not for that boy." She brought me close. "The one who stayed with you that night at the party?"

The party...

That was the night everything had changed, and my mom had recognized I had an issue. I'd been so good at hiding how bad things had gotten. I'd gotten drunk and high right under her nose by going to random parties behind her back.

I had hit my all-time low at a party. I'd gotten wasted and passed out with a cocktail of drugs in my system. I probably would have died on that floor if someone hadn't found me.

Mom rubbed my shoulder. "Thank God he called me that night. That boy?" she stated, sighing. I guess the guy who'd found me had scanned my phone's contacts and called her.

Not that I'd remember.

I'd been so far gone that night, and Mom never did get the guy's name. I remember asking around after I was sober enough to, but no one had been able to tell me anything about him. He'd apparently just been a good Samaritan and helped a girl he didn't know.

"Oh, would you look at this," Mom said, noticing something in a box. She had to let go of me to get it, and once she did, I smiled at what she had. She faced me. "I haven't seen this in years."

I hadn't either. Dad had given it to me.

Mom was smiling too by the time she handed the gift to me. It was an old phone case and seeing it was like something out of a dream. I'd worn the hell out of the thing, and it'd been on a couple of phones before it had made it into the box. It was a pink glitter case, a birthday present.

"Your dad gave that to you, right?" Mom asked, and I nodded. My dad had given me a lot of things before he'd passed. He had like any dad would have, and his absence made letting go of anything he gave me hard. Even an old, broken phone case.

The case was broken, an accident, and I turned the case around to study it. It had a crack right down the center, but that wasn't what I looked at when I shifted the case around.

What the...

I stopped, everything stopped when I noticed the design on the back. It'd been a design I'd seen a million times, but it'd been years.

"Honey..."

Mom watched me as I left her and began rooting around for the letter I'd been reading. I'd just been reading it. I'd *just* been looking at it, but I couldn't find it.

Where is it? Where is it?

"Honey, is everything okay?" Mom asked, suddenly beside me, and I wasn't sure. I wasn't sure everything was okay until I found that letter.

I spotted it with my mom by my side. With all the rushing around, the letter had slipped beneath a box, and right away, I unfolded it.

I studied the paper, my gaze zeroing in on something in the corner.

No way.

The resemblance was uncanny. The flower at the bottom of the letter and the one on the back of the phone case were duplicates.

Identical.

My back touched the wall, trying to find a flaw, something to distinguish the flower on Wolf's letter from the one on the case. I loved the one on the case. So much so that it'd been the inspiration for my tattoos. The watercolor flowers had been a tribute to my dad and even the artist hadn't come close to the design on the case. It hadn't been their fault as I'd had them sketch something from my memories. I hadn't seen the case in years, and all I'd had was the memory of it.

I touched my mouth, the case a literal duplicate of the flower in the corner of the letter. Wolf had this same flower as a tattoo on his hip, which was why I'd assumed he'd put it on the letter. The flower represented him.

I didn't know what I was looking at here. In fact, I was so confused, and my mom squeezed my shoulders. From some far-off place, I heard myself tell her I was fine, and the phone case slid from my fingers easily when she took it from me.

"It's a shame what happened to this," she said, and I assumed she meant the crack on the back. Her thumb went down it, the crack right in the center of the flower. She frowned. "I know how much this meant to you."

It did mean a lot to me. Everything my dad had given me did.

I couldn't answer her, too busy looking at the flower on the case and then the letter in my hand. I had no words.

Mom's head tilted. "I remember he felt so bad about that," she said, giving the case back to me. "That boy who sat with you that night at the party. He felt so bad. He said it broke before he called me."

It'd been the last time I'd seen the case. That night at the party it had broken, but I didn't remember that. Mom had told me after the fact, and I supposed that was how it had ended up in the box. She'd put it there.

"He'd looked so sad," Mom continued, staring off as if to a memory. Maybe she was. After all, she was the only one who'd seen him.

I didn't remember.

"What did he look like?" I asked, my thumb lazily brushing over Wolf's letter. I felt like I'd asked the question over a dozen times in the past. It was natural because he did come up whenever Mom and I talked about my sobriety. My recovery had started that day of the party.

It'd been the beginning of it.

Mom's laughter hummed beside me, but I barely heard it. I suddenly felt high off the ground, the place where sound escaped and oxygen was lost. I swallowed, reminding myself to breathe. Mom opened a box. "Dearest, you are asking me to pull from middle-aged memories for something that happened so long ago—"

I faced her, and upon making eye contact with me, Mom's head tilted. "I don't know. I suppose I recall him being hand-some. A handsome young man." She smiled to herself. Again, as if to a memory. Her shoulders lifted. "Not that I could make out too many of his features. He had a lot of hair. These big, vibrant curls that—"

I had my phone in front of my mother's face, a picture I had to scan a second to find. I'd gone to social media, easy.

Mom took my hand, bringing the phone closer. Her eyes narrowed, and the longer they did... the longer she didn't say anything, my heart raced.

"I don't understand," she said, awe in her voice. Her awe was at the photo, the image in front of her. "How do you have this? A picture of him..."

I said nothing, goose pimples lining my skin. "That's him?"

"Yes, um," she started, but then stopped. "Honey, I don't

understand. How do you have this? Do you know the boy from that night?"

She knew the boy from that night.

She apparently just didn't know.

I'd shown my mom pictures of my boyfriend in the past, but none of them had been the description she'd just given. She'd seen Wolf after treatment. She'd seen images of him with buzzed hair, and later, short curls. She actually hadn't seen a picture of him since he'd grown his hair out.

Not that he looked the same.

Wolf was a man now. He was a man who'd been through so much, and I stared at the image my mom recognized. A boy in the middle of three friends. Younger versions of Dorian, Wells, and Thatcher were with him, and Wolf himself barely looked at the camera. His expression was tight, his eyes downcast.

My gaze fell from that image to the letter. It glided over the flower at the bottom to the one on the phone case. They were the same flowers.

They'd always been the same flowers.

CHAPTER
FORTY-EIGHT

Ares – age 16

Dorian: Where the fuck are you? We've called you a million times, and you need to pick up!

Wells: You need to come home, Ares. Your parents are worried sick...

Thatcher: We're worried sick.

I shut off my phone after reading the guys' texts. The phone started to ring again, so I shut it off.

There wasn't a point to answering it.

After I did, I drew back a swig of beer. I'd stopped tasting it about five beers ago.

Flick. Close. Flick. Close.

I didn't know where I'd gotten the old pocketknife, but I liked watching the blade.

Flick. Close. Flick. C—

Some fucker ran into me, and with a growl, I stood from my chair and shoved the dick to the floor. He called me an asshole or something for shoving him, and I bared my teeth.

His eyes flashed.

That's right, asswipe.

It kind of astounded me how I didn't even need my name to intimidate people. I was at some random party in a city far away from where I lived and the influence my family's name had there. I'd been to a lot of cities lately. Some small. Some big.

This one was big.

Flick. Close. Flick. Close.

The guy on the floor cringed when I stepped over him. He probably thought I'd stomp his face in after he called me an asshole.

Lucky for him, I didn't care enough.

Flick. Close. Flick. Close.

Some girl easily half a decade older than me tried to kiss me on the way to the bathroom. I shoved her ass to the floor too, but she didn't cringe when I slammed the bathroom door in her face.

She laughed.

There were a lot of fucked-up people at this party. I didn't know how many people I'd seen passed out or on the verge of it. This was a nice house, and nice houses typically had good drugs and lots of booze. People who had money threw the best parties.

I took my fill of the alcohol but stayed away from all that drug shit unless it was weed. I didn't need any help being fucked up.

Flick. Close. Flick. Close.

I was in the bathtub now. I came into the bathroom for quiet and ended up going to the shower and pulling back the curtain. I sat there and finished off my beer.

Flick. Close. Flick. Close.

The world started to blur after a while, but I didn't think it had anything to do with all the beer in my system. Lately, I'd been in nothing but a brain fog. It was some deep shit. Dark shit.

You're an asshole. A failure...

They'd all be better off without you.

I wished I had more beer. I wished I could block out the noise in my head.

End it. End it so they don't have to deal with you.

They shouldn't have to deal with me. Not Dorian, Thatcher, or Wells, and hundred percent not my parents. My folks were good people, and they shouldn't have to...

Flick. Close. Flick. Close.

I saw the blade move toward my arm, a good vein.

End it. They'll move on. It'll be better for them.

I had so much guilt surrounding my friends and family. They got this fucked-up version of me all the time. They got me and my mental shit, and it was even worse for my folks. They'd lost a kid and ended up with this one. This fucked-up, *broken* kid.

End it. Just end it.

The voice in my head was always mine, but I never listened.

I thought today I would.

It'd be easier for my family if I was gone. They didn't need me, and they would move on. Dorian and the other guys too. They'd all be sad for a while, but in the end, things would be so much better for them.

End it. End it.

The voice was so loud, and I had no more beer. I just had a blade and a vein. Two veins.

End it. End it. End it.

The blade was so close to my skin, and it'd be easy. The metal was inches from my flesh. Centimeters...

The door opened from the other side of the curtain.

A thud followed, then a crash like someone had dropped glass. I opened the curtain to see a broken beer bottle on the floor...

And a girl.

She lay next to the bottle. Like she'd dropped it. The thud must have been her hitting the floor, and I got out of the tub, forgetting about the knife and leaving it there.

Fuck.

The girl wasn't in good shape. She was passed out like half the chicks in this house. I got beside her. "Hey."

She barely responded, mumbling as her lashes flickered. She wasn't any different than any of the other wasted girls I'd seen, but for some reason, I touched her face, tapping her. "Hey. Hey. Wake up."

She was so out of it, moaning. I decided to help her sit up and brought her to sit back against the wall with me. She was a redhead, big wavy hair like mine on my worst day. I had curly hair and hadn't been thinking too much about vanity when I'd been hopping cities.

I'd been traveling for so long, and I lost count of how many places I'd been to. I had one mission, escape, and always ended up where the action was. I'd heard about this party while eating a hot dog downtown, two college kids talking about it. They'd had university hoodies on, so I assumed they were in college.

"Hey, you need to wake up," I said to the redhead. Her head was sagging, and I froze when she laid it on me.

Flowers. A literal meadow of them hit my nostrils, filled my lungs. She made a little noise and started curling into me. She got deep, and I sat there with my arms open. I didn't know what to do.

Especially when she wrapped her arms around me.

She looped them around my neck, holding on to me like I was some safe haven and not some dude just as fucked up as she was. I think I was worse. I knew I was worse.

Another moan left her lips, and she was dragging her head up. She looked right at me. These hazel eyes that captured all the faint light in the room. Every ounce of it found her tawny irises, the light color a mix of soft golds and browns. She smiled. "You're so beautiful."

She passed out after she said that. She fell asleep with those words between us, and I forgot for a second that I was trying to keep her awake. I lifted her. "You need to stay awake, okay?"

She was only half listening to me and her hold got tighter. She wouldn't let go of me, and the harder she held, the weaker my resolve became. I didn't know this girl. I should just leave her.

You're so beautiful...

She was too, and she didn't even have to show me her eyes. She had these freckles all over, each one different than the last. A smattering of them was all over her heart-shaped face, and I never wished for my sketchpad more. I'd left all my art stuff at home, and I wanted to try at capturing all those freckles. Those and the soft sweeps of her lips.

So soft.

She was soft, her full curves settling warmly into my hands. I suddenly found myself not wanting to let go of her. She was so warm.

You're so beautiful.

She was wrong about what she'd said to me. I wasn't beautiful. I was a fucked-up friend and broken son.

You're so beautiful.

Her voice somehow replaced the one in my head, and instead of leaving her, I gazed around the floor. I found her purse and got her phone out.

I dropped it.

Between holding her and trying to unlock the device, I let the thing fall from my fingers.

Fuck.

I managed to keep the phone screen from shattering, but not from breaking the case that held the phone. The glitter case now had a crack down the middle, and I noticed the flower on the back. It was a nice flower and reminded me of the way this girl smelled.

Focus.

It was hard with all the beer in my system, and her holding me so close.

So warm. So soft.

I studied her as the phone rang in my ear. I'd found a contact labeled *mom* and called it. This girl needed her mother. She didn't need me.

You're so beautiful.

My mouth dried, and suddenly, someone spoke in my ear. It took me a second to respond to the girl's mom. I got lost in all those imperfect freckles, studying them...

And how beautiful this girl looked when she slept.

CHAPTER
FORTY-NINE

Ares – the present

"You really messed this one up, big."

I passed a glance over my shoulder, my sister behind me. She stood in the snow, out here in Dorian's letterman jacket like it wasn't cold as fuck.

I faced forward. "How did you find me?"

I'd come to the graffiti wall to be by myself, a history there. My dad had helped me use it as a way to channel my aggression when I'd been younger. We used to spray-paint it, and I'd get lost in that instead of in my head. Much later, my sister had joined us. We didn't come to the wall a lot, but we did from time to time. It was our place, my dad, my sister, and me.

We'd invited Bru a time or two, but he didn't do art for shit. Actually, that was like the only thing he sucked at when it came to school.

I rubbed my arms as Sloane arrived beside me, my own coat keeping me warm. It wasn't blistering cold, but it was chilly. She shrugged. "No one had to tell me. We're twins, remember?"

I eyed her, and she laughed.

She nudged me. "You know I can find your phone through the app. I tracked you."

Of course, she had. None of us had any privacy, and honestly, none of us should. More than one of us in Legacy had a history of being separated. We didn't let each other get lost anymore and having that locator app on our phones helped.

"And I would have come here too," she said, her head cocked. "It's a great place to think. Quiet."

She knew why I was here, what had happened between Fawn and me. I'd told her, Bow, and the guys everything after Fawn had left.

She'd left.

I hadn't blamed her. In fact, I'd given her another reason to when I'd sent my letter. She'd needed to know that detail about Kurt, and I'd known what I was doing when I'd sent the letter. I was letting her know it was okay to leave.

She should leave.

After I'd told Sloane, Bow, and the guys everything, I hadn't continued on with the conversation. The only reason I'd told them at all was because I knew firsthand what with-holding truths did. Lies ruined *everything* and had lost me the one thing I'd ever dared to let myself have.

My chest locked up just then, tight. The group of us had come home to Maywood Heights after the ski weekend. Everyone wanted to spend time with their folks before school started again. I did too, but I'd never felt such distance from Red. She was in New York with her family. She'd told me the information willingly. She'd said she thought it was best she spend the rest of break with her own family, and I remembered being happy that she'd told me. She didn't have to, and maybe because she had, the pair of us had a chance still. We could still be together when she got back.

Like you deserve that.

I didn't really, which was why I'd sent her the letter. Again, I'd known what I was doing when I'd sent it. Did I want that girl like I wanted fucking air? Hell, yes, but I also knew I didn't deserve her. I'd done nothing but hurt her, and I was so fucking tired of doing that.

Beside me now, my sister squeezed her arms. "So, what are you going to do about everything with Fawn?"

I'd already done what I should have. I pocketed my hands. "Nothing more needs to be done. She's where she should be."

She was far away, *away from me* and my bullshit. The best thing I could have ever done for her was let her go and not go chasing after her.

Tell my insides that, the burning inside even more intense with my thoughts. The thought of not seeing Fawn again... holding her...

My sister was in front of me now, and she was taller than most girls. We got our height from our father. "So you're just going to let her go," she said, frowning. She shook her head. "I have to say, big. That doesn't sound like you. Since when do you or any of the guys give up on anything?"

I glanced away. "She doesn't want to see me."

"And if she did?"

"I don't know, little." Why was she pushing this? This shit that hurt so much... My jaw moved. "She doesn't want to see me, and she shouldn't want to."

"But what if she did?" Her head tilted. "Would you be open with her? Open and honest about anything she'd want to talk to you about?"

Of course, I would. I'd fucking die before I lied to her about anything again. "Yes. A million times yes."

I heard the ache in my voice, and my sight hit the ground.

I stared off into the rolling hills of our hometown. Those hill-tops were covered in snow, thick until it all melted away for spring. I wished for spring. I wished for something beautiful in all this fucked-up shit.

Sloane nodded. "Okay, then."

My sister stepped away from me, and suddenly, a smile was on her face. She cupped her mouth. "You hear that? He says he's done being an idiot."

I veered a look in the direction her voice carried off to. Someone else was in the distance, and that someone else made my heart stop.

She also made it kick back to life.

Fawn had that coat on that made her look like a little marshmallow, her hands deep in the coat pockets. The sunlight in her hair made it look more auburn today, the charged red complementing the color in her cheeks. She was so flushed from the chill, glowing.

God, she's so beautiful.

It was hard to even look at her, the urge to run to her... hold her deep in my muscles. I wasn't allowed to just go over to her and do that.

I shouldn't do that.

But I did meet her halfway, my sister in the corner of my vision. Sloane stayed behind, and eventually, I noticed her head off in another direction. She left Red and me here, and she must have told Fawn where to find me.

Why did Red *want* to find me? She shouldn't want to. In fact, she should be with her family, and I loved that she was there. The fact that she'd reconnected with her mother was a good thing. She needed her mom. She didn't need...

I stopped breathing, but not because of where my thoughts had been about to go. Red's arms came around my waist, and the air escaped my lungs. I stopped moving. I stopped doing everything.

Until I wasn't.

Until I had my arms around her too, my body completely shaking, shook.

"God, Red." I pushed my hands into her vibrant hair, breathing her in and getting drunk off her sweet smell. So sweet, so floral. I closed my eyes. "*Fucking God*, how I missed you."

I wasn't supposed to tell her that. She'd left, and I wasn't supposed to engage, go after her…

But I hadn't. *She'd come to me*, and currently, her fingers were digging into my coat. Like I was her lifeline too.

"I missed you," she said, and my insides charged to life again. She sniffed. "I missed you so much."

I saw why she sniffed when she rubbed her eyes, her eyes red, glistening. She appeared to be on the verge of tears, but I dared not reach out to comfort her when she pulled away.

She missed you.

It didn't matter. It couldn't. I couldn't let how I felt weave into whatever was about to happen. If she chose something else other than us, me… I should let her.

But standing in front of her, being this close to her was killing me. All I wanted to do was grab her and kiss the fuck out of her. Instead, I was being forced to watch when she pulled something out of her pocket. It was a rectangular object, and my letter appeared to be wrapped around it. I recognized my handwriting on the notebook paper.

Red held it out, as if for me to take it. I did, but I didn't understand.

"Open it, please," she said, and I didn't hesitate. I did what she said and the folds of the paper revealed an object. A pink, glittery object.

No thoughts. No words formed on my lips as I stared at it, and when I gazed up, Fawn wasn't just fighting back tears. She was full-on rubbing them away.

"My mom and I found that when we were cleaning out the attic," she said, and my chest squeezed. I thought I hadn't been breathing before, but here in this moment, the ability to breathe at all didn't exist. It was like I'd forgotten how. Fucking frozen. She lifted her hand. "Show me your tattoo."

I was frozen again by the request, but like before when she'd handed me the object, I didn't hesitate long. I eased the side of my coat up, my T-shirt with it. I had to push down on my jeans a little for her to see, but one thing I noticed right away was I hadn't asked her to clarify her request. She'd asked to see my tattoo, and I hadn't gone to show her the one on my back. That wasn't the one she wanted to see.

It just wasn't.

The one she wanted was the one I was showing her, the one that looked just like the flower on the back of the glittery phone case she'd handed me. I didn't need to turn the case around to see the flower, compare them. They were the same ones.

And that was intentional.

I'd seen that flower in my head for almost a year before I'd gotten it on my body. It'd been like an anchor, a goal to get to. I wanted to see the beauty in me that some girl I'd met at a party had seen.

You're so beautiful.

The words that girl had said that night had stuck with me. So stuck and embedded. I'd never been uglier than the year I'd taken to get myself better. I'd been in a dark place, but eventually, I'd started to crawl out. I'd found light, and at the first sight of it, I'd gotten my tattoo. It was like a goal post for me and the start of something. It was new life, hopeful, *beautiful* life. I hadn't given up during those dark times and had gotten the tattoo as a symbol. It was like the finish line for all the work I'd done to get to that point in my life.

She was the finish line.

She always had been. Even when I didn't want to see it. Even when I'd written her off and I'd told myself I wasn't completely and *obsessively* in need of her. After the stadium fight, I'd been angry at Fawn, enraged. I'd put the girl I'd met once at a party on a pedestal because she had been my beacon for a whole year. She'd been my light source, and I'd given her that responsibility regardless of the fact that she'd never asked for that. I'd done that, then had the nerve to hate her for taking those photos of the fight.

But you never hated her.

No, I never had. No matter what I'd told myself, or how hard I'd tried to be when it came to her. Our history was always in the background, always, and it couldn't be helped.

Lost in thought, I came back when Fawn touched me. She touched my tattoo and ignited all that history again. Me holding her on the bathroom floor. Her holding me and calling me...

You're so beautiful.

"Ares..." Fawn was blinking, her eyes red. She pushed her fingers beneath them, then gazed up with glassy irises. I remembered wanting to make art with them as the focal point. Fill sketchbooks. Paint murals. She swallowed. "Ares, why didn't you tell me it was you? That it was you this whole time that..." She pressed her fingers to her lips. "That it was you who saved me? My mom got me into rehab after that night you called her. You saved my life, Ares. I wouldn't be here if it wasn't for you."

She wouldn't have endured so much pain, trauma, if it wasn't for me, and she didn't know all the facts. She'd thought it was me who had saved her.

Like it hadn't always been her who had saved me first.

I tucked that in the back corner of my mind when I'd tried to hate her. I'd rejected the thought and the girl with the flower.

You're so beautiful.

"Do you know how fucked up I was that night?" I asked her, knowing I was still fucked up. It was in a different way, but I still had darkness. The things I'd done to her regarding our fake relationship were terrible. I shook my head. "I was about to end it that night before I saw you. I was going to take my own life, Fawn."

Things had been so bad back then, and she knew about my demons. I'd told her all about my guilt when it came to my sister's absence. I was what my family had left after Sloane had been taken. I had been nothing but anger, grief, and the people I loved the most had had to deal with it. I had been such a burden for the guys and my folks. My depression was something they'd *all* had to deal with, and I felt so guilty about that.

Fawn tried to touch my face after I said that, but I put the phone case and letter in my pocket, then grabbed her wrists. She shouldn't touch me. She shouldn't want anything to do with me.

"All that guilt I had regarding my sister..." My throat worked. "I was going to end things. I was so my family and friends didn't have to deal with me. My depression..."

If intense sadness was a person, it would have been me during that time. My fucking face would have been next to the definition.

"Ares..." She was still looking at me like I was worthy. Like I was worthy of empathy or love, but people who did the things I had to her weren't. We were damned and should be.

"It was you who stopped me, Fawn." I put my hands on her cheeks, my thumbs gliding over her freckles. "It was you who's always saved me. I got help after that night. I told my family what was wrong and got help and that started with you. It was you who saved me."

No truer words had been said, my guilt hitting once again. I really had been a monster.

I glanced away. "I didn't tell you because I'm a piece of shit. I'm the guy who intentionally hurt the girl responsible for *everything*," I gritted, nostrils flaring. I faced her. "For everything I have. Everything good and wonderful I have is because of you. I'm living because of you."

And that had just been the beginning. She was still responsible for my reason for existing. My cancer treatment had been hell, and she'd made me fight. She was there, still fucking saving me.

I ended up not being able to look at her and pressed my forehead to hers. Fawn gripped my wrists. "Ares—"

I wouldn't let her speak, shaking my head. "I'm a piece of shit, Fawn. You saved me, and then I told myself I hated you after that stadium fight. I made myself believe it." I guided her head up. "And I used you at the first opportunity. I knew you wanted to go to Pembroke. I knew you wanted that internship. I basically stalked the shit out of you after the stadium fight. I'd finally found out who you were then and dug up everything I could."

She obviously hadn't known who I was back then, and that hadn't surprised me. She'd been pretty out of it. My surprise had come from seeing her. I'd never found out who she was, but as soon as I had, I'd looked up everything I could find about her. There hadn't been much back then, but I'd easily unearthed her dreams and desires. Everyone wanted to talk to the girl who'd provided the photos for the *Chaos in the Heartland* story, and Fawn had done interviews. She wanted to be a photojournalist like her dad and enroll in Pembroke University's prestigious photojournalism program. She wanted to work at the *New York Times* like her dad and make her mark on the world.

She'd already been making her mark. How many articles had I found with her photos, pieces she'd done within her community. It was small stuff in her local newspaper back then, but it'd always been humanitarian pieces. She showed people and their experiences. She uplifted, already doing so much inspiring work that young.

Years later, Thatcher obviously got me more details about

her, and I'd written off the search then like I'd done in the past. I'd told myself my initial searches into Fawn's life were backed by anger. Anger because she'd crossed me and destroyed the image I'd created of her. I'd thought she owed me something after the stadium fight and told myself that was why I was looking into her life. I'd told myself that for months, years, but never the truth. The fact of the matter was, I was completely obsessed with Fawn Greenfield.

Because I loved her.

It was a desperate love, and it made it so easy to do stupid things. Loving her scared me, and I'd fucked it up at the first opportunity.

I studied her, my beacon, my light. Her mouth closed after what I said. Like she wasn't sure what to say.

I'm sure she thinks you're insane.

She had to, and I guess she had reason. I mean, I'd gotten a tattoo that *reminded* me of her. A girl I'd seen once and barely spoken a word to.

I stepped back, but she got my arm. She squeezed. "Is that why you're trying to punish yourself?"

I didn't understand what she was saying, and she tugged me closer to her by my arm.

"You're punishing yourself. Pushing me away." She took my hands, weaving them together. Hers were small compared to mine. "I see what you're doing, Ares, and it's obvious. You're trying to push me away because you feel guilty about hurting me."

But I had hurt her, so badly. The things I'd done to her were unforgivable.

"That's why you lied in your letter," she continued, and I stared up from our hands. Her head was tilted, her expression sad. "Well, I guess you didn't lie per se, but you tried to make something look a certain way. Something you did."

I said nothing, and when I tried to look away, she didn't let me. She brought my face back with her hand, and it was so hard to look at this girl. I felt so much shame when it came to her. I could write a book on all the ways I'd fucked things up.

She fingered my hair. "You said you'd gotten me my internship with Kurt and made it seem like you did that to use it against me, which isn't true. It couldn't be because his office reached out to me about the opportunity before school started. It was toward the end of summer, and you said you got diagnosed again after school began."

I had, no lies there.

"I realized all that after I thought about it. Took a second." Her touch felt like heaven against my cheek, and it burned deep in my soul. Everything she was saying was true. So true. She nodded. "You did that, my internship, and that had nothing to do with your cancer. You did that for me. Someone you believed you hated."

She read between the lines better than I had when everything was happening. I'd told myself I did hate her, but my actions clearly said different.

They always said different.

Fawn was shaking when she placed both hands on my face, and I was too. I was quaking down to my fucking shoes, and I held on to her arms. "You always cared," she said, her little nose so red. Her smile was small. "Even when you thought you didn't. *Believed* you didn't, but for some reason, you tried to pass that off in your letter. You did, and I thought why would he do that? Why would he want me to believe he didn't *care* when he clearly always did?"

Shame once again had me redirecting my focus to the ground, but Fawn brought my head up. "Fawn—"

"You're trying to punish yourself," she repeated, swallowing. "You're keeping yourself from me. You're hurting yourself *for me*, but I know what you did, Ares. I know you made mistakes. I know you used me because you were desperate and *dying*. I know that."

My eyes shut tight, and I fought when she guided my

brow to touch hers. I wasn't worthy of it. I wasn't worthy of her.

"Haven't you suffered enough? Haven't we suffered enough?" She was keeping me stable with her hands on me, and I couldn't let go. I didn't. This girl was my anchor, always. "I've forgiven you, so now it's time to forgive yourself. Forgive yourself like you taught me to do when it came to my dad."

My arms wove around her then, tired of fighting. I had taught her that, the student better than the teacher. I breathed into her neck. "My heart wanted everything for you even when my stupid fucking brain didn't," I admitted, aware of that now, all of it so clear. "I wanted everything for you, Fawn. Your internship and dream of being like your dad…" Again, I knew all about that, researched her. "In high school, I read interviews about you. You talked about it and all the work you wanted to do, and I thought that was so fucking beautiful. I found your community work. It was so fucking beautiful, Fawn. You're beautiful."

She gasped in my arms, and I held her tighter.

"I made a call to Kurt's office, but you did the rest," I said, wanting her to know that, needed her to. "They just needed to see you over there. Them and the school… They just needed to see the beautiful fucking things you were doing."

She pulled away, tears in her eyes when she scanned me. "The school?"

I'd made calls to them too, admissions. I wiped away her tears. "I wanted you to have everything."

Again, even when my fucking brain didn't. I'd written off all those things I'd done and it had become even easier to do when I did need her. I'd used those actions against her, payback.

But she didn't need to pay up. She didn't because I owed her fucking everything.

"You got me into school," she said, touching my hair again. "Ares..."

She was looking at me like I was her savior, but it was so fucking hard to forgive myself. I touched my forehead to hers. "You never owed me anything, Fawn. Not a fucking thing." My arms gripped tighter around her, fusing us both in the heat, the warmth. The energy she and I created... The safety in the space... It radiated through me, and I fed off that shit like I had that day on the bathroom floor. "I owed you. I owed you *everything*, Fawn." My voice cracked. Broken. My hands caged her face. "I've loved you since I was sixteen."

She made me obsessed with her. In feral need of her. That may be some toxic shit, but it was true. It'd always been true, and again, even when I hadn't wanted to see it. My love for Fawn Greenfield was inevitable. I hadn't stood a chance that day on the bathroom floor.

I didn't know who was crying at that point, if it was her or me. I just knew, when one of us started kissing the other, I didn't allow it to stop. I brought her arms around my neck, guiding her to stand on my feet as I braced her against me. I wasn't letting go of her again, and I wasn't entirely sure that was my choice. My soul couldn't physically allow hers to leave mine, and even if it did, I refused to let it. My entire being needed to be with this girl. Everything I was *needed her*. Fawn Greenfield was my forever place. My forever...

And God did I love the fucking sound of that.

EPILOGUE

Fawn

"Marry me."

Wolf stroked the tattoo near my pussy. It'd been my idea to get it, but he'd picked the placement.

The caveman.

He'd always been a possessive ass, and when it came to my next tattoo, that fact had been no different. I wanted to get one to represent him. The flower near my tiny curls he'd designed, and I couldn't help getting it after he'd told me when he'd gotten his and why.

He called me his anchor.

The way this guy and I were weaved together... the deep and all-consuming way should be overwhelming for me. A love like that might drown some, but I was uplifted by it. It made me reach for the sky and filled me with incredible light. I loved this man, and I wasn't overwhelmed.

I was made whole.

It was a wholeness I didn't even know I needed, and I think I'd heard Wolf wrong when he'd spoken. I had to admit

I was a little sex drunk. We'd barely left this bed since I'd gotten back from New York, his bed. We'd started spring classes recently, but after our days, we always ended up right back here.

"Hmm?" I could hear the lazy tone in my voice. Again, I was sex drunk, and Wolf looked like a fucking *god*. He was on his own hip while he stroked mine, his vibrant curls all over the place, his smile coy. His eight-pack was on full display as well as his dick, always fucking hard, ready. The stamina this guy had.

He brought me up against it, his length teasing my sensitive pussy. I wasn't so ready and was still pulsing from the last time he'd taken me. His mouth hovered above mine, our nose rings touching. "I said marry me, Red. Make me the happiest guy alive."

Okay, so I had heard him correctly. I put some space between us, my hand on his abs. "What are you talking about?"

He must have been sex drunk too, and I'd never seen him so happy. Actually, that was a lie. This last year I'd seen him incredibly happy, and I had been too.

It couldn't be helped.

This guy and I just belonged together, and now, I understood why. He'd been my anchor too on the bathroom floor of the party that night. He'd been my source for home and brought me out of my own dark place. Ares Mallick had saved my life that night.

We'd saved each other's.

We were always passing the baton, and I didn't know what else to say in response to what he'd said. I was still kind of wondering if I'd heard him okay.

Wolf brought me to my back. His mouth instantly went to my neck, and I giggled like a kid.

"I said," he spoke between kisses, and I stopped giggling when he licked my flesh. I panted then, holding on to his neck. He smiled against my skin. "What I said."

Another kiss touched my skin, and it turned out it was just as sensitive as in between my legs. A sharp buzz between them caused me to rub my thighs together, and Wolf traveled down my body, his curls in my face.

"Marry me," he said, breathing the words over my trembling stomach. He spent a lot of time there, nuzzling, and the tingles hit straight into my core. "*Please* marry me, Red."

The desperation in his voice caused me to lift his head, and fuck, how gorgeous this guy was. It wasn't just how he looked, though. It was everything about him that sent a burn through my body. I touched the smattering of dark freckles across his nose. "Are you being serious?"

He certainly sounded like it, looked like it. All of a sudden, the smiles were gone and replaced with serious Wolf. *Ares* stared at me with those deep dark eyes. He guided the hair out of my face. "Please marry me, Red."

My stomach jumped. Flipped.

Please. Marry. Me. Red.

I swallowed, my mouth dry. "When?"

The response was... natural, easy. I honestly hadn't thought about another response.

Once more, it'd been natural.

Wolf's response to this was a blink, but then an easy smile formed on his lips. He brought my forehead to his. "When do you want?"

Holy fuck.

In all the time Wolf and I had been together, we hadn't had the *marriage* talk. I think we just hadn't had time. His health had been priority, and it just hadn't come up.

It was now, his focus on me, and I still didn't know what to say. This was all overwhelming. This was...

Wolf pulled me out of my head. He guided me to lie back on the pillow, then caged me in. His thumb brushed my cheek. "I've seen a life without you, Red," he said, his Adam's apple jumping. He nodded. "I've lived every painful moment of it."

A light tremor hit his voice, and I touched his cheek. I'd lived it too, and it was painful. Extremely.

A small smile touched his mouth. "But I've also seen the opposite. Experienced the depth of you, us, and what we can be. What we are." He took my hand, kissing it. "I've seen our futures, Fawn. I've seen you working and doing your thing." So much light touched his eyes, and inside, my chest fluttered. That couldn't be helped either. His mouth brushed my nose. "You work for the *New York Times*, but you're always on your feet. You travel all over the world for your stories. You're living your dream, but I am too. I see myself in your dream, Fawn, and I see you in mine. We fit, and it's fucking perfect. Gorgeous. *You and I* are gorgeous."

God, if he made me fucking cry *again*. I fingered his curls. "We are?"

"We are." He took my fingers, kissing both my hands. "My focus is in design with my art, but I can do that anywhere."

I could too in a way. He was right my job would require travel. That was how it had been for my dad, and though he'd technically worked in New York, his job had taken him everywhere. He could've been anywhere, but he'd chosen New York for Mom and me.

"I'm done denying us," Wolf said, nuzzling my nose. "I need us."

I needed us too.

"Marry me, Red," Wolf stated, smiling. "Marry me today. Tomorrow, or even in a fucking year or two. I don't care. It can be after we both graduate. It can be anytime. Just…" He breathed me in. "Promise me our future."

He simply wanted a promise from me. He wanted my heart and his to be together.

As if it already wasn't.

As if this guy hadn't already changed my life and weaved his way in. I hadn't had a chance when it came to our fake relationship, and apparently, he hadn't either.

"Please," I said, nodding, smiling. I hugged him close. "Please be my home."

It was wherever he was. We could be each other's home bases.

Wolf's big hands pushed into my hair, his golden chest rising and falling with heavy breaths. "Is that a yes?" he asked, sounding awed, and almost a little anxious, nervous. His thumbs brushed my cheeks. "I don't have a ring right now in this very moment to give you, but I swear to God that'll be fixed by the end of the fucking day. It'll be the best goddamn ring you've ever seen—"

I kissed him, done with all this talk. I didn't care about a ring right now, and it excited me he didn't have one. It meant this moment was impulsive and he'd asked because he felt something. He'd asked because he needed me and us and that awoke so much life in me. I loved this man. I *fucking loved* him.

"It's a fuck yes," I said biting his mouth, and he grinned against mine. "*Fucking* yes."

He bit me right back, then kissed the hell out of my mouth. He kissed me like I was everything.

He was everything. He was everything I both needed and wanted, and the next thing I knew, he was inside me from behind. He had my arms pulled back, pinning me beneath him.

"I'm going to fuck you like it's our wedding night," he said, his teeth tugging my ear. Pain pulsed through the delicate shell, my body writhing beneath his. His hand covered my throat. "*Wife.*"

Ooh... I liked the sound of that. My body surging, I

nudged my ass against him. My hips rocked for him to move, but he wouldn't.

Wolf held me back, and even slid out of me. I groaned from the release, and he pressed a kiss to my back.

"So impatient," he said, pressing a firm hand to my spine. My sensitive nipples touched the bed, and he tweaked one. "So needy."

I was needy, and so very frustrated. My fists balled, my fingers knuckling. He still had my arms behind my back, and I couldn't do anything. "*Please.* Please, I need you inside me."

I was desperate for him, and Wolf's response was to hug me. That weighted, muscular body caged mine. He ran his dick against my sex.

"Patience, Red," he murmured, teasing me. He started placing hard kisses down my spine, and I wriggled.

Especially when he sunk his teeth into my ass.

I nearly came right then, my whole body seizing up. He sucked my cheek into his mouth before releasing it with a pop. He caressed the area. "Fuck does this look good on you," he said, pinching where he'd bitten me. "My mark on you looks so good, baby."

He spoke as if he didn't already have his mark on me. As if he hadn't already worked his way into my entire soul.

We both had. Our flower tattoos matched for a reason, and when I tugged an arm free, he let me reach back and kiss him. He submitted to me and just as quickly as I had to him.

Because we owned each other.

"Fuck," he gritted, finally entering me again. He pumped in slowly, out slowly. Our tongues danced. "Fuck, Fawn. I love you."

I loved him too, so much.

Wolf's thrusts picked up, our hands woven together. His powerful hips slapped my ass with vigor. He fucked me wildly, fiercely, like he would if we were in the throes of passion and bliss. Like he would if we were married.

I could see that day. I could see our future just like he could. It was pretty fucking gorgeous like he said.

"I love you," I called out, kissing him when I came. I bit his lip, and his thrusts intensified. He hit once, then twice before his body stiffened, and he filled me with so much cum I felt it leak between my legs.

Wolf played with it, using it to run up and down my clit. His tongue flicked mine.

"Mine," he said, and my body electrified once more. Pulling out, he pressed our mouths firmly together. "Mine. My beautiful fiancée."

Hearing the title felt nearly as good as him calling me his wife. In fact, it felt equally as good.

Wolf brought me to my back, and I'd never felt such bliss. I'd never felt such heaven. I couldn't remember a world in which I didn't have this, and I didn't want to.

Wolf wrapped me in his arms later that night, and just when I thought he was asleep, his deep voice rolled softly into my ear.

"Move in with me," he said, and almost sounded more vulnerable than when he'd asked me to marry him. He did sound more vulnerable. His mouth touched my ear. "Make me the happiest guy alive."

He'd said that when he'd asked me to marry him too, and the answer to this new question was just as easy. I had a feeling this was just the beginning of easy answers when it came to us. Our journey hadn't been easy, but we'd finally reached a place of effortlessness. *Happiness* and ease.

I didn't make him wait for the answer to his question. We'd passed the place of suffering, and I kissed him deeply when I told him yes, passionately. The answer would always be yes when it came to us.

Again, it was effortless.

Thank you so much for reading *Eat Your Heart Out*! Get the next book in the Court Legacy saga, *Pretty Like A Devil*, on Amazon today!

Amazon

ACKNOWLEDGMENTS

I want to take a moment to thank all my patrons on Patreon for all their support! I appreciate each and every one of you. Thank you so much for supporting me and my work <3

My Lovely Patrons:

Abbycadabby	Camryn B	Jennifer F	Mack_1	Samantha M	
Adrianna	Candelaria A	Jess M	Mackenzie W	Samantta Z	
Alaina M	Candice K	Jess M	Madison G	Sara S	
AleesaR	Carolyn K	Jessica C	Malaika M	Sarah A	
Alex	Carrie	Jessica R	Manuela F	Sarah D	
Alex J	Cass S	Jessica W	Mariana R	Sarah J	
Alex K	Cathi T	Jordan F	Marianela V	Sarah V	
Alex M	Cecilia V	Jordyn B	Marissa P	Sarai G	
Alexandra W	Christen	Josie H	Mary J	Schella D	
Alexis	Christina S	Justice	Mary O	Sei	
Alexis R	Cici K	Kaitlin S	Maya N	Shaunna D	
Aliyah I	Claire M	Kaitryn S	Meg O	Sherry7813	
Alysia B	Coffee Break With Books	Kara S	Meghan B	Sophie	
Alyssa G	Cynthia C	Kari V	Meghan P	Sophie B	
Amanda B	Daisy M	Katalina A	Melissa H	Staccy K	
Amanda C	Dana A	Katelin	Melissa M	Stephanie	
Amanda J	Daniella	Katherine	Melissa W	Sunni	
Amanda S	Danielle B	Katherine M	Micaiah	Supernatural Creations	
Amandha K	Danielle P	Katherine M	Michaela P	T Diamond	
Amber H	Danni S	Katie	Michele S	Tabitha O	
Amber L	Darby	Katie J	Michelle	Tammi H	
Amber M	Delayne	Katlyn M	Michelle M	Tarryn S	
Amber O	Devan M	Kay	Mickenzie	Tatayana	
Amie N	Diana C	Kaylyn M	Mike L	Tawnya M	
Amy H	Dixie	Kaylynn F	Morgan B	Taylor G	
Amy K	ecantoni1	Kaytlyn	Naely R	Taylor Hutton	
Andi S	Ej	Kellie P	Natalia M	Taylor L	
Andrebelle	Elanor C	Kelsey	Nati	Taylor M	
Angel G	Elf_2000	Kelsey M	Neli	The Visual Museum	
Angelica	Elka L	Kelsey M	Nichole T	Torri L	
Annalisse G	Ellie T	Kim B	Nihad P	TrollerBridge	
April R	Elsa A	Kimberlyn D	Nikki S	TurtlezBooktok	
Ashley A	Emi B	Kimly	Nikki W	Valarie G	
Ashley H	Emmarose S	Kirsty A	Olga R	Vanessa	
Ashley P	Erica	Kittycat	Olivia A	Victoria M	
Ashley R	Erica	Kristen	Olivia L	Victoria P	
Aspen H	Erin G	Kristen	Paige L	VPC	
Aubrie O	Fanny L	Kristina	Patricia	Vr2011	
Audrey M	Frances A	Laina	Rachel	Whitney C	
Becca	Frances G	Lakeisha E	Rachel F	Xen G	
Becky B	Gabriella F	Leah A	Rae	Yilda M	
Bettina	Goriola I	Leah C	R	Yvo	
Blair H	Grace	Leah R	Ren		
Book Obsessed	Hailey C	Leah S	Renee O		
Breanna	Haley	Leanne	RGreen		
Breanne T	Haley R	Leighton G	Ro		
Bree B	Haley T	Lexi F	Robin R		
Breister Family	Heather L	Lindsay A	Rosa M		
Brianna B	Isabel C	Lindsey W	Rose C		
Bridgett Z	Jackie P	Lisa W	Ruby H		
Brittany	Jacquelynn R	Lissa	Sam		
Brittany E	Jasmin W	Liz M	Samantha		
Brittany V	Jasmine A	lizbit1979	Samantha		
Brooke	Jenascia L	Loni M	Samantha C		
Bryn M	Jenna B	Lorena P	Samantha G		
Callie	Jennifer	Luise K	Samantha L		

If you'd like to join me on Patreon (and be listed in the acknowledgements page in my next book!) You can join me at the link below:

https://www.patreon.com/edenoneillwrites